PRAISE

THE QUELLING

"An addictive page-turner with a compelling heroine on a thrilling journey of rebellion."

—**W. Bradford Swift,** eco-fantasy author of *Rainforest Shaman*

"A definite must-read for fans ready to immerse themselves in an adventure of ingeniously detailed world-building, vivid imagery, and quests that take you across the realm."

—**Hannah Pennington,** author of *The Tindoria Chronicles*

THE QUELLING

C. L. LAUDER

RIVER GROVE
BOOKS

Published by River Grove Books
Austin, TX
www.rivergrovebooks.com

Distributed by River Grove Books

Design and composition by Greenleaf Book Group
Cover design by Greenleaf Book Group
Cover art by Christopher Taljaard. Copyright © 2023 by Christopher Taljaard. All rights reserved.
Map of Aurora Saura by Jimmy de Ruig. Copyright © 2023 by Jimmy de Ruig. All rights reserved.

Publisher's Cataloging-in-Publication data is available.

Print ISBN: 978-1-63299-765-4

eBook ISBN: 978-1-63299-766-1

First Edition

JOIN THE CREW

If you enjoy this book, you'll want to join The Crew and get notified when the next instalment hits. For a limited time, Crew Members will receive two exclusive items of fan memorabilia. Firstly, an audio file of "The Forgotten Song," unavailable on mainstream media. Secondly, an undisclosed map of Merrocha, shared exclusively with members of The Crew. Don't miss this chance to sign up for these exclusive items available for a limited time to subscribers via my website:

www.CLLauder.com/reader-sign-up

For my brothers, who survived it all with me.
A pair of my favourite humans.

1

KYJTA

I t's cold down here. Cold and miserable, and I wish I hadn't come. But wishes are like curses, as my mother used to say. I should have asked her what she meant. I thought we'd have time. I was wrong.

There's a girl nearby. She's not the only one; about a hundred of us are crammed into this dank subterranean space, but she's the one who has my attention. She's small and thin. Silently crying. I could probably touch her shoulder if I stretched out my hand. By now, Helacth's ghoragalls must be circling. Hideous winged creatures with shards of bone protruding from their moulting black feathers, and long limbs perfect for snatching up anyone left wandering around in the dark. I'm sure she's scared. She has no family. None that I can see, anyway. I could put an arm around her and warm her scrawny arms. I could rub the chill out of her bare legs. She isn't dressed for the cold stone floor.

I lean my head against the wall and do my best to ignore the painful jut of an old man's hip bone in my side. How long until morning? It's impossible to tell. Some people are sleeping, gently snoring. The young girl must be tired but has nowhere to put her head. I could offer her my leg, but it's not my way.

The walls are hypnotic, not your typical cellar walls. They've been strung with zionate; the ceiling too. The delicate threads overlay each other in a crazed, haphazard pattern that shimmers in the lamplight. The protective canopy makes us invisible to Helacth's ghoragalls. Not us, exactly, but our Stains: glimmering silver-gold markings that brand the lot of us. The Rheman overlord's ghoragalls may be merciless abductors who attack us in the dark, but at least they're blind. It's when you're stained that they can find you. Day or night, inside or outside, they know where to look. Except where zionate is at work. Something about the shimmering strands disturbs their sense of our Stains, and we go unnoticed while it shields us.

The young girl is from the north. Skin the colour of polished darkwood, hair bright as the setting sun. She wears it in a braid that crowns her head. How old is she? Eight or nine alignments? Maybe. Too young to be on her own. Too young to be here. She turns and catches me looking. Sniffing, she lowers her long copper lashes and wipes at her eyes. I lost my mother young, so maybe I don't have a caregiver's nature. There are other women here, though, older than me and experienced, women with children of their own. Why don't they comfort her? Isn't that what mothers do?

The floor is hard and icy cold. I shift uncomfortably, nudging my boot past the town carpenter's ample bottom. She treats me to a pointed look, and I smile, but my eyes send a different message. She looks away. It's not that I scare her. I'm just a girl, nineteen alignments and a rawhide sack of bones. But she won't want to offend me. I might be wearing a field hand's clothes, but she knows me as something more than a farm girl. I am my father's daughter, and she has no alternative but to hide her scorn if she values his deliveries.

I wish I hadn't come.

Wishes are like curses. Wishes are like curses.

I should have asked my mother for the meaning. Not knowing bothers me, and the words stick in my head.

If only I hadn't been at the market when the warning bells chimed. These people scare me about as much as the wraith-like ghoragalls whose pouches are full of Stain. I remember the day many here got their mark. There was a stampede to get away. The ghoragalls flew low on skeletal wings that spanned the sky. The sun was bright, and then it wasn't. The shadow raced across the baked earth, sweeping people up like scattered dust. I fell, and the rest kept running. Some ran over me, digging heavy heels into the backs of my hands, spraining my fingers, tripping over my legs; but they didn't stop.

They didn't stop for me, and they're not going to comfort the girl.

She's not crying any more. She has hiccoughs. The irregular spasms look painful, contorting her tiny frame. They say a good scare will chase them away, but she's had one of those already.

'Hey. Girl.'

She turns her violet eyes on me, shimmering and luminous.

'You play Top It?' I pull a set of shells out of my pocket and splay them across my palm.

She nods, her expression serious.

'Come over here. I'm bored as a monolith.'

She crawls over on hands and knees, not minding who she bumps along her way. When she reaches me, she squats. Her feet are bare. They must be freezing. Her expression is a little hilarious. She's wide-eyed and solemn enough to lead a death march.

I distribute the shells. The young girl picks each up in turn and examines it. I let her go first, but I don't let her win. That would be a false lesson. She's good, though. Smart. She's definitely played before.

'Who taught you?' I ask.

'My brother.'

So there is someone to look after her, at least.

'Your Stain looks like a fez; anyone told you that?' Someone must have. The silver-gold marking at the back of her neck is a perfect silhouette of the tiny blue birds that swarm over the meadows.

'Yours is like—' she stalls, suddenly shy.

'Like I'm crying. I know. Unfair, isn't it?' I chuckle softly so she knows I'm not offended.

'I'm Kyjta,' I tell her.

'Calipsie,' she says.

We play five rounds. She wins one when I topple the stack, and I take the other four. Now that I have all my shells, I slip them into my pocket.

'If you're tired, you should try to sleep.'

I straighten my legs and flatten my shawl over the stone floor. It's a makeshift bed that will offer little protection from the chill, but it's better than raw skin against frozen masonry. I tap my thigh where Calipsie can rest her head. She looks uncertain but then crawls forward and snuggles up like a forest animal on a nest of reeds.

I return to resting my head against the wall at my back, giving the radiant zionate mesh covering the opposite wall my attention. Don't ask me how the House of Judgement figured out that zionate blocks whatever attracts the ghoragalls to our Stains. Sion Ignoti worked the Parched Lands and probably tweezed all this from the wings of giant satermijtes, cart-sized desert insects that scavenge the dunes, preparing for his retirement. It used to be the stuff was only good for brooches and trinkets. He couldn't have known it would be our first defence against the ghoragalls. Not that the beasts are the enemy. They only serve their master, Helacth, the Rheman overlord, and the reason I'm cowering in a basement with a small stranger curled up in my lap.

My world, Aurora Saura, used to be home to only two sentient species. My people, the Aurora Saurins, populated the habitable climes of Fareen and Sojour, while the Tarrohar kept to the equatorial Parched Lands. Only the most intrepid explorers ever made it past the Tarrohar into the Ice Realm of Thormyth, south of Sojour.

Everything changed the day the Rhemans landed their ships. There were six in total, and they scattered them across the three continents. Three ships in Sojour, two in Fareen, and the last in Thormyth, which Helacth occupies.

The Rhemans are not people; they are creatures. Just like the Tarrohar are not people. Both species are parasites. They use my people to fully experience the world. Their methods may differ, but the outcome is the same. My people suffer under their control.

With the Tarrohar, at least, there can be no deception: the monster is as plain as the victim it rides. Rheman control is more nefarious— they're invisible, hidden inside your body, controlling you. They could be anyone. They could hide inside your own mother—you wouldn't know. I favour the monster I can see, but that doesn't make the Tarrohar any less repulsive. It's not that I'd opt for having an eight-legged sack of organs suckered onto my back over being quelled by a Rheman. The sight of a Tarrohar turns my stomach, all squishy tentacles and shiny translucence—like a pudding that's sat too long in the heat. It's just that, with the Rhemans, you can't see it coming. A Rheman travels from person to person with no visible sign. You won't know they're there until your consciousness is pushed aside. Probably not even then. We call it being quelled. The Quelled are my people, Aurora Saurins just like me, but under Rheman control.

I close my eyes and try to listen for the sea. I can almost feel the sun on my back, if I sit very still. The cold walls burn. I wish I could just get up and leave. Not just this place, but *this* place: Merrocha, my hometown in Sojour, and everything it represents. Past. Memory. Pain. I want to go somewhere new. Somewhere the ghoragalls can't follow me.

The Rhemans landed in 4036, the same alignment I was born. Some might call that an omen, but I call it palm's luck. The Hands, our guiding deity, dole it out, and I've had more than my fair share. I've never lived a life out from under Helacth, and I've stopped wondering if I ever will. The Rhemans came here looking for bodies because they didn't have enough of their own. Now that I'm marked, my body is theirs for the taking. With my Stain, I'll be taken. One day—probably soon—a ghoragall will swoop down from the sky and carry me to the Ice Realm, where I'll behold their mother ship and forfeit my mortal shell. It's a fate I accept.

Wishes are like curses, and I did this to myself.

A shift in the light catches my eye. Movement at the top of the stairs. Calipsie stiffens. I thought she was sleeping, but the girl is smart. A young man and an old woman descend the stairs. I know the man. More of a boy. A farmhand called Merrick, who used to do part-time work on the farm. I lower my head and let my shaggy curtain of hair hide my face. All I need now is another reminder of my mistakes.

Peering through my mess of blondish hair, I watch Merrick lead the old woman down the stairs, making sure she doesn't trip. The woman's skin is milky white and sparkles like starlight. It isn't right how Merrick holds her by the hand while supporting her at the elbow. Merrick is a labourer and not a bit gentlemanly. He's built like a farmyard elvakan, and she like one of the fez that flutters over the meadow. It's like watching two different species caring for each other.

It's all wrong.

I lean into Calipsie, my field hand's cover-ups scrunching in the eerie silence.

'Sit up,' I say quietly.

She twists in my lap, her enormous spectral eyes fearful. She rises and quickly shuffles forward.

Merrick and the old woman reach the bottom of the stairs. He's only a few alignments older than me, but you'd think him older to look at him. His face is all hard angles—parts pleasing, others brutish and sun scuffed. He's fit, though, beneath his farmer's shirt. It's a terrible cut, but I can see the triangular jut of his muscled torso through the ill-fitting material.

Merrick leads the woman to a wobbly stool, which Sion Viandti vacates for her. Viandti owns a textile shop, and that gives him title of Sion. In Sojour, any man past his middle alignment and without title is belittled in private and snubbed in public. There's a thriving market for the smallest sliver of earth. No one wants to be branded with the opposing prefix of Hok, meaning a man without standing.

The shopkeeper doesn't look pleased to see Merrick. Once the woman is seated, he pulls him aside.

'It's past curfew. What are you doing here?' I can't really hear Sion Viandti from my position at the back of the room, but I think that's what he says. Merrick is facing away from me, so I don't get his response.

'The rules are there for a reason,' Sion Viandti continues. 'It's a disgrace,' the shopkeeper says, eyes darting toward the older woman with the starlight skin. 'What use would they have for her?'

I stare harder. Merrick doesn't seem himself. I've watched him take a scolding before, and he always stuffs his hands in his pockets and studies the floor. Not so today. He's engaging with Sion Viandti, trying to explain something to the old man. He might even be succeeding.

I settle back against the wall and motion for Calipsie to get comfortable. I don't want to think about Merrick. The fact he's here is bad enough. The last time he got a scolding in front of me was when he lost his job. My stepfather was angry. He caught Merrick lurking around the farmhouse, peering in at the windows. Sion Cromenk, my stepfather, hadn't an inkling of what I'd done to make Merrick follow me around. If I was ever found out, my days of moonlighting as the potion master's delivery agent would be over.

Boots stomp on the floorboards above. The focus of the room shifts. A heavy clunk resounds as the wooden trapdoor to the basement impacts the floor above. Light streams down the stairwell. Calipsie goes rigid, her eyes wide. Then, like a plague of insects funnelling through a breach in a wall, the Quelled rush in. I lose count of their number because, screaming, everyone around us surges to their feet. Their momentum lifts me as I try to hang on to Calipsie. Most rush for the stairs, thinking they can make it past the Quelled. I stand firm, battling the tide, too scared to attempt an escape. Outside, the ghoragalls are surely circling. The thought of those waxy talons sliding under my arms sickens me, and I don't trust my legs.

The Quelled seem so much less terrifying. Some are even familiar. I see a boy I spent a summer with when we were small. Though he's quelled, and not the kid I recall—a Rheman is controlling him— his face is still that of my old friend. The boy—the Rheman—leaps the balustrade and lands with astonishing balance, scattering the crowd. The Rheman clamps its arms around the meaty torso of Sion Turbotol, who's twice the boy's size and wrought from hard-earned muscle. In no time, the Rheman has the larger man tucked under one arm and wrangles him up the stairs. I've heard stories about Rhemans bringing superior strength to the Quelled—the bodies they occupy—but I never believed them. I guess I should have. I do now.

When Calipsie wraps her arms around me, I realise how badly I'm shaking. She doesn't notice. Her eyes find mine, and her upward gaze is expectant. She trusts me to find a solution. That's what adults do. Find solutions to impossible problems. But I'm no adult. Still, I search the room. There must be some way out. Calipsie has faith in me, and that faith creates an obligation. If it weren't for the tug of her slender arms around my middle, I might take my chances on the stairs.

On both sides, people pummel us, trying to get away from the closest Quelled. This one is tall with greying hair—probably some kid's grandfather. It wears a floor-length maroon frap, typical of merchants from Oblix. I pull Calipsie low to keep her out of its sights, and when I look back, it's bundling two of the Stained toward the stairs. They're screaming for help, kicking and biting it, but resisting is pointless. The Quelled don't feel pain. Being unconscious, they've no means to experience it. The Rheman is running things, and pain doesn't translate to them.

Someone has given us away. We might be safe from the ghoragalls down here, but we're never safe from the Quelled. Five more rush down the stairs and the cellar's occupants fall back, crushing Calipsie and me into the cold webbing of zionate strands crisscrossing the walls.

Whether guided by the Hands or pure desperation, my eyes hunt for Merrick. He stands out from the crowd, not because he's Merrick and we share an uncomfortable history, but because he's successfully fighting back. His right arm is locked around the neck of one of the Quelled, and he uses the other to free one of the Stained.

I grab Calipsie by the arm and use the crowd's momentum to work my way forward. It's not easy, we're constantly shoved off course, but the throng is thinning. Some were taken; others have escaped, or if they're unlucky, they've been lifted away by one of the ghoragalls as they fled the shelter. By the time Calipsie and I reach Merrick, he's managed to free the man and is searching the room for his next challenge. I step up and meet his gaze.

Merrick squints at me, his expression a little wild. Then, his attention shrinks down, and he sees me.

But he doesn't recognise me.

'Need something?' Amid the chaos, it looks genuinely curious.

It . . . Because whatever I'm talking to, it isn't Merrick.

I'm still clinging to Calipsie's arm, but I've tucked her behind me. The creature glances down, sees her, and waves its hand in the air, tilting it quickly back and forth in an Aurora Saurin gesture that means 'Are you okay?'

I look down and find her waving back at it. With a grunt of admonishment, I push her firmly behind my back. She should let me establish this Rheman's motives before we join hands and prance our way across the Parched Lands.

'You're Rheman,' I say.

The creature looks briefly apologetic, then launches at us. I've made a mistake. A staggering force pushes us backwards, Calipsie wailing as we collide with Sion Uberick. The alchemy master collapses into a chair, taking our weight. Winded and reeling, I suck down air, scanning the room for an escape route.

One of the Quelled leaps off the balustrade and lands precisely where Calipsie and I were a moment ago. It lunges for us, but Rheman Merrick grabs it by the arm and jerks it backwards. The Rheman controlling Merrick is trying to protect us, I realise, launching to my feet. Rhemean Merrick and our attacker circle each other, and the people fall back, clearing the area. I grab a chair, my knuckles white around two legs of the makeshift shield.

The attacking Rheman is broad-shouldered and wears a teal tunic edged in silver. It swings like a fighter, but Rheman Merrick ducks and then brings a knee into Teal Tunic's side. The attacker retaliates by grasping Rheman Merrick in a brutal chokehold. Without thinking, I raise the chair and slam it down on Teal Tunic's back. Teal Tunic doesn't even flinch. It pauses to scowl at me though, and Rheman Merrick strikes back, head-butting it on the chin.

'Get the child to safety! The latrine. Go!' Rheman Merrick demands.

I was so focused on getting up and out that I never thought of going down.

Teal Tunic rises behind Rheman Merrick.

I shout a warning, then grab Calipsie by the arm. If we can get to the latrine, we can take to the tunnels that serve as the town's waste works. I fight the crowd's momentum, forcing my way to the back of the room, but progress is slow. When we're partway there, I look back. Rheman Merrick has gotten the better of the attacker and is sweeping the crowd, looking for us. Our eyes connect, and I wave it toward us just as the mass swallows Calipsie and me. Through the crush of bodies, I catch another glimpse of it, unnervingly steady on its feet, immune to the pummelling tide of people it leaves in its wake.

Passing all the desperate faces makes me uneasy. I should tell them how we plan to escape, but I can't risk it. If they panic, the crush of bodies might kill more than the Rhemans can carry away. Calipsie's behind me and barely able to keep on her feet with all the shoving. If everyone were headed for the latrines, she'd never make it. I pull her closer, urging her to keep up. We struggle against the crowd until Rheman Merrick pushes in front of us, clearing our path ahead.

Calipsie tugs my arm, and I turn back to check on her. She's fighting our progression, looking back the way we came.

'What is it?' I shout.

'My brother,' she says. 'He's outside, waiting for me.'

I scan the stairs. They're swarming with the Quelled now. The Rhemans are empty-handed on their way down, but they carry armfuls of Stained going back up the stairs.

'Is he stained?' I yell to be heard over the screaming chaos.

'No,' she says. Her eyes are wet, but she's holding herself together.

'Then he'll be fine,' I lie. If he isn't stained, the ghoragalls are unlikely to carry him away, but I can't say the same for the Rhemans. I tug on her arm to get her moving and point to a small door. 'Over here.'

We travel down a short flight of narrow steps. When we reach the landing, there's another door on the right. Behind it, we find the latrine. We struggle to close the door with the three of us inside. The room is gloomy, lit by a pitiful basking lamp that sheds no more light than a candle. The smell is fetid, but I expected that. Rheman Merrick wastes no time, pushing between us and gripping the wooden seat. It comes away with a splintering crunch. Rheman Merrick sets it against the wall and turns.

'Who's first?' it asks.

We can't drop Calipsie into the dark, foul-smelling hole; I don't know what's down there. I clamber onto what's left of the seat. One of my feet rests on a crumbling wall of rocks, while the other balances on a section of distressed wood.

I hold my hands out to it. 'A little help?'

The Rheman hesitates.

Like every kid in my generation, I've been taught never to touch a Rheman. When they make skin-to-skin contact, their essence, being—whatever it is—can transfer across to you. When that happens, you lose control. Your body becomes their body. If you're lucky, they'll transfer away again, and you'll get your body back, but you won't remember any of what was done while you were quelled.

'Are you helping us or not?' I demand.

Rheman Merrick takes my hands and lowers me into the sewer. I'm not exactly heavy, but I'm almost of age and have done nearly all my growing. Still, my weight seems trivial to the creature. My feet touch down with a wet slap, and I stare up at the square of light above. Then Rheman Merrick leans down, holding the basking lamp in one hand. It must have snapped it off the wall. I take it and look around. The tunnel is dank and grim, meandering off in two directions. I set the lamp down to help lower Calipsie to the floor. I've no idea when the sluice water will flow, but we need to be out of here before then.

Rheman Merrick leaps down and lands with a splash. The putrid mess splatters my legs, but I don't complain. I still don't know what I'm dealing with. The creature has been friendly until now, but that could change.

Rheman Merrick drops to one knee, squatting before Calipsie. 'You did all right in there. Being small has its advantages.'

I shuffle on the spot, keen to be on the move. 'We can't go uphill; it'll take us deeper under the town,' I say. 'We should head to the farms.'

'I know where there's shelter,' it says, standing. 'We can get cleaned up. Maybe even have a meal.'

A banging door echoes from somewhere nearby, and the creature looks up, its expression suddenly hostile. With a quick gesture for us to follow it, Rheman Merrick sets off down the tunnel toward the farms. At first, we run, then we slow to a fast walk. It's quiet except for our feet slapping the putrid waste coating the floor. For a long time, no one says anything. When Calipsie finally speaks, she strikes bone with her question.

'If you're Rheman, why'd you help us?'

The Rheman's response is quiet, and its words send a chill through me.

'Some of us are tired of being someone else's nightmare.'

'Who are you really?' asks Calipsie.

'My name is Kranik,' the creature says. 'What do they call you?'

Calipsie shares her name and then introduces me. She doesn't share my reservations about the Rheman, and I can hardly scold her here.

'What about your body?' asks Calipsie.

'This body belongs to Merrick,' Kranik says.

Interestingly, it can name the owner, and correctly too.

Calipsie goes quiet, probably plotting her next line of interrogation.

'I'm just borrowing it,' Kranik says, filling the silence. Maybe it thinks it owes us an explanation. For a fleeting moment, I pity it.

'Your Asaurin is very good,' I say, surprising myself. The Rheman has had nineteen alignments to learn Sojour's continental language. It probably speaks perfect Farich too.

The creature—Kranik—nods. 'Thank you. Communication is essential. Change is impossible without understanding.'

I feel annoyed. No one would need to change if its kind hadn't invaded our world.

'It's not much farther,' Kranik says, picking up the pace.

The tunnel gets narrower the farther we get from the city, and I have the clawing sense that the walls will crush us. Sharing the tight space with a Rheman isn't helping.

'Can we take the next outlet?' I ask. The smell alone is nauseating.

'But your Stain . . .' it says.

'I don't care about my Stain,' I snap. How much worse can it be outside, with the ghoragalls circling, than being trapped underground with a Rheman?

'And the girl?'

The Rheman has a point. If we're stumbling around outside in the dark, we'll be begging to join Helacth's army of Quelled.

'Where are we going?' Not knowing is making me crazy.

'Nortjie Farm. I know the owners,' says Kranik.

Most of Sojour could say the same. The farm is run by Sion Chaffrot and his sister Maisi. It's one of the largest in all of Sojour. Thinking about it, I haven't seen either of them at the market for an age.

'And you think they'll be there?' I ask, making an effort to keep the worry from my voice.

'They're both home,' says Kranik.

'How can you be sure?'

'The Sion had an accident,' replies the Rheman. 'He's unable to walk.'

2

KRANIK

The older girl, Kyjta, struggles with being underground. I don't blame her. It's dismal down here. It reminds me of the mines back on Rhema. There were few enough bodies to go around back then, and on the days my team and I were assigned one, we were confined to the bowels of the planet, tunnelling for terrinium. The indestructible metal was our planet's most valuable resource, and Helacth always demanded more of it. Without the precious metal, we couldn't build ships, and without ships, we were doomed. Helacth, our leader eternal, was resolute on the subject—our only hope of salvation lay off-world.

This planet is nothing like I expected. Nothing like the desolate expanses back home. It's not only the place but also the people. Every one of them is unique, while our manufactured bodies, which were grown in animation casks, all look alike. There was a time when the casks produced enough bodies to go around, but, as time wore on, every manufacturing batch produced smaller numbers of viable hosts. More and more bodies were dysfunctional or diseased. In Aurora Saurin alignments, I might be a grandparent, but by my count of days inhabiting a body, I've yet to come of age.

We landed with so few bodies still working that we had to borrow from the locals. We needed to keep things running on our ship, the *Rhema Bolajio*, and for that, we needed hands and feet. Tiberico, our crew master, schooled us to ensure our usage went undetected. So we borrowed at night, while they were sleeping; or during the day, if they happened to nap. It didn't seem very wrong in the beginning.

Then, Helacth sent orders from the mother ship stationed in Thormyth, a region in the icy south of Sojour. The crew were mandated to outfit ourselves with a permanent body, since we'd be staying indefinitely. Rhytheus, the captain of the *Rhema Bolajio*, gave us Helacth's orders and directions to the homes we should visit to stake our claim.

The staking did not go well. At least for me, it didn't.

I went to the address. I couldn't disobey a direct order, especially one from Helacth, but I almost turned and fled when the door flew open, revealing a woman with a small child wrapped around her leg. The red welt above her eye held me, fresh and bloody.

She looked annoyed, called over her shoulder.

'It's one of them dupes that fell outta the sky, Gerish. You better come.'

A man trundled down the hall holding a bandage. His steps slowed until he knelt before me with alarming reverence.

I was too busy checking the woman over for other injuries to pay him much attention. Her hands and arms were covered in cuts and bruises. She gave a derisive huff, snatched the bandage from the man's loosely curled fingers, and started to wind the shabby strip around the seeping gash on her forehead.

'What do you want?' she demanded.

'I . . . we're . . . looking for volunteers—' I started.

'I volunteer.' The kneeling man raised his hand.

'No you don't.' The woman slapped his wrist, dropping his arm. 'It's not the Hands here to lift you to a mightier plain. It's nothing more than a sky creature, landed and stuck.'

The man crawled forward on hands and knees, taking hold of my ankle. To him, I must have looked like every other Rheman: replica, upon replica, upon replica. If, for some reason, he found that theological, I wasn't going to be the Rheman to set him straight.

'I volunteer,' repeated the man, his face so low that his brow hung just shy of my sandal.

'You dare.' The woman bared her teeth and pulled a pair of shears from her apron, holding them as if they were a stake. 'You'll regret this, Gerish. I told you before—my cutters'll make a swift delivery of your—'

The child, a boy, started to cry.

'Hush,' said the woman. 'Your da'll want to leave us more if you keep up snotting.'

'Please. I wish to serve,' said the man.

The woman raised her shears and glared at me. Taking a step back, she made to shut the door, catching the kneeling man on the elbow. The thought of returning to the ship empty-handed terrified me. The quick movement, coupled with the man's shout of pain, caused me to panic. I slipped along the path leading from my manufactured body into the man. His hand still rested on my ankle, forming the perfect conduit. My mass-produced body slumped in the archway, lifeless, and I got to my feet, quickly adjusting to the unique weighting and lilt of the man's body.

At first, the woman didn't look at me. She was transfixed by the motionless form lying crooked on her threshold, with its vapid expression and flat, staring eyes. The boy saw through me, though. He raised a stocky arm to point at me as he started to sniffle.

'Gone.'

It was his heartbroken expression that got me moving. Those watery eyes were set to topple my resolve. I hoisted the limp, vat-grown body into my arms and walked away. The man had volunteered. Show me a coward anywhere who wouldn't have done the same.

Things got worse after that. The Aurora Saurins retaliated, attacking our cask-grown bodies whenever they came across them. They sabotaged our vehicles and disrupted our supplies. The crew of the *Rhema Bolajio* were nothing but a bunch of miners. The only enemy we'd ever known was the dark. We were losing a war we had no intention of fighting. Then Helacth stepped in, banishing the king and putting the Tarrohar in charge.

Before that alliance, the Tarrohar kept to the desert. Helacth didn't have enough Rhemans to control every Aurora Saurin, but the Tarrohar, with their Mind Pain and mental manipulation, could control the cities through fear and suggestion, at no cost to Helacth. No one knows exactly why they agreed. Some say they fear the Rhemans because their Mind Pain has no effect on us. Others think greed drove the accord. Regardless, they've grown quickly accustomed to living very lavish lives.

Things are different now. Sojour is governed by a system. The Body Trust isn't perfect, but it's better than the permanent quellings of the past. Coin for life. Life for coin. Just a day here and there. Nothing meaningful. I can fool myself into thinking that the exchange is mutually beneficial.

We reach the outlet closest to Nortjie Farm; the young girl is limping and leaning into Kyjta. I'd carry her, but it's not done. Tiberico has explained it many times. Physical handling is an invasion of their sanctuary. So I trudge alongside them, keeping my pace slow. It's ridiculous. Kyjta took my hands when I lowered her into the sewer, and after that, I helped Calipsie. If I wanted to quell either of them, I would have done it already. But society has rules, and we must abide by them. Tiberico instilled these lessons into the crew of the *Rhema Bolajio*. Similar care wasn't taken by the crew masters of the other ships, who see the native Aurora Saurins as possessions to own and discard. I used to believe things would change with the Body Trust, but that fantasy has passed. We Rhemans are an occupying force, and the Tarrohar use our presence as an excuse to extract more tax from the people of Sojour, while doing little to protect them.

At least the ghoragalls won't trouble us way out here. They're occupied elsewhere. My worry is getting this body back to the House of Judgement. The system has rules, and it's way past curfew. If I don't return Merrick soon, Azaire, our ship's liaison officer, will have to explain our non-compliance to the Tarrohar. It's not that the Tarrohar care for the Aurora Saurins, rather, they're careful to protect the integrity of the Body Trust. Under the Body Trust, the Rhemans pay Aurora Saurins for the use of bodies, and on every contract, there's a tax. That's what keeps the Tarrohar in finery. If people didn't trust that their bodies would be returned on time, no one would sign up for non-mandatory quelling.

Nortjie Farm is nestled at the end of a winding road, edged in hubery bush. The night flowers are some of the best I've seen in Sojour. They light the path with their iridescent petals, absorbing and reflecting the moonlight. When we reach the farmhouse door, I knock three times and stand back. The heavy door opens, and Maisi peers out into the night. She's a tall, broad woman with snowy hair that she combs across her voluminous forehead.

'Fair favour,' I say. 'I'm sorry for waking you, but we must get out of the night.'

She takes in the three of us on her doorstep and wrinkles her nose at the stench.

'What a pleasant surprise. Who do we have here? It's little Calipsie, isn't it? And Kyjta. I saw your stepfather just this morning. Come in. Come in.'

'The Quelled raided Sion Ignoti's basement,' Kyjta says, glancing back at me as she nudges Calipsie over the threshold. I'm not sure what she's thinking, but the accusation in her violet eyes sends a jolt through me.

'The Quelled in Merrocha? Thank goodness you're safe,' fusses Maisi.

'They wanted the ghoragalls to get us,' Calipsie says. 'Except for Kranik. He took us through the latrine.'

'Well, that explains the smell. Let's get you washed up before we do anything else.'

Maisi sends me outside to use the shower pull while she prepares a hot tub for the girls. I spend too long under the water. It's hard not to. I keep thinking this might be my last experience in an Aurora Saurin body. If Azaire finds out that I've missed the curfew, it probably will be. I towel myself off and dress in the farmer's shirt and loose trousers Maisi provided. Then I join Sion Chaffrot and the girls in the sitting room, where Maisi has laid out a feast of biscuits and steaming soup.

Sion Chaffrot is propped up in an armchair, his splinted feet swathed in bandages and elevated on a stool. He's a slim man with thinning chestnut hair and inquisitive eyes. Calipsie sits on the carpet near his feet, playing with a rag doll and eating biscuits, while Maisi collects blankets. Kyjta sits in another armchair, facing the hearth, and looks up as I walk in.

'We thought you'd left,' she says, her luminous lilac eyes darkening as I enter the room.

The ferocity of her beauty makes it all the more intimidating. Her wild, sun-coloured hair fans around her face like flames, and her eyes have an unreliable quality, shifting through shades like storm light.

It's still disarming, seeing the myriad faces on this planet. So different to Rhema, where every face looks the same. Here, on Aurora Saura, every face is unique, capturing beauty in its own extraordinary way. I often find myself staring, but with Kyjta, it's more compulsion than curiosity. Kyjta's warm, beige skin is stained along both arms, and there's more, highlighting her cheeks and dusting her collarbone. I like the way it reflects the firelight. It looks like the gleam is shining from within. Complimenting a Stain is reckless, and I'm not about to speak my thoughts. I've only just met her, and I don't know how she'd react.

'Kranik.' Sion Chaffrot greets me warmly, but there's apprehension in his grey eyes.

If someone reported me for fighting in a borrowed body, there would be trouble. The system has rules, and Rhemans aren't permitted to endanger anyone who loans out their body. But I couldn't stand by and do nothing. The attacking Rhemans were sent by Helacth, who quells his victims indefinitely. Helacth, our leader eternal, doesn't support the Body Trust. Stationed in South Sojour, he sends his ghoragalls to invade the more densely populated regions farther north. No one knows where they came from, or why he continues to use them. All that's known is that they belong to him, and him alone. The blind beasts brand their prey by day, raining their homing stain down from the sky, then return by night to make their abominable collections.

The Aurora Saurins have their defences. First, towers installed with warning bells, used to raise an alarm at the first sign of a ghoragall, and more recently, the zionate bunkers. These protective sanctuaries, strung with filaments extracted from the wings of giant satermijtes, are set up in a number of clandestine locations throughout the land.

Helacth shouldn't have any knowledge of their locations, yet he must, because he sent his Rheman crew using the bodies of those they've quelled.

Like me, Sion Chaffrot is convinced that someone is leaking the shelter locations. He sent me to Sion Ignoti's bunker tonight so I could help him get a list of everyone's names. He plans to question all who were present individually to try to piece together this puzzle. We must act quickly. Helacth's appetite for bodies far outstrips the number of Rhemans aboard his ship. No one knows what becomes of them, and now, with the protection of the zionate bunkers, his hauls are diminishing—that's why he sent the Quelled. There's no telling what he's capable of, or to what lengths he'll go to reap more bodies.

'What about the others?' asks Sion Chaffrot.

'Many were taken,' I tell him. 'Others escaped.'

'Why didn't the Vigilance Men stop them? Weren't they stationed at the door?'

'There were few enough of those when I entered. They might easily have been overwhelmed.'

'My brother was outside,' says Calipsie, suddenly alert. 'Do you think he got away?' She turns to Kyjta, cheeks rosy with firelight.

'Why not ask the Rheman?' says Kyjta, looking at me with unexpected harshness. Unexpected but not unwarranted. I have no illusions about what we are or what we've done. I only hope that our shared experience might . . . well, I don't know what I hope exactly.

'Kranik won't know. He was with us,' says Calipsie.

'We'll send word at first light so that your family know you're safe,' Sion Chaffrot tells Calipsie.

'Let's get down to the basement,' says Maisi, wringing her hands. She's anxious about harbouring the Stained during a raid. 'I have a blanket with a zionate weave down there. It will keep you girls hidden.'

I stand, waiting for Sion Chaffrot to bookmark his page, and hoist him into my arms. He's a decent man, whom I've come to respect over many alignments. He sees his wealth not as a boon, but as a tool, and uses it to help those in need. Aurora Saurins mostly, but Rhemans too, where he can. I don't have any wealth, but with his guidance, I can also be a tool, helping those in need. Making good on my transgressions.

We descend the stairs to the basement, Maisi in the lead. I carry Sion Chaffrot, angling him sideways to avoid bumping his injured feet. The basement is cluttered and colourful, the way Maisi likes things. The floor is a patchwork of carpets and cushions, and paintings of inkopels and carriot flowers decorate the walls. I set Sion Chaffrot onto a day bed in the corner while Maisi pulls a mattress from a pile near the wall. The girls climb on, and Maisi covers them. With its zionate weave, the blanket reflects a shimmering gilded pattern onto the ceiling, mesmerising Calipsie.

I should go, but I put off leaving by asking Sion Chaffrot about his feet. 'Are you sure you don't want me to arrange a mending? Bones are the easiest to heal. It would be quick. Painless.'

He looks at me like he knows I'm stalling. He's an intuitive man, and I'm no good at hiding my thoughts. Something about Kyjta's fiery demeanour makes it impossible for me to divert my gaze. I'm sure he's noticed me looking.

Sion Chaffrot chuckles. 'And have you punished for breaking my feet?'

'How did you get your injury, Sion?' asks Kyjta. I can't see her from my position, but I sense her attention like she's watching me for a reaction.

'I must go,' I say, standing.

'Stay for the story,' urges Sion Chaffrot. 'You're in it, after all.'

'Please,' begs Calipsie. 'I can't sleep without a story.'

I pull up a stool. I'm late already—how much more trouble can I get into?

Sion Chaffrot's storytelling voice is pitched just right to encourage listeners to lean forward, as though he's inviting them to share a secret.

'Let me take you back to the day of my first quelling,' he begins. 'I was nervous, I must tell you. I had a limp back then; nothing as bad as this'—he indicates his feet with another chuckle—'and I was sure I would be late.'

When Helacth put the Tarrohar in power, they made it mandatory to submit for quelling. Under the Body Trust, citizens must give up at least one day every moon cycle for which they are compensated. If citizens choose to contribute more time during Ursala's forty-day moon cycle, they're paid more. This is how Sojour has curbed long-term quellings for almost a decade. The ghoragalls still raid the towns, scooping up the Stained and flying them to Helacth in the south, and the Quelled still raid the shelters at Helacth's command. Yet, the north abides under the covenant, and the system has prevailed.

'Have you seen the Sorbs?' Sion Chaffrot asks the girls.

They tell him they haven't. Calipsie is riveted, listening for every word. It's harder to tell what Kyjta's thinking. She's trying to hide how much the presence of a Rheman affects her. Especially one who's playing friendly with her kind.

'Kranik, why don't you explain?'

I pause, trying to figure out how to describe the oval environments that support our existence when we're not being ferried by a body.

'The Sorbs are our natural state,' I venture. 'They're like a home for our essence, somewhere we can feel closer to, well, to . . .' How do I explain Ezerya? Aurora Saurins worship the Hands. A simplistic concept of good begets good and evil begets evil. Ezerya is not a concept, and is far more difficult to describe.

'They look like spheres,' says Sion Chaffrot. 'Completely trans-parent. You can see right inside them.'

'What's inside?' Calipsie presses.

'Inside, it's like a storm. Cloud spears raging. Mist rising. You've never seen anything like it. They call it transference. Did you know that? You touch a Sorb, and the Rheman comes across to you.'

'Was Kranik inside your Sorb?' asks Calipsie.

The Sion claps a hand on one knee. 'Yes! How did you know?'

Calipsie looks suddenly shy.

'And when Kranik departed, guess what?' The Sion pauses for effect, but neither girl ventures a response, so he continues, 'I had no limp.'

Both girls stare at him, looking confused.

'But I thought he broke your feet,' Calipsie says.

'That was much later. Way before that—when we hadn't even heard of their miracle healing—he fixed my limp. Miracles are the real reason the Body Trust is important. It's not only the framework of our economy; nowadays, it's the source of our longevity. Under the current contracts, Rhemans compensate us for using our bodies, and we can use that coin to evade death and disease.'

'You're leaving out the part where a single treatment can cost more than an alignment's worth of our days,' says Kyjta. 'Not to mention the taxes that are syphoned from both sides by the Tarrohar.'

'Indeed. The system is far from perfect,' says Sion Chaffrot. 'And we're still working to persuade Helacth of its validity as an alternative to the raids . . . but that's another story. I wanted Kranik to tell you about the day he broke my feet.'

The girls angle their heads toward me. Everyone is silent, expect-ing me to complete the story . . . but what can I tell them? Not the truth. Just the same lie I told Sion Chaffrot.

Seeing my hesitation, Calipsie offers support. 'It was an accident, wasn't it?'

'It wasn't intentional,' I agree. 'It was a miscalculation.'

Kyjta is staring at me as though I've caught fire. I have the awkward sensation that my body is malfunctioning. It's difficult to speak, and my frame feels jittery and unmanageable.

'Let's not embarrass our guest,' says Maisi, as she makes her way down the stairs carrying a plate of moist lotils cake. The heavy slices, already crumbling, glint golden in the lamplight.

The story I made up, that I slipped from a cliff into the sea while gathering gossif thread from the nests on Nortjie Farm for garment production, was believable enough, but it's far from the truth. It's not that I want to lie, but the truth puts the entire system at risk, and I couldn't face that. Couldn't face going back to the way things worked before the Body Trust.

If the siblings reported me for breaking Sion Chaffrot's feet, I would have been relegated to my Sorb for eternity. The Tarrohar have a strict 'no injury' policy. It's not just that they worry word of injury to a loaned body would get out and impact their tax targets, it's deeper than that. Rhemans don't feel pain, and that fact disturbs the Tarrohar. It's as if they think we'll suddenly realise we're immune to the Mind Pain, and could overpower them. They don't fully appreciate that Helacth is in control. Thankfully, Maisi offered to ferry me back in time for curfew and lied that Sion Chaffrot had a business emergency. Without their aid, I would never have laid eyes on Aurora Saura again. I owe the siblings my freedom; it's a debt I'll never repay.

As I struggle to figure out how to approach the lie, someone beats urgently on the farmhouse door.

3

KYJTA

The pounding at the door makes me jump. The Rheman looks up, just as startled by the intrusion as the rest of us. If it's one of the Quelled, we won't have the same luck escaping. The latrines on the farms are in outbuildings. I have the ridiculous thought that it's my stepfather. He wouldn't be out looking for me, though. If the ghoragalls lifted me away, he'd applaud them.

Maisi sets the tray on the day bed at Sion Chaffrot's feet. She smooths her floral skirt, gives her brother a piercing look, and goes upstairs. Kranik rises before she makes it past the first step. I stand, the blanket falling from my shoulders. If anything happens, I want to be near the Rheman. The creature saved us once; it might do so again. Calipsie must feel the same because she stands, gathering the shimmering blanket around her like a shield.

'Girls,' says Sion Chaffrot in a reasonable voice. We don't wait to hear his sensible suggestion; we're already climbing the stairs.

The front door closes as we enter the hallway. Someone is in the kitchen with Maisi and Kranik. It's not my stepfather, thank the Hands. It's Sion Aldemin's youngest son. He's a drifter, or so I've heard from Halli—a Charmore, who's a fount of intrigue and one of my real father's most dependable customers. Halli once told me he refused to take his apprenticeship, giving up the title of Sion and the chance of taking on his family's brewery.

The boy Aldemin and Kranik wrap their hands around each other's forearms and knock shoulders in a Rheman greeting. Touch allows Rhemans to identify one another, so the contact is second nature. I know this because it's a good way for an Aurora Saurin to spot a Rheman, which is something we're trained to do from a young age, so we can quickly make ourselves scarce.

'Maisi, this is my good friend Lakhan,' Kranik says.

I can't remember the name of Sion Aldemin's youngest, but it's not Lakhan, so our guest is definitely quelled. If Maisi didn't appear so calm at the introduction, I doubt I'd hang around to eavesdrop on the conversation. I'm already cataloguing the exits and plotting the best route for escape. The three huddle on one side of the kitchen, in front of the main door. There's a large window to their left, but it's too dark outside to see the sprawling farm beyond the glass.

'I've looked all over town for you,' Lakhan says, addressing Kranik. Then, turning to Maisi, the Rheman continues. 'Merrick's parents are threatening repercussions if their son isn't returned immediately. They didn't know he'd signed up to the Body Trust, and we told them to expect him back in time for curfew.'

'Well, if you must travel at night, let me fetch you a lamp,' Maisi says, then disappears into a storeroom beyond the kitchen.

'You missed the curfew,' Lakhan hisses at Kranik; the Rheman doesn't realise Calipsie and I are standing in the darkened hallway.

It's no wonder Kranik's friend came searching. The Tarrohar wouldn't show Kranik mercy for saving the two of us. If the Rheman missed the cutoff for returning a body, it would jeopardise their precious Body Trust.

'The Quelled raided Sion Ignoti's basement,' Kranik says. 'I wanted to help.'

Lakhan waves dismissively. 'Save it for Azaire. I'm just glad I found you. He's talking about committing you to your Sorb. He says you've no respect for the Body Trust. He called you dangerous.'

'Dangerous?' Kranik says.

'Don't look so smug. It's not a compliment,' Lakhan says.

'I'm not being smug. It's funny.' Kranik smiles.

'We should leave now. It's hard enough listening to the meteoritic scrap Azaire spouts when you're around to defend yourself. When you're not—'

Calipsie fidgets at my side. The reflected light from the zionate weave grabs Lakhan's attention. 'Friends of yours?' it asks Kranik.

Kranik glances over, eyes brightening at finding us there. 'Yes. Friends, only just met.'

'Fair favour,' Lakhan responds. 'I see you're both stained. I'm sorry for that.'

I've never been pitied by a Rheman, and it doesn't sit well. I'm rifling through my reserve of biting comments when the window explodes. At first, all I see is the sprinkling glass; the glossy black feathers are indistinct until the shards settle on the darkwood floor. The ghoragall puffs its chest, agitating its colossal wings. Its size claims the entire room, trapping Maisi in the storeroom and obscuring the Rhemans. I've never seen one up close like this. It's so big, so terrifying, my darkest nightmare doesn't contend. It caws, and I jump, backing down the hall. I knock into Calipsie, who stumbles.

'Get up!' I scream at her, clawing at the blanket. My shaking hands can't find her. I look back, terrified by what I'll see. The beast lowers its great head into the hall. Its eyes are the white of wriggling larvae, its face a carnage of exposed bone. Calipsie shrieks, but I can't help her, I'm frozen in place. The ghoragall sees me, and its glistening claw reaches. I recoil and it snatches the air in front of my face. Its legs are long and lean, sheathed in pale, mottled skin. Through their sheer translucence, I see the mechanical workings of raw muscle and sinew gyrating the bones.

Terror paralyses me. I can't move out of its way. It's as though part of me wants the ghoragall to take me. The beast is drawn to me; that's its purpose: find the Stained and take them to be quelled. I hadn't considered that I might be drawn to it. But it's not the ghoragall I'm craving, I realise—it's a life without pain. I've lived so long believing my mother left me for a better life that I can't shake the hurt. Even now, knowing the truth, that shadow still blackens my heart, and I know I'll never be free.

Somewhere in the distance, someone shouts my name. A moment later, something cool brushes my skin. There's a tug on my arm, but I don't dare look. One talon snakes around my wrist, cool, slippery, but also comforting. The ghoragall flaps its wings and jerks me into the kitchen. Then it draws me in. Its bulging belly looms just ahead, covered in a dark, matted coat of feathers. I have time to scream before I'm bundled into darkness. But it's not the ghoragall's belly I'm burrowed into; it's Maisi's zionate-weave blanket. Somehow Calipsie has managed to throw the thing over my head. We're both tucked beneath it, staring at the ghoragall's claw loosening and retracting, as though it's forgotten why it's here.

Calipsie takes my hand. We edge backwards. We can't see where we're going, but we can guess how to navigate the hallway. The ghoragall caws, a mournful sound that makes my skin crawl. I once delivered a stillborn elvakan on the farm, and the mother's cries were eerily similar. She never drew a cart again. There's a sharp crack, and the cry is cut short. One of the Rhemans must have silenced the thing. I don't lift the blanket to inspect their work; seeing the ghoragall alive was nightmare enough for me. Calipsie and I muddle our way down the hall on unsteady feet, only lifting the blanket when we reach the stairs. When we make it to the basement, Sion Chaffrot tells us to take cover on the mattress, repeating, in a soft placating voice, that Kranik will deal with the ghoragall. We have nothing to worry about, he says. We should sleep.

Calipsie and I do as he suggests, pulling the protective blanket over our heads. The young girl snuggles into me and quickly falls asleep. I lie awake, listening to Sion Chaffrot as he turns the pages of his book. A long while later, I hear boots on the stairs. I tense, my arm wrapped protectively around Calipsie, whose body is nestled under my arm, and listen to the exchange.

'It's done,' Kranik says. 'We buried it at the back of the orchard. You're safe.'

'Good,' says Sion Chaffrot. 'Now go. Get the boy home.'

Boots clomp up the stairs. When the door closes with a gentle click, I turn over. 'What did Kranik mean? Why has he buried it? Because feather dust is illegal?' I ask.

From my father, Hok Poltiqe, the town's potion master, I know ghoragalls accumulate granules, which hold certain properties, in their feathers. The substance is banned by the Tarrohar, who feel threatened by anything they can't understand or control. My father is careful not to use the dust in his recipes.

Sion Chaffrot shifts under his covers. 'It's not the dust,' he says. 'Ghoragalls travel in pairs. If you have the misfortune of killing one, you must kill its mate or cover your tracks. Bury it, burn it, whatever it takes. Else the mate will haunt the site.'

'Haunt? With what purpose?' I ask.

'To find the culprit and carry them away to be quelled, I expect,' he says, adding, 'It's late. You should take some rest.'

I lower myself onto the mattress beside Calipsie and wait for morning.

I'm woken by the creak of floorboards above. I sit up, half expecting to hit my head on one of the low beams above my bed, the night and all its horrors sinking back into a dream. But this isn't my bedroom, and Calipsie is sleeping beside me. Sion Chaffrot looks up from his book. He hasn't moved from his reclining position on the day bed. I doubt he's slept at all. He's been watching over us, listening for ghoragalls. Bracing for the Quelled. Not that an early warning would change our fates. If the Quelled come for us, we've no means to escape.

I stretch and wish him fair favour. Maisi's rocking chair is empty; she must be upstairs, preparing the morning meal. Boots clomp overhead. The floorboards up there could do with a few well-placed nails, they squeak horribly, but that could be for the best.

'That'll be Kranik. He's got some tread,' says Sion Chaffrot, placing his book on an end table.

A mauve blanket covers the Sion's legs and most of his middle. The movement jostles something angular hidden beneath his coverings. I assume it's something deadly: a crossbow or similar weapon. I've misjudged him. He wasn't only listening; he was guarding us.

The cellar is warm, heated by basking lamps glowing white-hot in each corner. It's nothing like my home, where my stepfather only lights the basking lamps on the coldest nights and, even then, only in the living room. The heat never reaches my bedroom at the top of the house.

You'd expect it to be snug, tucked neatly under the thatched roof, but it gets cold up there. I sleep in four or five layers of clothing during the colder moon cycles. Even then, my nose is numb come morning.

Calipsie is still fast asleep, balled up like a startled curl worm. Her copper braid has come loose from her crown and slinks around her neck. I'm sure she's exhausted, and I don't want to wake her, so I get up carefully and tuck the blanket around her.

'Maisi sent a farmhand to Minuet Farm at first light. Your stepfather knows you're here, and safe. There's no need to rush home. Calipsie's family won't get here till late afternoon. You should stay, Kyjta. Keep her company.'

'All right.' There's no reason not to. Words don't come easily between my stepfather and me. I'm too tired to explain everything and listen to him rant about his obligation to look after me.

Gently, I pin Calipsie's braid back in place, taking care not to wake her.

'Any news of her brother?' I ask, not looking at Sion Chaffrot.

'I'm afraid I neglected to ask,' he says. I battle the sinking sensation in the pit of my stomach. Calipsie will blame me if her brother was taken. Though I might not see her again after today, she'll always think of me as the girl who dismissed her brother, intent on saving herself.

'Go on upstairs. Maisi and Kranik will come to get me when it's time for breakfast,' says Chaffrot. He must think I need Maisi's cheer.

As I leave, I ask, 'Why don't you just let Kranik get your bones mended? Isn't that the point of the Body Trust? They get Aurora Saurin bodies, and we get Rheman miracles.'

'There are greater rewards in life than mere mobility,' he says cryptically.

'Like reading your books?' I lift the tome from his side table and read the title: *The Trail of the Old Soro*. He's reading about the former king of Aurora Saura—banished into the Parched Lands by the Tarrohar and now only ever heard of in tall tales and imaginings.

Sion Chaffrot laughs. It's a pleasant, soft sound, like the gurgle of rushing water.

'Possibly, but that's not what I mean.'

'You think they'll put Kranik back in its Sorb if they find out the Rheman broke your feet?'

'There's a good chance.'

I'm sure my disdain shows on my face, but Sion Chaffrot doesn't seem to mind.

'If it broke your feet, why do you care what happens to it?' I ask.

It's a moment before the Sion responds, and what he says surprises me.

'You're so very like your mother.'

'My mother? You knew her?' I choke out. How did we go from a conversation about the Rheman to this?

'Yes. We once helped each other. A courageous woman.' I get the sense he wants to say more, but he stops himself.

'Helped each other with what?' Emotion constricts my throat. After all this time and even knowing that she's dead—even knowing who killed her—I'm still desperate for information.

She was here. She shared this world with me. Once, in a distant, murky past, she loved me.

Sion Chaffrot sighs deeply, and I know that, like most questions about my mother, this one will go unanswered.

'We'll speak on it one day,' he says gently. Placatingly.

My flesh burns with indignation. Why does everyone in this town shy away from the topic of my mother? It's as though they're all terrified I'll shatter at the mention of her name.

I won't. I'm long past that.

'For now, as a favour to me, you and Calipsie will help Kranik on the farm this morning. When you're done, come back for lunch. Your opinion of the Rheman may change if you spend some time with him.' Sion Chaffrot's eyes are gentle.

'Half a day won't change anything,' I tell him firmly. The Rheman may have saved my life, but I owe it nothing. Its kind are a plague on Aurora Saura. I have no idea why Sion Chaffrot is entertaining them, but he took us in, fed us, and protected us. If Calipsie and I owe any debt, it lies with him.

I'm about to head upstairs when Sion Chaffrot surprises me again. 'Kyjta,' he says, stalling me at the door, 'have you noticed how the Rheman favours you?'

His comment feels so inappropriate that I can't help checking on Calipsie, who remains snuggled under the covers, still fast asleep.

'What's that supposed to mean?' I demand.

'Only that a friend made of an enemy is no ordinary friend,' he replies.

Still struggling to pull my thoughts from the ghost of my mother, I bow my head and jog up the stairs.

The kitchen is darker than it should be this time of day. A wooden panel covers the window, which probably offers a grand view of the jade fruit orchard. Someone, I assume Maisi, has already cleared the glass and feather dust from the night before. I don't immediately spot Kranik, but Maisi is at the cooker. She wipes her hands on her apron when she sees me. Steam wafts off the pot at her back, and the scent is homey, taking me back to a time when family mealtimes were an honoured tradition.

'Breakfast's about ready.'

'It smells delicious,' I say softly.

Sensing a presence behind me, I turn, scuffing my boots on the floorboards and almost tripping. It's Kranik; the creature stands beside the dining room table, holding a bucket of jade fruit. Merrick's hair is blond, like most Merrochans', and has a slight curl. His face is hardy, but he has soft eyes and girlishly plump lips to offset the brutish nose and solid, angular jaw. I remind myself that this isn't him; in my mind, I must remake him as Kranik.

If Kranik is using Merrick's body again today, then Merrick must have gone to the village green this morning and agreed to give up another day of his life in exchange for coin. Once I'm of age I'll be expected to contribute to the truce between our two species in a similar way. The price of peace is one day per moon cycle, and every citizen is expected to pay. Some, like Merrick, may submit more often, and take the creatures' coin, but anything more than a day every moon cycle is a personal choice.

'Sleep well?' Kranik asks.

'Yes. Fine.' I don't ask it how it slept. I don't even know if it does sleep.

Maisi sets the dining room table. The clatter of crockery is unbearably loud. Kranik enters the kitchen and sets the bucket of fruit on the counter as I'm looking around for something to do. It takes a large knife from the rack and picks up one of the ripe fruits to peel it. Not seeing anything else that needs attention, I join in, taking a knife and lifting a piece of fruit.

'The Sion's asked us to help out on the farm this morning,' I say, slipping the blade under the fruit's thick purple skin.

Kranik looks startled by the suggestion, and accidentally cuts Merrick's finger with his blade. Blood runs a circuit across the fruit before dripping to the floor.

'You're bleeding,' I tell it.

Kranik looks at the finger, realising what it's done. I forgot that Rhemans don't feel pain. Physically, they don't feel anything. Kranik seems embarrassed by its lapse in concentration. I yell for Maisi, who sees the blood and grabs a towel. The Rheman is wrapping Merrick's finger when, for some reason, I rattle off my farm skills: I can milk yakkats, tend alzogs, reap gossif, and the list goes on. You'd think I wanted a job.

The Rheman stares at me, its mouth a little ajar. I guess I've stupefied it with my eagerness. Disgusted with myself, I drop my jade fruit into the mortar and take my aggression out with the pestle. Soon there's nothing but mulch and juice in the bowl. Kranik holds out a cup in Merrick's uninjured hand, and I pour in the juice. With one hand bundled in the towel, Kranik sets the cup on the table and gets another. The interaction is an unwelcome reminder of the foolish antics that cost Merrick his job. I had just returned from one of my father's deliveries, feeling annoyed. One of the Charmores ordered an infatuation potion but only turned up with half the coin. It was a long journey to the luxurious live-ins, quarters to the Charmore serfs, and I was angry not to take my full fee. Feeling spiteful, I shared the story with Serain, my stepfather's niece, who manages his stalls at the Meghaven fair. I should have kept my mouth shut. It's my job to be discreet.

'Are you telling me you have a pocket full of infatuation potion, and all you can think about is coin?' she scolded. 'Give it here. I'll buy it from you.'

I took her coin, not for a moment dreaming she'd spike Merrick's drink when my back was turned. She'd planned to hand it to him herself, but my stepfather stormed in ranting about something, and she was forced to leave the drink unattended. When Merrick took his water break, it was me who bewitched him as the potion took effect. I still experience a sickly wave of misery every time I think back on it.

'I'm learning about the farm,' Kranik says. 'You should take the lead.'

I pour the remnants of the jade juice into the fresh cup the creature holds out to me.

'Yakkats first. They get sensitive if they're not milked early in the day.'

'Maisi usually takes care of them,' Kranik says, a little warily.

'We won't need her help today.'

Once we've made the juice, Kranik collects Sion Chaffrot. I rouse Calipsie, and we all sit for breakfast. We discuss the day's chores while Maisi serves us bowls of creamy muleei. When the aroma reaches us, Kranik closes its eyes and breathes in. For a brief moment, I get to look at the creature uninterrupted. Merrick has large farmer's hands, but Kranik uses them elegantly and expressively; now that they've settled on the table, I'm drawn to look at them. Sunlight is streaming in from the living area, across the table, illuminating his tawny skin. The blond hairs on the back of his hands shine like crystal beams. I've never noticed Merrick's hands before; they were always wrapped around the handle of a farm implement or stuffed into his pockets when my stepfather scolded him.

I keep expecting Merrick to say something combative; he still hates me for spiking his drink. The creature, Kranik, doesn't share his hatred, though, and is pleasant and contemplative. It's like trying to have a conversation while a door opens and closes in my face; I'm not getting all of it. One moment I think I'm talking to Kranik, the next Merrick. It's impossible to concentrate on what the creature is saying. I muddle through it, somehow, and it's soon time for us to go.

4

KRANIK

After breakfast, Maisi and I help Sion Chaffrot into his rocking chair. It's a weather-beaten old thing that looks like it won't take his weight. It creaks as we set him down but doesn't fall apart. Maisi places a blanket around his legs, and I hand him his crossbow. The weapon is broad and probably heavy. He sets it on his lap. He can see a good portion of the farm from his position here. The stables, their rooftops anyway, are visible beyond a copse of yellowing trees. The rapzette cliffs are on the left, where these flying reptiles hatch their young. The crops and some of the animals are farther down the valley. He won't be able to see us, but his job is to watch the skies.

Maisi takes my arm. I don't notice her until she forces me to face her.

'You look after these girls, you hear.' Maisi hands me a lethal-looking pitchfork while raising an equally lethal eyebrow.

She's no fool. When she opened the main door this morning, carrying a sack of glass and feather dust, she didn't look surprised to see me. She didn't look pleased either.

'You're back early,' was all she said, but her look was reproachful.

I can't blame her. I've put her through a lot. We're fond of each other now, but we weren't always. I badly injured her brother when borrowing his body. Crawling back here on Sion Chaffrot's hands and knees, trailing his broken feet behind me, didn't set us up for a good start. Still, her disapproval didn't change anything. I took the bag from her and carried it to the pit.

Although I didn't ask after either of the girls, I was loitering too obviously. Maisi must've taken pity on me. She told me they were still asleep and suggested we have breakfast together. She said talking about last night would benefit everyone, especially Calipsie.

I'm sure she's right, though I have no experience with children. Back on Rhema, bodies aren't released from their animation casks until they're in their prime. Here on Aurora Saura, the young are bred to fear us, and their parents tend to spirit them away.

Maisi kept me occupied with chores, repeatedly sending me to the other side of the house for obscure items unrelated to her tasks. I thought she just wanted me out of the way until I noticed how much noise I was making. I tried to be quieter when she sent me back to collect a bucket of jade fruit, but when I returned, Kyjta was standing in the archway between the kitchen and the dining area. That's when I realised I hadn't thought of anything to say.

When she turned around, I stood there, gripping the bucket, and asked her something trivial. It felt wasteful; there's so much I genuinely want to know about her. Morning light sloped in from the lofty windows, kindling the Stain on her cheeks so it shimmered like tears. Seeing the markings every day must fuel her hostility, surfacing everything her kind has suffered under us.

'Stay in range,' Sion Chaffrot advises us, bringing me back to the present.

We all agree that we will, and then we're on our way. The morning is fresh, the grass long. We carve a passage through it toward the stables. The air is sweet with the tang of ripe jade fruit, and the breeze tousles Kyjta's fiery blond hair.

We visit the yakkats first. They're in the stables, curled up and still asleep. The sun streams through slatted walls, and there's a pleasant, sticky closeness about the smell. Three yakkats, gently snoring, are tangled together on a soft bed of springy gossif thread.

'That one.' Kyjta points to the largest of the furry beasts lazing in the sun. 'Scratch it under the chin. It might roll over.'

Calipsie settles on her knees. She leans forward and digs her fingers into the thick mane of russet hair growing from the animal's jaw. The yakkat yawns and rolls over, exposing a long belly thick with golden fur.

'Give it a really good scratch.'

The harder Calipsie scratches, the more the yakkat's fur curls back from its stomach, until three white teats are exposed.

Kyjta settles herself on the gossif bed. She takes a teat between finger and thumb and aims the nib into a tubular receptacle. A stream of yellow fluid arcs into the tube. The yakkat doesn't stir.

'Are there yakkats on Rhema?' Calipsie asks.

Absorbed with watching Kyjta work, I don't look up as I respond.

'Everything we need is manufactured,' I say.

Kyjta looks back at me. 'Haven't you milked anything?'

I shuffle in place. 'I don't know how.'

'You should be doing this.' She gets to her feet and passes me the receptacle.

'This isn't going to work.' I try talking her out of it, but she's already ushering me into position.

'Go on.'

I squat on the mat of gossif and stare at the three teats. Which one should I milk first? I go with the teat she was handling. I take it between finger and thumb and try to mimic her movements, but the milk doesn't come.

'You need to tighten your grip,' she says.

She fearlessly braces her hand around mine. I look at her, alarmed. If she's touching me, she's forgotten what I am. When she remembers, she'll pull back and we'll both be embarrassed.

'Tighter,' she says when our eyes connect. She doesn't remove her hand, and it's plain she's not afraid of me.

But she doesn't like me either.

I turn my attention to the teat, letting Kyjta guide my hand. When she lets go, she does it slowly. She thinks I can manage now.

I do something wrong; the yakkat's head jerks up and it hisses at me.

'Get back,' Kyjta yells, but it's too late. The yakkat's sharp tail whips forward and lances my palm. In my periphery, I see Calipsie edging for the door. The yakkat hisses again. Then, Kyjta is behind me, pulling me away.

When we're outside the stables, she inspects my wound. It's the same hand I cut earlier. I'll have to get the skin mended in Restoration before returning the body.

Kyjta digs in her pockets and withdraws a small tub. She opens it and smells the contents.

'It's for healing. My father's recipe.' She scoops up what's left of the salve and smears it onto the wound. Although the cream is primitive and unnecessary, I don't say so. I'm still in awe of her willingness to handle me, skin to skin.

After she pockets the empty salve, I do something Tiberico would call irresponsible. I take her hand and turn it over in mine;

her Stain gives me a reason. She stands quietly, not pulling away, and we both stare at her hands. The Stain glistens brightly, reflecting prisms of gold and silver light. Without thinking, I brush my thumb over her fingertips.

'How did you manage this?' I ask. I must say something, or the moment will get strange.

She pulls back, balling her fists. The fire is back in her eyes. 'How do you think?'

I attempt to recover. 'I only mean, I haven't seen the Stain so concentrated before.'

The Stain falls like raindrops, binding on contact. It's unusual for the pads of one's fingers to be thoroughly coated, while the fingers and hands are not.

Kyjta calls out for Calipsie, who comes running. When she reaches us, Kyjta grabs her hand and stalks away. I stare after the two girls, unable to believe how stupid I've been. Kyjta might not flinch from my touch, but I'm still Rheman. I wanted to share a brief connection, but instead, I've deepened a rift. By calling out her Stain, I've underscored our differences. If she didn't see me as a villain before, she will now. It was foolish to believe it could be any other way.

I follow slowly, keeping a respectable distance. My idiocy hasn't upset Kyjta enough to change our plans; she's leading Calipsie to the cliffs. If I'm careful, I might still get to spend the morning in their company.

5

KYJTA

At the cliffs, the hatchlings are unsettled. They bustle around my hands, pecking at my fingers. One particularly vicious brat nips the flesh between my finger and thumb when I try to collect the mesh of amber gossif, and I chase it away. The others smell the mote of blood and start to crip. It's a horrible sound, like knocking smooth stones together, right beside your ear. They hop in frantic circles, begging for food. I stay focused; rapzettes can be deadly. Maybe not the babies, with their oily, ineffectual wings, but the mothers are ferocious. We must finish before they're back from hunting, but I'm distracted.

I wasn't expecting the Rheman to question the markings on my hands. I should have done the milking myself. Why did I involve it? My Stain isn't something I can explain. Not without incriminating myself.

When the ghoragalls flock, they target crowded, noisy places. They're blind, but they can pinpoint large gatherings using sound alone. The Stain rains down from their splatter tubes as they soar overhead. If you don't get to shelter, you're marked for life. You can't wash it off. Most people hunch over when the warning bells sound, tucking their faces down. Hands clench into fists or protectively pull up their collars. The markings are usually splatters of silver Stain on the backs of necks or shoulders, heads, ears, and sometimes their hands. For me, it's palms, fingers, chest, and neck. My face too. My finger pads are coated like they were dipped in a puddle of Stain. But only zionate can hold the Stain. Melted down and crafted into a vessel, zionate has the power to maintain the Stain in its purest form. Use anything else and the liquid instantly turns into shimmering dust.

I work faster; the commotion will bring the mothers back. I grab the nearest nest and tear off the top quarter. More like the top half, but I don't have time to be precise. There's enough left for the mother to mend and probably enough to prevent her babies from plunging to their deaths.

I risk a look down and regret it. The cliff drops straight off into the Onaway Ocean. I stuff the threading into my sack and move along. I'm not comfortable with heights, but Calipsie is too young, and I couldn't take Kranik's weight if the creature fell. There's a rope around my middle, and Kranik holds one end. It's funny—I trust Kranik to keep me secure, but I don't trust the Rheman with the story of my Stain.

Calipsie hangs over the lip of the cliff, throwing dried cocchi fish into the nests. The meal smells of rot, turning my stomach. My Stain flashes, reflecting the morning sunshine; I hope it doesn't give me away to the mothers. They'll have my eyes for disturbing their offspring.

I haven't been stained very long. Not a full alignment has passed since that day at the fair. I'd stashed the zionate beaker in my dress. It was part of a collection my mother built up during her Rheman-free childhood. It knocked against my thighs as I walked the dirt path to the Meghaven field where they held the fair. The gentle tapping comforted me as I walked.

I spent the morning helping Serain sell my stepfather's produce at a stall near the wooden playground. A cover had been erected over it. That's what gave people the courage to come out. Most of the time, the fair was poorly attended; few children used the playground. Their parents always hovered nearby, ready to pull them under the awning if they stepped out of its bounds. It had been a while since the last staining, and people were getting braver. Small groups gathered, murmuring in the sunlight.

When the first yelp of panic sounded, a perverse quiver of excitement came over me. I stepped out from under the stall's little awning to get a gauge on the ghoragalls. They were flying in from the south; they always did. Their massive wings beat in unison, as though they shared a single mind.

Merrocha's bells chimed their warning, and everyone screamed. Serain yelled at me and grabbed me by the arm. People ran for the playground; no one wanted to be out in the open when the creatures swooped. I ran as fast as anyone, headed for the covered playground. But I wasn't looking at the skies; I was looking back at the zionate beaker. It sat glinting in the harsh sunlight, carefully positioned on the rim of a defective water fountain. It wasn't easy to tell yet, but I thought I had estimated their flight path correctly this time.

'The mothers are coming!' Calipsie shouts from above.

I yelp with fright, teetering on the ledge. Kranik pulls the rope taut and starts to hoist me up.

'Wait,' I demand, halfway through separating another nest. 'Let me finish this one.' Already my feet have lifted off the ledge; I have to drop the nest and use my hands or risk scraping my face and knees on the rocks.

'No time,' Kranik says, pulling me over the lip. 'Get to the barn.'

'Hurry.' Calipsie pulls on me as I'm trying to get to my feet.

Looking over my shoulder, I see them. They're not as large as the ghoragalls and not nearly as menacing. But if you value your sight, you don't upset them.

Kranik scoops Calipsie onto its back and tries to lift me too. The Rheman's strength is alarming. I shove its arms away. 'I can look after myself!' I shout.

We run. The rapzette cripping is getting louder; the rabid beasts are gaining on us. I imagine them swooping down, tangling themselves in our hair, and pecking out our eyes.

Kranik runs, snapping a branch off a tree. When one of the rapzettes swoops down, the Rheman uses the stick to knock it off course. Kranik reaches the barn first, shoving Calipsie through the door. It only follows once I'm through, slamming and bolting the door behind us.

'The windows,' I say, my terror escalating.

If we get trapped in here with one of those things, it'll tear us to bits. Kranik races to the back of the barn where a large stable door stands open. I dash for the nearest window and see an open shutter hanging limply. I grab it by the corner and look out. A colony of rapzettes is diving for the opening, each wrestling for the lead. I slam the shutter closed, but the wood is warped, and I can't lock it. The colony bombards the wood, cripping madly, their oily wings thrashing. I give the shutter another shove and wedge it into place. After I've locked it and stepped back, I see the tip of a wing caught between the window frame and the shutter. The sight makes me shiver. As I back away, I hear Calipsie's startled cry.

I look around, trying to spot her in the dark barn. When I see her, huddled near four barrels of rolled gossif, she's transfixed.

Something's lurking behind a heavy beam and a bunch of rusting farm equipment. Treading as softly as I can, I close the gap between us and follow her gaze. A rapzette hides in the shadows, and its lone dark eyeball, cradled on a volcano of puckered black skin, swivels and centres on me. Its beak opens, exposing a greyish-blue tongue, and it crips. I know never to take my eyes off of a rapzette. If you stare it down, you might have a chance, but if you lower your eyes, it'll peck your face full of holes.

Calipsie is waving something, but it's a blur in my periphery.

Then a second rapzette steps out of the darkness.

'Run!' I shout, turning to her. She doesn't run; she's holding something out to me. It's a spade. I grab hold of the handle as the rapzettes flap their wings. The sweeping movement blows gossif dust in our direction, and I try to shield my eyes, but it's too late. The granules sting, and my lids squeeze shut. When the grit clears, allowing me a fuzzy view of the barn, the rapzettes launch at us. I swing the spade, trying to deter them. Kranik comes out of nowhere, careening into one of the creatures and tumbling across the floor. The other comes for me. I bat it away, sending it spinning in Calipsie's direction. It flies at Calipsie, who screams and flings her arms over her face. The serrated beak slices down, tearing her forearms.

I swing the spade again. The rapzette careens into the corner but instantly gets to its feet. There's a slight hobble to its step, but it charges at me regardless. I swipe again, but this time I miss and then it's on me. I defend myself with the shaft of the spade, planting it in the rapzette's open maw. With a quick twist, I force the creature onto the ground. I clamber onto my feet, putting my boot on its neck. I slam the spade down, severing its head. I know it's dead, but that doesn't stop me. I stomp on its head with the heel of my boot four, maybe five times. I can't stop. Not until I hear

Calipsie whimper. Kranik hovers over her, and though blood covers her arms, neither seems to notice it. Instead, they're both staring at me, looking startled, like they think I might snap and turn the spade on one of them.

'What?' I shout, and both avert their gaze.

The beast is dead. I won't apologise for that. It can't hurt them now. It can't hurt anyone.

6

KRANIK

Kyjta insists on sterilising Calipsie's wounds in the ocean. She's fiercely protective of Calipsie, and I can't refuse her after questioning her Stain. So, I lead the girls along the rutted path, scanning the tufted grass and pointing out the tiny fez that flutter near the mauve blossoms. They're small enough to seem impossible. How tiny their little bones must be, like miniature needles, grafted together in a complex system that somehow keeps them afloat. Calipsie stops, fascinated by their whisker-like probosces, unfurling and draining the inkopels of black nectar. When Kyjta tries to hurry us along, Calipsie hesitates, spotting the more colourful male fez flying to greet its potential mate. I don't feel Calipsie's hand slipping into mine so much as sense her sudden and unfamiliar proximity. The young girl pulls me into the grass, hoping to get a closer look at the pair of fezzes, who dart up and down, inspecting each other.

'Look!' she shouts, pointing.

I don't look; I'm staring at her little hand, tucked neatly into mine. For some reason, the sight of it makes me smile. I'm used to children hiding behind their mothers' skirts, if I see them at all. Calipsie tugs at me like she can sense my distraction, and I marvel at the next thing to grab her attention, seeing one of the nothopi bleaching its thick skin white in the sun. Her excitement adds a fresh dimension to the experience, one I often enjoy alone. The sun is bright and touches everything, and the brief snatch of time is easily one of the best I've ever spent. I lose myself in it because I know how quickly it will all end. Soon, the girls will return to their lives, and I will return to mine. I will think of this often, but I'll never experience anything like it again.

Eventually, we move onto the beach, where I sit and watch as the girls splash in the surf. Kyjta's orange dress billows like a sail and clings to her wet legs. Calipsie has hers tucked up high to keep it dry, but it's no use. The spray is merciless. Kyjta's already cleaned Calipsie's wounds; she said the saltwater will start the healing process. I would take Calipsie to Restoration, but they're selective about who gets treatment. Someone like Merrick, who volunteers for the Body Trust, will be seen immediately, but the girl doesn't, and her cuts aren't very deep. It would probably be a wasted trip.

Calipsie points to something in the water and squeals with delight. Kyjta tries to shepherd it toward Calipsie, but the girl shrieks and dashes away. The water splashes Kyjta as Calipsie races through the waves. They look like they're enjoying themselves, and I don't want to call out for them to stop, but we should be heading back. Maisi will be fussing over lunch by now. Down here on the beach, we're out of range. Sion Chaffrot can't see us, and if he could, his arrows wouldn't reach us, no matter how good his aim. The zionate-weave blanket is folded up beside me on the rocks. I check the skies. Cloud cover is gathering in the south, but it's clear and blue overhead.

Dripping wet and giggling, Kyjta and Calipsie run onto the beach.

Kyjta shakes her head, spraying water beads in my face and making me gasp.

'What?' she says. 'Afraid of a little water?'

She grabs the blanket and drops it over Calipsie, whose hands are full of shells. The young girl trawls the sand for more treasure. She keeps hold of the blanket, trailing it along the sand.

'I thought Rhemans couldn't feel anything,' Kyjta says, sitting on the rock beside me. Water, in thick rivulets, runs down her body onto the stones.

If I don't tell her something, she'll think everything she's heard about Rhemans is a lie, which is worse than the truth.

'I can sometimes feel the rain.'

'You feel the rain, but you can't feel this?' She pinches my forearm, squeezing Merrick's flesh between her forefinger and thumb.

'Your hands are wet. I feel it.' I've told her now; no point hiding it. Strangely, after hearing my confession, she seems to drop her guard.

'So you feel water?' She leans into me, and her eyes have lost that distrustful squint. They're large and violet and beautiful.

'Sometimes. Not always.'

'Is it the same for other Rhemans?'

'I don't think so. I think it's just me. And so far, only in this body.'

She laughs like I've made a joke. 'Merrick's body?'

She leans over her knees to wring her hair. Her shoulders and back are smooth and flawless. There's not a drop of Stain on her. Not from this angle. I follow the gentle dimpling of her spine until it's lost in the coral folds of her dress.

When Kyjta sits up and angles her head in my direction, she looks mischievous. I don't have time to wonder what she's up to. Her wet hand is covering mine, where it rests palm down on the rocks.

'Do you feel this?' She presses her fingers between mine.

I do feel it. My mouth opens to speak, but I don't say anything. I don't want to ruin the moment. There's no way to describe what it feels like, and she'd probably laugh at me if I tried. She's toying with me. For her, this experience is pure intrigue, but for me, it's something else. My silence frustrates her; the distrustful squint returns. She pushes harder, sliding her hand slowly over mine. I stop breathing. The sensation is like nothing I've experienced. No one has ever touched me through water before.

'Yes. Just about,' I say.

She lifts her hand away, and my body starts to regulate. Normal breathing. Typical lack of sensation. Good, I think, and close my eyes.

'Are you a boy, Rheman?' she asks.

My eyes fly open. 'Does it matter?'

'It might to some.'

'I suppose I'm whatever form I take,' I say. 'Would it be better if I were?'

Kyjta doesn't answer; she seems to have lost interest. She's watching Calipsie stack shells in the sand. When she next speaks, it's about something else.

'What about the Sion? Are you going to tell me how you broke his feet?'

I don't know if I can explain it without making myself look callous and self-serving. Probably because it was both of those things.

'It was stupid,' I say. 'One day, I could feel the water. The next, I couldn't. I didn't realise it might be because I was using Sion Chaffrot's body that day. I thought if I jumped from the rocks, the increased pressure might—'

'You jumped from up there?' Kyjta points to the ledge jutting from the cliffs, towering over the Onaway Ocean.

I shrug. 'I've done it before, and I thought it was safe. I didn't consider that some bodies can withstand more than others.' I drop my head; the water is a shameful addiction. The Body Trust would be abolished if news of my anomalous talent got out. It's our non-tactile nature that makes the contract remotely palatable. Give Rhemans the sense of touch, and people will start to wonder what we do with their bodies.

'What about now?' Kyjta says. 'Will you do it with me?'

7

KYJTA

We stand at the apex of the world, looking out over the smoky-blue ocean. The restless wind blows my hair across my face. I run my hands through the whipping strands, pulling them away from my eyes.

Looking down, I'm terrified. The rocks drop away to the rushing water. Waves, crested with white fluff from the sea flowers, crash against the rocks and fall back. I take a breath and slip my hand into the Rheman's. Heights make me nervous; I don't want to lose him as we jump.

Him, not it. It is whatever form it takes. Today it is a boy.

Kranik looks at me; I wonder if he sensed me slip my hand into his. When he drops his gaze, he seems surprised and closes his grip. My hand is still loose in his; he's careful not to hurt me.

'Ready?' he asks.

I volunteered for this, and there's no backing out now. Leaping from a cliff edge into the ocean isn't my idea of fun, but this is a different kind of leap. Sion Chaffrot's comment about befriending the Rheman provoked something in me. The more I think about it, the more I wonder what my mother did to make him remark on her bravery. Intentionally or not, I've already learned something about this Rheman. I wonder what my mother might do if she were in the same situation. Everyone knows Rhemans aren't tactile. I saw Kranik slice open Merrick's thumb without flinching. Even when the yakkat's tail speared him, the worse kind of sting, he didn't jerk away. My heart hammers. Though I don't know what to do with this information, I know instinctively that it has the power to bring down the Body Trust.

We swing our arms back and launch into the sea breeze. My stomach lurches as the wind rushes to greet us. It rips at my dress and twists it up around my middle. When I hit the water, the material billows around me; I have to fight it so I can see Kranik. At first, I can't make out his face, but then I get a good look at his expression. What must it be like to go from not feeling anything to plunging into the ocean and having the sea surge all around you? He looks enraptured; I've never seen an Aurora Saurin enthralled by such a simple act.

When Kranik opens his eyes, I release my breath, and bubbles cloud my vision. When they clear, he's staring at our entwined fingers. This time his grip is just right. My stomach tightens. When he looks up, his expression is searching, like he's trying to figure out what I'm thinking.

Desperate for air, I kick and feel my fingers slip from his grip. I gasp when I break the surface, filling my lungs with salty air, then laugh. I'm still laughing when Kranik joins me, his expression soft with wonder. He looks overwhelmed and a little confused. Tears roll down my cheeks.

'You're amused?' His grin is cautious.

'No,' I manage, trying to get myself under control. 'I'm just—'

'I felt you,' he says.

My hysteria subsides as quickly as it began.

'I can feel you when we're in the water,' he says.

My dress is floating around me and my waist is bare. The material tickles my exposed flesh, sending shivers through me. Kranik and I are treading water, neither of us sure what to say or do.

I'm about to tell him we should head back when a shadow passes over us. I look up, aware that something is changing. The quality of the light seems to dim. Then I catch sight of it, and my thrumming heart loses its rhythm.

A ghoragall.

An icy dread washes through my veins. Calipsie is sitting on the sand, playing with her shells. The zionate-weave blanket lies in a heap farther up the sandy strip, forgotten.

8

KRANIK

The ghoragall swoops. There's nothing we can do. Calipsie is too far away. The horror will take her by surprise.

'Take cover!' I shout. If Calipsie looks up, there's still a chance she can save herself. The blanket isn't too far away—she could still reach it.

Kyjta doesn't bother shouting; she must know Calipsie won't hear her at this distance. She dives into the water and swims for the shore. She's fast, but she'll never make it. I plunge into the water and quickly pass her. I break my stroke only once, seeing the ghoragall glide down to the beach and scoop Calipsie up with its claws. I'm not close enough to hear her scream. A moment later, she disappears into a breast of thick black feathers. The creature flaps its great skeletal wings, causing a sandstorm on the beach, before taking to the sky. Helpless, I watch it fly away.

The shock deadens my limbs. I scan the beach, convinced I'll find Calipsie, and see nothing but the heaped blanket. I tread water, struggling to process what's happened. She was right there; it doesn't seem possible. Is it a trick of the light? If we can get to the beach, we'll surely find Calipsie right where we'd left her.

I reach the beach before Kyjta and stand on the shoreline, unmoving. There's nothing on the thin strip of sand but a small pile of seashells and the zionate blanket. Kyjta rises from the sea, chest heaving. She stumbles forward, trying to look everywhere at once.

'Where is she?' Her voice is raw with emotion.

'She's gone.' My words sound strangely hollow.

Kyjta falls to her knees, her hands in the sand, grasping at the shells. She picks them up in bunches and stuffs them into her pockets. When she has most of them, she stands and runs across the beach, screaming Calipsie's name.

She searches the rocks. Her voice is almost gone, but she keeps shouting. I follow her, not searching or calling out. An awful dread has settled over me, heavy and absolute. Calipsie is gone, and there's no coming back from Helacth's Ice Realm.

After Kyjta has scoured the small beach twice, she finally turns to me. 'You saw the ghoragall take her?' she demands.

'Yes.'

'Why didn't you stop it? Call out to it?' Kyjta snarls at me, her distrustful eyes squinting against the midday sun.

'It doesn't work like that.' I reach out, wanting to comfort her.

She jerks back. 'Don't touch me!' Her eyes are aflame.

I draw back. We stand together on the sand like opposing forces ready to war. Neither of us speaks for some time. Kyjta glares at me, breathing like someone who's been running for days. I feel trapped, caught in her gaze, as if I'll never stop seeing myself the way she sees me. I'm a monster to her, and that's all I'll ever be.

9

KYJTA

The walk back to Sion Chaffrot's farm is long and silent. I struggle to climb the rocks; my legs are weak. Crossing the plane is just as bad, the tufted grass creating an obstacle course for my rickety ankles. I spend most of the journey dreading the conversation with Sion Chaffrot. How can I explain what happened without falling apart? I resist the urge to cry. I don't want the Rheman to see my grief. I won't be able to hide how badly I blame him. And there's no one to turn to. My own kind are too afraid to act. Aurora Saurins are supposed to live by a code. The Hands govern us, one pushing us toward the light, on a righteous path, the other nudging us into the dark. To achieve harmony, a wrong must be set right. Only then can balance be restored. Way back, before I was born, when the Old Soro ruled over the three continents, Sojour, Fareen, and Thormyth, that was how things worked. But the Old Soro was usurped, banished by the Tarrohar when Helacth helped them take his throne. That disturbance upset the balance and our people have been paying the price ever since.

How foolish I was, thinking I could make a difference. I let myself get drawn in by an old man's silly schemes. *A friend made of an enemy is no ordinary friend,* isn't that what Sion Chaffrot said? What was it I thought I was going to achieve by befriending the Rheman? Some kind of truce? An end to the Body Trust? Just thinking about it now, I'm nauseated by my naivety.

My stomach tightens when we crest a low hill, and I glimpse the farmhouse. I stop, and Kranik slows, then turns to face me. He eyes me cautiously, his expression pained.

He's waiting for me to say something, so I do.

'I guess you'll always be someone else's nightmare and I'll always be the girl who lost Calipsie,' I say. Nothing really changes. I'm still the same girl whose mother left for a better life, even though I know that's not the truth.

Kranik looks lost. 'We could go after her,' he says quietly.

I laugh. It's a horrible sound. 'You and me against Helacth?'

'We could find others, people who are willing to help.'

'There is no one willing to help. Don't you get it? We are all cowards. That's something your kind have gifted us. Absolute clarity on our true nature. Because of you, we know exactly how deficient we are.'

The rest of the journey is made in silence. By the time we reach Nortjie Farm, I can no longer hold back my tears. Sion Chaffrot tries to comfort me, but I know what he really thinks. I took us to the beach. I neglected the girl. I don't need to be an apprentice at the House of Wisdom to know this is all my fault. But if the Rhemans hadn't invaded our world, the beach would be safe!

Sion Chaffrot hooks up a cart, and we head to the House of Judgement to confess. Maisi takes another carriage to inform Calipsie's parents. I'd take my punishment over hers, any given day.

I'm led into a small booth inside the House of Judgement. One of the Justice Men squeezes onto the bench opposite me and the doors to the little room slam shut. A crossbar clangs into place.

'My name is Sion Behesfy,' the Justice Man says. We sit close enough that I can smell perspiration. He's an obese man with jiggling jowls and a sallow complexion. A face like a bowl of souring yakkat milk, is what my father would say.

'Tell me what happened, in your own words.'

I want to get this over with. I know nothing can be done for the girl. Thousands have been taken from Merrocha, and we're just a small town. No one has ever returned.

'We took the girl to Sion Chaffrot's because there was a ghoragall raid in town. The next morning, Sion Chaffrot asked if we'd like to help out on the farm until—' this part is hard, 'until the girl's parents could—'

'Did the Rheman lead you out of range?'

'No,' I say.

'Did he make it difficult for the girl to reach the zionate blanket?'

'No.' I pump a little defiance into my response this time. Was I, or was I not, tasked to describe what happened in my own words?

'Why do you think the ghoragall took the girl by day?'

'I don't know. They sometimes do that, don't they?' I don't tell him Kranik killed a ghoragall in our defence the night before, that the ghoragall that grabbed Calipsie was likely its mate, and probably took her out of revenge. I hope Kranik is smart enough to do the same.

Sion Behesfy stares at me over his enormous nose, nostrils quivering like an elvakan drawing a heavy cart.

'Did the Rheman harm you?' he grunts, making a considerate appraisal of me. My torn dress is dry now, but still sticky with salt and clinging to me.

'No.'

When the big man is finally satisfied that he'll get nothing useful from me, he bangs on the door and it opens. I step from the claustrophobic space into the waiting area. There's a couple here now who weren't around before, standing, when there are plenty of chairs. They are dark-skinned and gaunt with worry. Their eyes are red. They must be Calipsie's parents. Then the double doors swing open, clanging against the walls, and Halli strides in. She's from the north, one of the big cities like Toro or Oblix. Probably from a wealthy family. Her skin is the deepest ebony, beautiful and flawless. She's tall too— people from the north usually are—and slim. She's wearing a short silver dress that exposes her lovely legs. Her beautiful bald head and face take everyone's attention.

'Tell me it's not true,' she demands. She's staring at me.

I could call her a family friend, but there's more to it than that. Still, that doesn't fully explain why she's here, or the look of acute anguish on her face.

'Where is my daughter?'

I blink at the Charmore, wondering if she's stalked into the wrong room.

'Where is Calipsie?' she demands.

Halli has been buying my father's potions for longer than I've been alive, and I've never heard her speak of a child. I look at Calipsie's parents—at least the people I thought were her parents—then back at Halli, my confusion evident.

'She's your half-sister. Didn't they tell you?' she says, gesturing at the grieving couple.

I shake my head, unable to speak.

'The eyes, Kyjta. Violet, like yours. And like your father's. The copper hair?'

My throat is tight, my head spinning.

'I settled her with these people,' Halli gives the couple a look of vile contempt, 'to separate her from your father and me. I wanted her safe.' Halli shakes her head. 'Now I'll have to tell your father he has another daughter.'

I remember Halli being absent from our lives for a time. It was after my mother's disappearance, and it destabilised me. I guess she was a little motherly and I'd taken her as a stand-in. Did she leave to have the baby? Head back north to be with her parents?

Halli turns her venom on the couple, huddled together against the wall.

'How could you let this happen? You were supposed to protect her.'

'Calipsie's brother,' says the woman, weeping, 'our son.'

'He's very protective of her,' says the man. 'He stood vigil outside the bunker. He's missing. We were out looking for him. That's why we didn't collect Calipsie.'

'This is not what I wanted for her,' says Halli. 'It's why I gave her up.'

Halli spits at the couple's feet, then storms from the room. She may be a Charmore, but she's no lady. I didn't think things could get worse than they already were, but I've been wrong before. I'm numb now. But overwhelm isn't a lasting anaesthetic. There's a darkness waiting for me, and it's worse than anything I've faced before.

Sion Behesfy drops me directly at the main doors of Minuet Farmhouse. I climb down from the House of Judgement's ridiculous gilded carriage, desperate for my stepfather to be out in the turtis fields, harvesting the brittle stalks for our tea crop, and unavailable for Sion Behesfy's briefing on today's calamity, but my luck is out.

'Fair favour, Sion. Be with you in a moment.'

Sion Cromenk, my mother's second husband, is on the thatched roof above my bedroom. There's a patch where the coursing is so thin I sometimes glimpse a sliver of sky through it. He looks the doting father, pausing the threading of fresh thatch to wave to us. Sion Behesfy doesn't know how the patch has been bare for almost half an alignment, how cold my bedroom is at night because of it. It's just like my stepfather to put on a show for the House of Judgement.

'Morning, Sion,' bellows Sion Behesfy.

I exit the carriage and duck inside the cottage, leaving Sion Behesfy to secure his elvakans. At least his grey mounts look well fed, their greedy trunks slurping up water from the trough I keep filled just outside the house.

Once inside, I climb the rickety ladder leading to my room. I like it up here, but it doesn't feel the same knowing my stepfather's just above me.

The room is long, stretching the entire length of the thatched roof. A panel runs the centre of it; if I keep to its path, I can stand to my full height. My bed sits under the eaves. It's a single bed frame tucked neatly below the low beams supporting the thatch. I swipe at the scattering of grit loosened from the thatch and settled on my quilt. There's a scuffling on the roof, and another layer of grit falls, catching the slanting window light.

The rasping reeds surface my buried anxiety when I recall the terror I felt one night when the ghoragalls came scratching at the roof. It was half an alignment ago, but the dread feels fresh enough. They knew I was here, cowering beneath my bed, because they sensed my Stain. They were trying to burrow through the roof to get at me. I replay their mournful caws when I lie here at night.

If my stepfather heard them, he didn't come up to check on me, and I'd sooner be quelled than seek comfort from him. I stayed in my bedroom and waited for them to break through. They grew bored, eventually, and left. Sometimes I lie awake wondering what might have happened if they'd scratched through.

'Kyjta,' calls my stepfather. He must be close to my window, making his way down the ladder to greet Sion Behesfy. 'Fetch the Justice Man and me a cup of your famous turtis stalk brew. I'm sure he's parched.'

The request triggers a familiar quiver of excitement, muting, but only briefly, the horrors of the day.

'Yes, Sion,' I yell, playing at the obedient daughter.

My stepfather has no real idea what I'm capable of, and neither does Sion Behesfy. I quickly change my clothes before making my way down the little ladder and into the kitchen, where I set water to boil on the black stove beneath the chimney. There's a ritual to preparing turtis, and I use the steps as a distraction. I must not dwell on what's happened. I'm sure my mind will break. Fastidiously, I crush the tawny stalks with a pestle to release the flavour, and sprinkle them into a net, aerating the crushed stalks to deepen the flavour. Next, I put them to boil for precisely twenty-seven counts. The turtis stalks are a speciality of the farm. We can only plant them when the twin moons—Urther and her baby sister, Ursala—align. They're tended at night, when the delicate white flowers open, and harvested in the winter for drying, right here on Minuet Farm. I spin the net and place it in the water. Then I head to the basement, counting in my head. I like it down here. It's cool and quiet, but most of all, it reminds me of my mother. Its shelves brim with the zionate tea sets she collected in her youth; it's like she had a premonition of their future worth. I take the small jar of yakkat cream off the shelf. The little basement is the coolest place on the farmstead, ideal for keeping fresh produce. Once I've arranged the tray with biscuits, the pot of strained brew, some sweet bariss root, and the jar of cream, I carry it to the small living area.

My stepfather looks up. His round cheeks are as rosy as a child's. He has listless hair, a shade that brings to mind the burnt clay mounds scattered about the Parched Lands.

'Wonderful. Here's the brew now. A true treasure of Minuet Farm, you'll not find tea to rival its flavour.' He uses the cheerful tone he reserves for guests and merchants.

The Justice Man doesn't look me over now that he's being treated to my stepfather's hospitality. He doesn't lift his head as I enter, carrying the tray, or even as I lower it onto the small woven table in front of him. Instead, he fixedly examines his bloated, interlinked fingers resting in his lap.

As soon as I set down the tray, I turn to make my retreat.

'Take a seat, Kyjta. You must listen to what the Justice Man has to say,' my stepfather says firmly.

I would have preferred to eavesdrop on the conversation. Still, the couch offers a better vantage point than the notch I carved in the floorboards below my bed. I can't refuse, anyway; if I did, I'd ruin the dutiful stepdaughter ruse. With only the briefest downward glance to hide my resentment, I flatten my dress and take a seat.

'So, tell us, what's to become of the Rheman?' my stepfather asks.

'It's possible he'll be encircled,' Sion Behesfy says. 'The Tarrohar won't stand for such flagrant disregard of the Body Trust. Many witnesses will testify they saw him fighting in a borrowed body.'

Although I'm sitting quietly, my heart beats at a violent crescendo. Kranik will be encircled? That's no justice. At best, it's unpredictable; at worst, pure entertainment. The Tarrohar know just how starved of amusement we Aurora Saurins are. If I've learned one thing from my true father, the potion master, it's the power of supply and demand.

'Indeed, we can't expect people to sign up if there's no guarantee of their safety, but this Rheman was trying to prevent further abductions,' my stepfather says. He must be feeling unusually charitable today.

The Justice Man leans back in his chair, resting his bloated hands across his belly. 'If he's encircled, the people will decide.' The thought seems to please him, but the process is barbaric, instigated by the Tarrohar after they usurped power from the Old Soro with Helacth's aid. They claim the punishments handed down at these encirclements are a collaboration gleaned by scanning our minds. But they're just mining our heads for information, secrets they can use to extract more coin and buffer their treasury.

'What about Kyjta?' my stepfather says. 'She was only looking after the girl. Surely they won't drag her into this.'

'People are taken every day. Kyjta can't be blamed for the girl's fate,' the Justice Man says. His eyes have a greedy sheen. 'The rules are clear. Rhemans are not to put Aurora Saurin bodies in jeopardy, and this one started a brawl.'

Though my expression never changes, I take his words like a hammer to the gut. Kranik will be encircled for saving us.

'You think an encirclement is more likely than confinement?' asks my stepfather.

'If the Rhemans want to be a part of our society, they must take part in our system. Being confined to a Sorb is no hardship for a Rheman.'

Anger fills me like a black mist. The House of Judgement and their rabid watchdogs, the Vigilance Men, are incapable of going after Calipsie; incapable of stopping the raids, no matter how many Aurora Saurins sign up to the Body Trust. None of that's surprising—it's been going on my whole life. But prosecuting a Rheman for protecting us from his own kind? What message was the Tarrohar sending here? That their precious Body Trust is more important than their citizens' lives?

That treasure has more worth than blood.

Sion Behesfy leans forward, groaning as he crests his ample girth. He reaches for a block of translucent bariss root and drops it into his cup. I wait, carefully holding my expression, to see if he'll add the cream. I can't imagine a man of his size abstaining. He lifts the cup and stirs the brew, releasing the root's sweetness. The act prompts my stepfather to shift in his seat and lift the zionate jug between finger and thumb. I smile sweetly as he pours a healthy dollop of yakkat cream into his cup. When he takes his first sip, I drop my gaze and enjoy the slightly sickening burst of power.

It took me three moon cycles to figure out how to mask the taste of the liquid Stain I kept hidden in one of my mother's ornamental zionate jars. It took longer to perfect a method that didn't curdle the cream. There was no reason to hurry; the preparations gave me the strength I needed to keep going. In the end, it took a shaving of knot wood and a pinch of crushed melton seeds. I felt sure he'd realise what I'd done the first time I served it. I watched at the windows for days, expecting the Vigilance Men to turn up and take me away. But they never came, and my stepfather started to expect his turtis to be prepared that way, even complimenting me on the flavour.

Sion Behesfy reaches for the cream, as I knew he would. He pours generously, sits back, and takes a deep sip. When he lowers the cup, a satisfied expression settles over his engorged features, and he looks at me.

'Brew like that, you'll make a fine bride.' He chuckles, that greedy sheen taking his eyes again.

The comment might anger me if I weren't imagining the Stain sliding down his throat, coating his insides. I smile, but my eyes must give something away; the leer slides off his face, and he looks suddenly uncomfortable.

My Stain is unsightly, but at least I know it's there. There are things I can do to reduce my chances of being taken. These men don't know they're stained; they won't protect themselves with zionate, or keep indoors at night, and with Minuet Farm on the direct flight path from Thormyth, it will only be a matter of time. Acquiring the stain has cost me so much. It's too painful to imagine my hard work won't pay off. It was dark the night I snuck back to the fair to collect my prize. The loom weed was recently cropped for a marriage ceremony. Usually, the light from the luminous seeds brightened the pathway, but that night, the path was in deep shadow. I was relieved when the little fountain finally took shape in the darkness. I lifted the jar with my bare hands, not thinking the liquid Stain might slop down the container's sides. It was only once I made it home and lit the basking lamp in the living room that I realised my mistake. I stood there, still disbelieving but teetering on the edge of a terrible realisation. The pads of my fingertips glittered. More than glittered; they shone. There were concentrated patches of Stain at the corners of each palm.

My heart stopped dead in my chest. There was nothing I could say to explain the marks. Lying would only jeopardise my plans. Instead, I made my way to the tiny basement, horrified by what I had to do. I lifted the jar and tilted it forward, making sure to cover my chest and speckle my arms. A noise startled me, and I jolted, the jug lurching in my hand. The Stain splashed my cheeks. I tried to wipe them clean, but it was no use. I was marked. Doomed to wear these perpetual tears.

10

KRANIK

I t's late afternoon before I reach Inner Town, an area near the centre of Merrocha where the House of Judgement and a few of the other Houses, namely Vigilance and Wisdom, stand. I spent the journey trying to figure out how to convince Tiberico and the others to let me go after Calipsie.

The House of Judgement squats at one end of a vast square. It's a yellow-tone building, up-lit by a run of tall basking lamps that are always aflame. As usual, there's a stream of Aurora Saurins exiting the building at this time, on their way home.

I'm climbing the broad stairs, taking them two at a time, heading for the entrance to the House of Judgement, when I notice a man and woman running across the dusty pavement. They're coming to intercept me. Immediately I'm on guard, knowing how temperamental Azaire can be. Perhaps he has sent some of his goons to escort me inside. These two don't look like Azaire's Rheman henchmen, though; they're not wearing the standard uniform. One day he'll announce the establishment of the House of Rhemans and his own appointment as the Zhu. It will surprise no one.

The man and woman running toward me wear plain clothes. Barrel-chested, he's dressed in a rough-cut farmer's shirt that exposes muscular, tanned arms. Beside him, the woman appears miniature, drowning in an oversized, russet-coloured dress. Now that they're closer, I see the woman's pained expression. The man hobbles a little behind her, unable to keep up. Not quelled then, I think, slowing to a stop.

'Merrick!' cries the woman, speeding up. She lifts her arms, reaching for me.

Before I can think of a way to respond, she's collided with me, wrapping me in her arms. I'm careful not to touch her with my hands; both my arms hover, a little ridiculously, at her sides. I look down to see her sobbing into my chest. They must be Merrick's parents, here to collect their son.

The father arrives, panting.

'Your boy is fine,' I say, reassuring her. 'I just need to get him inside.'

The man tries to pull his wife away. 'Don't touch him,' he says. 'He's not our son.'

The woman releases me and takes a step back. Her husband pulls her protectively into his arms, and they stare at me, the mother bewildered and the father furious.

'You—' says the man, raising a finger and pointing. His cheeks are red, his breath short and laboured. He doubles over, clutching his chest and gasping.

'What is it? What's the matter?' cries the wife. She's so petite that she doesn't need to bend down to see his distressed expression.

When Merrick's father falls to his knees, I step closer but stop short of touching him. My hands hover at his sides, ready to catch him if he falls.

Passers-by stop to stare.

'We must get him to Restoration,' I tell Merrick's mother. 'I'll need to carry him. Do you consent?'

'Yes,' she stutters, wide-eyed and frantic.

I hoist the man into my arms and carry him like a baby. He weighs three times what Merrick does, but the weight isn't a problem; it's time I'm concerned about. If I don't get Merrick's father to our ship, he'll die, and I can't allow that to happen. I don't know Merrick in conventional terms, but he's shared his body with me on more than one occasion, so I owe him.

I set off with the ailing man in my arms. There's a kinatoid on standby behind the House of Judgement. It's used for Rheman transportation to and from our ship, the *Rhema Bolajio*, but Azaire monopolises it most of the time. I hope it's there.

'Hey!' someone yells. 'Stop there.'

I speed up. If I stop now, Azaire's henchmen will march me inside, and I'll have to wait for Azaire to finish his political ramblings. Merrick's father doesn't have much time. When I reach the courtyard, I hear synchronised footfalls at my back. I don't turn around, because the kinatoid is prepped and ready for Azaire's next engagement.

'Open!' I shout in Rheman. The craft obeys, the ice-blue side doors lifting like wings. I load Merrick's father inside and scramble in after him.

I count eight henchmen marching across the courtyard, set on apprehending me. I recognise the lead, a Rheman named Hirco who reports to Azaire. Thankfully they've been instructed to appear peaceful and are unarmed, else Hirco might give the order to incapacitate me. A non-lethal shot, perhaps, but the delay would be lethal for Merrick's father.

'To the *Rhema Bolajio*!' I shout, and the doors close in response.

'Destination *Rhema Bolajio*. Authorisation granted,' the kinatoid confirms.

'Halt!' shouts Hirco, raising a hand to me.

'Ignore him,' I say. 'Take us to the *Rhema Bolajio*. Fly through them if you have to.'

Whirring, the kinatoid lifts from the ground.

'Kranik!' yells Hirco into the wind. 'You aren't scheduled for flight. This will get you into more trouble.'

As the small aircraft surges forward, Hirco only just manages to duck out of the way of the landing gear. The machine lifts into the air, cresting the looming rock walls that ring the House of Judgement. Through the transparent floor, I see Hirco shouting instructions at his henchmen.

The kinatoid powers forward, leaving Merrocha behind. To the south lie the Parched Lands and, beyond that, the inhospitable Ice Realm of Thormyth, where Helacth's flagship, the *Ebisu*, came to ground. We fly west, crossing the swamps until we reach the Golden Plain: a deserted strip of shimmering sand that runs parallel to the Onaway Ocean. Here, Aurora Saurin fishing boats speckle the coastline. I try to fix the sight in my mind. If I go after Calipsie, this could be the last time I see anything like this.

'Set us down alongside the *Rhema Bolajio*,' I say as our ship comes into view.

I squint at the black specks moving about and realise they're people, thousands of them.

'Careful not to injure anyone,' I say.

The kinatoid descends, producing a spray of sand that forces the Aurora Saurins to fall back. A moment later, the small ship settles. I leap out and collect Merrick's father, whose skin is tinted blue. I lift him out, listening for his breathing, but I can't hear much, just a few shallow, intermittent gasps.

Thousands of Aurora Saurins block my path. I force my way through the crowd, yelling for them to make way. It's not only people, but also their belongings. Some have erected tents. Many look malnourished or ill. I hate to think how long they've waited for care. I understand why they are here—their primitive medical system makes them reliant on us. They can submit for quelling and take the coin we Rhemans offer in return, but it might be alignments before they can afford the treatment they need.

A young woman with a crutch tucked under one arm hobbles into my path. She's swaddling a baby in her other arm and leans heavily on the crutch, breathing hard. Her face is gaunt, her hollow eyes pleading. I almost stumble when she offers me her baby.

'Please,' she begs. 'I can't donate to the Body Trust. I must look after my children. Even if I could,' she indicates her malformed leg with a downward glance, 'my body is no use to you.'

I glimpse the sleeping infant's rosy cheeks and upturned nose within the swaddling folds of his threadbare blanket.

'My baby needs a Rheman miracle. He's sick. Please take him.'

Surely an infant would be helped?

'I can't carry him,' I tell her. 'This man is dying. You'll have to follow me. Can you walk?'

She nods. 'I manage.'

'Stay with me then.' I weave around her, careful not to knock her off balance.

I'm conflicted, needing to move fast but not wanting the woman to overexert herself. When I check on her, she's lagging behind, struggling to make progress across the sand. A deformity like hers isn't easy to correct, but it's achievable. Once the baby is seen, I'll get her looked at.

I scan the crowd, trying to find someone who can help. If the woman trusts another to carry her baby, we might make better time. I weave through tents, looking for a friendly face. I try to find someone capable of helping her, but the people here are sick, wounded, or busy helping others. Through the lines of tents, I spot people distributing packages to the growing crowd. I assume it's food. How else would these people eat? The *Rhema Bolajio* has an entire floor of hydroponics that would produce enough to feed these people, or at least keep them from starving.

I'm so focused on watching the crowd that I walk through a gathering of children and only just avoid treading on them. They barely look up. Their attention is taken by the motion display on the ship's side. I glance upward to see what has them so enthralled. It looks like a live feed, a row of Restoration Pallets gleaming in the artificial light. The camera zooms in on a man lying back in comfort. His leg has a deep gouge, and the bone protrudes at an eye-watering angle. The Restoration Technician checks the pallet's display before making minor adjustments; then, the pallet starts its work. First anaesthetising, then setting and fusing the bone, before knitting the skin. The man steps off the plate, like the accident never happened.

'Hey, could we get some help?' I call out, focusing on the oldest kid in the group. She's a tall, gangly girl with wide-set eyes and a flat, freckled nose.

She looks up at me and then jumps to her feet.

'Can you give her a hand carrying that baby?' I raise my eyes, indicating the woman hobbling toward us.

The girl jogs across the sand and takes the bundle in her arms, a look of wonder on her face as she ogles the baby.

'Let's move!' I shout; Merrick's father's breathing has become ominously quiet.

Progress is faster now that the woman is unencumbered. We're soon close enough to the *Rhema Bolajio* to make out the Vigilance Men stationed near the entrance to the antechamber. Each of them carries a pair of illing swords, their signature weapon. Beside them is a row of tables and chairs. The chairs are populated by Justice Men. One by one, the injured and unwell step up to receive quotes or make payments.

When I reach the Vigilance Men, the ship recognises me, and the door opens, but the Vigilance Men block my path. The Vigilance Men aren't here as peacekeepers; they're serving the Tarrohar, blocking treatment for anyone without the coin. Tiberico would never turn the needy away.

'Let us through. This man is dying, and we have a baby who needs treatment.' I face the Vigilance Man directly in front of me: Brezan, the son of the Zhu, who heads the House of Vigilance and is most likely in command. He's young and handsome, with soft blue eyes and wavy golden hair, but there's something predatory in his gaze, and even before he speaks, I know our communication won't go well.

'Queue up and make payment. There's no special treatment here.'

'If this man isn't seen right away, he will die,' I tell him.

'I've heard it all, farm boy. Get yourself in line.'

If I wasn't holding Merrick's father in my arms, I would punch him in his entitled face. I consider setting the man down and taking on the entire troop, but that would violate the Body Trust's covenant and get both Merrick and me killed. I look around for someone with a little common sense. A commotion builds behind me, and when I turn, I realise why. The large crowd gathered at the base of the *Rhema Bolajio* has noticed the open doorway, and their numbers are growing as they encroach. People are shouting and jostling, and the turbulence catches, rousing others to join in. In no time, people are at my back and sides, demanding Restoration for themselves or those they love.

The Vigilance Men unsheathe their swords.

A man shouts. Then the crowd surges forward. I duck under the flying swords, passing through the line unscathed. Among the crowd, I spot the girl carrying the baby. I flinch as she ducks to avoid a near-fatal blow. She's fearless, though, weaving after me, hunching herself protectively around the child. When she reaches me, we run together, targeting the open door. The antechamber is empty; the white walls and tapered ceilings are like another world after the chaos outside. I look back for the baby's mother, but I can't see her among the riotous crowd. I do, however, see Brezan fighting his way toward us.

'Close the doors!' I shout, but it's too late. Brezan stands on the threshold. The *Rhema Bolajio* wouldn't crush him between her doors, even if I asked.

'You're no Aurora Saurin,' he says, squinting at me. 'You Rheman? You're going to regret this. Inciting a riot . . . that won't play well with the Tarrohar.'

I hoist Merrick's father a little higher in my arms, then take a swift step forward and boot the Zhu's son squarely in the chest. Brezan flies into the crowd; flailing arms and legs close around him.

I may be a monster made for nightmares, but I have my limits.

'Close the doors!' I shout again, and the doors slide shut this time, cutting off the noise. In the sudden silence, I listen for Merrick's father's breathing but hear nothing. I take off at a run, shouting for the girl to follow me. I pause before a crossroads in the corridors to check for company, stopping just in time to avoid being spotted by the Zhu—Head of the House of Vigilance—as he exits the comms room.

At least thirty Aurora Saurins are in the Restoration Facility when we arrive, but very few there are quelled and ferrying Rhemans. If I can find a Rheman, I might have a chance of getting the

Restoration equipment working. I search for an empty Restoration Pallet, striding purposefully toward the closest, carrying my load. Three Justice Men block my way, but I barge through them, whisking their maroon cloaks into the air as I pass. I set Merrick's father onto the pallet and step back. Four Aurora Saurins in grey cloaks, signifying the House of Wisdom, gather around him. One of them looks up and yells for assistance.

'Kranik?'

I spin, and recognise the assured gaze and subtle swagger.

'Lakhan.' I grip my good friend by his navy-clad shoulder and point to the Restoration Pallet. 'Can you work any of this?'

'I have some training.' Lakhan ushers the scholars out of his way and sets to work.

With Merrick's father in safe hands, my focus shifts to the baby, who's crying nearby. The girl jogs him in her arms with practised ease. She must have younger siblings; she seems to know how to calm him. I beckon to her, indicating a nearby pallet we can use to treat the child. A Vigilance Man steps into her path, blocking her from reaching me.

'Where's your quittance?' he asks her.

Her eyes go wide, and she looks at me, nervous.

'No treatment without proof of payment,' he says sternly.

I tap the man on the shoulder, and he turns to face me.

'Yes?' He's young and full of bravado. A typical Vigilance recruit.

'That baby needs medical treatment,' I tell him. 'Let the girl pass.'

'Show me proof of payment, and the child can have whatever it needs.'

'Unless you want to visit a Restoration Pallet yourself, get out of her way,' I warn him.

The black cloak stares me down.

'I may not be wearing navy, but I assure you I am Rheman,' I say.

I put my index finger to his chest and push. He tries to resist, leaning his weight into me, but he's forced backwards. My demonstration complete, the Vigilance Man backs away.

I usher the girl forward, and we settle the infant onto a Restoration Pallet. Someone in a navy coat walks over, reaching out a hand in greeting. I return the greeting, getting instant awareness of who they are. Though I've never met them, I know they are Telha, a Restoration Technician.

'Thank you,' they say. 'I've been aching to punch that specimen in the solar plexus. One of the Tarrohar's deputies, a constant irritation. We have so many pallets, and he stops us from using them.'

I glance back at Lakhan. Merrick's father is lying on the Restoration Pallet in front of him, disturbingly still. The machine is active, its bright light illuminating the blue tint of his skin. I hope I wasn't too late.

The Restoration Pallet beeps. Lakhan checks the screen, looking pleased. It may be self-delusion, but I think the man's colour has improved. I turn back to the baby and watch as Telha loosens the blanket. The tiny form is unsettlingly pale and covered in blistering red welts. The infant scrunches up its body as it reaches for something to hold on to.

'What's the matter with him?' I ask.

'It's well you brought him,' says Telha. 'He has rupey. Almost always deadly without treatment.'

'You can restore him?'

'We'll need to keep him a few days, but he appears strong. He'll recover.'

Hearing Merrick's father gasp, I turn to face him. The Restoration Pallet powers down, and its lights wink out. Merrick's father tries to sit up. Our eyes connect, and I hope that the sight of me doesn't set him off again, then I'm grabbed from behind.

'You've done it this time. There's nothing I can do to help you now.'

It's Azaire. There's no one else with such a bold ego.

It's no use fighting. His henchmen have my arms, and they won't be gentle. I can't let anything happen to Merrick; he's volunteered more days than anyone. If he's killed, the Body Trust won't recover. Not the 'trust' part anyway.

I will myself to be calm. The room has fallen silent. Every face is angled toward me. Old men in grey cloaks, gripping manuals in their gnarled hands, stop taking notes. As I pass, their pointed reeds drip black nectar onto thirsty parchment. Younger men in powder-blue cloaks pause, mouths still shaped around their most recent word. The black cloaks regard me with suspicion, stirring up memories of Kyjta's distress on the beach. I might have saved Merrick's father, but what about my plans to go after Calipsie?

'This is the last time you jeopardise everything we're working for,' Azaire growls. 'It's as if you want us to fail.'

'You still think you can bring the other ships around to the Body Trust?'

'Take a good look around, Kranik. The next time you surface from your Sorb, these people will be long dead. You'll awake to a new Aurora Saura. One where your actions don't continue to threaten us.'

When the door opens, the glare is blinding; I don't immediately see the woman. She's propped up on her crutch, managing, somehow, to hold her position at the front of the encroaching crowd.

'Stay back!' yell several Vigilance Men.

The people ignore the warning. They funnel toward the open door. The disabled woman is pushed forward, fighting to keep herself upright while battered from all sides. When our eyes meet, her expression changes. It's obvious that I'm a prisoner. Her mouth opens, and horror washes over her. She scans the Vigilance Men, looking for her baby. Before I can call out, she's knocked forward by the surging horde and disappears beneath their stampeding feet.

I struggle against the grip of Azaire's henchmen, desperate to pull her to safety, but they're too strong. Oblivious to her peril, they jerk me onward.

I look back, trying to get a sense of her predicament. I can't tell if she's been knocked down; there are too many people. If she's trampled beneath them, she may not recover. I might have saved the baby, but lost his mother.

'That woman . . . She's crippled,' I beg Azaire. 'You must help her.'

'I warned them to stay away from the ship,' Azaire says.

'If you want them to leave, you just have to heal them!' I shout at him.

'Our equipment is our only bargaining chip. If we heal them all, we might as well abolish the Body Trust. Do you prefer Helacth's approach?'

'Are those really our only options? Helacth's approach or this?' I demand.

'I suppose you have some better alternative that's eluded the rest of us,' scoffs Azaire, shoving me on.

'We could start by showing one another a little respect,' I throw back at him, but my words are lost in the wind.

11

KYJTA

sleep fitfully, my stomach in knots, thinking about Calipsie. Where is she now? What might have happened to her? Is she already quelled? By morning I'm exhausted. I throw off my bedclothes, not bothering to straighten them, and move to my dresser. It's three days since we lost her, and sleep isn't getting any easier. Last night was worse, because today, I come of age. Old enough to marry, and old enough for mandatory quelling.

Choosing something to wear feels overwhelming. What does one wear to get quelled? Something black, perhaps. Something noxious. I'm pulling out a tatty charcoal dress when I hear shoes clomping up the ladder to my room. It can't be my stepfather; he always yells from downstairs.

Serain pokes her head through the hole in the floor. I must look a mess. She gives me a bright, pitying look. She's younger than me but still comes across as motherly.

'Hey there,' she says, all sunshine and radiant smiles. 'I brought you something.'

Serain climbs the remaining rungs and crawls to the centre of the room. Like me, she has to get to the centre plank before standing up. I greet her briefly, wondering how quickly I can get rid of her. Today is not the day for company.

She holds some gathered white material in one hand; I know she's up to something because she's wearing her most innocent expression. 'Surprise,' she says, opening the tunic so I can read what's scrawled on the front of it. 'What do you think?'

The tunic is two sizes too large. Serain probably picked it up from one of the thrifties at the market; there's a hole in one pocket, but that's not what has my attention. Big red painted letters spell out the words, 'Can't talk now. I'm quelled.'

'I wanted you to have something nice to wear,' she gushes. 'Here. Try it on.'

I start to say how badly I just want to be alone right now, but I think again and say, 'Thank you,' instead. She's younger than me and probably doesn't understand what today will be like.

'I'm kidding!' she howls. 'Don't let those body beggars drain your sense of humour. It's bad enough we're letting them drain our lives.'

She's only trying to cheer me up. I'd crack a smile, but I don't have the energy to fake it.

'Anyway. I'm coming with you. You look like you could use a friend.'

'There's no need. I'm fine,' I say.

'When it's my turn, I want you to come with me. I'm desperate to find out who I get.' She looks at me with utmost sincerity, then says, 'I bet you get that snooty one.'

'What? Why?' I laugh despite myself.

In the end, I let Serain tag along because her silly chatter is distracting, and I prefer not to think about what's ahead.

We take the elvakans into town. I ride Bloodbane and Serain is on

Materare. The lumbering beasts aren't the fastest mounts, but they're sturdy and tough, with thick grey hide that's unaffected by the harsh sun. We stable them at Moll's. Since we're there and need to pay Moll anyway, I tell Serain I'll treat her to a bowl of chute and a jade juice. Instantly her cheeks turn a fresh shade of pink, and I realise I've embarrassed her. I can't mention jade juice without reminding her of the day she spiked Merrick's drink. She laughs it off, but I can see it unsettles her.

Moll's is a windowless drinking house that smells of wet elvakan. It pretends to serve food, but everyone knows the menu Moll writes on his arm in black nectar for reference is from Tab's Eatery across the street. Serain and I grab the only empty table, the distressed wood puddled over with spilled ale. Moll comes over to wipe the mess onto the floor with a rag that must have been white in the distant past.

'What can I get you?' he says, showing us the inside of his forearm.

He's a big man with long curly hair, braided. I expect one of his seven young girls plaits it for him each morning. Quite often, there's a pink ribbon at the tail end of one of the carefully styled plaits.

'What's that one?' asks Serain, pointing to a blackened smudge near the crease of his arm.

Moll lifts his arm to take a better look. 'Ah . . . I'll have to check with the kitchen.'

'Don't bother,' I tell him, laughing. 'Two bowls of chutes and two jade juices.'

He nods. 'Excellent choice.' He turns away, flipping his braids to display his daughter's handiwork. Today there's a cute red ribbon and another in a rather mature beige. I wonder how old his daughters are now and how long before one of them is drafted for mandatory quelling.

The door bangs open, and Merrick walks in with his younger

brother, Dew. There used to be three boys, but the oldest died before his seventh birthday. The boy was in a playground when he fell to his knees screaming and collapsed. They found out later that the Mind Pain killed him. One of the Tarrohar, extracting tax from a business-man nearby, accidentally included the boy in the sector it was targeting. Merrick's brother wasn't strong enough to withstand the pain. Merrick hates the Tarrohar even more than he hates the Rhemans.

When he sees me, he stops dead, the smile sliding from his face. In its place, several emotions battle. He leans down and whispers something in his brother's ear. Dew looks at me with unsettling ferocity before the two turn to leave, banging the door behind them.

I stare after them, feeling like I've been bludgeoned with a stick.

When I asked my father about his infatuation elixir—if there was any remedy—he told me that the effects wore off once the love was requited. In my eagerness to avoid the guilt, I imagined the same would be true if it was unrequited, but I'm not sure that's how it works.

Once Moll drops off our order, Serain turns serious. 'You can tell him it was me, you know. I can handle it.' She raises her chin, trying to give the impression she's above it all, but I know better. She'd be crushed if Merrick diverted his anger to her.

Two old men are sitting at the table next to ours, the kind who laze around all day drinking and bemoaning the state of things, but never utter a word of protest when the Vigilance Men walk past.

'That boy,' says one of them, pointing after Merrick with a gnarled, dirty finger. 'No trouble taking their coin, that one. Keeps signing up, day after day.'

Did he? A sinking sensation settles in the pit of my stomach. If Merrick is signing up to be quelled daily in exchange for coin, that has to be my doing. I lost him his job.

Serain looks pale and pushes her juice aside. Neither of us speaks. 'Come on,' I say, 'I don't want to be late.'

We walk out of Moll's and along the wide street, which takes us past the House of Vigilance. At this time of the day, its tall windows are in deep shadow; it feels like a place filled with musty carpets and cold stone. We move past the House of Judgement and keep walking until we cross the river and finally reach the green. By now, our steps have slowed; there's so much to take in. I hardly ever come this way, so the state of the green is a surprise.

Except for some patches around the edges, the grass is completely gone. They've erected a wooden roof atop five blackened pillars at the centre of what was once a well-kept park. A handful of Vigilance Men walk up and down the roof and scan the skies. Around the edges of the roof there are pallets of wood tied together with zionate. If there's a raid, these will be lowered to protect people from the ghoragalls. Two separate queues line up under the roof, and more Vigilance Men police the system. I strain to see past the queues to the other side of the green, where the Sorbs are arranged. More Vigilance Men have gathered there, and it looks like two Tarrohar are presiding. I should be able to tell the Tarrohar apart by now, but I've rarely seen one, and they all look the same. Just a coiling mass of tentacles and a bulbous head of mottled purple and white. These two are hunched over two immaculately dressed Charmores, as if feasting on their living beauty. Like the Rhemans, the Tarrohar control us. The difference is, they take physical form. They sit like heavy sacks on the shoulders of the two Charmores, strapped in place by their unctuous coils. There are five tentacles to a Tarrohar, which works out well for them. One to control every limb of their victims, and another for the head. It's why the Charmores are all bald. I expect their suckers would have a hard time navigating a head of hair.

When the Tarrohar think, the Charmores speak. When they want to be somewhere, the Charmores walk. It's much the same with the Rhemans, minus the slippery coils.

I look down at my hands to see they're trembling.

'I'll be fine from here,' I tell Serain. 'You can head back.'

'I'm staying until I find out who you get, remember?' She laughs, but it's clear the scene has her spooked.

One of the Vigilance Men walks up, asking if we're mandatory or voluntary. I recognise him as Brezan, son of the Zhu. He's notorious for his striking good looks and fickle temperament. I don't know him personally, but my father has had dealings with him, and his name always prompts an outburst of bitterness.

'Mandatory,' I tell him.

He grabs Serain and me by the arm and tries to lead us toward the queue on the right, but I shake him off and pull his hand off Serain.

'She's not of age,' I tell him. He stares me down.

'It's not a show,' he says. His eyes are tight little slits that brim with aggression. 'Do you see a ticket stand?'

'She's just travelling with me,' I tell him.

By now, Serain has backed up and camouflaged herself in the crowd. If it's not a show, someone should talk to the throng at the edges of the green.

'Let's go, mandatory,' he says, marching me forward.

Brezan forces me into a queue forty people deep. I'm going to do the whole day and get the ordeal over with, for this moon cycle, at least. In a way, Calipsie's abduction has spared me from spending too much time obsessing about this experience. But now, with the

Sorbs lined up on one side of the green, I struggle to move with
the queue. Whenever I glimpse the Sorbs, my stomach does a flip.
They're set out in rows of ten, each resting on a squat sandstone dais
that's waist high.

A middle-aged woman with limp blond hair is led forward by
an old man in a black tunic. The old man speaks kindly to her,
guiding her toward one of the Sorbs. I wonder if he's Rheman; I
can't imagine an Aurora Saurin doing the job. When they reach
the dais, the woman puts her hand to the Sorb without hesitation.
The Sorb's bright purplish-white light goes instantly dim. Then
the woman—the Rheman, I suppose—turns and walks away. It all
looks so simple.

I turn back to check on Serain and notice Merrick standing in
the voluntary queue behind Dew. His eyes darken with hostility the
moment he catches me staring.

'What you looking at?' he barks.

I lower my eyes to avoid a scene, but Dew is already at my side,
shoving me.

'You think you're so much better than us, with your big farm and
potion master daddy . . . You think you can go around experimenting on people.'

'I don't—' Serain cuts me off, flying in to defend me. But now
Brezan is back, breaking things up. Dew doesn't seem to care that
the Vigilance Men are wearing swords; he's ready to throw a punch.
Merrick pulls his brother back to stop a full-on brawl, but it's too
late. The Tarrohar have noticed the commotion, and the targeted
pain splinters my vision. I would welcome death over this. I grab my
head, losing focus completely. I must be on my knees because my perspective changes. I sense a body nearby, but the face is a blur. Still, it's
something to hold on to. I lean against them, my head buried into

their neck. Their hands have me, clamped around my arms, fingers deep in my flesh. The ache is insignificant, a welcome distraction from the real pain in my head. I grasp my partner in pain and dig my fingers into their flesh.

When the anguish subsides, I find myself crushed to Brezan. My fingers are stiff and have left bruises on his skin. My arms are already shaded with the marks from his fingertips. Slowly we get to our feet. Serain and Dew look ashen and unstable. Not Merrick, though. He stands quickly, brushing himself off, not taking his eyes off me. If anything, he looks pleased, triumphant even.

Seeing all the staring faces, I try to look unaffected. Most of the crowd appears stunned, including the Vigilance Men, but then the black cloaks who stand nearby laugh like someone told a joke. I didn't hear the quip, but the Tarrohar are well-known for speaking right into your head.

Brezan glares at the chuckling Vigilance Men, then shoves me back into the queue.

'Go on! Get out of here!' he shouts at Serain. 'Didn't I tell you this isn't a show?'

Merrick and Dew have already decided to forego the coin. They're headed away from the green, looking for something else to do for the day. I long to do the same, but I'm here now and this initial quelling is mandatory.

The incident has shaken me; the Mind Pain can be deadly. People occasionally go into a coma. It seems ridiculous to think I got off lightly.

When my time comes, I step forward. The Tarrohar are twenty paces away, surrounded by Vigilance Men. They cling to the backs of their Charmores, who are seated on a pair of backless chairs. One of the serfs is fair-skinned, with hazel eyes; the other is dark, with eyes the colour of the deepest ocean. Both wear long red dresses that flow to the floor.

Time slows to a crawl. I observe the Sorbs, wondering if there's some way to select Kranik, a Rheman I can at least claim to know. But the Sorbs are indistinguishable. All I know is that the duller ones are empty while the brighter ones house a Rheman. The choice isn't mine anyway. The old man takes my arm and directs me to one of the luminous Sorbs.

'Your name?' he says, positioning my hands above the Sorb.

'Kyjta Cromenk,' I answer. I have to use my stepfather's name if I want this day to count toward my mandatory obligation.

I sense mild heat emanating from the Sorb. I don't know what I'd expected, but it wasn't warmth. I know everyone is staring, and I'm taking too long, but I can't go ahead with it. Then, inexplicably, my attitude flips. The Sorb seems suddenly beautiful. Harmless. The Tarrohar have seeded this thought; I could fight it, if I wanted to. Others have. But why would I? The thought is a gift. Accepting it, I lean forward with a sense of heightened euphoria and settle my hands on the smooth surface. Then my world fades to black.

***

It's as though nothing happened. My world brightens and takes shape once more. I know time has passed because the sunlight is now sloping under the roof from behind the Tarrohar, and the little old man who ushered me to my Sorb is no longer at my side. I retract my hands from the surface of the Sorb and look around. I recognise Vigilance Men from earlier in the day, but the crowd has thinned out. Now it's mainly family members returning from a day's work or mothers with children in tow, here to pick up their loved ones. Standing immobile, I watch as others, freshly reacquainted with their bodies, stumble away from the green, a little unsure of their footing.

There's no one here to collect me. I wouldn't expect there to be. Serain could hardly stand around all day, waiting for me to return, and I didn't tell my father. This is how I prefer it. I need time alone to process what's just happened; I couldn't face the questions from Serain, nor the words of consolation from Father.

I take my cue from a tall Vigilance Man, thick stubble shading his hollow jawline, and step off the green, then head back to Moll's to collect my elvakan. Being quelled was anticlimactic. It started on the village green in the early morning and ended the same way that afternoon, with nothing but a gap of memory in between. I have no unaccountable bruises, and nothing has changed about my wardrobe or my hair. I'm still me.

But I feel different.

Once, when I was younger, the farmhouse was burgled, and the Vigilance Men were called in. When we returned home, everything looked like it had been scrambled by a forceful whisk. Our clothes were spread across the floor, books were torn from the shelves and scattered across the room, and a half-eaten jade fruit dripped its purple juice onto our dining room table. My mother cleaned up and put everything back in its proper place, and my father confirmed nothing was stolen, but the house never felt like our home afterwards. I could see the thief's finger marks everywhere. I feel that way now, only it's not my things that are spoiled; it's my body. My private headspace feels polluted, and I can't find sanctuary there. When I look down at my hands, they look foreign. It's like I'm the one borrowing a body. Perhaps I'll get used to it over time, but it's hard to see how I'll ever get over it.

At Minuet Farm, I house my elvakan in the stable and walk to the farmhouse. As I open the kitchen door, my desolation gives way to turbulence. My stepfather stands by the kitchen sink, his dinner bowl in one hand, eating while staring up the dirt road that leads to the farm. Had he watched my approach, or was he just staring vacantly into the distance? He doesn't look at me as I enter, nor when I close the door gently behind me.

'Dinner's on the table,' he says flatly. He scoops up another mouthful and continues to chew.

I try to recall the last time we shared a meal. It was before my mother disappeared. Before she was murdered.

Relieved to be dismissed, I walk into the dining room to collect my dinner. The purple stain is still there, seeped into the wooden tabletop, as though that long-ago thief is still haunting us. My mother was never able to fully reclaim the wood. The stain, the finger marks, these mementoes will always remain.

The evening after my first quelling, I stand in the twilight, waiting for my stepfather. I hold a tray in my arms, heavy with the ceremonial articles of a turtis smoking. There's the tea, loom weed, the fire stick, and a plate of biscuits moulded to look like veegizs, the tiny insects responsible for the turtis yield, and its failure if proper precautions aren't taken.

It's customary to share tea before the smoking. I wouldn't bother honouring the tradition if the yakkat cream weren't laced with Stain. When he greets me, I keep my expression clear. He offers to carry the tray, but I tell him I can manage. Together we walk to the edge of the turtis field. The turtis flowers will bloom tonight under Urther's full moonlight. We must light the dried loom weed and smoke out the veegizs that live inside the turtis stalks, or they'll calcify, which will mean the death of the harvest. The veegizs are bitter little beasts.

I lower the tray onto the sun-baked earth that crusts the edge of the field. My stepfather lifts the fire stick and lights the basking lamps I placed near the field earlier in the day. The fire sticks are Rheman technology. I've been told that when the Rhemans landed, they handed them out like sweet cakes. If the sudden appearance of a ship descending from the starry sky wasn't evidence enough, the fire sticks proved that the Rhemans could perform miracles. This particular fire stick is distinctive; the colour leeched from it when it sat in a puddle of one of my genuine father's potions. Before my mother disappeared, the fire stick belonged to her. She was there the day the Rhemans landed. Now it belongs to my stepfather, like the farm.

When I was young, my mother often told the story of the Rhemans landing. Five of them exited the ship that first day. They were short, she said, and stockily built, with greyish skin, strange wide eyes, and ears that seemed to have slipped down the sides of their faces to rest near their jaws. The Rhemans seemed peaceful at first, gifting us marvels from another world, but when the ghoragalls started coming, the people quickly turned against them.

Preparations finished, we sit and share the tea and biscuits; twilight gives way to night. I wear coveralls stuffed into yakkat-skin boots to protect myself from bites, but it's not the veegizs we need to protect ourselves from. I scan the sky; Ursala, the baby sister moon, is nothing but a dim sliver in the west, but Urther is bright. My stepfather sips his tea. He takes his thick with cream—I take mine dark, of course, and we talk to pass the time.

'I visited the House of Judgement today,' he tells me.

I stare out over the turtis fields. The slim stalks sway in the darkness, yellowing like a sickening sea.

'They confirmed that the Rheman will be encircled for fighting in a borrowed body. Your name will be kept out of it.'

I suppose I should thank him. It's a long journey to the House of Judgement by road.

'I know it's—' He stumbles on his words. He's charming when he addresses tradesmen or the men of the Houses; but he's so awkward with me. I sometimes wonder why he didn't get rid of me when he killed my mother, but a child's murder would weigh heavy, and I was only eight at the time.

'Just don't do anything that'll get you into trouble,' he says.

I turn sharply. 'Like what? Go after Calipsie? Isn't that what the House of Judgement should be doing?'

I've shocked him with my comment. His cheeks flare red, and there's a flash of aggression in his eyes. 'I can see how it must seem that way to you,' he says hotly, like only I want to see the House of Judgement actually deliver justice. 'But you mustn't involve yourself.'

I sigh and kick the dirt at my feet.

'Look. It's time,' my stepfather says.

The turtis flowers are opening. The field turns white almost at once. My stepfather hands me a bouquet of dried loom weed and lights the top of it, watching the seeds crackle and spark. The flame flares briefly as the seeds incinerate, giving way to billowing smoke. I get to my feet and walk along the neat rows of flowers, bending low so the smoke wafts beneath the leaves in lazy curls. The tiny insects scurry for the safety of loose earth.

Seeing them burrowing into the rich soil stirs something hideous inside me. A monstrous cocktail of rage and hostility. Nihilism so intense it's like a blackening crust coating my insides. The memory makes me gag. The day I found the bones. More than anything, I wish I could unsee what I saw. When the lie is so much better than reality, it can seduce you, even when all evidence points to the truth.

But the Hands must have wanted the truth discovered, and they must have arranged events accordingly. It started with a storm that raged all day. When it finally abated, I checked on the animals and noticed some branches had been blown onto the alzog pen. My stepfather was away buying supplies, so I climbed onto the roof to remove the branches and check the roof for damage. I remember the shadow and the sudden sense of fear. A stiffness that immobilised me. I braced for the claws, expecting to be carried away, but nothing happened. I simply clung there, my bones aching from the taut stretch of my muscles. When I found the courage to look around, I discovered it was only a tiny grey thriggot soaring overhead. Harmless.

I don't know why I fell. Maybe my muscles were fatigued, and then, sensing the lack of danger, they relaxed. A nudge from the Hands, maybe? I landed in the sloppy muck covering the front of the alzog pen. The beasts love to roll in the filth on hot days. Although it was only about a hand's length deep, the splatter covered me. When I pulled my right hand free of the muck, there was a soft sucking sound, and I held a bone. It was slim. Finger length. I screamed and hurled it across the pen. One of the alzogs looked up and grunted. More bones were underneath me, digging into my thighs like blunt molars.

I scrambled for the side and, when my back hit the side of the pen, I found my feet and leapt over the gate. I landed, spun around, and fell to the ground, shaking and trying to catch my breath. Although alzogs aren't carnivorous, they'll eat just about anything dropped into their troughs. Still, meat wasn't part of their diet, which mainly consisted of bulbs. Shaking, I crawled forward and pushed one hand through the fence and into the muck. With my eyes closed, I searched the mud; I had to be sure. My hand finally closed around something. I pulled it free. It was long and slim. The length of my shin. Trembling, I measured it against my lower leg. I couldn't think of a single farm animal that would have a bone like that. Not an animal, then, and that meant they were the bones of an Aurora Saurin.

<hr />

The field is vast, and the smoking takes time. We've been at it for the better part of the evening when I sense a change in the night, a queer mix of apprehension and excitement hits. I don't let my stepfather see me glance at Urther's night sky. Minuet Farm lies in the flight path from Thormyth to Merrocha. The ghoragalls pass by on the way to the more densely populated cities. I change direction, walking alongside a line of turtis back toward the barn. I hold the loom weed low, but the smoke is no longer wafting under the plants. My pace quickens as I walk. At the sound of the first mournful cry, I drop the loom weed and sprint for the barn. My stepfather and I prepared everything earlier, bolting the shutters and propping open the barn door. He said that if I had to run, I could sprint straight in. He emphasised my safety since I'm the one who's stained. It was farcical; I doubt he'd bother to look up if a ghoragall lifted me away.

I run at top speed, boots pounding the clumped soil. My breath is so hot it scalds my lungs. In the weak light, I spot the barn. There's no guarantee I'll reach it in time; ghoragalls hunt in pairs. If my slow administration of the Stain to my stepfather's digestive tract marked him on the inside like I'm marked on the outside, they still might scoop both of us up. I tread on a mound of soil, and my ankle gives way. My knees buckle, and I fall. As I get to my feet, I look back and see my stepfather running. He's heavier than he was before my mother's disappearance, not exactly built for speed, but he's gaining on me. I lengthen my stride, accelerating up the hill. It helps that I'm tall; I inherited my long legs from my father.

I don't look back again, and I don't slow. When I reach the open barn door, I run straight through. I careen to a stop so I don't collide with the low table laden with my mother's zionate jars. Then I head back to the barn door. From the safety of the barn, I spot my step-father running up the slope. He's a hundred paces from me when I slam the door and jam the crossbar down.

My stomach squirms. It would have been better if they'd taken him before it came to this. I stand close to the door, listening. When I hear him slam against the wood, I jump.

'Kyjta!' He beats the door with his fists. 'Kyjta, it's me! Let me in.'

I take a step back and clasp my hands to my chest.

'Kyjta! Let me in.' He's begging, slamming his body against the door.

I take a few more shaky steps backwards. What if the ghora-galls didn't notice us? What if they flew overhead and on toward Merrocha? I can't stand it; I must get away from the sound. My calves collide with the low table. We carried it into the barn that morning, and I topped it with my mother's collection of protective jars. It looks like a shrine. Desperate for the banging to stop, I get on my knees and crawl under the table. There is a sudden, awful scream. A scream that rises upward, over the barn and away.

Hunched over and trembling, I wait. My shins ache, crushed against the cold earth floor. I'm not sure what I'm waiting for. Relief? Remorse? Something.

I feel hollow; a nothingness that's more there than not.

After some time, I shuffle out and stand. I grasp for what I'm feeling. Loneliness?

No, aloneness.

I walk to the barn door and lift the crossbar. I don't open it immediately; I rest my hand on the cool metal handle and wait. When I feel ready, I lower the hammered metal lever and push the door open wide. Stepping outside, I look up at the empty sky. Something I can't name rushes into me; a chaos of emotions that makes me stagger. I drop to my knees, holding my head up to the sky.

'Curse you!' I scream into Urther's pale, looming face. My hands are stiffly balled like tiny rocks at my sides. 'Curse you to a dead life!'

Though I'm laughing, tears roll down my cheeks. My face twists into a grotesque grimace. It feels monstrous. When I fall forward onto my hands and knees, the violence of my sobs sends spasms through me, and each breath fires a sharp pain between my ribs.

My mother is gone. There's nothing I can do to get her back. I wasn't expecting relief from the pain. All I wanted was some peace. I have no guilt. My stepfather deserves a fate worse than the one I engineered for him. Telling me she left us for a life of luxury. As if my mother would ever supplicate to the Tarrohar. Imagining her as a Charmore serving the Tarrohar was ridiculous. She was graceless and would never dance; the idea of having one of those monsters suckered onto her body while she ambled between the luxurious live-ins and the House of Judgement would have repulsed her. Looking back, it's easy to see the deceit. But I was so young when it happened. I trusted too easily.

It's a windless night. When a fetid gust whips my hair, I know what's coming.

I scramble to get up and stumble backwards, trailing my fingers on the ground for balance. The ghoragall is on me, snaking its smooth claws beneath my armpits, and lifting me onto my feet. The stench of something metallic, buried in moist earth for too long, is unmistakable.

My back hits the barn wall, and my hands pan out, searching for the door. The flapping wings sweep the smell into my face. My right hand finds purchase on the doorframe just as my feet lift off the ground. The ghoragall has me; I'll join my stepfather for my sins.

I swing my other hand back and grip the doorframe. My body levels out, rising with each beat of the ghoragall's wings. My joints strain. Pain tears at my muscles. My grip is slipping, my fingers slick with sweat. I kick out, striking the ghoragall in the belly. A dark cloud of feather dust puffs into my face. There's a loud crack as the doorframe gives. Then I'm lifted free, a chunk of wood coming loose in my hand. We rise, and I look down at the farm, convinced I'll never see it again. I bested my stepfather, but the Hands are fickle deities. I should have known that the mate would lie in wait.

My hands shake, but I must keep hold of the splinter of wood I pulled from the doorframe. If this is the end, I'd rather die falling from height. I don't want to see Thormyth. I don't want someone else using my body.

I did this to Calipsie! Blood of my blood, and just a child. The horror twists something inside me. She's half my age—she'd have been terrified. I can't leave her in the Ice Realm. I can't desert her like my mother deserted me, dying when I was Calipsie's age. I have to go after her. I have to fight for her.

I tighten my grip around the stake and plunge the jagged point into its black belly. A cloud of feather dust hits me in the face, scratching my eyes and blocking my airways. As I cough and sputter, I twist the stake. The ghoragall caws as its wing beats oscillate, but it doesn't release me. I attack its claws, jabbing them with the spike, but it doesn't react. So I wedge the splinter between my shoulder and the ghoragall's claw and try to lever it free. There's no give at all. I'm weak, and the bird is gaining height. With the last of my energy, I power the spike into its chest. I must hit something because the ghoragall cries out and dips. Then it lets me fall.

The branches rush past me, smacking my arms and legs. Some gouge my flesh before cracking and giving way beneath my weight. The sound is like thunder, unnervingly loud and close. They must be breaking my fall, I think. Still, I hit the ground with bone-crushing violence, and lie inert. Not breathing. Giving my body time to figure out if I'll live or die, a turn of the Hands. I'm surprised by the gasp when it comes, followed by small ragged sucking sounds. Once my breathing regulates, I push myself onto my elbows and check my injuries. There's a lot of blood. Most of the cuts are superficial, but there's a deep gash in one calf and a dull ache around my ribs that's agony when I breathe deeply. But nothing's obviously broken, and I'm still on the farm. Not quelled. Perhaps the Hands took pity on me after all.

I get cautiously to my feet and venture to the edge of the trees. I look for my feathered nemesis. Urther's slate sky is stark, without so much as a cloud. I can't hide in the woods all night; my wounds need tending, and I'm exhausted. I want to curl up in my little bed, so I decide to chance the Hands at getting home. If I can make it to the barn, it's a short run to the safety of the house. I hobble forward; it's only two hundred paces from the wood to the barn, but the journey seems to take forever. Halfway, I spot a dark mound ahead and walk toward it. A sense of foreboding thickens my limbs. It's the ghoragall.

I knew what it was the moment I saw it, but I had to see it up close to be sure. I killed it. The Hands haven't had their fill of me. If the mate returns, looking for its partner, I'll never be safe.

The creature is three times my size and ghastly in death. Its white sightless eyes are pointless, like the dry bone shards protruding from its face. The ghostly eyes and splintered bones have just one function: to strike fear into the hearts of its prey.

It would take a long time to dig a hole big enough for the beast and fill it up again. I don't have a Rheman's unnatural strength, and what little I do have is waning; I need a different plan, where I'm not exposed to the night.

I circle the beast, trying to figure out the best place to take hold of it. The legs are long and bend backwards at an unsightly angle. But they offer traction. I grab the feet. The flesh is strangely spongy. The legs stretch out as I start to pull, the tendons visible beneath the soft skin. I have to lean back, using my full weight to get it moving, but it's still lighter than it looks. Slowly I haul the corpse across the grass and dirt toward the barn. The band of pain across my ribs screams with every lunging step. Gritting my teeth, I keep at it. I cross the dirt road, navigate a ditch, and finally reach the barn. With its wings outstretched, it's far too big to force through the doorway. I pit myself against each wing, hearing the bones snap beneath my weight. I drag the bedraggled creature through the door. There's still work to be done before I'm free. The fireplace at the back of the barn is huge, far bigger than the one in the house. It could fit the entire ghoragall. Something other than exhaustion stops me disposing of the body. My mind is hard at work, the outline of a plan taking shape.

12

KYJTA

The next morning, when I retrace my steps to the barn, the ghoragall is right where I left it, lying lifelessly on its back. Seeing how battered and broken it is, I almost feel bad for killing it. Then I see the eyes. Sightless and horrible, they chill me. I lift a burlap sack from a nearby hook and cover its head. Then I set to work.

By midday, I need a shower. Everything that isn't protected by my clothes is ash black with ghoragall dust. My nails are filthy. With my masked face and dusky skin, I must look like one of the mercenary Grulo from the Parched Lands. I can't bring myself to use the shower stall next to the orchard. After I was stained, my stepfather assured me he'd erect a roof over it, but he never did, always claiming there were a thousand other things to get on with. I stopped asking after I started lacing his tea.

I head to the stables to saddle up my elvakan. We keep three on the farm, Bloodbane being the strongest. I delivered him myself, around my twelfth alignment. He nudges me with his smooth trunk.

'You thirsty, old boy?' I ruffle the tufts of black fur sprouting from his thick-skinned shoulders.

I named him Bloodbane after his bloody and near-fatal birth. I spent half that day up to my shoulders in blood, trying to free him from the birthing canal, but he was too big. The mother grew exhausted and quit trying. I had to forfeit one or the other. In the end, I chose Bloodbane. I think he knows it.

I sling my saddle and porter pockets over his back. Bloodbane is a stubborn beast but lets me mount him. With a bit of persuasion, I get him walking. My eyes grow heavy as we travel through the afternoon's blistering heat. I'm desperate for sleep, but my stepfather's screams startle me awake whenever I drift off.

By the time we reach the shack at the base of the Qetheral Mountains I'm slick with sweat and in a temper. My father's living quarters are modest, and I feel a familiar stab of resentment seeing the hovel. The shack was loaned to him by the House of Judgement when they left him homeless, eleven alignments ago. It's a single room with a small latrine and a shower stall farther down the hill.

I dismount and tie Bloodbane to a tree, where he sets to grazing. My father must have company—another elvakan is tied up near the shack. It's not unusual for the potion master to have company, and I know better than to interrupt. My father's customers are secretive, and he's respected for his discretion. It's still hot, and I'm happy to be in the shade; I sit on the grass beside Bloodbane and wait.

Soon the door swings open, and someone steps out. The shock hits me like a blanket full of needles. I gasp, half rising to my feet. Then I change my mind; it's not who I thought it was.

It's Merrick.

He spots me, his attention drawn by my sudden movement. There's an awkward moment where we both stare at each other. I'm acutely aware that I've paused awkwardly, halfway between sitting and standing, and I'm holding the unnatural position. My breath stills; his expression wavers between slack-jawed stupefaction and forlorn bitterness. Seeing him, I thought of Kranik, and that was enough of a shock. This is worse. He's still angry, and I don't need a confrontation out here, in front of my father's shack.

'Kyjta,' he says, suspicion in his eyes. 'Why're you here?'

I shrug. 'Just visiting my father.'

'Up to your old tricks then. Who're you lookin' to ruin now?' His eyes have the wet look of an injured animal. He shoves something into his pocket and stomps over to his elvakan.

I stand to my full height and fiddle with Bloodbane's saddle, trying to look like my actions have purpose. I understand why he's angry; he thinks I experimented on him. Worse, he thinks I gave him the infatuation potion because I wanted to seduce him, and then I changed my mind. I told him it was an accident, but he never believed me, and I couldn't bring myself to point the finger at Serain.

Merrick mounts his elvakan and trundles past me. 'Fair favour,' he says, but he doesn't mean it.

I walk up to the door and knock. There's a shuffling inside.

'Just a minute,' comes my father's lazy voice.

The door opens. The frame is filled by a tall figure dressed in black. He has a long nose and thick, greying copper hair that falls to his shoulders. His lilac eyes light up when he sees me, and a big, slow smile follows.

'My girl, come in. Did you ride in through a sandstorm?' He fingers a strand of my hair, still chalky with feather dust.

I step into the small space, ignoring his question. It smells like fallen fruit, grown overripe in the sun. Something is always brewing in the cauldron over the fire and today is no exception. My mouth fills with saliva; the smell is too close in the tiny space. He could afford something larger, closer to the city, and less creepy, but he stays here as a self-inflicted penance.

The cabin is a room built from shelves that are crammed with bottles and jars of every shape and size. I recognise most substances by sight or smell. Every one of them links me to early childhood, an idyllic time when I still had both parents, back before my father was first encircled by the Tarrohar. Everything was normal then, or as normal as I can recall.

Scanning the crooked shelves, I see turtis stalks for bone aches, woc weed for cranial pain, tamper powder for constipation. I could go on and on. I used to sit for ages, smelling the contents of each jar and proudly naming the remedy.

'I saw Merrick outside. What was he after?' I ask, feigning disinterest.

My father gives me a look of mock admonishment. 'If you want a secret tightly kept, tell it to a potion master,' he says, repeating the age-old adage.

Closing the door behind me, I secure the bar. Then I turn to face my father, 'Did Halli come by yet?'

'She did. She told me of the child.' He looks down, quiet for a moment. 'I didn't know,' he says when his eyes meet mine again, and I believe him. 'I wondered why you hadn't been by. You were giving her a berth.'

'She said she gave Calipsie up for the girl's protection. Why?'

I should have been more tactful. If it's possible to break a broken man, those were the words to do it. My father takes a moment to gather himself. He looks tender, as though the slightest breeze would bruise him.

'Potion masters are notoriously one draft shy of trouble, and the live-ins are no place to raise a child,' he manages.

'How are you coping with it all?'

'I have suffered countless cuts, but none so deep as this.' It's a quote from a book he used to read me about a man who reaches his breaking point, and completely transforms. Meek and mild one day, crazed and conquering the next.

I should have visited before. There's only me to console him, but how could I after the role I'd played? I'm here today because I know what to do. With a plan to set things right, I can finally face him. I can fix this.

'You were right,' I say. 'The Stain worked. A ghoragall took Cromenk last night.'

My father closes his eyes, relieved to have the wrong finally put to right.

'You've done well, child.' He takes my shoulders in his hands and pulls me to his chest. I rest my face against his black robes, breathing in the complex mix of aromas that permeates his clothes.

'Once I've cleaned up, I'll head to the House of Judgement and propose your motion, but Father, I have a suggestion.'

'Of course,' he says, turning to stir the steaming concoction. The room is stifling with the fire on the go and the sour steam rising from the pot.

'You talked about a mixture once . . . something that could be administered as smoke. A susceptibility potion. You said it would make others more open to your ideas. Why not brew a batch before your appeal? I can place the dispensers around the circle before your allotment. That should bend the people's favour.'

My father was encircled before; he understands the treacherous unpredictability of the Tarrohar better than most. I'm sure he won't risk going up against them again without taking proper precautions.

'Indeed. The empathy smoke, Salechet Marapet.'

He drops the ladle and turns to face me. Scrutinising my face, he raises a hand, brushing his thumb over the skin beneath my right eye before thoughtfully examining the pad of his thumb.

'For that, I would need dust from a fallen ghoragall.'

'You can have the dust of an entire ghoragall,' I say, dropping my porter pockets on the bed. I free one of my mother's zionate jars and hand it to him.

He opens the lid and looks inside. 'An entire ghoragall,' he repeats, arching an eyebrow at me.

'Just about,' I say. 'I ran out of jars.'

'Well, there's enough here to—' A smile brightens his face. 'Should I ask how you came by this much feather dust?'

I shrug. 'You know what they say: the less you know . . .'

'The less you can be encircled for.' We complete the sentence together, laughing comfortably.

I sit on the small bed; the mattress feels terribly thin. My father turns back to the pot and stirs his potion. The room suddenly reminds me of the basement at Minuet Farm, cluttered with my mother's zionate collection and so very small. I wrap my hands around the cool metal of the bed frame and rock in place.

'How do you do it?' I ask, my voice tight with sentiment. 'How do you go on without mother?'

My father's eyes mist up; he shrugs his large shoulders. 'You know,' he says, 'a wound of the heart is no different than a wound of the flesh. Scars form. They give you strength.'

He's right, I suppose. If I hadn't endured what I have in my short, cursed life, I would never have escaped the claws of that ghoragall, and I definitely couldn't have killed it. I'm not that different from him, I suppose. He had everything: a wife, a child, a large farm, though it never felt like a farm when he'd been Sion. It felt more like land imbued with magic, with every stem, leaf, and seed embodying a mystical power that could be wielded for good or evil. But then he lost everything on the back of one foolish move. A squabble with Sion Cromenk outside the man's house. Some debt for a potion my future stepfather claimed had already been paid. Sion Cromenk slammed the door in my father's face. The story told is that he immediately left through the back door in a violent mood that needed walking off. I can picture him storming through the fields, ranting to Urther's pale face. My father, fuming, lit a bull reed stuffed with dried solarass weed. The smoke had a calming effect, and he needed to centre himself. When he'd sucked it down to a nib, he flicked the tiny bud into the night sky, as is the custom on Aurora Saura, then left. The globe of hot coal landed on the fishing cottage's thatch roof. The house burned to the ground, taking the lives of Sion Cromenk's wife and daughter. During his encirclement, my father was ordered to hand over his farm, his wife, and his daughter for the home and family Sion Cromenk lost. And that's where my troubles began. One foolish move led to another, until my entire life was a tapestry of errors.

I use my father's shower stall. It has no running water, just a bucket and sponge. There's no roof either, but it's set under a copse of thick trees, and the branches offer some protection. It's cold, and the shower floor is muddy, but there's nothing here to remind me of my stepfather.

Cleaned up and wearing fresh clothes from my backpack, I return to the shack to find my father preparing our evening meal. There's a spit behind the shack, and he's roasting plump honapeac over the flames. The smell makes my mouth water. He must have caught the forest grazer in one of his snares. My father is animated as we sit near the fire, discussing our plans. The prospect of having my mother's beloved farm returned to us has awoken something in him. Seeing his eyes bright with promise stirs memories I didn't know I had. We talk late into the night, and I start to believe we might be able to go back to some sort of normal life.

That night, I sleep in his bed, and he takes the ragged old chair. We've done it that way for as long as he's had the shack and I've been old enough to visit unaccompanied. My father rarely sleeps through the night, but he often naps. When I was a child, I'd find him all over the house with his eyes closed and a book in his lap. He'd open his eyes the moment I entered the room, almost as if he could sense my approach. I used to make a game of it, but I never won.

The bed is uncomfortable, but seeing him has lifted some of my burden. My dreams are quieter now. I did what needed doing. A wrong must be set right; it's the Aurora Saurin way. Around mid-morning, we say our goodbyes. I promise to be back soon, bringing him news of my journey and the date of his encirclement.

The House of Judgement is half a day's ride from the Qetheral Mountains. The slow, monotonous lumbering of the elvakan, and the exquisite warmth of the morning sun against my back, makes me drowsy. It's easier to stay awake later when we're crossing the plains of the Nobi Depression. A cooling wind whistles through the channel, tangling Bloodbane's mane and flinging sand in our eyes. When we reach the Caperero River, we stop. My father packed a small lunch for me: a wedge of soft bread and a jar of lotils pulp. I settle on a rock that crests the rapids to cool my feet in the water and eat. The river rushes around my calves, bucking my legs in the current. With my feet jostled by the water, and the sun on my back, I'm taken back to that day on the beach. The moment before we leapt into the sea, my hand resting in Kranik's. As I think about it, my blood rushes like the rapids. I must find him; Calipsie's life depends on it. If I must make the journey alone, I will, but I don't believe I can save her without him. The Rheman is strong, and he'll know the path to follow through the Parched Lands to reach Thormyth. I only hope my plan works.

Just before sunset, I reach Inner Town and stable my elvakan behind Purple Dew Dawn, a brew house favoured by the Charmores. It's a decent-size cabin constructed from wood and perched a hair's breadth from the edge of Skylorn Cliffs. A sign swings outside the door, curly letters spelling out 'a brew with a view'. And the view never disappoints. To the left, as far as the eye can see, is the turquoise expanse of the Onaway Ocean. On the right are the jade sheets of the Tibetha Sea. Where they meet, a darker line forms, straight as the path of a well-aimed quill.

I scan the room, then slip my right hand into my pocket and finger the pouch my father gave me. I'm looking for Halli, but I can't see her among the cackling bald women occupying almost every table. I walk over to the counter and lean forward to get the barmaid's attention. A burly woman, bald, as is the custom for Charmores, saunters over.

'Ain't you a little yoke to be coming in here, farm girl?'

'I'm not here for your brew, Dixie. I'm looking for Halli.'

'Halli? She's back in her live-in with the Tarrohar. You going over there, you tell her she owes me.'

'If I'm not old enough for brew, I'm not old enough for bill collecting,' I say and wish her fair favour.

The live-ins are set back from the cliffs in the Nersea Woods. They're built high into the trees, connected by a network of wooden walkways and stairwells. The Charmores' residences are opulent, furnished with every luxury on offer. I make my way along a pebbled walkway toward the bank of trees. Some of the cabins emit a warm glow now that night is falling. With mounting dread, I climb the stairs closest to Halli's cabin; a visit to her live-in risks an encounter with the Tarrohar. The ruling race are repugnant, and I have trouble hiding my revulsion. The idea that my mother gave up life on the farm and her only child to live like Halli is so absurd that it sickens me now, though I believed it for so long. If my stepfather had been bothered enough to come up with a better lie, he might have gotten away with murder. As soon as I was old enough to ride an elvakan, I volunteered to take on my father's deliveries, and it didn't take long to figure out my mother wasn't here. The Charmores have a real yen for nebuga azermi, one of my father's more mysterious concoctions.

I knock on Halli's door and her statuesque form fills the doorway, one arm lazing against the doorframe, the other cinching a gold gossif-thread gown at her slim waist.

'Well, if it isn't fair-faced Kyjta.'

Calipsie's abduction has taken a toll on Halli. Her flawless mahogany skin looks jaundiced, and there are crescent-shaped shadows under her eyes.

I peer around her, checking for the Tarrohar.

'She's in the tub,' says Halli. 'Spends most of her time there. It's rare you'll find us strapped. You farm folk don't seem to get that. You all think we're hobbling 'round the place like a bunch of drunken hunchbacks. Better for us, I say. Less competition. Come on in.'

Halli steps aside and sweeps her arm into the room. Her gown slips from her shoulder, exposing a pattern of circular blood blisters. There are seven that I can see, each the size of the bottom of an ale mug. The stigmata of the Charmores. The bare-headed serfs of the House of Judgement might not be continually subjected to the Tarrohar's demands, but Halli has taken on this burden recently.

'I didn't say anything,' I tell her, stepping into the room.

'No harm done.'

The live-ins are beautiful inside and out. Decked out with luxurious couches and gold-threaded cushions. Heavy curtains are carefully draped over large ornate hooks that jut from the walls, and beyond the window, all the way to the horizon, there's nothing but treetops.

'Did you bring me something?' Halli asks.

I pull the velvet bag from my pocket and dangle it in front of her. It spins on its string, displaying the embossed silver feather that is my father's trademark. The bag contains a considerable stash of nebuga azermi. I don't know the ingredients, but I know its import. The bald woman reaches out to take the bag, but I snatch it back. Without a steady supply, the Charmores' thoughts would be totally exposed to the Tarrohar when under their control. The salts make it possible for them to keep their deepest secrets hidden.

'I need something,' I tell her.

'And I've proved myself useful many times,' says Halli, beckoning for the bag. 'What is it?'

'There's a Rheman in town. His name is Kranik. He was with me when the girl was taken.'

'Heard about that. Looks like he'll be encircled and judged the Aurora Saurin way. Recommend you keep yourself out of it, Fair Face.'

'When's his trial?'

'Fami phase. At quarter day. Why?'

'With Sion Cromenk gone, my father wants to appeal for the return of his land. I need his appeal to back onto Kranik's,' I tell her.

She's listening, but her attention is on the bag.

'I can get you an answer right away,' she says, looking at me sceptically.

I bite my lip, then pass Halli the bag and wait as she opens it. She wets two fingers and dips them in the bag, then runs the salts along the underside of her tongue. She takes a deep, steady breath, staring out over the trees. Her eyes mist with tears, and she blinks them away. When she's levelled out, we walk from the living area, through the bedroom, which is equally lavish, and stand outside the washroom door. Halli knocks, and we enter. At the centre of the washroom sits a vast metal tub, filled to the brim with sand from the Parched Lands. A fireplace is housed in an archway carved into the wall between the bedroom and washroom. Someone has lit it, though the evening is warm.

I stop just inside the doorway, but Halli keeps walking until she gets to the tub and squats beside it. A moment later, a gelatinous limb breaches the surface of the sand and wraps around the edge of the metal rim.

Halli strokes it with one hand as she speaks. 'I've a friend here,' she says. 'Her father wants to appeal a ruling long past. The state of affairs has changed: the debt no longer stands. He's asking to have his farmland returned to him. We can fit him in before the Rheman. What say you?'

Stomach squirming, I watch as the glutinous limb slides up Halli's arm, exposing a scattering of mauve suction cups that glint in the firelight. The tentacle attaches to the back of her naked skull. I do my best to keep the horror from my expression. The Tarrohar's puppetry may be no more sinister than the Rheman's, but it's far more disturbing to look at.

When Halli speaks, her voice is deeper and has more resonance. Her mouth moves to form the words.

'Fair-face Kyjta, daughter of the potion master.'

The Tarrohar couldn't possibly know the nickname Halli coined for me. Is it scanning her mind? Reading her thoughts? My mouth is dry; I'm not sure I'll be able to speak.

'We recall your father's encirclement. He was unremorseful.'

My fear ebbs beneath a sudden rush of anger. My father mourned the incident every day of his life. He was angry at his encirclement. His entire family was awarded away.

'He has paid his debt,' I say, my tone measured.

'You believe it is so.' The Tarrohar don't know what it is to ask a question; instead, they make statements and rebuttals.

'By rights, the farm is yours, if you marry.'

It's difficult to think, seeing Halli puppeted like a theatre doll. Still, I know enough to understand the Tarrohar motivations for seeing me wed. With my stepfather gone and the land falling to me, there would be a healthy nuptial tax if I marry.

I want this conversation over with; I'm not sure how long I can stand here and watch Halli like this.

'My skin is stained. I expect to be quelled before I'm married. My father is welcome to the land.'

'Very well, fair-face Kyjta. An encirclement there will be. The people will decide whether your father has paid his debt and deserves title to the land.'

I don't care for the way it smacks Halli's lips when it uses Halli's nickname for me. Two more tentacles slip from the tub and wind around her. Unable to watch any more of this, I back away.

'We did not expect such generosity after the way your father deceived you,' it says.

My father?

The unexpected accusation stuns me.

'What are you saying?' I demand.

Its agenda met, the Tarrohar draws the unconscious Charmore over the lip of the tub and onto the sand. I'm desperate to leave before its treacherous words can imprint their madness on me. I track back through the bedroom, knocking into a table on my way. My father is a decent man. Why would he deceive me, his own daughter?

I stumble out of the live-in. I expected to be reeling from an encounter like this, but for different reasons. I can't think why the Tarrohar would go to the trouble of lying to me. There must be some mistake.

My father's encirclement is some days away, so I bury myself in chores. I worry that I won't have the coin to pay the farmhands, but there is coin enough beneath the floorboards in my stepfather's room. My stepfather was no farmer, but he was frugal. My father's transition will be smooth.

On the third day, as I break for a quick midday meal, Serain comes to the door. Seeing her, my heart skips painfully. I don't know what I'll tell her if she asks after her uncle. I have to summon the image of my mother's bones to keep myself together.

Serain has other things on her mind, though. She slips into a wild monologue, cataloguing events that occurred the day I was quelled.

'I followed you,' she gushes. 'I told you I was going to find out which Rheman was quelling you.'

I drag her onto the couch, forgetting my anxiety. 'Wait,' I tell her. 'Start from the beginning.'

'After you were quelled, you just walked off. I had no idea which of those Rhemans had you. I was worried, so I followed you.'

I give her my most reproachful look but want to hear more.

'I followed you to the cliffs of Timmil. I had to hitch a ride with Bury Matol in his father's waste cart. I got Bury to drop me at the crossroads near Bater Meadow; his father wasn't going the way of your Rheman. I watched your wagon take the path that leads to the cliffs. There are gathering rooms there, you know the ones I'm talking about. I ran up that road, then took this little off-ramp when a wagon came past and found a trail that led along the cliffs. It led to the gathering rooms. It must be some sort of secret path; it led right to a ledge that ran to the open window. That's where I stood to listen.'

'You spied on the Rhemans?' I ask her, aghast.

'I suppose I did,' she says, looking smug.

'What did they say?'

'I'm getting to that part,' she says, enjoying tormenting me. 'I'm almost sure one of them was that evil captain—I heard them call him "Rhytheus." Others were there too. The reasonable one who sometimes sneaks about healing the sick with that silver contraption of theirs.'

'Their crew master?'

'Yes! And the snooty one was definitely there. The one who runs around in spectacular bodies.'

'I know the one,' I say quickly, so she'll get on with the telling. 'They call him Azaire.'

'I think there were more, but I didn't dare lean in to check.'

'What did they say?'

'They were talking about the usual stuff—the importance of the Body Trust, current subscription rates, taxes to the Tarrohar . . . but then they said something about the zionate safe houses. The Tarrohar have launched an investigation. Someone is leaking the locations to Helacth and the Zhu has been charged with figuring out who.'

She's brazen now, but what must it have been like hearing this revelation firsthand and realising that no matter what we do, we're never safe?

'The captain started shouting about Helacth, saying that the Rheman overlord didn't lay sole claim to the Aurora Saurin population.' Serain's voice wobbles, and she rushes the last part. 'The captain said that at the rate Aurora Saurins are disappearing, there'll soon be none left for the Rhemans in Merrocha.'

I can't speak because the memory of Calipsie overwhelms me. She was so young. Imagining her being puppeted around by some Rheman sickens me. I want to rise to my feet and break for the stables, but I can't go after her yet, not before Kranik's encirclement. If there's a chance I can do this with Kranik, I must take it. The odds of success will be greater if I'm ferrying him.

'If anyone is leaking the locations of the zionate bunkers to Helacth, I would have thought it would be the Tarrohar. But if it is them, they wouldn't assign the Zhu to investigate, would they?'

'The Tarrohar wouldn't give Helacth the bunker locations,' I tell her. 'The last thing they want is for more Aurora Saurins to be taken. It'd interfere with their tax forecasts.'

'Who then? Who would do such a thing?'

'Any of the Rhemans, I suppose. They'd be able to find out the locations easily enough. They'd only need to slip into the body of one of the Justice Men and check the records at the House of Judgement.'

We're both silent for a moment, thinking. Then Serain continues, looking even more spooked. 'There's more.' I give her my full attention. 'They said there are far more people disappearing than they can attribute to the ghoragalls.'

'So . . . you're saying the Quelled are taking them?'

'It didn't sound like that to me,' she says. 'It sounded more like people are going missing from Merrocha unaccountably.'

'Missing,' I repeat, struggling to make sense of everything I've heard. 'Missing how?'

'Don't ask me. I couldn't even work out which of the Rhemans you were ferrying. Anyway, I've been desperate to tell you all this, but it's market day, so I need to whip around and collect everything for the stall.' Her tempo slows, and I brace for what's coming, summoning my courage. 'I still can't believe they got the old man. He wasn't even stained. No one is safe.'

I cast my gaze to the floor, sure she'll see right through my façade, but she's distracted when the house horn blows. We both jump at the grating sound. I go and open the front door. A uniformed delivery man is on the step, holding a package in one hand.

'Fair favour,' he says. 'Delivery for you.'

Serain slips past me, weaving through the open door and heading for the stables.

The delivery man hands me a small sack tied with string. I take it from him and shut and bolt the door. When I pull on the string, the sack slips open. The item inside is tiny and smooth, a vial, stoppered with a wedge of porous wood.

A small flask of potion.

I roll it in my hand, trying to figure out its purpose and why the package was addressed to me. There's a label scrawled untidily and pasted askew on one side of the bottle. I know my father's elegant handwriting, and this isn't it. I squint and read:

Vengance.

I drop the ampule like a lump of white-hot coal. It lands on the carpet with a soft thud. I kick it under the couch and listen as it tinkles across the stone tiles before coming to rest against the wall. My first thought, that if this is a gift of vengeance, it must have come from my stepfather, is ludicrous, but that doesn't stop me from reacting. He might have escaped the ghoragall and returned to take revenge. Escape is a real possibility; I've done it myself. But he wouldn't send me a potion he knows I'd never drink. He'd be more subtle and scrupulous than that. After all, he killed my mother, and he'd probably end my life the same way if he could. Our bones could linger together in the mud until they turned to mulch, ground to dust beneath the heavy hooves of the unwitting alzogs.

I wonder whether he could have sent me the ampule before he was spirited away, but that makes no sense. He drank the tea the night he was taken; if my stepfather knew what I was doing to him, he would have refused it.

No, it couldn't be him. Releasing the crazy notion allows me the mental space to consider the alternatives. I realise that 'Vengeance' is misspelt on the label—an atrocity my stepfather would never commit.

The vial has to be from Merrick. Didn't I see him at my father's shack? He's still angry about the infatuation potion and is looking for a way to make a statement. He wasn't expecting me to drink it. He just wanted to shake me up, and he's succeeded.

It's possible the fumes are harmful. Merrick might expect me to sniff the contents to figure out its purpose. It was foolish of me to drop it on the floor. If the glass broke, I might have suffered my intended fate; I doubt I'd even know what hit me.

13

KRANIK

I'm seated at a polygonal table with a vibrant sheen inside an extravagantly decorated room full of polished furnishings and gaudy ornaments on a high floor in the House of Judgement. Two Vigilance Men flank the only door. They transported me here from the Sorb Room aboard the *Rhema Bolajio*, where I've been imprisoned since my arrest.

'What day is it?' I ask.

Time doesn't work the same way inside a Sorb, and I couldn't track it. Neither of the black cloaks responds. Their eyes remain fixed on some point beyond the room's only window. I follow their gaze, hoping the view will reveal something about the day. The window shows a block of ice-blue sky. It's a crisp, clear morning; the sky turns a deeper shade in the afternoon. Below us, Inner Town is a bustling swarm of bodies.

I've spent much of my life inside my Sorb, and the loss of time has never bothered me. Something has changed.

Every day I spend inside my Sorb is another day Calipsie will never get back. Each passing moment feels critical.

I look down at my hands, Merrick's hands. He must have signed up for the coin again. You'd think he'd want to spend time with his father. I'm anxious for him, for the time he's losing.

The door swings open, and Azaire strides in with Tiberico at his back. Azaire has a rotating shift of bodies. He's rarely in his Sorb. Most are hewn of the richest ebony or sable, tall, and respectable. Today Azaire uses Vico, who is dark and muscled and also handsome. A prime body with a pedigree bloodline. Someone the Merrochans would respect. I wonder if he paid a premium.

Tiberico is ferried by a familiar middle-aged man with greying hair and dirty fingernails. Tiberico doesn't put the same forethought into body selection that Azaire does; he values consistency, which is probably why I'm so often ferried by Merrick.

Tiberico smiles and greets the guards, but they ignore him. It must be in their training.

'Kranik,' Tiberico says. 'How are you holding up? You've been Sorb-side for almost four days. I'm sure you'd like an update.'

Four days? I could be on the other side of the Qetheral Mountains by now, and heading through the Parched Lands. I almost get out of my seat, but one look from Azaire settles me.

'The date of your encirclement is determined,' says Tiberico, walking up to the window. He puts his hands on the sill and surveys the activity below. 'We need to talk before your hearing.'

Turning back, Tiberico motions for Azaire to take a seat.

Azaire takes a chair, flapping his blue cloak back as he sits.

'We must agree how to structure Kranik's defence,' says Tiberico, sitting opposite Azaire. 'The first charge is easy enough to dispute. He disregarded one of the stipulations of the Body Trust by fighting in a borrowed body, but in defence of two young girls. His actions prevented them from being quelled. The second charge is more difficult to argue. Attacking a Vigilance Man. The Zhu claims he has witnesses to both events, but Kranik was only acting to save lives. The people must see that.'

'There's no guarantee of that.' Sunlight from the window glances off Azaire's ebony skull as he speaks. 'The people are fickle; they enjoy punishing Rhemans.'

'We must guide them to a conclusion. Our statistics speak for themselves. All three ships in Sojour abide by the Body Trust. In Fareen, where we have two ships, one is considering conversion. In Thormyth, we have one, and there lies our problem. The system isn't delivering as long as Helacth keeps sending his ghoragalls.' Tiberico glances at the guards. Anything we discuss within these walls will be reported to the Tarrohar, so he considers his words. 'Any news from your contacts in Thormyth?'

Azaire leans forward before quietly responding. 'None. They've gone completely quiet.'

'If they don't manage to talk Helacth around, our delicate agreement will crumble. We committed to ending the raids, and we haven't delivered. We must send a team to discover the real reason for Helacth's insatiable need. He must have three bodies to every Sorb aboard the *Ebisu* by now,' says Tiberico.

'Have you forgotten how difficult it was to round up the bodies for the last expedition? The Tarrohar have made it impossible. It's illegal to put an Aurora Saurin in harm's way, and they'll know the journey is dangerous if the others haven't come back.'

'Regardless, we must try. We'll work with the Tarrohar to get a second contract drafted and ask for willing volunteers.'

'No one will sign up,' Azaire says.

'Kranik's heroics may help us there,' Tiberico continues. 'Let's not forget that Kranik saved a man's life using our Restoration equipment. There will be footage of Merrick's father being helped into the *Rhema Bolajio*. The man was moments from death; the Restoration was a complete success. He's healthier than ever; people will see that when they meet him on the street. Merrocha isn't so big, and good news carries no burden of telling.'

Azaire doesn't look convinced.

'We could build a campaign around that one incident. We could use Kranik's bravery to encourage people to sign up. We don't need many for the journey, just enough to appeal to Helacth. Let's help people see Kranik as a hero. We can gather people's trust, which will also help Kranik during his encirclement.' Tiberico leans in a little, all his attention on Azaire. 'We can't do this without you, Azaire. We need your creativity and influence.'

Azaire sits back, pleased by the compliment. 'Well, the footage would be easy enough to pull. If we splice it right and add a compelling narrative, we could package it that way.'

Tiberico looks satisfied, and for the first time since my arrest, I consider what I'll do once I'm released. I imagine myself running, the dirt road blurring beneath my feet. I'll find Kyjta. I'll tell her I'm going after Calipsie. If she stops seeing me as a monster, perhaps I can do it too.

Then the door to the holding room swings open, and I know everything's about to change. Rhytheus, captain of the *Rhema Bolajio*, has Lakhan in one hand and a boy in the other. Rhytheus is being ferried by a middle-aged man with ebony skin, silver hair, and an overbite, made more compelling by the captain's brutal expression. My friend, Lakhan, is still being ferried by the Aurora Saurin they call Herjit Aldemin, but the boy in the captain's other hand is not someone I've ever seen before and is too young to be ferrying a Rheman.

'Found these two trying to access the Sorb Room. The young one confessed. They were planning to break out your Rheman here.' The captain glares at me. He must think I put them up to it.

'The boy's the brother of the girl that got lifted away. They had plans to skip the encirclement and go after her,' Rhytheus says.

Tiberico looks grave. There's little hope of him talking Lakhan out of this if the captain caught him. I hadn't realised how thoroughly Tiberico's proposal had drawn me in until all the hope is leached away.

Rhytheus shakes the boy by the shoulder.

'Tell the room how old you are.'

'Sixteen alignments,' mumbles the boy.

The captain shoves the boy forward, causing him to stumble. The kid just manages to stop himself from colliding with the table.

'You sold me this alliance.' Rhytheus points at Tiberico. 'You told me it would guarantee a healthy supply of bodies for the crew. I won't have to worry about supply if every infringement gets another of my Rhemans confined to their Sorbs. Keep your Rhemans out of trouble, or we'll go back to the old way of doing things.'

My borrowed body tenses in its seat. We can't go back. It was carnage before; it'll be a hundred times worse if we revert. The Aurora Saurins will retaliate. On Aurora Saura, a wrong must never go unpunished. There will be slaughter in the streets.

Rhytheus exits the room, slamming the door behind him. We're left to consider his ultimatum. If the captain is upset about Rhemans being confined to their Sorbs, he's probably furious that I'm facing public encirclement. Azaire won't help me now. He won't associate himself with a lost cause.

There's a moment's quiet after the captain's departure. Azaire, probably offended at losing the room's focus, slams a fist on the table, eyes blazing in Lakhan's direction.

'What in the name of the stars aligned were you thinking?'

Lakhan knows better than to answer.

'Sixteen alignments!' Standing, Azaire bears down on Lakhan. 'Have you gone mad? This is exactly the type of juvenile behaviour that got us into this mess. I can't work like this.' Turning to me, Azaire continues. 'I can't campaign for a Rheman who has no regard for children's lives. Do you have any idea how this makes me look?' Azaire points at me. 'You continue to put our existence here at risk. You have no idea what you've done. No sense of the impact of your actions. Inciting a riot, attacking the Zhu's son, and now this. You can't be trusted to look out for Rheman interests.'

Azaire is right. I'd do the same again.

'Maybe you'll finally learn how to abide by the rules when the Aurora Saurins get to dream up your punishment,' Azaire says. 'I'm done protecting you.'

14

KYJTA

On the day of my father's encirclement, I rise at dawn. My father is awake, having napped briefly in his chair. I know this because I spent most of the night feigning sleep. My father is secretive about his more illicit concoctions, even with me. I couldn't risk asking him for the recipe and being turned down. He would want to know why I was interested, and I can't tell him. So I monitored through slanted eyes, keeping careful track of the ingredients, memorising the ordering and guessing the measurements. I can't be sure I saw everything, his back was to me, but I think I saw enough. I can re-create the smokers with ingredients from the farm. I still have the ghoragall, there's enough feather dust left for my needs. I only wish he hadn't waited until the night before his encirclement to reveal the recipe to me. I'd hoped to create another batch to use during Kranik's defence. Now I'll be forced to split these between the two of them.

After my father made the smokers and put them on parchment to set, he approached the shelves at the back wall, where the more malignant brews are kept. I watched as he dislodged one of the shelves, revealing a slim recess in the wall. He extracted a small black pouch and helped himself to the contents, swigging back a pill with a deep draught of water. Then he settled himself in the shack's only chair, bereft of most of its stuffing, and closed his eyes. I slept then, but my dreams were exhausting; I feel like I've been shaken awake from a terrible nightmare that still has its hooks in me. My eyes are stinging, and I yawn.

'You didn't sleep well,' my father says, examining each smoker before holstering them inside my porter pockets.

'Did you?' I ask.

'You know me.' He buttons the porter pockets and hands them to me.

He's not wrong. I do know him, and I know he's happiest when he's scheming. My father enjoys cooking up a plot even more than one of his potions. I've seen the satisfaction on his face when he gets the better of an adversary, and I can tell he's looking forward to the encirclement. The anticipation of victory is as plain on him as black nectar etched into skin.

The Tarrohar in Halli's tub called him unremorseful, and said my father deceived me. Seeing him like this, preening for a win, stirs up that anxiety. I shouldn't think about it; I'll make myself crazy. But I need to know the truth. The Tarrohar could have been lying, but for what purpose? It's not as though they need the nuptial tax. They might have gotten things confused. It can't be very exact, reading someone's mind like that, especially given Halli dosed herself with nebuga azermi. Still, it's troubling. Even more so now that I know my father was in a relationship with Halli. They've always been secretive, and I've often walked in on private conversations that quickly dry up the moment they see me.

'You ready?' my father asks, making me jump. 'Are you sure you want to do this? You don't seem yourself.'

'Yes. I'm ready.' I take a deep breath. I wish I still had the fire stick, but the ghoragall took it along with Sion Cromenk.

After we feed and water the elvakans, we throw their saddles onto their backs and strap on the porter pockets. It's another hot day, and we're both uncomfortably sweaty by the time we stable our elvakans behind Purple Dew Dawn. We've arrived early; the encirclement isn't until late afternoon. My father insisted we make some house calls while we're here. I soon figure out why. My father, Hok Poltiqe, the potion master, is nothing if not charming. The Charmores treat him like long-lost kin, welcoming him into their lovely homes and lavishing him with berook smokes, lotils cake, and spirits of cane, shrew, and gnarly. The potion master hands each of the women a small pouch. One for a malodorous foot, another for cramps. A love potion for Torie, surprisingly, since she's the oldest of the Charmores. She birthed five children before abandoning her husband to take up life as a serf to the Tarrohar, choosing to spend her days as a mount for one of the beasts, or entertaining the Vigilance Men for secrets and favours.

Later, at a dark table at the back of Purple Dew Dawn, I discover my father can brew a concoction capable of turning out the light of an unborn child. He hands the little pouch of ruination over in a surreptitious switch, but when the conversation gives away the potion's utility, I excuse myself to step outside and breathe the sea air.

The fifth house is Halli's. When she opens the door, it's almost a surprise to see her alive and healthy. The image of her being pulled into the tub, red gown streaming behind her, stayed with me, and though she looks more tired than when I last saw her, I'm pleased to find she's still breathing.

'Hok Poltiqe and his lovely daughter, come to see me. What a treat,' says Halli, ushering us into the living room. She wears a long black dress that trails to the floor, leaving her back bare. Her bruises are lighter, but they might have been dusted with amber sand to make them less conspicuous. I can see the tub through the double-sided fireplace. The sound of sand sifting onto the floor accompanies the crackling of the fire.

'You have something for me?' she asks, opening her hand to my father.

My father lifts a pouch from his pocket and hands it to her.

'I could offer you a brew, but I expect you had your fill on your way over here,' says Halli.

'Thank you. We're fine. I wanted to stop by and ensure we had your support. Once the farmlands are restored, production will increase. I will be more regular with my deliveries.'

Halli agrees. 'I speak for all the Charmores when I say we want you back in your rightful place. We've been open with the Tarrohar about our needs. In fact, my mistress wants to speak with you before the encirclement.'

My father straightens in his chair. It's the first time I've seen him look uncomfortable. I feel a tremor of dread at the idea of watching Halli submit to the Tarrohar again.

'Let's make it quick. It's a hard walk to the House of Judgement when you're strapped.' Halli stands, her black dress sliding neatly down her perfectly sculpted behind as she leads us to the washroom. She opens the door, and I see the tub brimming with sand. One of the tentacles has already slipped over the lip and is patting the side, searching for something, probably Halli's hand.

My mind is racing, seeking a clever way to ask the Tarrohar about its accusation without drawing too much attention. Then Halli closes the door in my face. My breath catches; I didn't expect to be excluded. There's probably no reason I should be part of the discussion, but it still stings. We have a long history, and she should know better than to shut me out of this. I lean forward, trying to hear what's being said, but I only catch a few words, with the crackle of the fireplace beside me. While I'm bent against the door, looking across the bedroom, I spot Halli's fire stick on her dresser. I leave my position to collect it and slip it into my pocket. That's one job taken care of. After Halli discovers it's missing, she'll think twice before leaving me alone in her room.

Soon the door opens, and my father steps out, looking deathly pale. His hands tremble; he struggles to stay on his feet.

'What's the matter?' I ask, coming to his side.

He looks at me as though I've startled him, his eyes wide and unseeing.

'What did she say?'

I worry that he won't tell me or that he's lost the ability to speak. Halli walks out behind him, her expression stoic. Her eyes have the glazed look they always get after she has a taste of the nebuga azermi.

'What happened to him?' I demand.

'He's in shock,' she says. 'They're going to encircle him for past crimes. They say he's a spy for the Old Soro.'

'A spy?' I shake my father, trying to bring him out of his stupor. 'What past crimes?'

I have the sickening sense that I'm to blame. That somehow my prior visit triggered this turn of the Hands. What did the beast discover about my father when it rifled through Halli's memories? Or did my own recollections give something away? I only went before the beast because I was desperate to ensure my father's encirclement backed onto Kranik's.

'Father,' I say, 'what past crimes?'

'Leave him, child,' says Halli, shoving me back. 'Can't you see how upset he is?'

Later that day, two Charmores lead my father to the centre of the Eye, a circular stage in the windowless atrium of the House of Judgement. The women wear long, blood-red dresses that scoop at the rear to expose a pair of flawlessly toned backs. The clefts of their buttocks are visible above the curve of the cowls at the backs of their dresses. When they reach the centre, they raise the potion master's hands in the air, beaming like they're introducing an act. My heart clenches painfully. My father is a proud man, and the ordeal has him hunched over; the stress must be crippling.

It's an intimidating venue. Five podiums ring the stage, each towering over the disk at an unnervingly extreme angle. A long maroon staircase leads to the pinnacle of each platform, and atop these sit five Tarrohar in judgement. Their unctuous limbs glimmer in the lamplight, suckering to the backs of the glamorously dressed Charmores perched on the elevated seats. I shudder, spotting Halli's slim form sitting stiffly beneath one of the coiling, shadowy masses. The Tarrohar has her inertly erect, looking like a wooden doll. I can't pull my eyes away. What is it like to be strapped? Is it like being quelled? A leap of faith followed by a hole in time and a desperate sense of loss? Or is it worse?

A gong sounds as a ceremonial crossbow shoots a sandbag-tipped arrow at the zionate disk suspended high above us. My father stands alone at the centre of the Eye. The proceedings haven't started yet, and he already looks defeated. The stage is ringed by elevated stands, and each successive row of seating tightens like a stranglehold. One of the serfs turns a lever, and the disk rotates. When the serf turns another lever, the seats tilt forward. The crowd gasps and cheers. Entertainment is rare in Merrocha since the ghoragalls. The curfews put an end to theatre, night markets, and street dancing. Apparently, music attracts the beasts.

The crowd seems particularly nasty. A volley of slimy sea crawlers strike my father's chest, then skid down his front, leaving glistening trails down his black robes. I'd hoped to save some of the smokers for Kranik's encirclement, but I can't risk it. If my father had brewed this batch earlier, I would have had time to make my own, but I've only five in my porter pockets, and my father will need them all.

I angle myself against a podium to prevent being seen, then surreptitiously remove one of the smokers and light it with Halli's fire stick. Once it's lit, I pretend to drop a zionate talisman. Leaning to pick it up again, I secrete the smoker in a wooden rapzette cage near my feet. The owner is probably headed to the market after the judgement and will find nothing but a small pile of black silt where it stood. Smoker emissions are opaque and have no scent. They'll be undetectable in the busy House of Judgement, but I can't get caught. The Tarrohar don't forgive disruptions to their justice system.

With four more smokers to place, I jostle my way through the crowd. When I reach the next podium, I pull a small woven bag from one of my porter pockets. I stuffed a sunset-orange scarf into it earlier and now nestle a smoker in the folds and place it beside the stairs. It'll look like someone grew tired of carrying their belongings and set them down. Once satisfied, I quickly move on to the next. It's only when I make it to the last podium that I finally hit trouble.

I'm stowing one of the smokers in the open pocket of a woman's backpack when I get the feeling I'm being watched. I look up and spot a boy with messily styled hair and a fierce scattering of freckles across his nose. The instant our eyes meet, he breaks into a run. He's young and gangly, and I hope that means he can't run very fast because I have to catch him. I can't let him report what he's seen. The Vigilance Men will hunt me down, find the smokers, and have me encircled for crimes against the Tarrohar. If my father's chances were poor before, they'll be far worse once our contrivance is exposed.

I race through the House of Judgement, knocking into someone as I detour around a tight group of men taking bets. I call out to apologise, but the hooded figure scuttles away so quickly that I've lost sight of them before the words are out. With no time to waste, I exit the House of Judgement in pursuit of the boy, taking the steps two or three at a time. The throng thins out as I cross the sandstone, weaving between the meandering lunch crowd. I snatch brief glimpses of the kid. He's wearing a brilliant green waistcoat that makes him easy to spot; until I lose him. Spinning in place, I'm cursing the Hands for my fate when he peeks out from behind the decorative shrubbery that hems in the House of Judgement from one side. The hedge has been carefully raised to prevent wandering Aurora Saurins from falling off the cliff, and the young boy is on the wrong side.

'Hey, come away from there. I'm not going to hurt you. I only want to talk.' It's my sweetest voice, but he's a smart kid and doesn't go for it.

There's a flash of colour. He's on the move again, leaping the shrubbery and racing for the live-ins. I charge after him and catch hold of his collar when we're just shy of the public latrines. I consider locking him inside one of them, but I'd have to let him out after the encirclement. The story he'd tell would be worse. So I pull him close, with my face right up against his. I bare my teeth and am doing my meanest impression of a Justice Man, hoping to terrify the kid into silence when someone calls a name, and the boy looks up.

'There you are. I thought I'd lost you.' It's the woman from the last podium. I'd stowed my last smoker in the open pocket of her backpack. She's as wide as she is tall, wearing a disarray of colours that flow from her like water from a fountain.

I release the boy and stand quickly, putting my hands behind my back. The kid streaks across the sandstone, collides with his mother's thighs, and hides among the plumage of material.

I'm attempting to explain the situation when the kid shouts, 'She stole from you, Mama. I saw her take something from your bag.'

'Your boy's confused. I didn't—'

The woman assesses me, her eyes narrowing. 'Well, let's see here,' she says, taking her backpack off her shoulder and sorting through it. I hold my breath, waiting for her to discover the smoker in the bag's outside pocket. 'Nothing's missing, Motjie,' the woman admonishes her son.

I let out a breath.

'Hold on,' she says, pulling her hand free of the bag. 'What's this?'

She lets a small black pouch dangle from her fingers in front of the boy's face. Imprinted on one side is a silver feather: my father's potion mark.

'Aren't you Sion Poltiqe's daughter?' asks the woman.

'Hok Poltiqe,' I correct her—my father lost his title when he lost his land. I have no idea what's going on, but there's no harm in playing along.

'You see, Motjie, she wasn't trying to steal anything. She was making a delivery for her father. Mommy's special medicine. Off you go now, and don't get yourself into any more trouble. I must pay the potion master's daughter.'

The boy runs off without looking back. I stare at the woman, trying to guess why she'd help me. She closes the distance between us, walking confidently and without menace. When only a few paces separate us, she introduces herself. 'My name is Tiberico, and if I'm not wrong, you must be Kyjta. Kranik asked me to find you.'

'You're a friend of Kranik's?' I respond, bewildered to find I'm talking to a Rheman.

'I'm the crew master of the *Rhema Bolajio*. Kranik asked to see you before his encirclement, and I told him I'd see what I could do.'

The Rheman's eyes are gentle, and the patient expression almost has me trusting her, but I can't let down my guard. A Rheman is still a Rheman, regardless of how polite they are. Besides, my father's defence may depend on me sticking around. The encirclement is about to start. The Tarrohar will state their charges, and my father will refute them. I need to be there to gauge the crowd's reaction and redistribute the smokers more effectively if required. I couldn't go with Tiberico, even if I wanted to; even if I had something worth communicating to Kranik. Which I don't. If only there had been time to make my own batch of smokers and use them during his encirclement. As things stand, I can't see how he'll get off.

'I can't—' I start, my voice cracking.

Tiberico doesn't flinch or try to persuade me otherwise. Instead, she waits patiently for me to finish my thought. I'm struck suddenly by how ridiculous she looks with the sturdy straps of her backpack offsetting the chaos of material that constitutes her dress.

The backpack! I almost forgot that one of my smokers is nestled inside it. If I turn her down and she walks away, I'll lose it.

I clear my throat and take a breath.

'I'll come,' I tell her, 'but I must first check on my father.'

Tiberico agrees, and as we walk, I slip my hand into the side pocket of her backpack to retrieve the smoker. When we get close enough to the Eye, I surreptitiously slip the smoker into the crevasse between some steps and an elderly man's mobile seat.

Tiberico positions herself beside me in the gathering crowd, a colourful pillar of quiet stability beside my jittery, expectant form. My father stands centre circle with his eyes on the floor. The Charmores ring him, spinning and swaying to the carnal beat. The dancers are impossibly supple, their bodies melding together like paste. Sliding like slippery tentacles, they grasp one another, first curling, then unfurling, in a seductive rhythm that mesmerises the crowd. At least their presence has distracted the spectators from throwing sea crawlers. Still, there are enough of the slimy sea creatures covering the floor at my father's feet to see that he's endured a proper pelting in my absence.

I've missed the introduction chasing after the boy, and my father looks ashen. His shoulders are slumped forward, his expression dejected.

'Silence!' booms one of the Tarrohar. I think it's Halli's. From where I stand, I can just see her head over the top of the podium. One purplish tentacle waves above her skull, looking like a living headpiece. I glance around at the stands, breath held as I await the charges. The Charmores sit erect on their pedestals, their faces blank and staring. Their heads are stretched uncomfortably high by the tentacles suckered to the backs of their heads.

When the Tarrohar speak, their voices resound as one. The harsh echo rebounds within the domed atrium, and the muted sound swaddles me in suffocating panic.

'Hok Poltiqe, for the first charge, we say you committed smuggling of ghoragall dust—a banned substance—between the alignments four thousand thirty-six and four thousand forty-four. For the second charge, we say you are a spy for the banished Soro, selling your secrets and illegal concoctions to the Grulo. Now you say.'

The crowd roars, stamping their feet on the metal grilling below their seats. There's a fresh volley of sea crawlers. My father raises an arm to cover his face as they bounce off him to join the growing pile at his feet. My throat feels sticky, and I struggle to swallow. Four thousand forty-four was the alignment when everything changed. My father accidentally burned Sion Cromenk's house to the ground, killing his family, and my mother and I were awarded to Cromenk as compensation for the family he lost.

My father clears his throat. The disk is spinning, and he lifts his head to address the crowd. He must get them on his side. Without their support, he has no chance of avoiding punishment.

'Tarrohar,' he begins, 'people of Merrocha, I am a humble man. I live in a shack at the bottom of the Qetheral Mountains. I own no land, and I have no title. If I were a smuggler or a seller of secrets, wouldn't I live a more lavish life? I am your potion master. I live to serve the people of Merrocha. I have served many of you all your lives. All I ask is that I be allowed to continue.'

The trick with using the smokers isn't in what's said but in how it's said. My father's voice is soothing and calm. The smokers take effect once the listener is relaxed, and any words spoken in that same relaxing voice will resonate. The effects wear off over time. Some are more susceptible than others, but most people remain under their influence for days. Already, the crowd have stopped throwing sea crawlers.

My father points to a man in the stands. 'Sion Norfi, I helped your wife rid her lunqet patch of nolves last autumn, did I not?' He points to another spectator. 'Meriqe, it took three doses of that ghastly medley, but your back pain hasn't returned, has it?' The list of people he's helped continues until he's called at least seven names. I'm sure many more people here have benefitted from his talents. Slowly, violet petals start to fall. I look up. More and more are flitting to the floor. It's a good sign. The people are on his side. My chest must loosen because suddenly the air feels lighter and my breathing gets easier.

'Saito and his Grulo spend most of their days harvesting zionate. Any smuggler servicing the desires of the Old Soro would want for nothing. Yet I want for much. Until earlier today, I wasn't aware I'd need to defend myself at this encirclement. I came here to apply for the return of my farmland.'

The petals are tumbling from the stands now. The flurry is so thick that I can barely see my father.

'Silence!' boom the Tarrohar. 'We have heard enough. Open your minds. The mining begins now.'

It's no use resisting. If you try, the Tarrohar will only make it hurt. I close my eyes and try to picture my father toiling away on our family farm. The Tarrohar will be looking for my verdict, and I can't afford for them to stumble across our deceit. I have the image of my father, as a free man, firmly affixed in my mind by the time the rustling sensation hits. It's not uncomfortable, more like wind and leaves swirling through your head. It's over quickly, and the crowd soon goes back to mumbling.

'Silence.' The Tarrohar lifts Halli's arm and slams it down hard onto the podium, quieting the room. 'A decision has been made; a verdict taken. We find Hok Poltiqe guilty of smuggling and espionage.'

I stagger where I stand, certain I've misheard them. The crowd is outraged, shouting their disapproval. Everything swims in and out of focus, and I think I might topple. Tiberico clasps my arm, holding me steady.

'The sentencing will be read after the show. Entertainment will be provided while we deliberate,' boom the Tarrohar over the uproar.

Oblivious to the sentiment of the crowd, or despite it, several Charmores sashay into the circle and start to twirl.

———

Tiberico leads me up a sweeping staircase in a part of the House of Judgement that's strictly forbidden to the public. The banisters are intricately carved, with newel posts shaped into gilded mythical beasts. The carpets are thick, and softer than my bed back home, under the eaves. Even the walls are patterned in gold. It's precisely how I imagined my mother living all those alignments ago, back when I thought she'd left us for a life of decadence.

Before I knew the truth.

My hands shake. It's hard enough knowing that my father will soon be sentenced for spying against the Tarrohar without my mother's ghost permeating everything. If my father really was a spy, then the accusation by the Tarrohar in Halli's tub finally makes sense. My father truly did deceive me. I didn't suspect a thing. I believed him to be as accepting of the injustice as everyone else. If I misjudged my own father, who else have I underestimated? Could others be willing to make a stand?

As I climb the grand stairway toward the unknown, I hold on to the idea. Its presence is faintly warming, like a spark trapped in ice. There may have been a time not so long ago when my father was willing to fight. The idea should terrify me, given what he's facing, but I can't help feeling a little emboldened by it.

When we reach the landing, Tiberico ushers me into a room further down the hall. Soft as the carpets are, every step jars my teeth. My jaw is tight, my face a grimace. I can't think what I'll say to Kranik. I try to regain my composure, focusing on the chaos of Tiberico's dress, but with all the tussling blues and greens, it only reminds me of the sea. The sea where we lost Calipsie.

I couldn't save her, and I can't save Kranik.

The room feels cold despite the auburn furnishings and sunlight dappling the ivory rugs scattered about the floor. There's a polygonal meeting table polished to a high sheen and surrounded by high-backed darkwood chairs, but besides Tiberico and me, there's no one else in the room.

No one corporeal, anyway.

A Sorb sits on a white dais at the centre of a tabletop. My feet stick in the rug's plush material, and I almost stumble. The Sorb is translucent. Inside it, streaming, flickering strands of light dance playfully while mist rises and clears.

I'm struck by a sensation of awkwardness, like I've walked in on someone who's only halfway through dressing. It's silly because I've seen Sorbs before. I've touched one. But this is different.

'Is it Kranik?' I ask.

'Forgive me. I'd expected him to be ready. Give me a moment.'

Tiberico exits the room. There's a cool gust of air as the door closes, and I'm suddenly on my own. The room is quiet, but my blood is rushing so fast it's humming in my ears.

Does Kranik know I'm here?

I take a step closer. The streaming light grows more intense, climbing the inner walls of the sphere. Leaning in, I hover my hand above the Sorb. The spears of light grow increasingly agitated, reaching up to touch the very top of the sphere.

If I touched his Sorb, would he transfer across to me? We could leave together. Be free of this place. If I could only talk to him.

Then the door opens. I take a step back, noting Tiberico's companion with a stab of apprehension.

'What are you doing here?' It's Merrick. He's just as surprised as I am.

I stare at him, unable to form a response. I don't think I could answer his question if pressed, not even to myself.

'Are you . . .' He points at me, and I give the finger a rueful stare. His presence puts me on edge. Thinking better of addressing me directly, Merrick turns back to Tiberico. 'Is she here to ferry the Rheman, or am I?'

'You're here to ferry Kranik for the encirclement. Kyjta is here at Kranik's request,' Tiberico says.

Merrick looks as though he's heard it all.

'You two know each other?' asks Tiberico, clearly confused.

Merrick ignores the question, preferring to glare at me.

'So, you're working with them now?' He tilts his head at Tiberico. 'Figures, given your skill set and lack of empathy.'

'Me?' I say sharply. 'You're the one taking their coin.'

Merrick turns to Tiberico. 'You lot using her to brew up her father's recipes? I'll tell you, she's real smooth at the delivery.'

I'm primed to argue with him, but my words catch in my throat. He's only reacting to events as he understands them, and he doesn't have a believable alternative to the narrative in his head.

'Can we get this over with?' says Merrick, stepping toward the Sorb.

I'm amazed at how casually he raises his hand and presses it down on the Sorb. By the time he turns to face me, all the venom has left his face.

15

KRANIK

Kyjta is the first thing I see. Her face hovers not far from mine. Her lips are parted, and her eyes glow like twin suns beneath that familiar scowl. She looks about to say something, but then her fierce expression shifts, becoming pensive and a little sad.

We're in one of the ostentatious gathering rooms, and the sheen off the furniture is almost blinding. I'm so relieved to see Kyjta, that I'm oblivious to Tiberico standing beside a monstrous marbled vase, until she speaks.

'You'll need to be quick with whatever needs saying; Kyjta must return before her father's sentencing.' Tiberico disappears out the door with a small 'hurry' gesture.

Kyjta and I are alone. Seeing her like this, just the two of us, is like standing on a stage in front of the whole world. I've lost my words, but there are things I need to say.

She's first to break the silence, tipping her head toward the Sorb.

'What's it like in there?' she asks.

Her question focuses my thoughts.

'It's nothing like it used to be,' I tell her.

'Nothing ever is,' she agrees.

She walks to the window and stares out, scanning the courtyard.

'Big crowd here today. It's a while since a Rheman was encircled.'

I join her at the window. She's right; hundreds of people are gathered on the broad sandstone steps, all dressed in their finest clothes.

'I should have gone after Calipsie when you offered,' she says to my reflection.

'Should haves are yesterday's burden,' I respond, as we turn to face each other. 'What happens now?'

'Calipsie is my half-sister. I didn't know it until after she was taken.' Kyjta lowers her head. 'It shouldn't make a difference. I know that.' I watch her struggle for her next words. 'It does though. I didn't know Calipsie long, but blood binds us. I have a responsibility to protect her.'

'What are you going to do?' I ask, suddenly fearful that she'll get herself killed.

'I don't know. Things are harder now. My father's been encircled. He's facing a serious charge. They say he smuggled ghoragall dust for the Old Soro, but I know him. He's not a fighter.'

'How did his rebuttal go?' I ask.

'Not very well. They found him guilty. The sentencing is after the show.'

I asked Tiberico to bring her here because I wanted to tell her how much I regret losing Calipsie. To tell her that I aim to go after her, just as soon as I get free of this place. I may have the makings of a monster, but it's my choice whether to behave like one or not. I prefer not.

'You should know that the Tarrohar passed judgement without considering the will of the spectators. They mine the crowd's imagination for cruel punishments, but they choose whatever outcome benefits them most. You might have a chance if you can figure out what they want.'

If I can escape encirclement, I'll be free to go after Calipsie. That's the only chance I need. I search my memory, rifling through snatches of overheard conversations. What is it that the Tarrohar truly want? My thoughts go to Azaire on the day of my arrest, and I hear the echo of his words as the wind whisked sand in my face outside the *Rhema Bolajio*.

'Is it Helacth's approach you prefer?'

I would not prefer Helacth's approach, and I doubt the Tarrohar would either. If the population was decimated, their tax revenues would be impacted. They'd lose their most lucrative stream of income.

'They want our taxes, but they also want control,' I say, musing aloud.

'They're threatened by you,' Kyjta says. 'They can't control you because you don't feel anything. They can't use the Mind Pain on you.'

Before my thoughts can coalesce into a plan, the door swings open and Tiberico strides in. He's changed, ferried by a silver-haired man in a grey jumper and charcoal trousers. It's the spirited eyes that give away his identity.

'Quickly,' he says, beckoning to Kyjta, 'the sentencing is about to start.'

16

KYJTA

'Death by giant satermijte,' boom the Tarrohar as Tiberico and I weave through the crowd, working our way toward the Eye.

I stumble, but momentum keeps me moving. Momentum and disbelief. That can't be my father's judgement. I must have misheard. Tiberico looks back at me, and his expression convinces me otherwise. Heart hammering, ears ringing, I shuffle on, shoving onlookers out of my way. My father made the journey here today to request the return of his farmland, and now he's going to be torn apart by monstrous insects. I can't make sense of it.

The crowd are shouting their disapproval. I wish they'd stop. Their fervour only makes it more difficult for us to reach the Eye. When I finally spot my father, I drink him in. Alive and standing tall, with his face upturned and scowling at the Tarrohar, he looks heroic. In this moment, it's impossible to imagine him any other way. But then the Charmores arrive at his side and lead him off the stage. It finally hits me that this is goodbye. I scramble, pushing and shouting at people in my path, but it's too late. He disappears behind a thick wooden door.

I stand, just breathing, like it's the only thing I know how to do. The Tarrohar are going to take him away from me again, and this time it will be forever. I can't endure it. Once was all I could handle. All I would ever handle.

Hands clenched claw-like at my sides, I mount the stairs leading to the closest podium. I won't be satisfied until I've mauled the creature squatting at the top to death. Let the Mind Pain take me. Skewer me on the end of an illing sword. It makes little difference. Inside, I'm already dead.

I'm scaling the stairs on all fours, like an animal stalking prey, when a hand closes around my arm. I turn back, expecting to be arrested by a Vigilance Man, but it's so much worse.

'Your family won't thank you for getting yourself killed,' says the man. I recognise him at once as Calipsie's adoptive father.

He offers me his other hand. The compassionate act takes all the fight from me. I step down, certain my legs will buckle. When I'm confident on my feet, I wipe my eyes with the heel of one hand.

'You're . . . You're here for the Rheman trial,' I manage.

'I'm here to appeal to the Tarrohar to get my daughter back,' says the man, squeezing my hand.

I can't bring myself to tell him how sorry I am. I'll only come apart. I want to flee, but he has my hand. Seeing my panicked expression, he squeezes.

'None of this is your fault,' he says, his gaze shimmering.

He's wrong. It is my fault. Calipsie. My father. Kranik. All of it.

I tug my hand free, spin around, and disappear into the crowd.

As I run, I search for sanctuary. A small space that I can squeeze myself into and get free of the masses. I find a dark alcove under the stands and slide into it, panting hard.

Death by giant satermijte.

My stomach churns, imagining my father torn to pieces by the glossy mandibles of these monstrous insects. We could surely appeal; my mother would have known what to do. I'll go to Halli. She must understand the process, and she'd have a vested interest in keeping my father alive.

There's a deafening roar of aggression from the crowd, and I know my time is up. Kranik has taken the stage; I hadn't expected it to be so quick. I get to my feet and shove my way back through the growing horde, ignoring the annoyed squalling as I trample their feet. Kranik is facing away from me when I reach the stage, but the disk is turning. Pretty soon, he's all the way around, and our eyes connect. I'm looking for some sign that he has a plan, but his face is unreadable.

The Tarrohar pound their Charmores' arms against the podiums to quiet the crowd.

'Rheman Kranik, for the first charge, we say you are responsible for multiple violations of the covenant of the Body Trust. For the second charge, we say you are culpable of rousing a riot and disturbing the tranquillity of Merrocha. Now you say.'

Kranik is facing away by the time he starts to speak. I can hardly hear him with the crowd stomping the metal grills at their feet. Someone must be selling fresh sea crawlers because the audience is showering Kranik with them. Merrick had better have negotiated a decent wage to have his body subjected to this. It's good he won't recall it.

'For the first charge, I confess I am guilty,' responds Kranik.

The crowd didn't expect this. There's a hush, followed by agitated rumblings. The people are angry but can't believe a Rheman would be daring enough to take responsibility for flouting the Body Trust. The Tarrohar will have him exterminated for this. If they want to control Aurora Saura without interference from the Rhemans, Kranik is giving them an easy way to reduce their numbers by at least one.

'For the second charge, I confess I am guilty.'

This time the crowd is stunned. I want to roar into the silence. Is Kranik so blind he can't see he's courting death? Does he want to be handed the same punishment as my father?

I take a step toward the circle. Kranik's not guilty. I'll have to say something in his defence. He's not thinking clearly.

'Aren't you tired of living in the shadow of the ghoragalls?' he asks the crowd, lifting his arms as he spins below them. 'Haven't you had your fill of the quellings?' His voice has gravitas. I hadn't noticed it before. Although people are still throwing sea crawlers, the quantity and velocity are diminishing.

'We Rhemans ask to borrow your bodies. In exchange, we mend your sick and wounded; but is that enough when you spend your lives cowering in basements and whispering in the dark? If a wrong must be set to right—if that truly is the Aurora Saurin way—then that is what you should demand of me. That is what you should require of all of us. There are twenty Rhemans in the Sorb Room, each of them consigned indefinitely. They are as guilty as I am. Inside their Sorbs, they are as useless to you as men awaiting execution.

'Put those able bodies and a Rheman's superior strength together, and you have a formidable battalion, capable of crossing the Parched Lands and the Ice Realm. A force strong enough to approach Helacth and negotiate an end to the ghoragalls.'

No one is throwing sea crawlers now. They're not throwing petals either, but that's probably because they didn't buy any for a Rheman encirclement.

Then the crowd mutters. It starts low but soon becomes a din, filling the atrium.

'I say you should be charged with bringing our people back!' yells someone from the stands.

'You'll only run off with the bodies!' shouts one of the women.

'You'll join Helacth!' a man hollers.

'Stop the ghoragall raids! Set this wrong to right,' wails an older woman from the sides.

Somewhere to the left of Kranik, Tiberico takes to the stage.

'These are valid concerns. Allow me to address them by reminding you of what we've already achieved.' Tiberico is used to speaking publicly, and it shows. A hush falls over the stadium. 'Of the six Rheman ships on Aurora Saura, three abide under the covenant of the Body Trust. Most towns surrounding the converted ships are no longer subjected to raids. Once we persuade Helacth to adopt the Body Trust, the abductions will stop here too.' He continues, and there's not a whisper from the stands. 'Send a Rheman convoy to the Ice Realm, and we will end the raids!'

I peer up at the Tarrohar. The Charmores lean heavily over their podiums so the Tarrohar can get a good view of the action below. As usual, I'm drawn to look at Halli. She appears stretched, like a heavy garment pegged up wet and pulled out of shape. Her hands dangle from her wrists like macabre ornaments.

Tiberico is about to go on when the Tarrohar demand silence.

'A decision has been made. A verdict taken. We find Rheman Kranik guilty on both charges.'

The crowd goes wild, shouting their agreement.

Tiberico joins me at the side of the circle as the Charmores take to the stage. They form a perfect ring around Kranik, each standing with one leg pointing inward as though gesturing toward him.

'Open your minds,' say the Tarrohar in unison. 'The mining begins now.'

I'm suspended somewhere between grief and relief, with no sense of how the sentencing will play out. If Kranik is consigned to his

Sorb, I'll never see him again. I'll be forced to go after Calipsie on my own. If he's successful, short of committing some awful crime and being served a death sentence myself, I'll have no way of joining the convoy. Joining them makes little sense, anyway. Their objective is to stop the raids, while mine is to rescue Calipsie.

Feeling the familiar rustling in my mind, I focus my thoughts, imagining Kranik setting out across the Parched Lands. Only he's not using Merrick's body—he's using my father's. If the Tarrohar have been taken in by Kranik's proposal, he's done more than save himself.

There's a brief interlude where the Charmores perform their dance, but the crowd seems to have lost interest, preferring to chatter. Even the finale, with their dresses whirling off the ground, exposing long sculpted legs, does little to distract them. There's an energy building, sparking off the spoken word, and people are rejoicing.

'Quiet!' demand the Tarrohar. 'A decision has been made.'

Silence falls like a thick curtain, snuffing out the conversation.

'As punishment for violations against the Body Trust, twenty-three Rhemans will cross the Parched Lands using the bodies of those sentenced to death. The Rheman leaders—Rhytheus, Azaire, and Tiberico—will join the Rheman convicts to oversee the mission,' boom the Tarrohar.

'Naturally,' Tiberico says with a wry smile.

The Tarrohar want rid of the Rhemans and Tiberico knows it, just as Kranik knew it. The encirclement is just a tool they're using to get what they want. A society free of Rheman leadership, where they will hold greater power.

'If the Rhemans return after delivering on their promise to free the people of Merrocha and end the raids, the criminals will be pardoned for their crimes. Should they fail, however, the Merrochans will face their original fates, and the Rhemans' Sorbs will be destroyed.'

17

KRANIK

I'm in the Sorb Room aboard the *Rhema Bolajio*. Tiberico is running through the list of Rhemans who've been confined to their Sorbs. Azaire and I are supposed to be helping, but Azaire's only contribution has been to pace the room, lamenting the Tarrohar's ruling and the part I played in getting him assigned to a mission that will almost certainly get us killed.

He has a point, but I didn't mean to involve them. I only wanted a chance to go after Calipsie, and though my plan worked, it has put many lives at risk.

Tiberico uses the ship's virtual interface to check which Rhemans have been encircled and for what crimes. I make my way through the aisles until I find my own Sorb. Like the others, it's nestled inside a claw of terrinium—the same metal I was forced to mine back on Rhema on the rare occasions I was assigned a body. The *Rhema Bolajio* is constructed almost entirely of its rare deposits.

I reach out and touch the smooth surface of my Sorb, not feeling it, but enjoying the sense of connection. Touching the sphere is like coming home. If we fail and the Tarrohar follow through with their punishment, our Sorbs will be destroyed, and we'll be drawn back to Ezerya. Our memories and personalities will be wiped clean, leaving only our energy.

Considering the number of days I've experienced outside my Sorb, it would be a short life by any standard. I would have liked more time here on Aurora Saura, with its clear skies and brilliant sun. I wish I'd explored more.

It's simple to tell which Sorbs house Rhemans. They're brighter, with strands of electric light pulsing through them. Empty Sorbs burn dimmer, and the strands simmer at the sphere's base.

'Wixnor,' Tiberico says, calling out the name of one of the Rhemans who fell afoul of the covenant.

'What were they encircled for?' I ask.

'It says here it was indecency. I remember the case. It was early on. A wardrobe mix-up. Borrowing an elderly man's body and wearing a dress.'

'A criminal mastermind,' I say.

'This is preposterous,' Azaire says, marching up and down, his blue coat-tails swishing behind him. 'If the last envoy didn't return, what makes the Tarrohar think we'll fare better? What good will it do the Aurora Saurins if the architects of the Body Trust are killed?'

I'm pretty sure Tiberico only invited Azaire down here so he could let off steam.

'Here we go. Loppard, a Restoration Technician. That will be useful,' Tiberico says.

'Crime?' I ask.

'Blasphemy. Playing ralish with a balloot,' Tiberico says.

'A what?' I ask.

'Let's see—' Tiberico scans the azure display. 'It's a sacred fruit.'

'You're not seriously considering this.' Azaire stands before

Tiberico, his ebony skull reflecting the purple and white light of the Sorbs like a decorative ornament.

'We may not have a choice,' Tiberico says. 'This may be just the push we need to make our stand.'

'The push? There's nothing but sand and snow on the path to Thormyth. We might freeze or be feasted on by giant satermijtes. If we're lucky and make it, Helacth will probably have us killed. None of what we've done is sanctioned.' Azaire puts a hand to his forehead, looking exasperated. 'We've been set an impossible task. They mean us to fail!'

'Nothing is impossible when death is the alternative,' Tiberico says.

'So, you think it's a good thing then, our Sorbs being threatened like this?' Azaire leans backwards as though he's taking a fresh perspective on Tiberico.

I walk back down the aisle to join them. I don't want to be part of the discussion, but my actions have led to this perilous situation, and I shouldn't expect Tiberico to defend me. Tiberico hasn't said as much, but I doubt the encirclement's outcome thrills him. There will be no defending Aurora Saurins from the quellings if we're dead.

'You did this,' Azaire says as soon as he spots me. 'You've ruined everything. Without me to oversee the Body Trust—me and Tiberico,' he recovers, 'the other ships will never adopt the framework. So much work destroyed. And for what? If we try to dictate terms to Helacth, he'll only retaliate and take more Aurora Saurins.'

'Then we'll have to stop him,' counters Tiberico. 'I don't want a return to the old times. I saw enough the first time around.'

'Stop Helacth? With twenty Rhemans?'

'Twenty-three,' corrects Tiberico. 'We won't have any chance at a decent life without the Body Trust.'

'So we're just going to kill ourselves?' asks Azaire, exasperated.

'Hopefully not.' Tiberico's face is up-lit by the azure display. He looks contemplative. 'The Tarrohar robbed us of our ability to take a stand against the raids by insisting no Aurora Saurin body be put in harm's way. Things will be different now. The rules will have to change.'

'That law is there to protect the Tarrohar as much as the Aurora Saurins. They'll never amend it.' Azaire continues to pace the room, his coat-tails trailing him like a sliver of sky.

'Yes. We're immune to Mind Pain, so they must control us by some other means.' Tiberico sighs. 'If the raids stop, the people will start to see us as heroes. Do you want me to try talking to your contacts in Thormyth? Perhaps I can—'

'No.' Azaire abruptly stops his pacing. 'No. That won't help. I told you I've lost contact with them. And what do we do then, as the people's heroes? Overthrow the Tarrohar? Have you lost your mind? They'll exterminate the Aurora Saurins. You've seen the effect of the Mind Pain.'

'I know what they're capable of,' Tiberico says, silencing Azaire with a stern look. 'But we have no choice. We must play this ruling to our advantage.'

Although Tiberico has a point, for once I agree with Azaire. The Tarrohar's talent for Mind Pain means no Aurora Saurin is safe, no matter how heroic we Rhemans appear.

Azaire turns away; he must not want Tiberico to see the look of disgust on his face.

'Fiderly,' Tiberico says, reading once more from the list. 'It says they're an authority on Rheman technical frameworks and interfaces. That's useful, isn't it?'

'They're letting us take the ship?' I ask hopefully.

'The *Rhema Bolajio* is the real prize. If we don't return, the

Tarrohar will pretend to accommodate our successors, just as they've pretended to accommodate us; the ship and its equipment are the real prize. It must remain here. We have the Sorbs of the other crew members to consider. The *Rhema Bolajio* is the only safe place to house them.'

'And the riot you started got the kinatoid destroyed.' Azaire glares at me.

'Well, as far as I know, the elvakan don't have a technical interface,' I say.

Tiberico reaches out a hand and runs it over the Sorb's transparent encasement. Streams of escalating pinks and purples traverse the housing and converge where his fingers rest. 'We're not the only ones with a ship.'

'Does this Fiderly's criminal résumé include hijacking?' I ask.

'Nothing so grand, I'm afraid. The charge is mountain climbing, cited as a dangerous activity in the covenant.'

'Is it too much to ask for a little sense?' rants Azaire, turning away in frustration.

I close the distance between myself and Tiberico, hoping to have a private word. 'I have a couple of things to do before we set off. Do you think I could—'

Looking like he knows what I'm going to say, Tiberico dismisses me before I get the words out.

'Go, but be back well before nightfall.'

I don't wait around; I can't risk Azaire raising an objection.

'Don't think I don't know where you're going,' Azaire says when I reach the door.

I ignore him and take the longer route through the Restoration Facility. There are only two occupied Restoration Plates and one Rheman in attendance. He hunches over a girl whose arm has been speared by tremble weed. I sidle past him, checking the contents of a tray that extends from the wall. Quickly I spot what I need and slip it into my pocket.

Hearing the subtle clink of metal behind him, the technician turns. 'Hey. What have you got there?' But I'm already on the move. 'Azaire will hear about this!' he yells after me.

'I doubt it could get me into any more trouble,' I shout over my shoulder, hurrying for the antechamber.

Merrick's elvakan is a lumbering beast, well past its prime and frustratingly slow. I could run faster, but I must conserve Merrick's strength, given what lies ahead. I have one stop to make before I head to Minuet Farm, where I hope to find Kyjta. I must convince her that, regardless of my party's objective, I will get Calipsie back. If she doesn't believe that, she'll do something reckless.

I find Sion Chaffrot on the porch, looking out over the farm. It's the middle of the day and the sun is toasting the decking where his broken feet rest, swaddled in bandages. Maisi must be out tending the farm because I don't hear the gentle clatter of pots and pans as I pass the kitchen window.

'Kranik,' he says, seeing me as I round the side of the farmhouse. 'I didn't expect to see you for some time. I heard about the judgement. When do you leave?'

'Sion,' I say as he sets his book on the three-legged table beside him. 'No date has been set. Tiberico and Azaire have a fair bit to work out with the Tarrohar before we can set off. Supplies, transport, that kind of thing.'

'I'm pleased you'll go after the girl,' he says. 'I shoulder the blame for her abduction. She'd still be here if I hadn't asked the two girls to help on the farm.'

'We had the zionate blanket; it should have been fine. If anyone is to blame, it's me. I was distracted. We shouldn't have ventured out of range. It was an unforgivable error.'

'No error is unforgivable. Unless you're about to tell me you Rhemans are predicting the future now.'

'Not that advanced,' I say.

'Then the Hands played you, as they play us all.'

'Speaking of advancements,' I say, pulling the Restoration Wand from my pocket. 'Since you refuse to come to the ship to have your feet mended, I brought some lightweight equipment to you.'

'This will make for an interesting story at the market.'

I get on my knees and unwrap his feet. I'm about to set to work when the swinging door squeaks open and a child pokes his head out. I look up, surprised because I've never seen this child before. Two pale arms slip around the child's middle and pull him inside. I hear someone making hushing sounds, and then the place goes quiet.

'We have some family visiting,' says Sion Chaffrot, not meeting my eyes. 'They'll be thrilled to see me on my feet again.'

'Is it the same family that visited last moon cycle? There was a young boy—'

'No,' he says cheerily. 'These are different relatives.'

I have a fairly good idea of what Sion Chaffrot does for his 'relatives,' but I'm not going to ask questions until he's ready to speak. There are places in Aurora Saura that are less frequented by the ghoragalls, and Sion Chaffrot has the means and motivation to assist the Stained with their passage if they've a mind to leave.

Judging by the number of mattresses stacked against the wall in the basement, I expect he's already helped quite a number.

I tap the book on the table beside his chair. 'You've started something new. Did the last book deliver? What was it called again?'

'*The Trail* of the *Old Soro*. Yes, it gave me much-needed direction,' he tells me.

'How long will you be gone?' he asks, changing the subject.

I shrug. 'Hard to say. It's a long journey by caravan, and convincing Helacth to adopt the Body Trust won't be easy.'

'Any idea why he's resistant?'

'I've never met him. It's hard to say what motivates him,' I answer truthfully.

'Well, that's all about to change. Whatever you do, make an impression.'

I settle my thumb over the pale oval initiator that's situated about halfway up the spine of the traveller's Restoration Equipment. The beam illuminates Sion Chaffrot's ankle and begins knitting the bones beneath. When the light quickly winks out, indicating the work is done, I move to the other ankle. Once both feet are mended, and I've watched the Sion crossing the decking with only a slight hobble as his muscles adjust, I bid him fair favour and am on my way.

By early afternoon, I crest the hill that leads into the slight dip sheltering Minuet Farm and its stables. The house looks deserted, with its doors and shutters closed as though a storm is coming. I tie Merrick's elvakan to the hitching post and climb down, glancing back the way I came to check the skies. The clouds are thickening in the south and rolling toward the farm.

I use the small horn dangling from a hook beside the front door to announce myself. All I know of Kyjta's family is what came out during the encirclement. At my insistence, Tiberico relayed everything back to me in detail. A missing mother, a condemned potion maker father, and a stepfather taken by a ghoragall. I wonder if there's anyone left and, if there is, how they'd feel about opening the door to a Rheman.

When my knock goes unanswered, I call her name.

Nothing.

I try not to panic, but I can't help worrying she's gone off alone. I can't face leaving for the Ice Realm until I'm sure she's safe. I must impress on her how foolish it would be to make the crossing herself. I try the handle, knowing Tiberico would discourage me from entering without an invitation. The door isn't locked, so I peer into the gloomy interior, with its shuttered windows, and call her name again. When I don't receive a response, I step inside and see a large fireplace of glazed sandstone. A family-size dining table crafted from chalky hore wood. A shelf of worn books with gilded spines lends the home an aura of prosperity. Everything is neatly in its place, except for the porter pockets slung over the back of one of the beige marook pelt couches.

I cross the stone floor until I'm standing in front of them—the pockets brim with an assortment of possessions, including clothing and a water pouch. The baggage might easily contain all the essentials for someone planning a long trip. But if the porter pockets are still here, Kyjta must be too.

I search the house. First the ground floor, then the cellar, which is barely big enough to stand in. There's a sketch on one of the shelves, an exquisite rendering of a woman shaded in charcoal. The face is that of a woman, older than Kyjta but just as beautiful. It must be her mother.

Finding no one, I climb the thin ladder to the loft, which leads to a bedroom with a single bed beneath the eaves and a chest. The bed is made but scattered with clothes, and the chest drawers are open. It shouldn't surprise me that Kyjta's been packing, given that her family farm is now the property of the Tarrohar. They'll probably evict her.

When I've searched the rest of the house, I head outside and try the stables. The elvakans have been fed and watered. A sturdy-looking brush, thick with main hair, is on a bench. Someone must have been here recently, tending to the animals. Next, I check the alzog pen, where the beasts are resting near the back. Sensing me, the larger one opens its eyes and lifts its head from its partner's hump. There's a loud grunt before they scramble to their feet and slosh toward me through the muck. It must be feeding time because the creatures stick their wriggling snouts through the fence and snuffle at my feet. A bucket sits nearby, brimming with bulbs. The alzogs lose interest in my feet and push against the wire fencing, trying to get to them. When I lift the bucket and throw the bulbs into their feeding tray, they jostle each other to get to their meal. Mud squelches through the fence, along with something else. As it nudges my foot, I lean in to lift it from the muck. It's long and slim. A bone, I realise, as I scrape away the mud. Strange. I apply gentle pressure and snap it in two. As the wind whistles through the enclosure, I have the awful sense that something has happened to Kyjta. Why else would this place feel so deserted? Her bags are here, but she isn't. My mind flashes to the scene at the beach, Calipsie's bare feet disappearing into a breast of dark plumage.

I drop the bone and break into a run, shouting, 'Kyjta!' I'm not sure where I'm running until I spot the barn. The ground outside the barn door is scuffed and full of grooves. There was a struggle here, and it looks like it happened recently. The barn door is a mess, with a sizable chunk of wood torn free from the frame and cracks in the doors as though a wild animal tried to hammer it down. I barge through the door, expecting to find the place empty, but it's not. A ghoragall is lying in the centre of the room, dead and plucked nearly naked of its feathers.

I stand frozen, bewildered by the sight of the sagging carcass. It's repugnant—its grey, creased flesh rutted where its feathers were plucked. Its long hind legs are doubled over and pulled against its body, sloping lazily to one side. A burlap bag covers its head, hiding the horror beneath.

Hearing movement beside me, I swing around to see a black-clad figure. I can't tell who it is as there's a cloth wound around their face.

'Kyjta?' I ask, noting the unmistakable shade of her eyes. They're the only discernible feature through the thick film of charcoal ghoragall dust.

'Kranik?' she asks, loosening the tie at the back of her head and exposing her face. Her long neck is dusted with midnight, and her blond curls cling to her skin in sweat-damp sickles.

I look from her to the ghoragall. 'Are you . . .' I struggle, unsure how to phrase my question, '. . . planning to cook this?'

Kyjta laughs. I smile but not very convincingly. Killing ghoragalls is a dangerous business, especially for the Stained. If there's an aggrieved mate on the loose, Kyjta will be an easy target.

She must note my expression because she stops laughing and stares at me, her eyes bright with contemplation. 'What are you doing here? Didn't they lock you up?'

'They wanted to,' I say. 'Tiberico can be very persuasive.'

'And you came to check up on me?'

She's speculative, but there's breezy confidence there too. She could see how panicked I was, thinking I'd lost her too. My feelings are plain.

'I came to tell you I *will* get Calipsie back. I needed to be sure—'

'That I wouldn't do anything stupid?' A stillness settles over her as she continues to stare at me.

'That you wouldn't worry.'

She shifts on her feet, dropping her eyes to the ghoragall. 'Help me with this, will you?' She walks over to the beast and grabs its spindly legs. 'I can't lift it on my own.'

I walk to the head. The skin is grey and putrid, but there's no point protesting; I can't refuse her. The hearth is deep and long, nearly half the width of the barn. We drag the ghoragall to a pyre she's built in its alcove. I wonder how regular a task this is for her. A stack of firewood has been neatly prepared, and we wrestle the creature onto it. Kyjta lights the fire with a fire stick she draws from her dress, and soon there's smoke billowing up the expansive chimney.

The distant rumble of thunder causes Kyjta to glance out the window. I follow her gaze. The cloud cover is writhing; the sky looks alive.

'It's going to rain,' she says.

It's impossible to think about the rain without recalling the gentle pressure of Kyjta's damp fingers slipping between mine. I study her expression, trying to figure out if she's making an intentional reference or simply commenting on the day.

'Where will you go?' I want to hear her say she won't go after Calipsie. I can't force her to stay put, but I must convince her it's the only way.

Looking at me, she bites her lower lip, wetting the ghoragall dust and causing the plump flesh to glisten darkly in the firelight. She's considering her response, trying to figure out how much she's willing to tell me.

'My father has a place in the mountains,' she finally says.

'Will I find you there when we return?'

'Why do you care where I'll be?'

I sigh. 'I want to know you'll be safe.'

'Safe,' she scoffs. 'I'll never be safe.'

'You might be safer if you stopped killing ghoragalls. It's a dangerous pastime.'

She laughs dismissively. 'You make it sound like a habit.'

'Isn't it?' I ask.

'One ghoragall is hardly a habit.'

'What about the bones in the alzog pen?'

She scowls at me. I've upset her; her eyes have a sudden wet sheen. 'What is it?'

'Those aren't ghoragall bones. They're my mother's,' she says, lowering her eyes.

'The bone I found was hollow,' I tell her. 'It couldn't belong to an Aurora Saurin.'

Her expression flickers. I don't know what she's feeling, but it's easy to see she's struggling with something. She passes me without another word. As soon as she exits the barn, she breaks into a run. I jog after her, confused and trying to figure out what I've said or done. Outside, the air is thick with moisture. Not a drop has spilt from the roiling clouds, but it's only a matter of time. Kyjta is almost at the alzog pen when the clouds open up. The rain is like a river falling from the sky; I can barely see her through the thick sheet that separates us. She hits the railing, and I think she's going to topple all the way over, but she comes up holding a bone in each hand. I watch her snap one bone and then the other. She throws them onto the ground and is back at the fence, doubled over it, looking for more. By the time I reach her, she's gathered three. She holds them by one end, wedges the other side against the wet earth, and then stomps on them until they give way beneath her boot.

I take her arm and turn her to face me, determined to understand what's made her so upset. The rain has collected on her lashes in heavy dust-filled spheres. Although it obscures her tears, she's clearly crying. The feather dust rolls down her cheeks, hiding her stain. She looks as though she's being washed away. Her sun-coloured dress is soaked, and I can feel the shape of her arm beneath my hand. Heat radiates from her, and I can feel that too. I've never used my hands to convey my feelings before, but I do now. I wipe at her face. I use my palm and fingers, pushing back her hair and sweeping the dark water out of her eyes and away from her cheeks. Kyjta doesn't pull back, letting me clear the dirty water from her face. Her skin is soft, but tiny granules of feather dust grate the pads of my fingertips. My movements grow gentler when I can see her Stain. Her expression changes; her focus shifts; she's looking at me like she's just realised I'm here. Her hair clings to her face, flowing down her neck in thick damp coils. I want to push my hands into the dripping mess and feel the wet strands coil around my fingers; the craving is torture. Then, without warning, Kyjta steps closer, and our eyes light a pathway that joins somewhere in the middle. I know where that pathway leads, and it's somewhere I can't follow. I place my hand—Merrick's hand—at the back of her head and pull her against my chest, where the pressure of her cheek burns like a gentle flame.

18

KYJTA

stand in the tall grass, watching Kranik go. When he reaches the ridge of the low valley that cups the farmstead, he turns back, looking like he doesn't want to leave. Probably worried for my sanity; I was weeping like a child, almost kissing him. I would have if he hadn't redirected me into an embrace.

Maybe wishes are like curses when they don't come true.

What was I thinking? Not just a different species but an enemy. *The* enemy. No matter how upset I was, I wouldn't kiss one of the Tarrohar. I didn't even consider Merrick, and it's his body, his lips, that I so badly wanted to feel the pressure from.

What would Merrick make of that? Flatly turning him down after 'spiking' his drink with an infatuation potion, but willing enough when he's ferrying a Rheman?

I know these thoughts are just distractions. The real atrocity is too big to wrap my mind around. I prefer to relive the humiliation of that near kiss. I made a fool of myself and that's good because it shields me from the true horror.

Kranik takes a few more steps, and then his form dips over the horizon. The moment his head drops from view, I turn away. I walk past the alzog pen on wooden legs, unable to look at the ghoragall bones that litter the damp earth near the gate. Ghoragall bones, not Aurora Saurin bones; they snapped too easily—just as Kranik said.

I cross the patch of wet grass that skirts the pen; the world shimmers and reverberates. The alzogs push their muddy snouts through the fence, grunting loudly. Always hungry and always wanting more.

'Be quiet!' I shout.

Something about their persistent greed rouses a distant memory. The night I'd spent beneath my bed, terrified of the awful scratchings coming from above as a ghoragall tried to burrow its way through the thatch and snatch me away. Something—or someone—distracted it. The scratching stopped and never returned. I know my stepfather didn't come to check on me because I lay awake under my bed the rest of the night, thinking he hadn't heard or didn't care.

But what if he had heard? What if he'd killed it? He would have had to hide the body. What better place than the muck at the bottom of the alzog pen?

These are the bones I assumed belonged to my mother.

I feel queasy, swallowing a large lump in my throat. Did my stepfather protect me? And for that, did I gift him a dead-life?

I enter the farmhouse, feeling the emptiness like a hollow in my chest. The sooner I can leave this place, the better. I take the steps to the tiny basement and stop in front of the sketch of my mother's face. I can't bear to look at her after what I've done. I take the picture, fold it in two, and slip it into the pocket in my dress.

At least when I believed she was buried in that muck, I had some certainty. Now the haunting questions are back. If she wasn't there, where was she? What happened to her body? My stepfather may not have killed her and buried her bones, but that doesn't exonerate him.

He lied about her leaving us to take up life as a Charmore. If her body isn't buried on the farm, it doesn't make her any less gone.

In the living room, I stare vacantly at my porter pockets, incapable of summoning the will I'll need to heft them into my arms and leave this place. I gaze at the couch, thinking I might clamber onto it, curl up into a ball, and wait for the Vigilance Men to evict me. The thought of journeying into the Parched Lands alone terrifies me, but I have no choice. I can't abandon Calipsie. I know what it is to be left by those you trust. Halfway across the room, I recall the small brown vial with its untidy scrawl.

Vengance.

It's somewhere underneath the couch, resting against the wall. I get onto my hands and knees to survey the sandstone. It's there, half-hidden by a fallen cushion. I crawl forward, scoop it up, and reverse from under the overhanging marook pelt. Sitting on the floor with the bottle in one hand, I wonder what horrors it contains. My father was careful not to expose me to the darker facets of his vocation: poisons, indelible sleeping drafts, paralytics. The vial could hold any of these. Merrick sent me the ampule to express his anger. He wouldn't expect me to willingly dose myself, no matter how badly I deserved it. Even facing up to my monstrous act, I can't bring myself to open it and drink. Alive and healthy, I can still make a difference. I'd rather give my life over to the search for Calipsie than waste it here. I'll follow the Rhemans at a distance. If I keep my mother's zionate jars close, I won't endanger the party by drawing the ghoragalls.

I'm fidgeting and absentmindedly plucking at the carpet when I stumble over the length of coarse twine Merrick used to seal the little parcel. I lift the string and examine the texture with the pads of my fingers. Still seated on the floor, I use the string to fashion a necklace, making a pendant of the little brown vial. The road to Thormyth is long, and I am Stained. If I'm gripped to the belly of a ghoragall, I'll have time to decide my fate, but I'll need the means. This little jar of vengeance may serve its purpose yet.

Once I'm back on my feet, I visit the barn and collect the smokers I made according to my remembered recipe. They stand on the low wooden table in the centre of the barn, a poor interpretation of a master's work. Most sag a little to the left, their sides bulging like the milk-fattened bellies of the baby yakkats. After scooping all six into my porter pockets, I head for the stables. Bloodbane snorts as I sling the saddle over his back. I secure the porter pockets and pat the thick hide on his rump. Then I nip to the drying room behind the stables and take down four large strips of dried alzog meat from the hooks dangling from the rafters. I roll the meat in thick parchment and scrunch it around the ends. These go into my backpack. Next, I add my stepfather's water pouches, after filling them at the pump. Lastly, I check to make sure I still have Calipsie's shells stuffed into my pockets—the ones she collected on the beach. One day soon, when I find her, we'll spend the day laughing and playing Top It.

I throw some reins over a second elvakan. Materare is a sturdy beast, as aggressive as Bloodbane is stubborn. Given any kind of scare, she can be counted on to buck, bite, or kick. Usually, I stay out of her way; her allegiance was to my mother.

As soon as I mount Bloodbane, we set off with Materare trotting at our side. We take the winding road through the orchard, exiting the farm.

I don't expect to return, and I don't look back.

19

KRANIK

I t's been three days since I last saw Kyjta. When I close my eyes, I can still feel her body heat against my rain-soaked chest. The present has no power over me. I travel back and forth in time like the memory of relinquishing that kiss wields gravity. I can't break free of it; I don't want to. So, I relive it, over and over again, wondering if I made the right choice.

In the here and now, I'm seated at a long, slim table, but the room does nothing to hold my interest. It's carved into the clay cliffs of Timmil, and though the outer wall stops at the knee, opening onto mauve skies and the Onaway Ocean, I'm barely aware of the view. Every thought is a trigger, and the seascape only catapults me back to the day on the beach when Kyjta slid her wet hand over mine.

Staring off into the distance, I struggle to bring reality back into focus. The landmass to the right of the Onaway Ocean, with its fingers stretching into the sea, is home to Merrocha, a town moulded mainly from the same orange clay as the cliffs. If I squint into the distance, I can make out the *Rhema Bolajio*, gleaming like a splintered star.

Tiberico and Azaire sit alongside each other at the table. They're both absorbed in looking over the manifests, and their handheld displays illuminate their borrowed faces, giving them an eerie blue glow. It's their job to ensure we'll have everything we need for our journey. Once or twice, I spot them conferring, and the strain between them is evident. Azaire, still riding the dulcet-skinned Vico, is irritated by every suggestion, while Tiberico is low-spoken and excessively calm.

Twenty-three of us sit at the table, most liberated from our Sorbs and enjoying the sensation of being reacquainted with a body. There weren't as many Aurora Saurins sentenced to death as Rhemans relegated to their Sorbs, so Tiberico has sought volunteers. Merrick and a few others have already signed up. In the lead-up to the trip, Merrick is spending time with his family. Today I'm being ferried by a short young woman with calloused hands and bitten-down fingernails. Things might have been different if I'd been in a woman's body the day I found Kyjta in the barn. If she'd looked at me differently, my decision might not torment me so much. Resisting her is the most difficult thing I've ever done.

The elaborately carved double doors swing open, and several men from the House of Vigilance march in. I stiffen at the sight of them. I'd thought we were meeting here to discuss preparations for the journey; did the Tarrohar need a full guard for that? The Vigilance Men line up along one side of the room, looking fearsome. Two Tarrohar follow them, suckered to the backs of a pair of elegantly dressed Charmores. The additional weight has the women unsteady on their feet.

Once seated, the Charmores stare vacantly into the distance, their heads held too high and at an awkward angle. Their arms rest, eerily inert, on the tabletop.

Preparations for the journey have been slow, and frustrations are mounting. The Tarrohar are uncompromising, and though we've met three times already, we cannot secure an agreement.

Once the Tarrohar are seated, the negotiations begin. Staring into the stoic faces of the Charmores when they're strapped has never failed to put me on edge. The Tarrohar coil at their backs, their movements disturbingly languid.

'Your presence is appreciated,' Tiberico addresses the Tarrohar. 'Our agenda, however, remains unchanged.'

One of the Tarrohar lifts its Charmore's head even farther and responds in an expressionless tone. 'You wish to discuss what is already decided.'

'We wish to reiterate that a Rheman will not be separated from their Sorb,' Tiberico says. 'If we are to make the journey, we'll need our Sorbs to be accommodated in the caravan.'

The larger Tarrohar is made distinct from its companion by the light feathering of green veins marking the left side of its bulbous head. It leans forward, crushing the Charmore against the table's edge. Her mouth drops open, and she speaks. 'Your Sorbs stay. This is how we ensure your return.'

Instantly, Rhytheus is on his feet. The captain leans aggressively across the table, his weight on his hands. He chose the roughest-looking character from the eclectic mix on a death charge, and his appearance fits faultlessly with his character. Messily styled dark hair obscures tawny features and their networked scars. 'Where we go, our Sorbs go,' he says. 'On this, we have no bend. Have it, or we'll not go.'

I doubt Tiberico could have said it better. The captain may be unpredictable and harsh, but he's still a worthy ally. If he disagrees with the condition of a thing, he'll do something about it.

'Take as many caravans as you will,' the Tarrohar says, 'but no Sorb leaves this place.'

Rhytheus slams a fist against the table. 'We are one with our Sorbs,' he barks. Three Vigilance Men appear at the captain's side, gripping the hilts of their illing swords.

The thin filaments that shade the tops of the Tarrohar's heads tremble. It must be an innate response to the threat because, by now, the creatures know we Rhemans are immune to their grievous talent.

'This is a waste of time,' says Rhytheus, glaring at the closest Vigilance Man as though he means to commit his identity to memory and visit future violence on him.

'This needs to be a discussion,' Tiberico says softly.

'Rhytheus is right,' I say, despite my unease. 'The more time we spend planning, the more people will die.'

'To be quelled is not the same as dying,' says the Tarrohar. 'Unless your kind has been lying to us all this time.'

'Helacth's Rhemans are nothing like the Rhemans who live among you. They have no empathy for living things. They use them to live; then they discard,' I say.

'If I could recommend just one thing?' Azaire cuts in on the conversation. 'One of us needs to stay to oversee the Body Trust. Of all of us, I have the most experience, and I—'

'You all will go,' say the Tarrohar. 'There will be no concession.' The tentacled creature lowers the Charmore's head to the table with an audible thump, as though this abuse signifies the end of the argument.

Azaire melts back against his seat, looking like he's lost the will to go on. He's by far the most uninspired by the prospect of trekking across the desert.

'Our ship will remain here, as will many of our crew and their Sorbs,' reasons Tiberico. 'We wouldn't ask if it weren't essential. Where a Rheman goes, so must their Sorb.'

We must find some way to appease the Tarrohar, or we'll never leave for Thormyth. Calipsie's chances grow slimmer every moment we delay. Kyjta gave me good advice the day of my encirclement, which is just as relevant today: We must appeal to the Tarrohar's interest and make them an offer they can't refuse. They fear only one thing: loss of control. They allow the raids to continue because Helacth permits them to keep their seats, but he's still a threat to them. Still, Helacth isn't the only threat to the Tarrohar. They dragged the potion master into an encirclement without warning, accusing him of smuggling feather dust. There had to be a reason they were suddenly alert to that threat. The dust has many properties and was banned by the Tarrohar many alignments ago. If they were worried about its use, something must have sparked their concern. The Rhemans can't be the only ones to notice how many people are disappearing, more than can be accounted for by the ghoragall raids. If Sion Chaffrot, or an organisation he fronts, is assisting them, they would need a way to persuade others to help. From what I know of the feather dust, it might be the perfect tool.

'If we're successful,' I say, taking a gamble, 'it'll mean an end to the raids. The people of Merrocha will be safe. It'll also mean an end to the ghoragalls. You'll no longer have to worry about spies and traitors getting their hands on feather dust. Where there is no supply, there can be no trade.'

The Charmore swivels in my direction, the bulbous tentacles of her appendaged Tarrohar quivering as she speaks. As soon as the discussion resumes, I withdraw from it, allowing Tiberico to take the proposal forward. I settle into my seat and retreat into my memories of the day on the farm. I did the right thing. Merrick's body isn't my body, and it would be callous of me to treat it like it is.

20

KYJTA

It's an uncomfortable ride to the little shack at the base of the Qetheral Mountains, especially with a heavy backpack in the heat. The midday sun is beastly; sweat cords down my midriff, tickling my skin like the feather-light touch of scurrying insects. When we finally arrive, I'm relieved, though I know I can't stay long. If the Rheman procession passes through the canyon before I reach the lookout, I'll have no way of reaching Thormyth. Without their trail to follow, I'll only lose myself in the desert. I wouldn't have made the detour to my father's shack if I didn't need the protection of my mother's zionate jars. I'm already cataloguing the list of potions and tinctures I'll collect from my father's shelves; zionate isn't the only thing I'll need in the desert.

I tie Bloodbane and Materare to a tree and head for the shack's only door. I don't know what I'll do if it's locked, but fortunately, it's open. I locate the zionate jars, empty now, stuffed into my father's porter pockets and hanging over the back of his beat-up old chair. The relief is staggering. I wasn't willing to admit to it, but without them, I doubt I'd make it as far as the desert. One by one, I sew the handles of each jar to a lightweight blanket I fashioned into a poncho. As soon as it's done, I slip it over my head, astounded that I never thought to do this before. I guess I never felt the jars belonged to me until now, with my stepfather gone.

I'm about to ransack the shelves for potions and elixirs that might be useful in the desert when I hear Bloodbane give an aggravated snort. Something about the sound unnerves me, so I walk to the door and check outside. The elvakans are where I left them, tied beneath the trees in a patch of long grass that's never failed to get them grazing. The slender stalks sway in the breeze at their feet, but the pair seems oblivious, staring out over the green hillside. I follow their gaze, awake to the noose of uncertainty tightening at my throat. With growing apprehension, I survey the mountain pass that meanders through the hilly landscape. Finally, I spot them. Black cloaks. The House of Vigilance. I try to think what they might want with my father's shack when they must know he isn't here. There isn't time to guess at their objectives.

I must act quickly. I dash back inside and quickly scan the shelves—no time to be selective. Some tinctures and potions look familiar; green bottles are usually medicinal. I find a pain reliever and something to help with fever. There are other potions I don't recognise by sight, and very few are labelled. I scoop them up indiscriminately and shove them into my porter pockets. I can figure out what they do later. I've always suspected the darker the bottle, the greater the potion's malignancy. I grab a few of them and then scan the room for my father's crossbow. Once I've retrieved it from its resting place beside the fire, along with his hat, I scurry back outside and load up the elvakans. Grabbing their reins, I run through the trees, hoping to get them out of earshot before the Vigilance Men arrive. I leave both elvakans tied to a dead tree trunk in a gully I used to play in as a child, and circle back. Something about the procession is nagging at me. The man in the middle, the one straddling an elvakan and sagging in his seat, is wearing black, but I didn't see a cloak. I find a hiding spot behind a group of trees with their roots reaching around some rocks and peer out. I hold the crossbow in my hand, feeling its weight.

There are six men in total. Five are agents of the House of Vigilance, but the sixth man is my father. The Vigilance Men dismount in front of the shack. One of them, the Zhu—I recognise him because his cloak is trimmed in red—issues instructions to the others. He's older than the rest of the men, with coarse, greying hair and a sturdy build. He orders my father brought down from his elvakan. My father's hands are tied in front of him. There's a smear of blood across his mouth and a bruise on his cheek. One of the men jerks him to the ground, forcing him to his knees on a pile of leaves. The remaining three men are ordered into the shack. Two are middle aged with broad shoulders and brutish dispositions; the other is younger, with wavy brown hair and piercing blue eyes. The younger one is Brezan, the Vigilance Man who the Mind Pain caught the day of my mandatory quelling. He looks back just before passing through the door and gives a whistle.

When I first spotted the party approaching, I didn't notice their companion. The norzett was unleashed and probably bounding ahead of them. With a sinking sense of dread, I spot it now, circling the trees that cluster near the bog, sniffing at everything. The animal breaks for the trees, doing a circuit of the spot where I tied up my elvakans not long ago. Then it peers up, its dark eyes scanning the opposite bank, looking for me. I hold myself still, not daring to breathe. If it sees me, I'll never escape. Norzetts are trained hunters, quick and merciless. Maintaining my position, I fight the impulse to blink until the Vigilance Man shouts the animal's name. The norzett gives one last sniff at the air and then charges through the door after him. Relieved, I consider making a break for it while the beast is occupied, but when I look back at my father, he's staring at me. With a jolt, he quickly drops his gaze.

'We must have a name,' the Zhu says, pacing.

'I've told you. I don't know who it is.' My father kneels before him, hanging his head.

'The House of Vigilance has been keeping tabs on you,' responds the Zhu. 'Someone is going to a lot of trouble to make it appear like your work. If we hadn't been tracking your movements so closely, you'd be in the frame. I convinced the Tarrohar to let you join the Rheman caper into the Parched Lands, but whoever's imitating your work, you owe them nothing.'

'You think I'm protecting someone, but I'm not,' says my father. 'You'll see when you follow us into the desert. No one's coming to our aid.'

It's a warning, I'm sure. My father pitches his voice, making sure I'll hear him. The Vigilance Men aim to follow the Rhemans into the desert; I must take extra care.

'What happened to you?' My father regards the Zhu with anguish in his eyes. 'We used to be friends. When did you become their puppet?'

The Zhu shakes his head. 'Trust me, friend—I'm puppet to no one, beast nor man. But I know war, and there are only three ways to end it. Fight; control; surrender.' The Zhu marks each off on a finger. 'To fight, you need an advantage. To take control, you must bend them to your will: lay siege, cut off their supplies, take their children. We might have had a chance at control, but you never made a smoker that worked on the Tarrohar.' The Zhu shakes his head as though admonishing a child. 'That leaves surrender—give the enemy what they want, and live. Everything else is just diversion.'

Inside the shack, the Vigilance Men are hard at work. The hovel looks alive, shaking on its foundations like it's trying to shed the deadweight and break free. The sound of glass breaking reaches me; then, the door flies wide open, and Brezan strides over to the Zhu.

'Father,' he says, standing at attention before the Zhu, 'the place has been looted. And Norek found traces of feather dust.'

'Feather dust,' says the Zhu, unsheathing his illing sword.

He thrusts the tip beneath my father's chin, using it to lever his head.

I raise the crossbow, resting it on the rocks, and aim, but my hands shake so badly that I'm as likely to hit my father as the Zhu.

'A banned substance, my Hok? How did you come by it?' demands the Zhu.

Panic heightening his voice, my father responds, 'The feathered beast attacked me. I shot it in self-defence. The dust flew everywhere. Check my potions—they're all pure.'

The moment the Zhu draws back his sword and swings, I pull the trigger on the bow. I gasp, half expecting to find my father impaled by my quarrel, but it only planted itself in a tree. The Zhu has used the flat of his sword against my father's cheek. The flesh is split there, and my father is reeling. The injury doesn't hold my attention long because the Zhu and his son are both staring at me.

'Get the girl!' shouts the Zhu, pointing his sword at me.

I push myself up from my hiding place and break into a sprint; heavy footfalls sound behind me. Brezan is young and physically fit. I doubt he'll have trouble catching me. I zip through the trees, desperately reaching for a decision. I could dash for my elvakans and try to outdistance the Vigilance Men, or keep the animals' existence secret and hope for escape. The choice is an illusion; the Zhu's son grips first my dress, then my arm, forcing me down. I lose my grasp on the crossbow when I'm flattened against the ground. Dust and grit fill my mouth. Then he straddles me from behind. His weight takes my breath away; I'm forced against the spiky vegetative debris covering the ground.

'You're the daughter, all grown,' Brezan growls against my ear, as though the idea pleases him.

He lifts me to my feet, bending my right arm upwards behind my back. I yelp in pain, and a gruff sound escapes him, like a chuckle but more menacing. 'The girl from the green. *You're* the potion master's daughter. I'm not immune to a little irony . . . but this . . . this is too much.'

He leans against me, his face in my hair, and breathes deeply. I jab an ineffectual elbow at his chest.

'All these alignments, your father's been the source of so much suffering, and then you turn up on the green, and suddenly I'm on my knees begging for the pain to stop. Stepping into your old man's shoes, are you? Getting all us Vigilance Men the Mind Pain when all we're trying to do is our job.'

I stop writhing against Brezan; he's far stronger than I am.

'I don't know what you're talking about. My father hardly ever leaves his shack, and I . . . I didn't mean to get you the Mind Pain. I got it too.'

'Ah, but the Hok used to be quite the roamer. You don't know; you were too young. How sweet that you defend him after the number he pulled on you. Letting you believe all that junk old Cromenk dreamt up.'

'What junk?' I'm angry and scared but I need to know what he's hinting at.

'Don't tell me. You still believe the stories about your mother?' He says the words like they're dipped in sweat nectar, an elderly aunt trying to pacify an upset child.

'Any man ever visited a Charmore knows the lies you were fed.'

Brezan pitches his voice, mimicking the Charmores. 'Sweet, gullible Fair Face, always asking after her mother when she drops by with our nebs.'

'You know what happened to my mother?' I twist to face him, but my arm can't bend any more than it is, the pain is like a pulsing cord of fire.

'According to the records, a ghoragall took her.'

'Ghoragall?' I repeat. 'Are you certain?'

'That's how your stepfather presented it to the House of Judgement. I checked.'

My mother could be alive, should the Hands will it. Living a dead-life but still breathing. The Tarrohar were right: my father *did* deceive me. He would have known the truth. Why didn't he tell me? Did he want his precious farm back so badly that he was willing to let me believe Cromenk killed my mother? He schooled me on the Stain. He encouraged me to lace my stepfather's tea. Did he use me—his own daughter—to achieve his ends?

Bile collects at the back of my throat as I consider how easy I must have made it for him.

Then I hear Brezan unsheathe his sword, the sound bringing me back to the moment.

'What are you going to do?' I ask, breathing hard.

'Finish something I started long ago,' he says, wrapping his hand around my hair and jerking my head back so my neck is exposed.

'Wait, please,' I beg as Brezan pulls my arm higher behind my back.

I brace for the cool metal of his sword against my throat. He's savouring my fear; it's the only reason I'm still alive. I make sure to lay it on thick as I slip my hand into my dress and extract Halli's fire stick. With our bodies so close, he doesn't see me target his flowing cape with the flame. I can sense the fire catching near my hand, working its way up the black material. Soon he'll smell the smoke, and then the Hands will decide whether to save my life or claim it.

'I'm not as blind as the Zhu. I know what your father is capable of.' Brezan pulls me closer, his low voice rasping near my ear. 'You know the Mind Pain—you've felt it yourself.'

Not waiting for a response, he jerks me closer, bringing his lips to my ear. 'That's the punishment inflicted on us every time the Old Soro's spies infiltrate the House of Judgement. And your father helps them with his tincture and potions. I've seen the smokers; I know what they—'

Brezan suddenly cries out, shrieking curses at me. His sword tumbles into a patch of dead leaves, worthless in his current predicament. He beats his cloak, trying to stifle the flames, but all the flapping only feeds the blaze. The flame is at his shoulder now, and taking hold of his sleeve. The fire licks at his neck. I'm transfixed by the horror, watching his pale skin sizzle and burn. His face is a grimace of the worst kind of agony. He drops to the ground and rolls in the dank leaves.

I force myself to turn my attention to my escape. Lifting the crossbow, I point it at the shifting, howling thing on the ground, but I can't bring myself to shoot him. With leaden legs, I break into a run, listening for the sound of his footfalls behind me. When I'm confident I'm not being followed, I change direction, heading for my elvakans. Bloodbane, agitated by my disappearance, snorts repeatedly. I mount him without pulling the hastily made protective poncho over my head. The noisy blanket, with its stitched-on zionate beakers, is as likely to attract the attention of the Vigilance Men as I am to attract a ghoragall. I ride Bloodbane at speed, trailing Materare behind me and checking over my shoulder, looking for signs of dust on the horizon. When I'm certain no one from the

House of Vigilance has given chase, I stop and dismount so I can pull the poncho over myself. The mountain looms ahead of me, with the woods and valley at my rear. I've no choice but to start my journey now; there's no going back.

We ride until dusk, and then we veer off the trail, looking for a secluded spot. When I find one, I tie the elvakans to a tree and let them graze while I munch on a strip of alzog meat and take a long drink of water. Though I'm starving, I must eat sparingly; there's not enough food in my bags to last the journey. When I'm feeling marginally satisfied, I hoist myself into the branches and secure my hammock. I lie there quietly, my father's crossbow clutched to my chest. What did he do to attract such intense attention from the House of Vigilance? He couldn't be spying for the Old Soro; the Zhu said as much. It was someone else, they said, imitating his work. And what work was that? From what Brezan said, I can only imagine it's the production of smokers. The Old Soro must be using them to gain access to the House of Judgement, or garner favour from the folks in Merrocha and the surrounds. My father couldn't possibly have a hand in that.

The Tarrohar's words replay in my head: 'the way your father deceived you.'

And he did deceive me. If he could do that and still appear to me like a loving and caring parent, who else might he deceive? Why did he allow me to believe my stepfather's lie? Why didn't he tell me that my mother was lifted away by a ghoragall?

When the sun rises, I'm still in my hammock. The Vigilance Men haven't come after me. Perhaps they're convinced I'll die in the desert. They couldn't know I was prepared for the journey.

I eat a meagre breakfast of lotils cake and water. Even with the crossbow, which I clutched to my chest all night, I can't be sure I'll find food. Not in the Parched Lands. It's this vast, treacherous terrain that's kept Aurora Saurins from going after their loved ones. Starvation, dehydration, and heat fever are obvious concerns, but there are worse things in the desert.

It takes me most of the day to reach the canyon, the one place I can be sure to see Kranik's caravan as it passes through. There's a slim chance I've missed it, but I can't dwell on that. Besides, there are no tracks on the ground and there's been no storm that might have blown them away. As I lead Bloodbane and Materare up a rocky slope to a plateau, the sun is like a physical force beating down on us. If I weren't wearing my father's wide-brimmed hat and a cloth to mask my face, I'd be suffering from heat fever already.

The earth is dry, and it's rare to spot anything not made of rock or sand. We stop once, finding an illustrious vatti plant, and snap off a few plump leaves. The milky sap is well-known for its moisturising properties. After I drain a little and apply it to my exposed skin, I strip away the wicked thorns and feed the moist leaves to the elvakans.

I spot a decent enough vantage point, protected on either side by rock and below by the skeletal branches of a scraggly baoy baoit tree. I lead the elvakans into the insubstantial shade and set to work. The Parched Lands are no place for a girl and two well-fed elvakans. Not at night. I spy a dead tree halfway down the canyon, sagging listlessly to one side. It takes several trips, but I manage to haul most of it up the slope. Then, I begin the gruelling task of weaving the dead branches together to create a makeshift fence around the elvakans and the sacred tree. Finding a baoy baoit is supposedly a good omen, a reason to believe that the Hands have smiled on you, gifting you a water source—but this one bears no fruit and only serves as a reminder that the Hands are playing me.

Every so often, I peer over the ridge, hoping to spot the caravan, but I'm disappointed each time. The dusty orange depths remain eerily quiet; there's no telling how long I'll have to wait.

Satisfied with the fencing, I sit between the two elvakans to eat. We share biscuits and some water from Sion Cromenk's leather pouches. As I eat, I spot a coil of noose vine, dark as dried blood, strangling the life from the baoy baoit tree. When I'm done with my meal, I unwind a length of the vine, releasing the tree from its deadly embrace and acquiring something useful.

My unease grows with the failing light. I scan the gloomy scenery for predators, but visibility is increasingly limited. Eventually, when I can no longer keep my weariness at bay, I tie one end of the noose vine around my ankle and the other to Bloodbane. Although I can't trust myself to stay awake after the day's exertion, Bloodbane is almost always alert.

I assume my position, cocooned in my hammock above the elvakans. The noose vine cuts uncomfortably into my ankle, but it won't keep me from falling asleep. I hug my father's crossbow, nuzzling the tip beneath my chin. I have only six quarrels, I must conserve them to survive.

Sometime later, I wake with a start. There's a tug at my ankle, short and sharp. Restless, Bloodbane snorts and shakes his mane. I lie stiffly in my hammock, clutching the crossbow, and listen, hearing the baoy baoit branches scratch against one another in the wind. There's something else too: the scurry, stop, scurry, stop of little feet crossing the shingles. I must act or risk losing my elvakans. I swing my legs over the edge of my rapidly swaying bed and leap into the enclosure. I pull Halli's fire stick from my dress pocket and light the dried twigs I packed between the branches. The flame takes a few moments to catch, but soon the fencing is ablaze, illuminating my attackers. There are at least twenty of them.

Small, thin creatures with large sorrowful eyes circled in white paint to make them look bigger. Their clothes are tattered rags tied around their pasty bodies in strips. Dusty material has also been wrapped around their heads, covering their mouths and noses. *Ravvids.*

They're armed with hollow shooters and jars of sharp skeets, tied to short strips of material cinched at their middles. The deadly insects buzz around their transparent encasements, looking increasingly agitated.

The Ravvids are after my elvakans. One of the animals could feed their entire tribe for a moon cycle. With shaking hands, I raise the crossbow. Without my elvakans, I'll be fortunate to survive a journey home; tailing the caravan definitely won't be an option.

'I don't want to waste my arrows on you,' I shout, 'but I will!'

The leader, I assume, given his extravagant headdress of ghoragall feathers, lifts his hollow shooter and blows. I feel the soft tap of a sharp skeet as the insect smacks into my neck. I slap the place where it hits, but the bug has already dropped to the ground, too confused by the smoke to deliver its deadly poison. Seeing it spin and flick in the sand, I crush it under my boot. The remaining Ravvids mimic their leader, dispatching a cloud of sharp skeets to join their fallen comrade. Unable to find them all in the frantic firelight, I dance on the spot, stomping the sand and hoping to crush them before they acclimate to the smoke. Materare rises on her hind legs, giving an almighty bleat, and comes down, only just missing my foot. Ignoring the panicked elvakan, I aim at the clan's little leader.

My first shot goes wide as Materare bucks beside me, but my second shot is true, and the Ravvid leader drops dead. I hoped the kill would deter them, but their chanting grows louder. I load my third quarrel and aim it through the thickening flames and smoke. Another Ravvid collapses, the sharpshooter tumbling to the sand

and, with any luck, loosing a skeet among his companions. I shoot another and another until I reach for a quarrel and find none left. Seeming to understand that my defences are spent, the Ravvids jab at the flaming fence with their poison-tipped spears, sending up sparks that make their comrades cheer wildly. More and more spears break through the interwoven branches, causing the circle to crumble.

Materare rears up, making frantic guttural sounds. I reach up, trying to calm her, but it's no use. Her hooves trample the ground, causing chaos within the circle. I can't see the Ravvids through the mounting dust; I have no way to tell how they'll next attack. I have no choice—if I don't act now, we'll all be killed. I pull the noose vine off my ankle and double the length in my hand. Then I bring the vine down hard onto Materare's backside. The elvakan rears up and emits a high-pitched shriek, then leaps the burning perimeter and charges through the chanting Ravvids, trampling a few before stampeding into the night.

I reach over the dying embers to grab a spear from an injured Ravvid. The instant I have it in my hand, I turn the poisoned tip on the creature and quickly dispatch him with a jab through the ribs. Then another, as he stands distracted by Materare's getaway. The remaining Ravvids set off after Materare, chanting their ghastly chorus. I watch their little bodies disappear into the darkness. When I hear the clan cheer, I know she's gone. Another link to my mother lost. Something else taken from me.

I work through the remaining smoke-drunk skeets, crushing them into the sand. My movements grow wilder with each successive kill. When I've exhausted my energy, I plant my feet together and lift my head to the sky to scream. Bloodbane nudges me with his trunk, but I shove him away. I don't deserve his compassion, not after murdering his companion.

Once I've packed our things, I mount Bloodbane, and we leap over what remains of the fire. I pull him around, circling the carnage on the outskirts of the glowing embers. I count eleven Ravvids in a tangled mess on the ground. I dismount and check each of them, retrieving my quarrels where I find them. Most come free with a soft crunch; I only break one as I wrestle it from a Ravvid's chest. I clean each quarrel on the Ravvid's tattered robes before sheathing them. I've started to collect jars of sharp skeets when I notice movement in my periphery. I spin, holding one of the spears raised, ready to defend myself. The movement was slight: a Ravvid, not quite dead and trying to crawl away, his mangled body a sorrowful sight. I lower the spear. It looks as though the barbaric little creature's left arm was mauled beneath Materare's feet. I stalk toward him, my hand gripping the spear, intent on delivering him to the Hands. The Ravvid's eyes are squeezed tight; he knows what's coming. It's not pity that stops me; it's the untried smokers in my porter pockets. It's the tinctures and potions without any labels. If I'm to use any of it, I'll need a subject.

Taking my cue from the Zhu, I settle the spear beneath the Ravvid's chin and lift the creature's face. Slowly he opens his eyes to take me in. 'If you believe the Hands have smiled on you, think again,' I say, kneeling beside him.

As I prod the Ravvid's arm, the creature bursts into a fit of chants that would probably make his mother blush. The break is bad, but the risk of infection is low. The creature is lucky the skin is only broken on a superficial level. The Ravvid eyes me cautiously as I snap one of the spears in two. I place the pieces beside me, then loosen strips of cloth from a nearby Ravvid and lay them on the dusty shingles. When I'm prepared, I prod the break again. The instant the creature opens his mouth to scream, I wedge a ball of material into his mouth. Then I reset the bone, using blunt pressure to snap it in place. Although the Ravvid's scream is muffled, it's still loud enough to travel some distance across the Parched Lands.

'That's for Materare,' I say.

I splint the arm with a piece of the broken spear and the strips of cloth. When I'm done, I glare at the Ravvid and jerk the wad of material from his mouth. With a whimper, his big white-ringed eyes stare back at me.

'Don't look at me like that,' I say. 'You brought this on yourself.'

After walking for a time in the dark, we stop, and I tie the Ravvid to a tree with the noose vine. With Bloodbane tethered nearby, I spend the rest of the night beneath a rock outcropping with the crossbow and two spears clutched to my chest. Although I checked the Ravvid's bonds three times, I still don't feel safe. I keep imagining I'll wake to find Bloodbane slaughtered and the Ravvid drinking his blood. All night I get no rest, rising before dawn with an appetite to kill the creature out of spite.

The morning announces itself by blowing sand in my face. I rub my eyes and peer into the spray of dust. There's a whistling wind, and I can't see the Ravvid or Bloodbane from the crevice that's kept me protected through the night. The Ravvid, when I find my way to him, is up to his elbows in sand. The wind is howling, and I have to shield my eyes as I dust him off. I curse, thinking I'll have no hope of tracking the caravan in a sandstorm.

The Ravvid doesn't look well. His powdery skin is glazed and yellowing. Chanting softly, he holds his injured arm. I dig through the porter pockets, looking through my father's tinctures. When I find a green one, I pop the stopper and pull on the Ravvid's jaw to open his mouth. He's in too much pain to protest as I drip the liquid onto his tongue. Waiting for the potion to take effect, I examine the other bottles. Apart from the two green ones, I have a small dusty-red vial, a couple of sallow brown ampules, and one of deepest black. I pop the lid off the red one and sniff the contents: restrippe, nauticks, and something unfamiliar. My father's recipes are fluid. He experiments, improving a little here, refining a scent to make it more palatable, sometimes blending two elixirs to create something entirely different. The potion from the brown bottle is even more elusive: perhaps a little mayamp and elterforp, possibly some nijet milk. Again, not a familiar blend.

I tuck the tinctures back in the porter pockets and shimmy up a nearby baoy baoit tree to knock free the two young balloot fruits near the top. Back on the ground, I shuck the nip and pour half the sweet water into my mouth. Then I toss the fruit to Bloodbane, who swallows it whole. The other one I reserve for the Ravvid, setting it beside him as I unwrap a little of the binding around his splint to check the swelling. Although the arm has turned a noxious, fermenting yellow, the swelling is mild.

I pick up the fruit and shake it, so the creature hears the liquid sloshing inside. 'You thirsty?'

The Ravvid's eyes go wide and he picks up the pace of his chant.

'We can trade,' I say. 'I give you water.' I shake the balloot. 'You sit for an experiment.'

The Ravvid doesn't decline. I don't know if he understands me, but he understands the water. Trying the smokers on the creature is pointless if he can't take instruction from my words; I'm not going to waste them. That leaves the tinctures and potions. I consider which of them to try first. The darker the vial, the more malignant the potion.

I unstopper the black and take a tentative sniff. The scent is unfamiliar. I could pour two drops onto the Ravvid's tongue, and the utility would be plain enough, but I may never learn the purpose of the other potions. It makes more sense to work my way up to the darkest vial. I dip back into the porter pockets and come out holding the red. By now, the pain reliever has done its work: the Ravvid's eyes are brighter. He's focusing better, and the fruit has all his attention. The desert creature licks his dry lips; he looks thirsty but largely recovered.

I pop the top of the red vial. If the Ravvid survives, I'll have to call him something. 'Ringface' seems as good a name as any. I take him by the jaw. Again he opens his mouth without protest. The pain reliever may have bought me a little trust. The unnamed tonic drips a sticky drop onto the Ravvid's tongue. I watch him swallow, but nothing happens. I study the creature as he eyeballs the fruit. The Ravvid fidgets as though something is making him uncomfortable. He twists and squirms on the spot, still tied to the tree but wriggling like he's trying to get free. If I could speak his language, I could ask him what he's experiencing, but our communication is limited to gestures. Time passes, and nothing much changes about the Ravvid's appearance or behaviour, so I lift the fruit to help him drink.

Unexpectedly Ringface cracks a grin. His powdery skin creases at the corners of his mouth as his lips widen, displaying a row of discoloured wedge-like teeth.

'Here,' I say, leaning forward with the balloot. Although he's wary of me, he recognises the fruit, and his thirst must win over his fear because he lets me pour the sweet water into his mouth.

I fashion a harness out of the noose vine, untie the Ravvid, and acquaint him with the straps. I tie the other end of the vine to Bloodbane and then turn my attention to my preparations for the day. First, I check the provisions. Two porter pockets went missing along with Materare. All that remains of our food and water is one strip of dried alzog meat, a single pouch of water, and a stale loaf of lotils cake. If the caravan doesn't pass soon, we won't survive long. Since I have no guarantee when they'll be along, I must hunt for food and look for water. After packing up the camp, I take a final look over the ridge. Although there's no sign of the caravan, at least the wind has died down. If we're successful in finding food and water, I should be able to climb down before sunset and check for tracks.

I hoist Ringface into Bloodbane's saddle. He looks terrified, round eyes bulging in his head. I point to the tufts of hair that sprout from the elvakan's impressive shoulders; the Ravvid is tentative but quickly grabs hold when I destabilise him by launching myself into the saddle.

We search for close on a quarter day but find only vatti plants. When stripped of their thorns, these are good enough for Bloodbane, but they'd make me sick. I offer some to Ringface, but he turns them down. I'm about to give up and head back to check for the caravan when I notice a mound on the horizon and feel my blood slow in my veins.

It's Materare. It has to be.

Desert ukirines circle above, with more on the ground, pecking at the carcass. We trundle closer. The heat from the sand is intense, and the scent of her baking flesh reaches me long before I can clearly make her out. The meat on her rump and back has been stripped, showing the white bone of her rib cage. As I drop from Bloodbane's back, I reach for the knife at my side. We must eat, and Materare's flesh will be as good as anything we can scrounge up in the desert. Still, the idea is terrible, and my stomach churns as I imagine chewing on chunks of my mother's trusty mount. I killed the beast as surely as putting a stake through her heart. I should eat the meat—if only to ensure her death serves the purpose of sustaining our lives. I can't do it, though. Instead, I shoot one of the ukirines, breaking away from Bloodbane and the Ravvid to collect it.

As I turn back to face Bloodbane, I'm disturbed to find he's wandered off. It's unlike him to walk away from me. I must be preoccupied with my guilt because one moment I'm walking, the next I'm falling. The pain, when it hits, splinters my mind. Incapable of stifling my scream, I cry out. My fear can't silence me, though I know I shouldn't draw attention to myself in the desert. I grit my teeth and hold myself static while trying to deal with the shock. The slightest movement has me wailing in agony. Blinking back tears, I try to make sense of my new surroundings. I see four walls, carved into orange clay, where there was desert before. Something is horribly wrong. A sand-coloured weave covers my feet, and something protrudes from the ground beneath. With trembling fingers, I grab an edge and tug, terrified by what I'll find. The cloth snags, but enough of it comes free for me to get a good look at what I'm dealing with. My breath hitches as I inspect the sharpened, evenly spaced stakes jutting from the earth, each the length of my forearm. Sucking a deep breath over my quivering lower lip, I lift the weave to check my foot. A whimper escapes me when I see the stake protruding from my boot. A dark mote of blood has gathered around the shaft, seeping into the leather. I bring a hand up to cover my mouth, my hand shaking so badly I almost miss.

Looking up, I'm relieved to see the rectangle of sky above me. I've fallen into a hole—a hunting trap. If I don't get free, someone will be along to check on it. If they're hungry enough, I might look tasty. Just then, a face appears at the rim of the pit.

'Ringface,' I gasp, never imagining I could be this pleased to see a Ravvid.

He makes a sharp tut-tut sound, which I expect translates as, 'You idiot.'

'Throw down that vine,' I say, gesturing to the harness I looped around him earlier.

Ringface ignores me, disappearing from view.

'Hey!' I call. 'Come back.'

It's no use. The Ravvid is gone.

I look back at my foot and shudder. Getting free is going to hurt. I shrug off my backpack and take out the last piece of alzog meat. Tearing off a strip with my teeth, I hope to fool myself into thinking everything's normal and this is just another mealtime in the desert. The salty meat only increases my thirst, but thirst is as effective a distraction as any. Chewing, I take hold of my leg under the knee. The world is in balance; there's nothing off keel. I recite the ballad of The Hands under my breath. I close my eyes and jerk my knee toward my chest. There's a gruesome sucking sound, followed by a scream, which brings Ringface running back. I sink to the ground, weeping and chewing on what's left of the meat.

'Vine!' I shout, but when I look up, four faces are staring down at me. They all have eyes circled with white paint, but only one of them has a splinted arm. Ringface has managed to re-join his barbaric little gang. Did they follow us all morning? I must've made it all so simple for them.

Reaching for my crossbow, I fumble with the catch. The heads are gone when I finally attempt to aim. Cursing, I haul myself onto my good foot so I can lunge to the other side of the pit. Above, the Ravvids are chanting. It doesn't take much experience to guess what's coming next. Almost immediately, spears fly into the pit. If I'd remained against the opposite wall, the pain in my foot would feel trivial, if their spears hadn't instantly killed me. I flatten myself against the wall and raise my crossbow above my head. The first Ravvid to peer over the lip is rewarded with a quarrel through the top of his head. The creature falls into the pit beside me, dead. I lift a few rags, checking for Ringface's splinted arm, but find both in good order. A search of the Ravvid's rags reveals a water bottle strapped to his side, which I untie while repeatedly checking overhead. Then I'm back against the wall, shimmying into a corner, hoping my attackers have run out of spears. I take a deep drink of water before stoppering the bottle and setting it beside me.

I'm starting to think they've cleared off. It's safer for the Ravvids to wait for me to die or come back when I'm too weak to lift my crossbow, but then I hear Bloodbane's grumpy snorts growing more indistinct and realise he's being led away. I can't allow that to happen. No amount of pain could prevent me from protecting him.

I hitch the crossbow to my belt and reach for a spear. With effort, I snap it in half across my knee. I do the same with the second spear, followed by the remaining two, so I have four spear tips, each connected to about a hand's width of wood. I pick up the spear pieces and muddle my way onto my good foot, facing the wall. First, I fling my backpack and protective blanket out of the hole. I don't want any extra weight for this, and if my crazy plan doesn't work, I won't need them anyway. The jars clang loudly as the blanket hits the sand. With all my strength, I shove the first two spear tips into the wall. I've set them apart; they're the footholds for a makeshift ladder. I gouge the other two spearheads into the clay above my head; then, I use them to pull my weight onto the lower rungs. When I put my weight on my left foot, the pain is so excruciating that my hasty meal of alzog meat threatens to revisit me. I have to remind myself that the pain will be far worse if I fall. I dislodge the first spearhead, hunching into the wall to keep myself steady, and quickly stab the clay a little higher. Now I must do away with the first foothold if I'm going to make it to the ridge. The sand-covered clay shelf is almost in my reach, but the wall starts to crumble when I pull out the second spearhead. Quickly I jab it back in, digging down as hard as I can, desperate to keep the traction. Then my final foothold buckles under the pressure, and my foot slips. I thrust upward, using my punctured foot to boost me up the wall, but it's too late. I'm losing my footing, falling backwards on to a bed of spikes. Free falling, I spot the tail end of the noose vine I'd attached to Bloodbane's saddle earlier. The Ravvid must have wrestled himself free. I reach for it, snagging it up as I topple to my death. It's still attached to Bloodbane and Bloodbane is being led away. I slam into the wall, my feet brushing the skewers jutting from the floor of the pit. Then, I'm pulled up and over the clay lip and onto the sand.

21

KYJTA

I lie on the sand, panting and staring after the three tribesmen as they saunter across the desert with the sum of my possessions. They're about fifty paces from where I lie, drained from exertion and shock. I don't have the luxury of getting my breath back. If I wait any longer, they'll be out of range. I rise quickly to my elbows and unhitch my crossbow. The longer I take to aim, the greater the distance between me and the targets; I'll need to be selective about which one to take down first because the others will run. In all likelihood, I won't be able to make a second shot.

Bloodbane's life is my priority; by the looks of it, Ringface is leading him away. The tall Ravvid, the one in the middle, has my backpack with all the food. What's left of the water is in there too, not to mention my father's potions. I almost weep at the thought of losing the small green vial of pain reliever. My foot feels twice its usual size and throbs with the slightest movement. The remaining Ravvid wears my poncho with its precious jars. They're not just protection from the ghoragalls; they're also the only link that remains to my mother. The choice is impossible but inevitable. As I centre my crossbow on the smallest of the Ravvids, I can tell it's Ringface because I see the sling I made for his arm. I aim, but it's not the same as shooting one of the others. Although we didn't bond, I did help mend his arm. I felt the creature's weight as I lifted him onto Bloodbane's back. I named him. I must be very lonely out here in the desert to have become so attached to a Ravvid in only half a day.

I drop my head to my arm, sweat trickling down my face. If I don't act now, I'll lose everything, including my life. This tribe attacked me in the night, and they just left me for dead. I owe them nothing. I raise my head, squinting into the shimmering heat, then fire.

Ringface drops, crumpling onto the sand beside Bloodbane.

The others run, as I predicted. I load another quarrel and take aim at the taller one. This time, I don't hit anything. Exhausted and sickened by what I've done, I lower my face into the sand. Lying in the baking heat, catching my breath, I try to rouse myself, but the heat keeps me down and at some point, I black out.

I'm awoken by Bloodbane, who nudges me with his trunk. I close my eyes and try not to think about Ringface lying dead in the sand.

'Hey there, old boy,' I say, wrapping a hand around Bloodbane's warm trunk. He must have stood over me while I slept, creating shade, because the sun is low, and while my skin is red from the heat, it's not sore to the touch. My foot is another story. I flip myself over carefully to take a better look. I'll have to remove the boot, and there's little hope I'll get it back on again. I lean forward, pull the straps free, gently grab the heel, and push down. I grit my teeth, feeling the wound sear at the pressure. Then I wriggle the boot from side to side, and it finally comes away in my hand. There's a hole clear through the centre, and the leather is stained with blood. I stare at it in disgust, then hurl it away. It bounces along the sand and tumbles into the pit. I cry out. I'll need that boot if the swelling ever comes down.

I don't want to deal with my foot, but I have to figure out some way of cleaning it. I'm trying to build up the energy to get to my good foot and search the porter pockets on Bloodbane's back, hoping to find a forgotten water pouch, when I hear a sound that sends a chill through me. I'd recognise that mournful cry anywhere: a ghoragall circling overhead. Without the protection of my zionate jars, my Stain will draw the beasts from all around. Quickly, I pull myself upward, using Bloodbane to stabilise me, then grab the tufts of hair at his shoulders and launch myself into his saddle. I yell in pain as my injured foot knocks against his rump, but I can't let the pain distract me.

'Go!' I urge, and he starts to run.

We gallop across the sand, neither of us sure where we're headed— we're just trying to get away. I'm cringing against Bloodbane's muscled back, imagining the ghoragall's talons wrapping around me, when I spot a gathering of large rocks.

'Over there!' I shout, giving Bloodbane a nudge in the right direction.

The elvakan turns, passing beneath a shadow. I look up and see the ghoragall swooping low. Somehow, I power myself off Bloodbane's back before landing and rolling across the sand. As I collide with a rock, I look up to see the ghoragall silhouetted against the sun. Hastily, I scramble into the cleft between two rocks. Bloodbane snorts and tips onto his front legs, kicking out with the back. The elvakan's large hind feet connect with one of the ghoragall's wings. Whether injured or outmatched, the grim beast retreats, breaking for the north where it might find easier prey.

I sit for a time, allowing the pain in my foot to dull to a still horrible but less overwhelming throb. The open wound is covered in sand, and while that's helped stem the bleeding, it's guaranteed to result in infection. The Hands must want to see me punished. If I had my father's potions, I could deaden the pain and reduce my coming fever, but without water, the wound will grow septic, which could mean my life.

With great difficulty, I pull the porter pockets off Bloodbane's back and nestle back into the rocks. I grab a blanket from one of the bags and try to dust the sand away from my wound. When I've had my fill of torturing myself, I tear off a strip of the blanket and bandage my foot. Then I wrap the remaining blanket around my shoulders. I've started to shiver. There are clothes, my hammock, and the smokers in the porter pockets, but there's nothing Bloodbane and I can eat or drink. Still, I check it three times to be sure. My stomach growls like it's reading my mind. It's almost dark, and I can't risk leaving the safety of the rocks to comb the sand in search of my backpack or to retrieve my crossbow. Not without my zionate poncho for protection. All that's left to do is sleep, so I hunker down and do my best not to think about the pain.

I wake with a burning thirst. The sun is up, and the heat is already unbearable. I sit up, noting how damp my clothing is. I'm surprised I'm still capable of sweating. My vision blurs as I stare across the unending sand. Shuffling, Bloodbane gives a rasping snort. He's probably as thirsty as I am. Just packing the porter pockets has me panting like I'm running for my life. How long have I slept? It must be mid-morning, but I feel like I haven't drunk a thing for days.

Every swallow is painfully sticky. The caravan must have passed by now. This catastrophe should have me anxious, but all I can think about is my thirst. Even when my father's warning replays in my head, I can't muster a response. The Vigilance Men will go after the caravan; the Tarrohar aim to find whoever is imitating my father's work. They must think my father is helping them, and that they'll stage a rescue. I expect the Vigilance Men are tasked to slay them all. The desert will hide their bodies, and my father will be among them. He can't even warn the Rhemans, because he'll be quelled.

I twist onto all fours, lifting my injured foot off the ground. The movement ignites a fresh burst of pain that throbs up my leg. Gritting my teeth, I crawl to the edge of the rocky crevasse to get an unobstructed view of the sky. It's clear, without a ghoragall in sight.

'Here, boy,' I call to Bloodbane, who stands with his head hanging, looking listless in the heat.

My voice is nothing but a brittle crackle in the wind, and it doesn't rouse the elvakan, so I wet my lips with what little moisture I can muster and whistle. Bloodbane looks up and trundles closer. I attempt to haul myself into the saddle, but my weakened limbs can't take my weight, and I give up. I consider climbing into the saddle from one of the rocks, but if I fall, I'm not sure I'd get up again. I opt for tying my hammock to either side of Bloodbane's saddle, then climb inside. It's a bumpy ride, trailing behind him in the sand, but it's better than walking. All the movement intensifies my pain, but I curl up inside the trailer and try to ignore the jostling of my limbs. We're heading for the spot where I felled the Ravvid. If Ringface's body is still there, perhaps he has a water bottle tucked beneath his rags. I focus on that to distract myself from the pain.

Every few moments, I peer through Bloodbane's ambulating legs to get a feel for our progress. When I spot the Ravvid, I whistle for

Bloodbane to stop. The body is half shrouded by sand; I crawl out. My thirst intensifies at the thought of water nearby. I retrieve my quarrel from where it's lodged in Ringface's back. Thirsty as I am, I don't want to snap it. Then I roll the Ravvid over and search his rags. I find a water pouch, but it's dry, punctured by my quarrel. Battling this level of disappointment should bring me to tears, but my body can't spare the moisture.

Ringface looks different. A short pelt of golden fur covers the patches of chalky skin visible through his rags. I've never heard of a furry Ravvid before. It must have been the potion. Some hair growth accelerant, or something equally useless. Why couldn't my father just label his potions? Even Merrick's system trumped the one used by my father, who mainly relied on colour coding and scent. With Merrick's potion, at least I'm clear on its utility: vengeance. I could drink it now. The thought of liquid passing my lips is almost enough to tempt me.

I lean back onto one of Bloodbane's sturdy legs, close my eyes, and take a few steady breaths.

The backpack is the one thing I need. Inside it, there is food, water, and pain relief. I scan the surrounding sand, hoping to discover that the taller Ravvid shucked it off when he fled, but the sand is immaculate. Then I recall the dead Ravvid in the dugout. I drank from his water pouch, but did I finish it? I don't remember; there was too much going on. I crawl back into my cocoon, and we set off for the pit.

I spend the journey trying to figure out how I'll collect the water pouch from the bottom of the dugout, but I'm too dehydrated to think up a solution. When we reach the pit, I climb free and peer over the lip, hoping inspiration will strike me, but it's not inspiration that makes my stomach flip when I look over the ledge. I jerk back, clawing the sand as if something threatens to drag me away. Bracing myself, I gingerly take a second look.

A giant satermijte—twice as long as I am tall!

They're the largest insects to inhabit the Parched Lands and one of only two safe water sources to be found in the desert. The thing is repulsive—worse than that, it's not yet dead. Its long spiny legs twitch while its front pincers dig into the clay walls. Two of its six stalked eyes swivel in my direction. Our presence has excited it; all ten legs lever at once. I cry out, imagining it'll lift its body free of the stakes, but its thorax is stuck fast. As it hisses and clicks its pincers in frustration, I look around for a large rock. I need something big enough to crush its head and end its misery. I find one not too far away and position myself at the lip of the pit with my legs hanging down. The satermijte must smell my wound or sense its fate because it's reanimated. It scuttles its legs, chipping away at the dugout's walls with its pincers. I hold the rock above its head, breathe, and let go. There's a wet crunch, followed by a soft hissing sound. Then the pit goes quiet.

I still have the noose vine tied securely to Bloodbane, and while I don't have the strength to climb down a rope, I no longer need to. The insect's hind legs are so large that they form a ledge for me to step onto. With the rope tied securely around my waist so Bloodbane can haul me out if he has to, I step cautiously onto the brittle surface. Then I lower myself onto it, one leg on either side of the insect's prickly limb, and squirm my way toward the thorax. I pause to pull one of the spearheads from the clay wall, then cross to the apex of the thorax, where I lever the wings upwards and saw through the fibrous sheaths. Each wing is veined with zionate and as close as I'll get to having my poncho back.

When I'm done, I take hold of one of the insect's horns and saw at them until they come away in my hands. I scoop the fibrous mess out from inside while doing my best to ignore the dead eyes, but I have the unnerving sense they're watching me. Then I move to the insect's abdomen, slicing through the thick membrane covering one of its moisture traps. My throat clenches painfully as I work, imagining the liquid inside. When I pull the membrane back and finally see the water, I croak an unintelligible sound. Forgetting the cup I crafted from the horn, I lunge straight in with my hands, scooping up water and swallowing it down. It tastes incredible. I drink enough of it that my belly feels swollen, and my throat stops feeling like it's meshed together. Then I remember Bloodbane. He's dropped his trunk into the hole and sniffs nearby. I snag the horn in one hand, scoop up some water, and hold it out to him.

As Bloodbane snuffles and slurps, I stare across the insect's giant body. There's a second cavity on the other side, and I'm hopeful it contains just as much water. Once Bloodbane has drunk his fill, I tear back the double membrane and fill the empty water pouches. First, the one I find at the bottom of the pit and then Ringface's punctured one, which I tie off with a piece of noose vine just below the puncture hole. Then I remove all but one of the insect's legs, hurling them from the pit. Roasted over an open flame, they'll make a good dinner. As I'm clambering out of the hole, relying on the beast's one remaining leg to carry my weight, I spot my boot in the corner of the pit. It's tattered and soaked with blood, and I wonder whether it was that boot or the Ravvid I killed that lured the hungry satermijte. Using the longest segment of one hind leg, I snag my boot and fling it free of the pit.

With the zionate veined wings tented over me to protect from the ghoragalls, I make a small fire and roast the satermijte's leg over the flames. After Bloodbane and I eat our fill, I pack the rest. The meat is fibrous, without much flavour, but I gnaw the white flesh cleanly from the cartilage without complaint. With my belly full and my thirst sated, my thoughts turn to the caravan. It must have passed already. Our only hope is to follow the tracks, assuming they're still there. The Rhemans will have supplies. Maybe even some medicine.

We set off in the late afternoon, when the desert sun sizzles our skin without incinerating it. The way into the canyon is perilous, and twice Bloodbane nearly loses his footing. Inside my hammock, I use the blanket to cushion myself, but I feel battered when we reach the canyon bed. My injured foot throbs with every step the elvakan takes, and I have a bad fever. It's getting harder to stay awake.

In the canyon bed, Bloodbane mercifully trundles into the shade. I sit up and try to focus. I can't see any tracks from inside my cocoon, so I whistle for him to stop and venture out to check the sand, keeping under the protection of my scavenged satermijte wings. When I locate the trail, I set Bloodbane on its path. We must keep moving, even as night falls. Urther's face is mercifully bright, and the tracks carve deep shadows into the loose sand, making them easy to follow. We stumble onto the campsite just before midnight, but it's deserted. The tracks into and out of the camp tell a story. Something came through here, subdued the Rhemans, and carried them away. It wasn't the Vigilance Men. The tracks are too unusual to be made by elvakan.

My mind is foggy with fever, and every decision overwhelms me. I can't think what to do. One option is to stay at the campsite, and the temptation is great. I could sleep comfortably inside one of the wagons, but I might not wake. I set Bloodbane on the fresh tracks, and crawl back into my cocoon. I fade in and out of consciousness, and my dreams are a hot succession of troubling scenes. I wake intermittently with a clawing thirst and drink sparingly from the water pouches. It's increasingly difficult for me to check the tracks. I'm weak and feverish, and I can't keep myself awake.

When morning finally comes, I'm hot and delirious, and the tracks are gone. Morose, and barely able to keep myself upright, I sit on the hot sand, struggling to make sense of my decision to follow the bizarre trail, when I spot something moving on the horizon. My stomach weakens, and I try to clear my vision, but the scene doesn't change. Four giant satermijtes, skimming the dunes. If they smell my wound, they'll come for me. I'm too weak to defend myself.

The procession slows. The lead satermijte scuttles briefly in our direction, looking like it has sensed something in the air. My heart rate escalates. The insects must have caught a whiff of my foot, the blood and the rot. Sitting rigidly, I hold my breath. This must be a hallucination. They're moving toward us now, and there's nothing I can do but wait.

I must be delirious because as the insects get closer, I see dark figures silhouetted on their backs. My fever is definitely playing games with my head; giant satermijtes could never be trained mounts. Then I hear a sound like a wail, one of the men yelling at another. My infected leg throbs, and I feel increasingly weak. The dunes sway before my eyes, morphing into sandy maws that threaten to swallow me. When the world tilts, I close my eyes and let myself fall.

22

KYJTA

wake to a sea of white. I expect to be dead, but my heart is racing, and a tent takes shape from the glare, supported by lengths of arched beams crossing at the apex high above me. Someone else is here, but I can't bring them into focus. The soft eyes, cascading blond curls, and tan skin seem familiar, and I wonder if this is another dream brought on by fever.

'Kyjta. You're awake,' the woman says.

I try to speak, but my voice cracks like splintering firewood.

'Don't talk,' she says, and disappears.

Panicking, I try to sit up, but I can't move, and then she's back. She'd gone to get me water. She leans down to help me drink, but something stops her.

'No touching.' The stranger's voice is startlingly sonorous.

'She needs fluids,' says the woman, but she's shoved away, and the voice's owner leans in.

'Open your mouth,' he says. The booming command says it all. This is not a man to be trifled with. He has deep ebony skin and beautiful turquoise eyes, underscored by twin scars cresting each of his cheekbones. I realise these aren't random scars of war but honorary brandings of the Old Soro's personal guard. Thirsty and still in shock, I open my mouth. The guard pours water from a pouch until my mouth is brimming, then stops, careful not to spill a drop. I swallow, and the sensation is agonising.

The guard steps back, and the woman takes his place.

'I don't—' I croak.

'Try to relax,' the woman says, though she doesn't draw any closer. Her eyes are wet.

'Where—' I manage.

'Save your voice,' she says, her hands fluttering close by. I sense she wants to touch me, but she doesn't dare.

She looks so much like my mother, but my mother was taken by ghoragall. That's what Brezan told me. It's too warm to be the Ice Realm. It must just be some dreamscape where my mother wears a dry weave tunic the colour of desert sand and looks like a mercenary Grulo from the Parched Lands.

I hear the tent flap open; then, someone else speaks.

'She's awake?' The voice is speculative, kind, and masculine, but not one I've heard before.

'Yes.' My mother looks back at me, her eyes brimming with love.

'Then all the mutterings about Rheman miracles are true,' says the man, his voice growing louder as he approaches.

What Rheman miracles? What a strange dream this is.

His face peers out from behind my mother. He's an old man, wizened by the sun's heat. Though he bears no resemblance to me, what with his rich complexion and thick black hair, my mother greets him like family, and he looks at me with deep affection.

'Soro Saiyto,' says my mother, 'meet my daughter, Kyjta.'

The Old Soro? What could my mother possibly have to do with the banished ruler of Sojour?

'It's a fair thing. A fair thing indeed. We thought the Hands had hold of you. It's a wonder—your strength is a marvel.' He looks from me to my mother. 'How's her fever?'

'Gone,' says my mother, looking bewildered.

'And the injury?'

'Healed.' She lifts the bedsheets and shows the Old Soro my foot. 'Nothing but puckered skin.'

The notion that the Old Soro would take the faintest interest in my anatomy convinces me that I truly am dreaming. Exhaustion claims me, and I close my eyes, allowing the dream to carry me away.

The sound of an argument wakes me. I don't immediately open my eyes, focusing instead on what's being said.

'I know my own daughter,' my mother says. She's having difficulty controlling her temper.

'Of course you'd think that.' This isn't the calm voice of the Old Soro from my earlier dream; this voice is stern and a little hostile. 'My responsibility is to my people.'

'She recognised me,' declares my mother.

'That's your proof?' scoffs the man. 'How far you've fallen in little more than a day.'

'What would you call it?'

'If she's quelled, the Rheman might have been shown a sketch. Helacth might have fed it all the answers you want to hear. You taught me never to let my heart guide me. Said I should always follow the logical trail to a problem's conclusion. We've barely started along that path, and you want me to release this . . . this thing? My faith in you grows slim. I don't dare let my men see you like this; your lack of judgement will reflect poorly on me.'

He's talking about me, calling me a creature. He thinks I'm ferrying one of the Rhemans. I test my ability to move, squirming unobtrusively, but quickly realise I'm restrained at my ankles and my wrists.

This is no dream. These bonds are real. Could this mean my mother is real too?

'Tell me then, what will convince you?' says my mother. I sense her walking over and kneeling at my side. I want to touch her, feel her substance, but I'm still feigning sleep. It seems important that I figure out if this new arrival is a threat to me. I can tell by his tone that he doesn't share the Old Soro's affection for me.

'Don't be blind. You see the girl's Stain—she's one of them. Taken and quelled,' he says, coming closer. 'I worry about you.'

'Name your test, Sha'yan, or stay the Hands. I'll cut her free myself.'

'Just look at her hands,' he says warily. 'They're covered in the Rheman's brand.'

My stomach twists. I don't want my mother to examine my hands. If she sees my Stain, she'll figure out what I've done. Better to be seen as a creature than for what I truly am.

I open my eyes and clench my fists.

'Look, she's awake,' says my mother, smiling down at me.

She is real. I am sure of it.

I look from her to Sha'yan. He's tall, with gleaming dark skin and the same regal features of the Old Soro, but in a much younger, handsome face. The son, I think.

'Ask her something only she would know. Think carefully on it,' Sha'yan says with unflinching resolve.

'Kyjta,' says my mother. 'This is important. Do you remember how much you wanted to watch the Charmores dance when you were younger? Do you recall how your stepfather forbade me from taking you, but we snuck away? What colour was the dress you wore that day?'

I do remember. Mostly I remember how my stepfather fumed at my mother when we returned, calling her irresponsible for exposing me to such a shameful tradition.

'Green,' I say. Easy to recall, since I only had one smart dress at that age.

'That's right,' she gushes, ushering Sha'yan forward to release me. Sha'yan doesn't look convinced.

'I'll do it, but if anything goes wrong, my well runs dry for you.' He leans down, eyeing me with suspicion, and cuts my bonds with a knife drawn from his belt.

The instant I'm free, my mother pulls me into her arms. I watch Sha'yan head to the tent flap. As he pushes through, he glances back, and his eyes are not friendly. When my mother pulls away to look at me, she attempts an explanation.

'Don't mind Sha'yan,' she says compassionately. 'He's finding his way in a world that robbed him of his position. It makes him very serious.'

'Is he—'

'My son? No.' She laughs. It's a sound I remember from a different time, back when happiness was a thing I recognised in others because I knew it myself. Now it feels strange and unfamiliar . . . especially coming from my mother.

'I'm done with all that. Two marriages and one daughter are quite sufficient. Speaking of which, if you're worried about your father, don't be. We have him. I was about to go and see him when you turned up, and I haven't left your side. We'll see him together once you're back on your feet.'

I nod, unable to think about my father because I already know her next question.

'What of your stepfather? How is he?'

I stare at the sand-covered rug, the irregular pattern shimmering like a distorted reflection.

I'm sure my words will give me away, but I can't ignore her question.

'Gone.' I breathe out. 'Taken.'

She shudders, then bundles me into her arms, my shoulders shaking as I weep.

The mere idea of revealing my involvement sickens me to the point of blacking out. I'm the one who stained him. Stay the Hands, may she never find out.

'I'm sorry, my child. I wanted so badly for things to be different for you. You were my conviction.'

I lean back so I can look at her. 'What are you saying?'

'All I ever wanted was for you to have the same freedom I had growing up. I never meant for any of this . . .' She waves her hands around as if the tent encompasses everything that didn't go to plan. 'It didn't start out this way. They were just small acts of rebellion. We'd shoot down a ghoragall or two, nothing serious. The farm lay so neatly in the flight path from Thormyth. It was almost too easy. Then your father started experimenting with the feather dust. Once he discovered how to make the smokers, there was no going back. We thought we could really make a difference. We arranged a meet with the Old Soro, and soon after that, we were smugglers.'

The tent flap opens, and a young boy steps in, carrying a tray laden with tea and cake.

'Can you eat?' my mother asks me, then takes the tray, thanking the boy.

'Tea may help my throat,' I say. Watching the boy exit the tent, I add, 'My elvakan, is he—'

'Stabled with the rest of the animals. Don't worry. He's being fed and looked after. There are many children in the village in the valley. They're taking good care of him.'

I can't imagine Bloodbane surrounded by a band of boisterous children, but I smile all the same.

'Thank you,' I say. 'So, you're an agent of the Old Soro?'

She stops fixing my tea and looks at me. 'It was foolish. If the Charmores hadn't been so reliant on your father's tinctures and potions, we would have forfeited our lives. That's precisely why I faked my abduction by ghoragall and came to live out here. I got word that the House of Vigilance had plans to arrest me. If they had me in a holding cell, with no access to nebuga azermi, the Tarrohar would have pilfered my memories, and I'd have given everyone away.'

'What about my father?'

'He wouldn't have anything to do with the rebellion after the fire. I had to do it all myself. Shooting the ghoragalls. Making the smokers, getting them to the Old Soro. Everything. He wouldn't risk losing you, and I guess I wouldn't risk losing hope,' she says, lowering her eyes, but not her smile, as she tops off the tea.

'No yakkat cream in the desert, I'm afraid.'

A sense of sick incredulity comes over me—could she know?

I'm struck by an idea, both terrible and lovely. 'Did you ever come back to the farm?' I ask her.

'Every now and again, just to check on you.' She smiles at me, her eyes bright.

Did she stand by and watch me administer the Stain, knowing my stepfather was innocent? No, she couldn't have. Was it my father? Did he tell her? Surely not. I watched him grieve for her; she wouldn't risk telling him her plans if the Tarrohar could so effortlessly pluck his thoughts from his mind. Just like me, he believed her dead. What then? Some cruel coincidence? The Hands toying with me again? It's not enough to know I've doomed an innocent man to a dead-life. They want my deed exposed.

My horror at being unmasked has its source, and it's not the Hands. It's my mother. Her existence should bring pure happiness, but it's a noose tightening around my throat. If she's alive, then I am the monster. My stepfather didn't kill her, but what have I done to him?

My mother passes me a steaming cup of tea. It rattles noisily on its plate as I lower it to the mattress.

'You're shaking,' she says, patting my arm. 'You should eat. Here, let me cut you some cake.'

She's sliding the cake onto my plate, and I know I must take the conversation in another direction or I'll fall apart.

'Can I ask you something?'

'Anything,' she says.

'You used to say something when I was young. I can't think why or how, but I remember it. Something like, "wishes are like curses" and I don't know the rest.'

She looks contemplative, even a little happy. 'It's a song I used to sing to you when you were small. How did it go? Let me think.' She purses her lips and starts to sing. Her voice is just as sweet as I remember, soft and lilting.

'A drop of dark, a flash of light
A circle's essence swirls with life
And comes to be, all things right

In the night when stars align
Our fates connected like the moons
We'll always be as one to me

I watched you burn like the brightest star in the sky
Follow your path, defying earth, wind, and fire

When I look upon the stars
Wishes are like curses, rough and cruel–'

Then, the tent flap opens, and the Old Soro's wrinkled face appears, looking even more lined than I recall.

'Nija, you'd better come. It's Sha'yan.'

My mother looks suddenly shaken.

'Don't go,' I say, grabbing for her.

'I must. We'll talk later.' She gets to her feet, squeezing my shoulder.

'But I have to tell you something,' I say, struggling to gain control of my weakened limbs. There was a reason I ventured into the Parched Lands. Meeting my mother has distracted me from it.

'I'm so sorry. It'll have to wait,' my mother says, and then she disappears through the flap.

I sit quietly, feeling winded. A vivid memory comes to me, like a draft let in to fill the space she vacated. In it, I'm a young girl coming home from picking jade fruit. My stepfather stands at the door; I sense he's waiting for me, and I know whatever news he has, it won't be good. When he takes my hand, the awkwardness of that sensation feels somehow worse than the announcement he delivers. Although I hear his explanation, the only thing I understand is that my mother won't be coming home.

23

KRANIK

I t's too bright to fully open my eyes, so I squint into the burning
heat. Shadowy apparitions assemble on the blazing sand. They're
too large to be the Grulo that materialised outside our barred
enclosure in the dead of night, and there are auditory cues that force
me to consider a more sinister alternative. Durable tapered surfaces
snick-snacking in an agitated rhythm and a low, droning rattle: the
satermijte's oscillating tumbler.

I panic and try to get to my feet. The closest blur is twenty paces
away. I get my legs up underneath me, but my torso and arms won't
budge. I'm pinned to the sand, I realise. Tied to a pole that's staked
in the ground. As I fight my bonds, I look around, trying to get a
sense of my surroundings. I'm not the only Rheman here. Ten of us
are in the same predicament. The row of giant satermijtes, crouching
before us, eyeing us patiently, look as though they're waiting for a
dinner invitation.

As the scene comes into full focus, I note, with surprise, how each
insect carries a rider. A Grulo sits astride each beast, wearing their
archetypal structured hoods jutting out over their brows like beaks,

with net veils to protect them from the glare. They are men for hire, but they seem to have found a home here, in the desert, though who's paying them is a mystery.

The insects wear harnesses, and a length of flexible core wood is attached to these. A smoking sack dangles from one end of the pole, and the smoke wafts beneath the insects' mandibles.

The satermijte in front of me rises when its rider pulls on two lengths of cord, hoisting the smoking sack away from its head. I freeze as it scuttles closer. The Grulo doesn't release the pole until the insect is almost upon me, but when he does, the insect instantly lowers itself to the sand. The satermijte is now so close that if I extended my leg, I could knock my foot against one of its pincers. I hate to think what those gnashing claws could do to Merrick's soft flesh.

I was groggy from whatever compound the Grulo used to knock us out before moving us, but the shock has fixed that. Whatever they dosed us with, it's strong enough to last half the day. It was dark when they came for us, and judging by the heat, it must be midday now. They have to know the party is ferrying Rhemans, or they wouldn't be so cautious moving us.

A man stands on an amber boulder, set back from the satermijtes gathered on the sand. He looks better kept than the Grulo, wearing long, sand-coloured robes and a matching shroud to cover his head. He surveys the scene with his arms crossed over his chest.

I turn to Tiberico, sitting staked to the ground to my right.

'Who's that?' I ask, nodding toward the stiff figure.

'Too young to be the Old Soro,' Tiberico says. 'Must be his son.'

There's movement on my left: Azaire finally stirring awake. I don't like that Azaire chose Kyjta's father to ferry him on the journey, but complaining won't achieve anything.

'What's this?' Azaire's voice shudders.

Pleased to demonstrate, the Grulo in front of me jerks the smoking sack back once more. The giant satermijte springs forward, looming over me with sudden ferocity. When the first pincer sails in, I kick out, connecting with the obsidian claw. There's a snap like a clap of thunder, and I quickly check for injury. Both legs remain intact. I turn my attention back to the satermijte, seeing Merrick's reflection in its glossy eyes. Whatever happens, I must protect this body. I check my surroundings, searching for something—I don't know what—there's nothing but sand and more sand.

Sand.

I dig my feet into loose granules, then fling the dirt into the satermijte's eyes. A scattering of dust rebounds, blurring my vision. By the time I can see again, the smoking sack is back in position, and the satermijte is docile once more. The rider has a good chuckle, commenting in the local dialect and pointing me out to his fellow riders.

I look to Tiberico and then Azaire, but neither has been attacked. They're both staring back at me, wide-eyed and horror-stricken.

There's a commotion building on the boulder, and it takes our attention. The boy—the Old Soro's son—is locked in debate with someone freshly arrived. By the look of them, I'd say it's a woman. The Old Soro's son has lost his calm demeanour, and his counterpart is in his face, shouting and waving her hands. I catch a few of her words: 'restraint' . . . 'opportunity' . . . 'risks.'

The woman breaks from the conversation and leaps from the rock. She's agile, but it's difficult to tell how old she is from a distance. I catch glimpses of her golden hair as she strides toward me, and there's something familiar about her, though I can't say what. As she gets closer, I realise I've seen her face before. Not her face, exactly, but a sketch of it. The day I searched Kyjta's house.

She stops in front of Azaire and stands as though waiting for something. A moment later, the Old Soro's son joins her, taking pains to appear unhurried.

'Sha'yan, this man can help us,' she says, pointing to Azaire, who looks pleased with the assessment and makes some agreeable noises.

'That man is infested,' responds Sha'yan, his expression dark. 'Can't you see how the presence of these Rheman parasites affects my Grulo?'

'What's your strategy?' she asks.

'To start, I'll rid Aurora Saura of these Rhemans,' replies Sha'yan. 'I'll show the Grulo there's nothing to fear. Rhemans bleed. They can be killed.'

'You need a plan, Sha'yan, not a display. You're not a Grulo, though you act like one. As Soro, you must protect all your people, even those who are quelled.'

Sha'yan isn't convinced. 'These Rhemans are a threat to our settlement. They could infect any one of us.'

'I agree, we must be mindful of the Rhemans, but consider what this means. I was at the encirclement where these Rhemans were promised a pardon if they travelled to Thormyth and negotiated an end to the ghoragall raids. As Soro, you can't stand in the way of that.'

'That encirclement was a farce. The Tarrohar only want rid of them.'

'This man'—she points at Azaire—'is the potion master. There's so much he could teach us. We need him alive.'

'And yet, here he sits. He failed to make smokers effective against the Tarrohar. I read your report.'

'But they work on Aurora Saurins. That recipe I've been using all these alignments, he's the one who mastered it. All I did was mimic him.'

'He can't cook for us if he's quelled.'

With a flick of one wrist, Sha'yan authorises another attack. The satermijte squatting in front of Azaire rises and scuttles forward.

The woman launches into a sprint, tracking and then overtaking the satermijte. Not bothering to slow, she slams into the potion master, her hands finding his.

'Transfer if you want to live,' she breathes, appealing to Azaire.

Azaire must do as she requests because there's a flare of recognition in the potion master's eyes.

'Halt!' cries Sha'yan. 'The creature has Nija. Seize her.'

In an instant, a Grulo is at Nija's back. The Grulo quickly loops a moon blade around her neck and pushes a star hammer against her spine, securing her in place.

'It's as I feared,' says Sha'yan, addressing his Grulo. 'The creatures have infected one of us. We can't afford to keep them as prisoners. We must kill them all.'

24

KYJTA

struggle to my feet, knowing I must warn my mother. My father wanted me to know that the Vigilance Men planned to track him and the Rhemans into the desert, but whether to kill them, or discover who they believed my father was working with, I don't know. The Tarrohar might even be using this mission to draw out the person they believed was imitating my father's work.

That person can only be my mother. She'd know all of his recipes; she said as much herself . . . and I might have led them to her in my feverish state. I would have worked it out earlier if I hadn't been unconscious, and now, my warning might come too late. I can't let this happen, especially after the terrible things I've done. I must get this right.

Finding my balance, I teeter forward. My injured foot is weak and sensitive, but it takes my weight.

My bigger problem is my clothes. My skin will blister all over if I head outdoors in the thin slip I'm wearing. I make it to the tent flap and peer out. If I call her name, maybe my urgent yells will bring her back.

I don't see her, but two of the Old Soro's personal guards are stationed on either side of the tent flap.

'Fair favour,' I say. 'Did you see which way my mother went?'

'Back inside,' bellows the larger of the two—the turquoise-eyed behemoth who poured water into my mouth earlier.

'You don't understand. I must warn her,' I explain. 'The Vigilance Men are coming. They're tracking the Rhemans.'

'You have desert fever, girl. Go lie in your bed.' The turquoise-eyed guard closes the flap in my face. I hear him mutter something, but it's some slang of the Soro's guards, which is meaningless to me.

Stonewalled, I turn back and face the tent. I have a new plan: find anything that can help me escape. There's a sizeable darkwood chest under one of the supporting beams, a tall mirror, a desk, some carpets—nothing useful. First, I dig through the chest and find a long desert robe, which I pull on over my slip. I had hoped to find something plain to help me blend in, but this one, with its bejewelled embroidery and patterned edgings, will have to do. I lift my satermijte wings from the bed, which someone must have placed nearby to protect me. Whoever it was has sewn a cord through the fibrous wedge that kept them connected to their previous owner. I tie them at my neck like a cape. Then I don my father's wide-brimmed hat and force it into a peak at the front, in imitation of the Grulo, and cover it with some loose netting from the bottom of the chest. It's a getup that supports the desert fever theory if I must explain myself.

What I need is a weapon, or at least something sharp I can use to cut a hole in the side of the tent so I can slip away. Searching the desk, I find a secret drawer hidden beneath the legitimate one. It was common sense to check for it, knowing my own home as I did, with its myriad hiding holes. Yet another clue about my parents' secret vocation I somehow managed to miss.

I find a slim silver wand inside the secret drawer. It's far too smooth to be Aurora Saurin made. I expect it's Rheman. I weigh it in my hand.

I've never seen anything like it; it might be just the weapon I'm searching for. I point it at the side of the tent and place a finger over the dark oval on one side. A beam of light sails out one end and hits the side of the tent, but nothing happens. I remove my finger from the pad and slip the thing into my pocket. I can work out how to use it later; right now, I must focus on escape.

I pick up my cup of tea, cool by now, and drink it down, then continue my search. Inside another drawer, I find a small black pouch. I check it for my father's potion mark but find none. When I loosen its maw, I don't have to peer inside to guess the contents; the acrid stench gives the utility away. I tie the bag off quickly, forcing myself not to breathe until I've stepped away from the lingering dust, but I'm already woozy.

A bag of sleeping salts . . . another of my father's recipes. Not a weapon, but not a bad find either. I secure the pouch around my wrist, and I notice a large brooch pinned to my fancy desert robe. The ensemble must be ceremonial; no one would wear this much decoration on a regular day.

I unclip the brooch and examine the pin. Long and sharp. Exactly what I need. I walk to the far side of the tent, stick the slender needle into the coarse material, and jerk it downward. The gash that forms takes me shoulder to knee. I squeeze through and look around. I'm barefoot, and the sand is hot but bearable, given that it's late afternoon. With my back to the tent, I peer toward the wider encampment, trying to intuit my mother's location. I don't know where I'm headed, and I'm not exactly inconspicuous. Hearing voices, I duck behind a boulder to let a pair of Grulo pass. The men grumble as they walk, and I only catch the tail end of their conversation.

'Don't know why we're bothering with feeding them,' says one. He's carrying a large tray laden with an assortment of cracked bowls.

'Waste of energy, if you ask me,' says the other, hefting a pail of water in each hand.

'And food.'

The bowls are still steaming. The Grulo are making a delivery. If I follow the Grulo, they could lead me to Kranik. My father too, though he'll be quelled. The prospect of finding my mother seems less overwhelming with Kranik at my side. But, if Sha'yan had me in shackles, convinced I was quelled, he won't be treating the Rhemans any better.

Quietly as I can, I trail the Grulo, keeping to the rocks, but when we leave the collection of boulders that must shield the Old Soro's tent from the worst of the wind, the plain opens up, and there's nowhere to hide. I spy a great outcropping of rock in the distance, and besides that, only dunes.

Given my bare feet and the soundless sand, I take my chances and follow the men. They're absorbed in conversation, and I keep ten paces behind them, listening for any lull in their exchange. When we get close enough to the large rock formation, I see two Grulo standing guard in front of a grill that blocks an opening into the cavern. I step in behind the man with the tray and hope I haven't been spotted.

When the Grulo stop, I pull up just behind them while doing my best to look like I'm supposed to be there. One of the guards leans to the side to look at me.

'Is it the alignment tonight, Soro? I thought that was—' says the guard beside the gate.

The tray bearer and the water carrier turn around, looking like the Hands just reached down from the sky and dropped me onto the sand. I take a deep breath and throw a pinch of sleeping salts into their faces. Both men fumble the items they're carrying. The tray topples, sending the bowls crashing to the sand. The bucket pitches, wetting the guard's feet. Planning to repeat the manoeuvre, I step forward just as one of the guards figures it out.

'You're not the Old Soro,' he says, drawing his moon blade.

He lunges for me, and I take a step back, standing on my robe and tumbling backwards. My father's hat falls from my head. The guard is on me instantly, his blade at my throat. I have my hands up to protect my face and another pinch of sleeping salts between my fingers. I take a breath, then let it go in front of his face. A moment later, he's asleep on my chest. I push him off and try to get to my feet. It's a struggle. There's too much material to manoeuvre properly. Smart enough not to get too close, the remaining guard stands back, holding his star hammer and moon blade.

'I didn't come here to fight,' I say. 'I'm just looking for my father.'

'Who are you?' he demands groggily. He must have gotten a good whiff of the salts when I threw them at the food bearers. His expression is weak, but he's fighting the salts, trying to stay on his feet. He staggers where he stands, and I think he might topple, but he quickly regains his footing and shakes himself awake. Then, an arm shoots from the grill behind him and claps around his neck. He panics, closes his eyes, and goes limp. When the arm releases him, he slumps to the ground.

'Kranik!' I yell. I can't see into the darkness beyond the grate.

With a suddenness that almost knocks me backwards, a face appears at the bars, but it's not the face I'm expecting. Not Merrick's face. The man has wild eyes and wilder hair. Dark strands hang in a scraggly mess about his pockmarked face, and there's a vicious scar beneath one eye.

'Kranik's gone, pretty. Sure you're not looking for me?' he snarls.

Instinctively, my hands go to my throat, checking my satermijte wings are in place—there's nothing my wings can do to help me here, but knowing they're there makes me feel safe. I take a step back, thinking I've made a bad mistake. I might have come to trust Kranik, but the same is not true for all Rhemans.

Then another face appears. 'Get back, Rhytheus. You'll only scare her.'

'Kyjta—it's me, Lakhan. We met on the farm.'

I don't recognise the face, but I remember the name—Kranik's friend who visited Sion Chaffrot's the night I met Kranik. He's being ferried by a tall, well-built man with dust-white hair.

'Where's Kranik?' I ask. 'And my father? Are they with you?'

'They were taken in the night,' Lakhan replies.

Taken? I recall my mother's shaken expression. And her insistence on leaving me when we'd only just been reunited. Sha'yan was up to something.

'They're in trouble,' I say.

'Yes,' says Rhytheus, eerily enthusiastic. 'Deep trouble. Let us out. We'll help you.'

'I don't know—' I start, thinking a better plan might be just to walk away.

'They'll be killed if we don't get to them,' Lakhan says.

As I trek back through the sand, I show my palms to the Rhemans. 'I don't have a key.'

'Over there,' says Rhytheus, his face pushing greedily through a square of core wood. Following his animated gaze, I spot the star hammer in the sand beside a snoring guard. 'That key's good enough for me.'

I don't like the eager glint in the captain's eyes. Kranik can't be the only Rheman to regret the Body Trust, but these Rhemans may only have agreed to confront their master to secure enough of our bodies for themselves. With a shake of my head, I back away.

25

KRANIK

'Stop!' a female voice yells from a distance.

I'm deflecting another attack. One of the pincers snaps shut, just missing removing Merrick's foot at the ankle. My trick of throwing sand in the satermijte's eyes won't keep me alive much longer. It's toying with me now, but it'll want to eat at some point.

'The Tarrohar know you're here! The Vigilance Men are coming!'

That voice again—distracted as I am, it's familiar.

The Grulo rider releases the pole, and the sack drops back into place. With the smoke wafting over it, the satermijte grows instantly docile and settles back on the sand. I lean out as far as my bonds allow, unable to trust the mirage sprinting across the sand. Kyjta, wearing an elaborate robe and a shimmering cape flowing behind her. She's without a hat, her Stain glittering impossibly bright in the slanting daylight blazing off the horizon as she races toward Sha'yan.

Two of the Old Soro's guards step forward, blocking her approach.

'Sha'yan,' she says, breathless. 'Please listen to me. The Vigilance Men are coming. The Tarrohar sent them after the Rhemans, knowing you'd act. They're using my father to draw you out. They believe he's still working for the Old Soro.'

'If the Rhemans have drawn our enemy to us, we will fight!' Sha'yan clangs his moon blade against his star hammer. The Grulo shout their support, raising their hammers in the air.

'Thousands will come,' reasons Kyjta. 'It'll be a massacre.'

'Sojour belongs to our people. My men are warriors—we will fight and we will win.'

The Grulo throw up another cheer.

Kyjta looks around, spotting her mother. Her fierce expression wavers as she takes in the Grulo with his moon blade looped around her mother's neck and the star hammer wedged against her back.

'What are you doing?' she demands.

'Nija is infested,' Sha'yan says, his tone accusatory.

'What are you talking about?'

'She touched one of the parasites, and now she's one of them.'

Kyjta scans the stakes, and the Rhemans tied to them, until her eyes find mine. Her body braces for motion, and I know she's headed my way. It's as though I can see her moving before she's begun.

Then her father calls her name, and the tension shatters. Her posture, rigid a moment ago, slackens, as though some invisible string has snapped. Relief is etched into her face, but she hesitates—she can't be sure he isn't ferrying a Rheman.

'It's me,' the potion master says, sensing her doubt. He takes a shaky breath. 'Kyjta, your mother. She's alive.'

When Kyjta looks back at her mother, fresh misery fills her eyes. Kyjta's mother is unreachable with Azaire riding her. Kyjta forces her attention back to her father, launching into a fast walk. Two Grulo cut her off.

'No touching,' commands Sha'yan. 'Can't be sure he's not infested.'

'And my mother?' Kyjta says, pointing to Nija, trapped between sword and hammer. 'Will you be feeding her to the satermijtes too?'

'She will be kept under guard until we figure something out.' Sha'yan motions to one of the Grulo, who grabs hold of Kyjta's wrist and jerks her toward the camp.

I strain against the noose vine, not caring that my abrasive movements shave flesh off Merrick's arms. All my struggling yields nothing, though—the vine is wound around my arms and torso too many times. I don't have enough momentum to get free.

Sha'yan raises a hand, flicks his wrist, and then yells, 'Let the beasts feast. Nija and the girl come with me.'

'No!' screams Kyjta, her attention snapping back to the stakes. Her panicked eyes dart between her father and me. The Grulo pull on their sticks, and the smoking sacks rise. The groggy satermijtes lurch on the spot, unsure whether to laze on the sand or fight.

Kyjta battles the Grulo as he drags her away.

'Please,' she cries. 'We must work together. War is coming!'

But Sha'yan is already walking away.

When he pulls up, it's not her words that stop him; it's the thirteen Rhemans stepping around the boulders to surround him.

The satermijtes turn their glittering eyes on the new arrivals. With a real fight taking shape, the insects' killer instinct is back. They click their pincers excitedly, limbs twitching with impatience. I hope Lakhan and Rhytheus know what they're doing.

Sha'yan raises his crescent blade. 'Attack!' he yells.

The satermijtes surge forward, whipping up sand in their wake. Their powerful pincers and agility on the sand make them an impossible adversary, especially given the small show of Rheman-held weapons. Rhytheus and Fiderly have star hammers and Allora a blade, but Lakhan's hands are empty. He won't win a fistfight against one of the armoured limbs.

The basin comes to life when the insects charge my travelling companions. A sandstorm rises as the two forces collide, and the raging particles obscure my view. I catch glimpses of pincers lancing out of the dust, attacking from every angle, but there's nothing I can do. A gleaming claw grabs Fiderly at the waist, shaking him violently from side to side. Fiderly hacks at the pincer while Rhytheus attempts a rescue, plunging a star hammer into an exposed joint, but this only provokes the satermijte. I lose track of the pair, spotting Lakhan under heavy attack. Allora sees the fray, leaping from the rocks to take down one of the Grulo riders.

Then, the battle scene is suddenly obscured, and Kyjta stands in its place. I look into her lilac eyes, startled by the complete contrast to war.

'Kranik?' she demands. 'How do I know it's you?'

'For starters, I'm the only Rheman who's mad at you for breaking this up. You're supposed to be at your father's shack.'

While the worry doesn't leave her face, the distrustful glare fades. She circles me to cut away my bonds. Despite the roaring fray surrounding us, I feel absurdly assured.

I get to my feet as soon as the noose vine falls away. Merrick's arms and legs are torn and bleeding, but there's no time to address that. Kyjta runs to free her father, and I almost follow her before I think to check on Tiberico. It's good I do because Tiberico's host is in far worse shape than Merrick. One of the old man's arms has been ripped open, exposing the white bone beneath. I untie him and help him to his feet.

'Kranik!' Kyjta yelps, her voice rent thin with pain. Wordlessly, Tiberico and I race to her aid. She's with the potion master, who lies slumped against his pole. His bonds are loose, but he can barely keep upright as blood soaks through his robe.

'Father, can you hear me?' Kyjta grasps his arms and gently shakes him, but he's staring off into the distance, barely breathing. There's a hole in the side of his robe, and the raw flesh beneath it pulses blood. I place my hands over the wound to stem the bleeding, but he's already lost too much.

Kyjta looks on, utterly lost, and I can do nothing to help her. I can do nothing but soak up her father's blood, dousing my sleeves and bathing my hands in it—knowing the task is futile, but unwilling to forego the act.

Her eyes shimmer as she kneels before her father, ready to whisper a few final words; preparing to say goodbye. She passes one hand across his cheek and the other slips into his bloody hand.

'I thought I'd lost you,' her father whispers. 'It's a miracle.'

With a sudden gust of shifting material, Kyjta is on her feet, frantically searching her robe. A moment later, her hand emerges, holding a slim wand.

'Is this one of those—' she stammers. 'I think it healed my foot. The Old Soro called it a miracle.'

It's the traveller's restoration equipment I used to heal Sion Chaffrot's broken feet. A guard relieved me of it during my first night of captivity. She hands it to Tiberico, almost fumbling the pass. Even with one arm hanging useless at his side, Tiberico quickly initiates the device. I pull back to give him access to the wound. My hands are slick with blood, and I wipe them on my trousers. The restoration wand should do the work of sealing the wound. At least he won't lose any more blood.

With the potion master in Tiberico's expert hands, I have the freedom to check on my friends. I squint into the dust storm but can see nothing. Then, Sha'yan is thundering out of the cloud, charging toward us on the back of a giant satermijte. There's no time to react; he's almost upon us. The most I can do is tuck Kyjta behind me and raise my arms to defend against the incoming pincers.

With my arms flung high, my body shielding Kyjta's, I wait, but the attack never comes. I expect to lose limbs, but I'm still standing as the clang of metal falls away and is replaced by shrieks of pain. I lower my arms onto a new vista. The Grulo have fallen from their saddles and are writhing on the ground, screaming.

Terror grips me as I turn back to Kyjta. The Mind Pain incapacitates, but it can just as easily kill.

'Kyjta!' She's convulsing on the sand, her arms flung protectively around her head, her eyes squeezed tightly shut. I drop to my knees beside her. She's chanting something under her breath, but I can't hear what it is. I lean in, listening hard.

'Kill me. Kill me. Kill me.'

Seeing her pain is like taking an iron bar to the back of the legs. I fall to my knees beside her, then lift her into my arms and rock her back and forth. 'It will pass. It will pass,' I chant in response to her death pleas, my voice cracking over every word. I tear my gaze from her to seek guidance from Tiberico. 'It's the Tarrohar,' I say, dread weighing down my words.

If the Tarrohar are here, there will be no survivors, or none that aren't ferrying Rhemans. If I want Kyjta to live, I only need to transfer. And leave Merrick to die.

I struggle with the awful decision.

'If they've come, they mean to finish this,' Tiberico says, shaking me from my stupor.

'What should I do?'

Foam is gathering at the corners of Kyjta's mouth now, and the whites of her eyes are visible through slatted lids. Her body is weakening, losing its ability to function.

'If I run with her, maybe—' I grasp at an alternative. Anything.

'There's no telling at what distance the Tarrohar have set their parameters, and her mind will give out before long. The best you might hope to do is find the Vigilance Men—there might be a pocket of protection around them.'

I stand with Kyjta curled into my chest. I must figure out which way to run, so I scan the sands. Not toward the camp; the Tarrohar will be targeting the Grulo occupying that space. Somewhere to the north, where the Vigilance Men stand in wait. They'll only attack after the Tarrohar have made everyone mindless with pain. They'll be tasked to slaughter rather than fight.

My eyes fall to the potion master. I don't want to leave him, but what choice do I have? If I try to carry them together, I'll lose both of them. Kyjta's father looks better than I expected. The gash at his side is no longer oozing blood, but that's not it. It's how he's sitting, cupping his head in his hands. He doesn't look affected by the Mind Pain. At least not as severely as everyone else. When he lifts his head there's a strange smile on his rumpled face.

'Is it the traveller's restoration equipment? Does it provide some sort of immunity?' I ask Tiberico, giddy at the prospect of muting Kyjta's pain.

'Unlikely,' Tiberico says. 'I suspect it's something the Hok cooked up himself.'

I kneel at the potion master's side. He's fiddling with the hem of his robe. His expression becomes sanguine as he extracts a black velvet pouch. After rummaging inside it with two fingers, he removes a powder-black pill.

'They're longer lasting than I thought,' he says as he pushes the tablet between his daughter's lips.

'What does it do?' I ask, struggling to get my mouth around the words.

'Fortification of the mind . . . a mental barrier,' he says, looking pleased. 'My life's work.'

I try to help Kyjta swallow the pill, and when I look up, the Hok is pulling on Sha'yan's jaw, about to drop one of the pills into his mouth. The Young Soro lies face-up beside the Hok, unconscious. He must have taken a hit to the head when he came off the satermijte.

'How many of those do you have?' I search Kyjta's face for the slightest sign of recovery.

The Hok peers inside the pouch. 'That's it. All done.'

As the boy Soro swallows, Kyjta stirs, her terrible expression of tight-jawed anguish loosening.

'Kyjta,' I say. 'Can you hear me?'

She doesn't respond, but I'm sure the colour in her cheeks is rising.

'You're going to be all right,' I whisper, pulling her against my chest.

After some time, her lips part, and she wheezes my name.

'Don't speak,' I tell her, taking the pouch of water Tiberico passes me. It was tied to Sha'yan's belt before Tiberico liberated it. I pop the cap and pour the water into her mouth. Her chapped lips close, and she swallows as her eyes flutter open. I stare into their lilac luminescence, and she stares back. The desert recedes, and for the briefest moment, there's only us. Then, Sha'yan sits up, appalled to find himself on the ground. He scans our faces.

'What's this?' Sha'yan asks, but the cries of his men distract him. He looks out over what was recently a battlefield and sees his unruly Grulo writhing in agony on the sand.

Sha'yan gets to his feet. 'We're being attacked.'

Rhytheus crosses the sand, carrying Fiderly. Tiberico beckons to them, keen to work on Fiderly's wounds. Fiderly is caked in dried blood, and maroon flakes scatter with the sand.

After setting Fiderly down, Rhytheus stands. The Young Soro looks at him and raises his hammer, but the captain only regards him blankly.

'Is it the Tarrohar, like the girl said?' says the Young Soro, letting his hammer fall.

Rhytheus walks up. An insect leg hangs limply from the right side of his tunic. The captain takes a moment to tease it free, then tosses it at the Young Soro's feet.

'They'll slaughter them all. It's a terrible waste of good bodies.'

'My father . . .' The Young Soro's expression tightens in pain. Then, features hardening, he continues, 'the Old Soro is in the camp!'

Allora steps in beside Lakhan, wiping a messy blade across the front of her robes. Sema and Noon step in behind Allora, just before Leviatha and Wixnor come to the captain's side.

The Young Soro regards each of us in turn. 'We must kill the Tarrohar,' he says. 'We cannot allow this atrocity to take hold.'

At first, no one responds. Most regard the captain, waiting on his command.

'I can't do it alone,' says Sha'yan, his roaming eyes assessing each of us, but ultimately, settling on the captain.

Rhytheus picks at his teeth with a stray piece of insect bristle. Sha'yan's appeal seems to dry on his lips, and for a while, all we hear is the agonised screams of the Grulo.

'If it's bodies you want, there'll be nothing left. They'll annihilate everyone in that camp. It's not just the Grulo—further down the hill, there's a second escapement filled with the Stained and their families. People rescued from Merrocha. Women and children. You can't just leave them to die,' Sha'yan pleads.

The captain raises a bushy eyebrow, unmoved.

'Your hosts have spilt much blood here today. I can promise you fresh bodies if you'll only help me. We will be in your debt.'

This last comment finally rouses something in Rhytheus. He raises his star hammer in the air and shouts, 'What are we waiting for? On with it.'

We break for the encampment with Kyjta and me at the rear. Kyjta's mother is gone. The Grulo led her away before the fighting started, but there's no telling how far she got. At least she's been spared the mind pain, since she's ferrying Azaire. There's a good chance she's safe. Still, we search the sands as we walk, looking for any sign of her.

'You meant it that day after the beach, when you said we could go after Calipsie,' says Kyjta. 'I didn't know it at the time. I thought you were just talking.'

'I still mean to go after her,' I say. 'That day on the beach was the best and the worst of my life. Finding Calipsie is . . . it's something I need to do.'

She reaches for me, taking hold of my hand. I can't feel it, not physically, but the sensation of closeness is there; both beautiful and inadequate.

When we crest the ridge of the tallest dune, the full macabre tableau spreads out before us. There are Grulo everywhere. Most are senseless, curled up on the ground and weeping. Some lie dead, having already succumbed to the pain. The Tarrohar's torturous intrusions must have ceased; Vigilance Men storm the encampment. They pull the Grulo from tents, slit their throats, and heap their bodies on the sand. It'll be a miracle if any of the Grulo survive.

The light is low, the sun dipping below the horizon. We keep to the ridge of the dunes and try to stay hidden. We find the wagons that transported the Vigilance Men, but they're empty, and there's no sign of the Tarrohar. We search the tents, looking for anything heavily guarded. The Tarrohar aren't fighters; their only weapon is the Mind Pain. If we kill them, we can remove the Vigilance Men's motivation for war. We progress through the encampment without drawing attention to ourselves; there's enough commotion to distract from the footfalls of our small army. We cluster behind a tent to peer into a clearing where we spot a gathering of Vigilance Men. The vast space is littered with chairs and tables flung out of position or collapsed into piles of splintered wood. There's a pit at the centre, overflowing with ash. A broad spit crosses the pit; toward this, we see the Old Soro being drawn behind two Vigilance Men. Sha'yan releases a garbled cry. His father hangs limply, his legs and feet trailing in the sand. When the men reach the pit, they fling the Old Soro into the ash, which swallows him in a puff of opal dust.

Sha'yan tries to charge forward, but we hold him back.

'You can't help him now,' I tell him, but he thrashes in my arms, unable to contain his grief.

'You traitors!' Sha'yan yells. 'Stay the Hands, I'll see you pay for this.'

Twenty Vigilance Men turn to look at us.

'It's the boy Soro!' shouts the closest Vigilance Man.

Instantly, the group are on the move, charging us.

I shove Sha'yan into Lakhan's arms.

'Save the Soro,' I shout to be heard. 'Kyjta! Go with Lakhan.'

Lakhan grips the Young Soro by the arms. He knows as well as I do that the people will need a new leader if we somehow manage to rid them of the Tarrohar. Without further encouragement, Lakhan bundles the Young Soro away. I watch for a moment, ensuring that Kyjta and her father get out of sight.

Then, those of us who remain turn to face our attackers.

26

KYJTA

akhan's grip is firm on my arm, and he holds Sha'yan in the other
hand. He's dragging us through the tents as quickly as possible,
but we're not making it easy for him—you'd think he meant to
kill us. Sha'yan is fighting him every step of the way. I look over my
shoulder, trying to check on Kranik and the others, but the tents
completely block my view.

My father staggers at my side, continually checking over his shoulder. He's weak, with a brittle, clenched-jawed expression. I don't know
if it's the loss of blood or losing my mother again, but he's struggling. I
must get him somewhere safe where he can try to recover.

I tell myself that my mother ferrying Azaire is a good thing. She
wouldn't have fallen victim to the Mind Pain. The Grulo escorting
her will have suffered like the others, and Azaire could have walked
free. But where is she? Where would Azaire have taken her?

We make it to the edge of the encampment without being spotted. As we're about to dash across the plain, I notice the wing of a red
dress disappearing into a tent.

'Charmores,' I whisper, my hand clenching around Lakhan's arm,
forcing him to a standstill. 'They'll lead us to the Tarrohar.'

'Where?' he asks, his grip loosening.

'That tent over there.' I point, but the slip of dress is already gone.

Lakhan stands quietly for a moment, thinking. If we can kill the Tarrohar, we can end this, which might save his friends, but he is committed to getting us safely away. I'm not sure he can be trusted to make the right decision. We can't lose an opportunity like this. My mother is out there. If we don't act now, it might mean her life. I'm sure my father would agree, but he's too feeble now to make a stand. I must make the choice for all of us.

I twist in Lakhan's grip, pulling my arm free. Then, I'm on the move, and the others have no choice but to follow. As I run, I pull the brooch from my robes. The long pin will make a decent enough weapon against the spongy flesh of at least one of the Tarrohar. They're powerless without the Mind Pain. I only hope Lakhan can handle the rest.

We're almost at the tent's entrance when seven Vigilance Men surround us.

Pulling up with my heart somewhere in my throat, I scan their faces. One among them stands out. I've only met him twice, but Brezan made an impression. There's a shiny patch of skin covering most of his neck. I'm sure his burns were tended by Rheman technology, but he'll always have a memento.

Lakhan lets go of my wrist; I want to run, but my father won't make it two steps before collapsing. I can't leave him here to face Brezan. My eyes dart around the circle of Vigilance Men, checking for the weakest among them, but Brezan's steely gaze never lifts, pinning me like a specimen to a board. Of all of us, my father keeps his head, releasing something noxious from his fist. A black mist fans away from us, curling toward the Vigilance Men, making them cough and splutter and back away. As the darkness descends, Brezan orders his men to cover their faces with a cloth.

I'm lost, not knowing which way to travel. I reach out for my father, Lakhan . . . but they're nowhere. Panic takes me, and my breath comes quickly. Black powder rides in on a tidal wave, choking me. I attempt to avoid a fit of coughing, spiralling away from the spot where I last saw my father. I don't want to give away his location. I pull my robes over my mouth to filter out the worst of the soot. I stumble around in the darkness, trying to get a sense of where I am from the things I make out in the sand. A stone, a shoe; I tread on a hand, and a scream lurches free. A moment later, I'm jerked backwards by my hair. Someone's at my shoulder, their heavy breath against my ear. Even with the soot clogging my mouth and nose, I can smell the sweetness on his breath.

Brezan.

He searches my pockets and comes up with my fire stick.

'Let's see your tricks get you out of this one,' he says, pushing me ahead of him. My feet grind into the sand. As much as I fight him, pretty soon, we're free of the mist, and he's dragging me toward the pit. When we reach the edge, I look down and see the Old Soro—just the jut of his brow and a single eye; the rest is below the ash. He looks so peaceful, lying there, as though he's only drifted off to sleep.

'Bring me firewood,' shouts Brezan to a clutch of Vigilance Men passing a canteen around. 'I have a debt to repay.'

I search the gatherings of Vigilance Men, trying to find Kranik and the others. There are bodies everywhere: some Grulo, others the Old Soro's guard. No Rhemans that I can see, and not a single Vigilance Man on the ground. Most of the dead still have their weapons sheathed.

From behind me, Brezan flips the switch on the fire stick and holds the open flame so close to my face that I can smell my eyelashes singeing.

'Didn't think I'd forget about you, did you? That's one good scar you gave me, and I make it my business never to owe nobody.'

The Vigilance Men return carrying tent poles and furnishings. They stack them on top of the Old Soro's limp body. I search the corpses for weapons, but there are so many Vigilance Men that I doubt one weapon would make much difference.

Brezan releases one of my wrists to set a tent flap on fire. We stand, watching the flames catch. Pretty soon, the blaze is building, licking at the furniture scraps.

'It began with fire, and it ends with fire.' Holding me by one arm, Brezan pulls me around to look at him. 'I made you what you are, and you made me this.' He points at the shiny patch of skin that mars his jawline and one side of his neck.

'You were just a bad day,' I tell him.

He scoffs, his dark eyes flashing manic in the firelight. 'I shaped your entire future with a single act. Your father knows it. He'll never tell you, just like he never told you about your mother. He doesn't think you can handle it.'

'You know nothing about my family.'

The longer I keep him talking, the better my chances of figuring out an escape. Brezan hates my father; that much is clear. He blames the potion master for every punishment inflicted on him by the Tarrohar, but what's his quarrel with me? Sure, I burned his face, but only after he chased me down and tried to slit my throat.

'Your father let you think he set that blaze that killed old Cromenk's wife and daughter,' sneers Brezan. 'All these alignments, you've probably been wondering if it was an accident like he claimed. You never thought to wonder if it was him at all.'

Brezan's eyes glint wickedly, reflecting the growing flames.

'What are you saying?' My voice cracks.

He responds like a child airing a malicious secret. 'Your parents were spies. They deserved what they got. I watched my father suffer the Mind Pain too many times, when he refused to implicate your father. He used to claim they were friends. But a good man doesn't stand by and allow his friend to be punished because he won't snitch. The Hok needed a lesson.'

I stare hard into his face.

'You should thank me. The Tarrohar would've encircled both your parents, eventually. You'd have been orphaned if I hadn't done what I did.'

The past ten alignments crash over me with a weight so vast that my knees almost buckle. My father encircled and banished into the mountains. My mother forced to marry a man she didn't love. My stepfather mourning his dead family, full of anger and recrimination. His grief made it so easy for me to believe he'd killed my mother.

Brezan's smile broadens, the firelight glinting off the pale enamel of his immaculate teeth. The curl of his lips detonates something within me, and I launch at him, bringing my knee hard into his groin. He crumbles and I grab a pole from the fire. The tent material looped over its end blazes brightly against the night.

'Get back,' I say, jabbing the end at him.

Brezan unsheathes his illing sword and takes up a fighting stance. 'You've never lost your fight,' he says, his shiny flesh shimmering like my Stain.

All around us, Vigilance Men cheer like we're the entertainment.

I'm no sword fighter, but I know how to keep animals at bay with fire. I jab the torch at him, trying to catch his cloak, since the previous one already proved itself flammable. He darts in with the sword but is unwilling to get too close. Noting his weak spot, I charge, swiping at him with the flames. In my urgency, the piece of tent draped precariously over the end of the tent pole flies off and lands in a flaming puddle on the ground.

With a yowl of frustration, I raise the bar like a bat.

A harsh voice sounds behind me. 'Enough.'

Brezan tenses, fractionally lowering his sword as the Zhu strides over. He turns to face his father.

'She must pay, father.' Brezan touches his neck with the palm of one hand.

'That will have to wait,' says the Zhu. 'We need her alive and in good shape. She's stained.'

Brezan must understand because a calm satisfaction settles across his features and he tilts his head in agreement. I should have killed Brezan with the crossbow when I had the chance. I won't make the same mistake if I get another opportunity.

'Take her to the tent,' says the Zhu.

Four Vigilance Men fall in around me; two take hold of my arms, and another relieves me of the smoking tent pole. The flaming tent flap is snuffed out by the heavy boot of a Vigilance Man.

I walk in silence, head hanging low. If Brezan was willing to give up on a revenge burning, then whatever the Zhu has in store for me must be worse, and I can't help running through imagined scenarios.

The Vigilance Men pull up in front of a large tent. Hundreds of the Zhu's men are gathered outside. Whatever's going on inside, it's closely guarded. The men who flank me take me through the tent flaps, and the first thing I see is my father. Standing in front of a table littered with potion-making paraphernalia, he looks weak but stable. He glances up as I'm shoved into a seat, and our eyes meet. I try to read his expression: relief, remorse, definitely fear. One of the Vigilance Men binds me to the chair with a length of coarse rope.

The Zhu steps between us before I can ask after Kranik. He wears twin blades, topped with gleaming ovals of brilliant blue.

'You have your ingredients. You have your daughter. Now give me what I want,' commands the Zhu. 'Every day you toil is another day I must feed my men.'

My father swallows like a man with a dagger at his throat.

'Iyko, I need time,' pleads my father, using the Zhu's childhood name. They *were* friends once, that much I know from my father's fireside retellings of a long-lost world. A wistful place, filled with night markets and street dances, where the two of them would streak between hiding spots, giggling while eluding the adults.

The Zhu turns away, his jaw tight. Pain flickers across his face, like shadows thrown by flame. Then he's gone, striding past me without a glance.

'What does he want?' I whisper as I catalogue the ingredients set out neatly on the knotted wooden bench that serves as a table.

'The impossible,' says my father, lowering his head to his work.

I can already see that the stacks of herbs, roots, and stalks are a pretty good match for the recipe in my head. He's making smokers. Nothing impossible about that, for my father at least. I want to push him to explain, but more important things are on my mind.

'What happened to the others?' I ask quietly.

'The Young Soro and that Rheman? I lost them in the black mist.' His hands never stop moving, stripping leaves, measuring powders, and folding these careful doses into a steaming concoction.

I watch him work. There's so much I want to ask him, but not here, with the Vigilance Men standing around, listening as we speak.

I'm still recovering from my fever, and the day's exertion, coupled with the heat, makes me drowsy. I doze in my seat until I notice that our guards have drifted outside. I swivel in my bonds to check their proximity. When the tent flap whips in the wind, I catch a glimpse of a red dress. The Vigilance Men must have moved outside to flirt with one of the Charmores who arrived along with the Tarrohar.

I'm finally free to ask my father why he lied to me. This could be my only chance, but I might not get the answer I want.

'Can I ask you something?'

'Certainly,' he says, distracted with the task of popping kho-kho berries and milking their black juice.

'Did you know Cromenk told the House of Vigilance that mother was taken by the ghoragall?'

The berry tumbles from my father's hand, trailing dark juice across the workbench. I track its progress, unwilling to look my father in the eye.

'I knew,' he says, the tempo of his voice increasing, even as he steadies himself against the bench. 'I just never believed it. Your mother wasn't stained, and we'd spent alignments shooting the beasts down to make our smokers. She understood their patterns and knew how to avoid them.'

'Why did you let me believe she left us to become a Charmore?'

'Your stepfather told you that story. He didn't want you spending your childhood believing your mother quelled. I wasn't about to replace one lie with another and tell you a ghoragall lifted her away. When you found the bones, it finally made sense. I assumed he killed her for revenge and lied to the House of Judgement about her being taken by a ghoragall.'

Dropping his chin to his chest, he continues, 'The truth is, I wanted to blame him. I couldn't go on with the haunting questions. I wanted him punished for claiming my wife and child while I lived alone.'

'So you schooled me on the Stain.' Hot tears roll down my cheeks.

'I'm not proud of what I did. Being a parent doesn't make you infallible; if anything, it only provides more opportunities to fail.'

I continue when my voice allows it. 'The bones belonged to a ghoragall. Someone killed it and buried it in the alzog pen. It might have been Cromenk. It might even have been Nija. She said she came back to check on me. Wouldn't that be an irony, my own mother, burying the bones I took for hers?'

My father's hands come up to cover his face. His tears spill onto the wooden worktop.

He'd encouraged me to the task of administering the Stain, and my hands went gladly to work. Which of us was more to blame? Him, because he's the parent? Or me because I never questioned him? Some days the only thing that kept me going was having that daily chore of lacing my stepfather's tea with Stain. I needed someone to blame just as much as my father did.

Someone gusts past, startling me. I realise it's a Charmore when I catch a glimpse of her red dress. When she takes my father into a maternal embrace, I see that it's Halli.

'What is it, my Hok? What happened?' she asks.

My father wipes at his eyes, mumbling a few words I can't hear. As they talk, I spot the sleight of hand. Halli grasps the little black pouch my father secrets in her hand and slips its strings into the band of her garter. There's a flash of thigh and something else. Quickly, I divert my eyes, unwilling to draw attention to the item strapped securely against her ebony skin.

It is a killing blade, long and sharp.

Brezan comes for me late the following afternoon. I spent the night in my chair, and my neck aches from the strain. My father hasn't slept and works with nervous, insatiable energy, even now. I don't know how he remains animate in the heat. My inactivity has me exhausted and fighting to keep awake.

An eyeful of Brezan is all I need to get my adrenaline flowing. Two Vigilance Men accompany him, and he introduces them to me like we're all the best of friends. First, Siggon, with his wild bush of sandy facial hair. I recognise him from the night before, when he seemed especially enamoured with Halli. Then Farat, who is clean-shaven, sunburned, and peeling. Farat stands with his hands behind his back, looking like he won't commit to anything without first being instructed. Siggon is the opposite, going straight for my bonds. He unties me quickly, pulls me onto my feet. The burlier of the two, he has no trouble forcing me into position in front of Brezan. Brezan looks especially pleased. Whatever the three have planned for me, it won't be pleasant.

'Wait,' my father protests, raising his hands to placate them. In his urgency, he knocks down one of the smokers lined up on the bench. 'Please, I'm close, really. Call the Zhu. I'm ready.'

He still hasn't told me what he's making. There are smokers on the bench, but he could make them blindfolded; there's no reason for all the fuss.

Brezan ignores him, indicating to Siggon that it's time for us to go.

We walk through the encampment toward the dunes. It doesn't take me long to guess where we're headed. I was scared before, but now I panic. I know what lies on the other side of the amber range.

'If you kill me, my father will never give you what you want,' I shout into the wind. When we reach the foot of the dunes, I refuse to walk, but it makes little difference to our pace. Siggon and Farat drag me up the dune, cursing and panting, my feet carving a deep gully into the sand. When we reach the peak, we can see down into the valley. There are ten stakes ploughed deep into the earth, their shadows elongated in the late afternoon sun, stretching across the sand and mounting the surrounding rocks. I shiver, thinking of the giant satermijtes lurking behind the boulders, their glossy eyes glittering in the dying sun. Wild-eyed and gasping with fear, I search for the beasts that will be sent to feast on me. Imagining the shifting mandibles at work, my stomach twists, and I retch, losing the small bowl of tepid soup I managed to eat for lunch.

Siggon strips me of my satermijte wings and ties me to a stake. Once satisfied that I'm securely fastened, the three Vigilance Men retreat, leaving me alone to face my fear.

Time passes, and though I jump at every sound, the most life-threatening encounter I have is with the sun. My flesh is roasting, even in the final slanting rays coming over the horizon. When the fiery globe finally sets, a cooling breeze picks up. Night falls, the stars shine, and the desert loses its inhospitable heat. Still, I wait, watching for the slightest hint of movement, every muscle tensed against imagined pincers, slicing toward me through the dark.

When the ghoragall swoops, it takes me entirely by surprise.

The winged beast grabs me by the leg and jerks me hard against my bonds. Its dark, agitated wings swirl sand into my face. I gasp, getting a lungful of its putrid stench. Then, spluttering, I kick out. But I have no real momentum with one of my legs hoisted into the air. Bit by bit, the ghoragall's wingbeats jerk me up the pole. It's impossible to feel the cool talons snaking around me without hearing the echoes of my stepfather's cries as he was lifted away. The way to Thormyth is long; did he spend the time trying to figure out why I did what I did?

There's a whomp from above, followed by a caw. The talons slip from my limbs, and I careen down the pole before hitting the sand with a thump. The ghoragall lands on top of me, its great breast crushing me and stealing my breath away. Knowing the thing is dead is no comfort. I panic, kicking out, trying to escape the warm carcass settling over me. Still pegged beneath its mass, I manage to free my face and breathe.

I try to spot my rescuer but see only Siggon, Farat, and Brezan strolling toward me. Siggon has a crossbow dangling from his right hand. When they reach me, Siggon and Farat grab the ghoragall by the feet and haul it off me, dragging it toward the camp. I'm alone with Brezan, who takes his time untying me. After lifting me from the sand, he cinches my hands behind my back with the rope.

'Ghoragall stew is not my favourite meal, but my father has a thousand men to feed. The elvakan meat only went so far,' says Brezan with a sigh.

Pain pierces my chest like a quarrel shot at close range.

Bloodbane.

I struggle against Brezan, desperate to land a single punch. My elvakan! I'd birthed him. I'd slain his mother to save his life. I would have lost them both if I didn't act, but that didn't make it any easier to bear. He was mine, and I was his. We were bonded by blood, and now he was dead.

'I'll kill you!' I scream, fighting my bonds, the coarse rope tearing my skin.

Brezan chuckles. 'The children were very quick to tell my men he was yours when they led him away. Don't worry, we didn't say he was for the slaughter.'

'I will kill you. I swear it.'

Brezan drags me across the sand, and I would die a thousand deaths just to wipe the smug look off his face.

27

KYJTA

It's an afternoon like so many before. I'm tied to a stake in the ground in the late afternoon sun, looking like easy prey. I just want to get the ordeal over with, so I can get out of the sun. I'm surprised when Farat crosses the shimmering sand to untie me, before shooting a ghoragall to feed the camp. Equally unexpected, Farat doesn't lead me to the tent my father and I share. I'm taken instead to a small tent on the outskirts of the desert encampment. Inside, I find a bucket and, next to it, a sponge nestled neatly on a crisp beige towel. There's barely any water in the bucket, but that doesn't matter. I can wash, finally lifting the layers of dust caking my skin and clogging my wounds. Beneath the dirt, my skin is raw from the sun, and there are deep ruts where my bindings have cut into my flesh. I examine the gouges on my legs, where the ghoragall's talons have perforated the skin. The wounds are raised red welts, extremely sensitive to the touch, and probably infected. My father would know how to heal them, but I can't ask him to mix something up when he's struggling just to keep himself upright. At least three wanings have passed since our capture, and he looks more haggard every day. I don't know how much more he can take.

I don't strip off completely, not with two Vigilance Men stationed at the tent flap, but I take off enough to allow myself to wash. When I'm done, the water is thick and murky. Farat enters the tent carrying a few scraggly catty plants and sets them down nearby, along with a bowl of soup and a wedge of bread. If not for the chunks of grey meat floating in the bowl, the meal would exactly mirror the bucket's contents. I push the soup away; I know where they get the meat.

The bread I devour, but I'm getting weaker by the day.

When I'm finished eating, I drip the milky sap from the catty plants onto my raw skin. The white puddles are quickly absorbed, though I try to smooth the soothing balm out evenly. I comb my hair, then dress in fresh leggings, a long-sleeve white tunic, and my boots, a gift from Farat. I haven't asked him where he came by them, and he hasn't thought to tell me. Not knowing is probably better, and I doubt the Grulo they belonged to is missing them anyway. I transfer Calipsie's shells from my tattered robes into the front pocket of my fresh tunic. So long as they are with me, so is Calipsie.

As usual, my satermijte wings are returned, and rest against a chest nearby. In an odd way, my Stain has made me valuable. It probably saved my life.

When I'm ready, my assigned guards, Siggon and Farat, lead me through the encampment, walking me past the tent my father and I share. My father's tent is quiet and dark, filling me with the sickening sense that something terrible has happened. What if my father has lost his usefulness, or if the Zhu has finally lost patience with him?

It's dark, but both Urther and Ursala are full, and it's easy to see the way ahead. The guards lead me out the back of the encampment and across the plain. When I spot the outcropping of rocks that once held the Rhemans, I wonder if they'll throw me in the cage to rot, but we keep walking.

Eventually, the consistency of the sand shifts. We cross a gully of stone shards and then move onto solid rock.

'I'm thirsty,' I say, stopping to take in the stark landscape. Above us, boulders hunker one on top of the other, blotting out the dusk sky, and below us, the land crests in gentle waves, rippling shadows across the plain.

Farat and Siggon pause to catch their breath and loosen their water pouches.

'Where are we going?' I ask Farat.

'You'll know soon enough,' Siggon responds.

Farat passes me his water pouch, and I take three sips. It seems so heavy that, when I pass it back, it almost slips from my grip.

'Careful,' reprimands Siggon, grabbing the pouch and shoving it into Farat's hands.

'I want to know where my father is,' I say, suddenly angry.

Farat looks startled by my outburst, but then he looks up at the sky, distracted. 'Something's off with your wings,' he says.

He must have heard it too—distant but unmistakable. The caw of a ghoragall.

Following his gaze, I search the sky for the glimmer of our winged companion. My hand instinctively checks for the strings that tie my satermijte wings at my throat. I'm relieved to find my protection still in place.

'There's a ghoragall over us.' Looking worried, Farat wipes his mouth with the back of his hand.

'It's not after me, not with my wings,' I say. 'One of you probably killed its mate.'

'Don't listen to her,' Siggon scoffs, shoving Farat so he'll stop scanning the skies.

'Quit it,' says Farat, dropping his gaze. 'Come on. We're almost there.'

Together we climb the rocks, with Farat trailing some ways behind. With each step, my limbs grow wearier until finally, when I'm sure I can't take another step, I hear voices. We round an enormous rock and, judging by the number of people gathered on the broad stone foundation, we've reached our destination.

Roughly twenty Vigilance Men are gathered in a semblance of a circle, and at its centre stands my father. My elation at seeing him alive is enough to drive back my exhaustion. He's preparing something, but I can't easily see what; too many black cloaks are blocking my view. Beyond him, the horizon drops away. I can't be sure whether it's a cliff edge or some less formidable fall. I walk forward, wanting to greet my father, but Siggon clutches my wrist. Just then, one of the Charmores strides across my path. She's wearing a dress the colour of night, her ebony head gleaming in the light of the two moons. I don't see the tentacle at first; it's out of sight, somewhere at her feet. Then, with unexpected agility, the Tarrohar launches up from the sand, wrapping its tentacles around her and pulling itself up her body. In no time, it mounts her slim frame. I jerk back, repulsed by the coiling mass of tentacles, unctuous in the moonlight as they settle into place. The Charmore staggers slightly, then, regaining her composure, she walks toward a tent erected behind an outcropping of rocks.

The tent flap whips open, and Halli strides out in a long silver dress that lends a striking contrast to her deep russet complexion. Seeing her, I fight back an unwelcome urge to weep. I wait silently at Siggon's side, unsure why I was summoned to this place. Seeing Halli approach, Siggon releases my wrist. She ignores me when she glides up to us, focusing her charms on him.

'Siggon, you made it.' For once, her eyes aren't glazed in preparation for her burden. She looks clear-headed and competent, if thinner than I remember.

'Yes. I said I would.' I imagine Siggon must be smiling beneath all that fuzzy facial hair, but it's impossible to tell.

'Thank you for bringing the girl. Brezan asked for her specially. Do you mind if I take her myself?' Halli's delivery is faultless; who could refuse such a request? Not Siggon, it seems.

''Course. Take her. She's yours,' he responds, then turns to me like he thinks I might resist and make him look bad. 'Go on, then. Off with you.'

'Fair Face,' she says as we walk hand in hand across the stone. 'You must prepare yourself.'

'For what?' I ask, my panic returning.

'Your Rheman is here.'

'Kranik? Why?'

'They want evidence that your father's claims are valid; that the smokers truly work.'

'What kind of evidence?' I ask, my heartbeat suddenly erratic. Let it not be what I think it is.

Brezan falls in beside us. 'Hardly recognised you without all that desert muck,' he says, looking me over.

Halli looks like she's bitten into something tough that she must spit out discreetly. She excuses herself, leaving me alone with Brezan. Leaning in, Brezan whispers into my ear, 'You ready for the show?'

His breath is hot on my cooled skin and sweet as fallen fruit.

'Your father tells me we'll be able to see better from over here,' he says, leading me to a narrow rock littered with the potion master's paraphernalia. He's right; we have a clear view of the circle and are away from the crowd. My father has set his smokers in a ring just big enough for a person to stand in.

It's not the ring of smokers that Brezan wants me to see, though. It's my mother. She's locked in conversation with the Zhu. It's easy to see that she's still ferrying a Rheman. The two are discussing something and the Rheman—Azaire, I presume—seems agitated. Nija's expression is sulky and a little petulant, which is not at all like my mother. It pains me to know she's quelled, but at least she's safe. I have that.

I stand perfectly still, my hands clasped at my stomach. If we're gathering here to witness the Rheman-strength smokers my father was tasked to produce, there's no good outcome. Brezan will win, regardless of whether my father delivers.

Spotting me, my father strides over. 'Kyjta,' he says, his eyes bright with his achievement. 'I did it. We'll soon be free.'

I wince at his announcement, and he tries to reassure me by taking my hands. Something cool slips into my palm.

'Let's get on with it,' shouts the Zhu. He strides away from the gathering audience, beckoning to two of his Vigilance Men. 'Get the Rheman.'

The men disappear into the tent; when they exit again, they have Kranik. Merrick's blond hair is grimy and plastered to his face. He looks like he's lost more weight than I have. His arms are strapped to his sides, and there's a noose around his neck, jutting from one end of a hollow pole, crafted from core wood. Kranik grimaces, forced forward by the star hammer wedged into Merrick's back.

'Bring him here.' The Zhu points to the spot that marks the middle of the circle. Smokers have been positioned at equidistant points around a central marker. When Kranik sees Azaire, ferried by my mother and standing at the Zhu's side, he glares at him.

'Is this how it is?' he shouts. 'You side with whoever has the most to offer?'

Kranik is forced to step inside the circle. The Vigilance Men aren't gentle, using the pole and star hammer to shove him into position, but he isn't done with Azaire.

'It was you, wasn't it? Telling Helacth the locations of the bunkers. Tiberico trusted you. You were the ship's liaison. You used your position to ingratiate yourself with the Helacth, didn't you?'

Azaire stares at the rocky ground, unable to muster a response.

'Did you do it alone or with the help of your contacts in Thormyth? The ones that could never be found when Tiberico wanted to talk to them. How long did you have us fooled?'

Azaire can't take it; head bent low, he skulks away.

I watch Nija leave, sickened by the Rheman's duplicity and the fact that he's riding my mother. I want to scream into the night, but the Zhu is encouraging people in range of the smokers to step back, and my father is animated, leaning down to light his creations. Soon, Kranik will be breathing the smoke and then . . .

'The smoke will need time to permeate his system. You must speak in a calm monotone. Any command you give should hold, even once he gets out of range,' says my father, stepping back and allowing the Zhu to take the stage.

My heart pulses painfully. I don't know what sort of test the Zhu has in store for Kranik, but I can't imagine it'll be a good fate.

As if sensing I'm at my weakest, Kranik raises his head and looks at me. He gives a small, encouraging nod and my throat constricts.

Brezan must notice because he glances at me.

'Are you two friends?' he says, his tone light and cheery.

I drop my eyes and stare at my feet, then remember that my father slipped something into my hand. Careful to avoid being seen, I open a few fingers to look. It's a fire stick.

I glance around, wondering what my father is expecting of me. The Charmores are gathered in groups of twos and threes. Each group centres around one of the five Tarrohar in attendance. There's one Tarrohar per group, suckered onto the back of a Charmore, while the remaining women are unencumbered, like they're forming tiny support groups for one another. Halli is one of these; she turns as if sensing my attention, then nods as though she's conferring some sort of permission.

But permission for what? I feel like I'm missing something. Does my father expect me to light Brezan's cloak again? There are about a hundred Vigilance Men here ready to put it out.

When the Zhu speaks again, his voice is resonant, holding the monotonous note required to ensure the smokers are effective.

'The time has come to test our potion master's fealty and skill,' he announces. 'If these smokers have the power to manipulate Rhemans, then this Rheman should answer my questions truthfully, no matter the consequences.'

My heart beats against my throat. What information might the Zhu want from Kranik?

'Your Sorbs are hidden somewhere in the desert. Tell me, Rheman, where will my men find them?'

Merrick's face contorts as Kranik struggles against the urge to confess the whereabouts of the Sorbs. If the Zhu learns of their location, he'll dispatch his men to destroy them.

'They're in our wagons,' Kranik says through gritted teeth. 'A storage space, hidden beneath the carriage.'

The Zhu motions to a party of Vigilance Men and they silently slip away. I want to chase after them and beat my fists against their chests, but they'd only cut me down. Any protest would be pointless. And my inability to act means Kranik will die. If his Sorb is destroyed, he will cease to exist.

'Is that the truth?' demands the Zhu.

To this, Kranik bares his teeth and growls like an injured animal.

'We'll know soon enough,' says the Zhu, circling Kranik. 'Still, we have an audience to please, and not all of them are willing to stand around for the time it'll take to confirm your story. We need proof that these smokers work, and we need it now.'

'They work, I assure you,' says my father. He stands away from the crowd and upwind of the smokers, tucked in beside the rock face. His face is ashen. If the smokers don't work—if he's failed—then he and I will pay the price.

Either way, Brezan wins. Wicked Brezan, who burned Sion Cromenk's house to the ground, killing his family and destroying mine. It isn't fair. My nails dig into my palms, fingers wrapped tightly around the fire stick.

What should I do with it?

The Zhu looks to my father, and something passes between them, though I can't say what. They've known each other since childhood, but in adulthood, they've always been at odds.

'The word of a potion master is insufficient.' The Zhu's hands are tucked neatly at his back. Whatever he's doing, it's theatrical. He's putting on a show for the Tarrohar. Delight radiates from Brezan, his face a shining oval of joy in the dusky light.

'As anyone in the audience might have guessed, I know precisely how this Rheman can prove the effectiveness of these smokers.' The Zhu pauses to ensure he has the crowd's full attention.

I'm gripping the fire stick so tightly that it'll probably snap before I figure out what to do with it.

'Walk, Rheman. Walk and keep walking. Don't let anything stop you.' There can be no mistaking the Zhu's intention; he's pointing toward the cliff.

The fire stick feels suddenly hot and heavy in my hand. Panicking, I fumble with it, thinking I'll have to resort to setting a few cloaks alight after all. But, with effort, I rein in my chaotic thoughts and focus on the facts. Fact one: I have a fire stick. Fact two: my father gave it to me. Fact three: my father positioned me beside his workbench.

I turn my head slightly to get an idea of what's available. Wok weed, berries, hamaz stalks, and a small sand-coloured smoker nestled behind a large bouquet of mostle thread. A smoker positioned here, just like I was. It can only be for me. My fingers ache with the urge to light it, but I can't get caught. I glance at Brezan; he's completely enthralled by his father's showmanship. I quickly construct a list of demands in my head while reaching behind his back. It takes three attempts with my shaking hands, but I finally get the smoker lit. Giving the smoke a chance to take effect, I return my attention to Kranik. It's worse than I thought. He's already on the move. I can tell he's fighting it, walking backwards with his feet dragging across the shingles, but it's not a battle he's winning.

I glance around, looking for someone to stop the madness, but the only person I connect with is Halli. She's staring at me expectantly, like she's waiting for me to do something.

I swallow, searching for my voice.

'The desert is cold at night and hot by day,' I say steadily. 'It's strange when you think about it. All that heat should build up over the day and keep it warm at night.'

'What?' Brezan looks at me like I've lost my mind.

It hasn't worked, I realise. The smoker is too small, I started too soon, or my voice wasn't pitched right. Still, I must keep talking. This is the only plan I've got.

'It's cold,' I say, 'so cold I need a jacket or a cape. Something warm to keep off the chill.'

'Yes,' he mumbles. 'Cold.'

I'm not sure I have his attention. His eyes remain firmly on Kranik, but something about his manner seems more accessible.

'I'm so cold,' I say. 'I could really use a cloak. A lovely warm cloak like yours. Would you loan yours to me?'

Brezan unpins his black cloak without looking at me and hands it over.

I accept the gift, but the real test is still coming. I take a breath, knowing I must be quick but equally that I can't rush it. If my tempo changes, even for a moment, I'll lose him.

'Do you see the Tarrohar?' I say with a steady voice, watching as his preoccupation with Kranik's slow shuffle to the edge and beyond is replaced with a sudden avid interest in the five Tarrohar gathered nearby to watch the show. Beneath them, the Charmores hunch like children forced to carry their parents' oversized baggage.

'The Tarrohar are our true enemy,' I go on. 'The real reason we suffer. You've seen the effects of the Mind Pain on your father. You've felt it yourself. We must act. We must free Aurora Saura.'

Halli is watching us, her eyes widening at the sight of Brezan's hands hovering over the hilts of his swords and the determined expression coming over his face.

'Kill them, Brezan,' I say. 'Kill the Tarrohar.'

28

KYJTA

can't waste another moment on Brezan. I must stop Kranik from going over the edge. I pull the strings of my satermijte wings as I run, leaving them dancing in the sand. From somewhere behind me, I hear Brezan unsheathe his swords. If he can kill just one of the Tarrohar before the Mind Pain claims him, it might create enough of a diversion. I hope my intuition about the Charmores can be counted on. If the little pouch my father gifted Halli on her last visit contained my father's secret weapon against the Mind Pain, like I believe it did, then the serfs may have their own plans for the Tarrohar. I don't have the time to confirm any of this. I must get to Kranik. I'm running as fast as I can, my breath like fire in my lungs, but he's getting dangerously close to the edge.

The Mind Pain hits as I sprint across the stones, but it's not impossible to overcome. My head aches, and the drumming between my temples almost forces me to close my eyes, but I'm not on the ground, clutching my head and wishing for death, so I run on, squinting ahead of me, trying to stay focused on Kranik's proximity to the cliff. I urge myself on, desperate to maintain my pace, despite the pain. Then, just as suddenly, the pain vanishes. Not reduced or conquered, but extinguished. I want to turn back to confirm my hopes, but Kranik is stepping into nothingness, and we're out of time. I hear the mournful cry of the ghoragall and breathe in the fetid wind to get a sense of the creature's proximity—it's not far now, but is it close enough? My eyes hold Kranik's as he drops off the edge of everything, and I leap after him.

───

The world falls away, and I collide with Kranik, wrapping my arms around him, my hair whipping my face. Brezan's cloak flaps behind me like I have wings, but we're falling fast, racing toward the canyon floor. One moment we're plummeting to our deaths, and the next, we're soaring above it all. It's not the first time I've thanked the Hands for my Stain in recent moons, but I imagine it'll be the last.

From high above it all, I peer down and try to make sense of the carnage below. All five Tarrohar lie prone in the sand, looking like leftovers from some gruesome meal. Our fight isn't over. There will be more to take their places, but with the aid of my father's little black pills, we might finally make a stand.

The Charmores huddle on the rocks below, kissing and hugging one another in victory. I scan the scene, looking for Brezan, finally spotting him among the Vigilance Men. A few of his cohorts look like they're trying to revive him, but the Zhu seems oblivious to his son's mindless condition, raising Brezan's hand in the air as though the entire attack was his idea. Other Vigilance Men are in a similar state, all victims of the Mind Pain, but many look unscathed and are rejoicing. In fact, the only one still on his feet and not cheering ecstatically is my father, whom I spot near the edge of the cliffs, peering up at me. His stark, lone figure sets a chill through me, and I wonder how things will play out for him now, with the Tarrohar gone and the Vigilance Men in control.

When he's just a dot on the cliff's edge, I lift my head so I can better see Kranik. 'You gave me a scare,' I say.

'You didn't look scared at all,' he tells me. 'For a moment there, I thought you could fly.'

'If I could, I would have timed your rescue better,' I say with a smile. 'Here, let me untie you.'

I reach for the vine that binds his arms to his sides. It's a tricky manoeuvre with the ghoragall's glossy talons clamping us to each other, but with a bit of shuffling, I'm starting to think I'll manage; then one of the claws loosens and retracts, sending a jolt through me. Sensing the movement, Kranik shudders, trying to grab me, but with his arms tied, we only bump our heads. Laughing, despite our situation, I look at him, expecting to see my reaction mirrored, but his eyes are joyless. My fingers go limp, unable to continue freeing him.

'What is it?' I ask, feeling idiotic for asking. We're on route to Helacth's ship, where I'll probably be quelled, and Kranik, well, I have no idea what Helacth's stance on him is. Yes, things are bad, but at least the Tarrohar are dead. It's all right to feel a little elation. 'We're still alive, aren't we?'

'We *are* alive,' Kranik says quietly. 'But we don't have much time.'

It's a strange thing to say, and I feel like I'm missing something. It must still be a decent distance to Helacth's ship, even by ghoragall. I lean in for a second time, my body pressing harder against him so I can reach the knots behind his back. The ghoragall's feathers tickle my neck, buffeted by Kranik's steady breathing. After a struggle, I finally get him loose. I pull back, my breath coming hard, and wipe the feathers out of my eyes to get a better look at him. He looks grave.

'You're not going to tell me your allegiance is still with Helacth?' I ask, only half-joking.

Kranik gives a wry smile. 'No. Nothing like that.'

'What then?' I ask, nervous.

'I . . . you—' he starts, struggling to find the words.

'Just tell me.'

'It's my Sorb,' he says.

His Sorb! In all the commotion, I'd forgotten about the Vigilance Men who'd been sent to destroy them. My body goes cold; my hands icily numb. There's no way to stop them from up here. Kranik's Sorb will be destroyed, and it makes no difference that I saved him from plummeting to his death.

'The Vigilance Men, they'll—' I stammer, tears pricking my eyes. I can't face what's ahead with him gone.

'Not the Vigilance Men. That might take a day or more,' he says, brushing aside the threat of death as though it is nothing more than an annoyance, 'but we don't have days.'

'You're scaring me,' I tell him.

'I need you to know it's not a choice—not my choice. I want to stay with you, but I can't fight my design.'

'What are you saying?' It sounds like he plans to leave me, but that's impossible. We're both trapped up here; he can't just disappear.

'I've never wanted to stay anywhere more,' he tells me.

'Then stay. Stay with me,' I beg him, without any real sense of what's happening. All I know is that I don't want to lose him.

'I can't. My limits are stretched already. There's a reason we brought our Sorbs along on this journey.'

I stare at him, still not comprehending. Brought their Sorbs into the desert?

'I'll be drawn back to it, Kyjta. Rhemans can't stray a great distance from their Sorbs. Now listen, we don't have much time, and there are things you need to know if you're going to survive.' He holds my gaze, and I find him in the pale translucence of Merrick's eyes: not a Rheman, nor an Aurora Saurin—just Kranik. Gentle and kind. More concerned for my safety than for his.

'You need to listen.'

I draw breath. Listen to what? Instructions on how not to die? This isn't the way this was supposed to happen. He's strong, and he's Rheman. He was supposed to save Calipsie.

'You *must* avoid the Rhemans. Are you listening?' Kranik says. 'I know you're scared, but you must take this in. When the ghoragall drops you into whatever system they've set up for collecting the Stained, you must hide until the Rhemans have done their rounds. Then find a way to keep warm and get to the mother ship.'

Kranik struggles to free a hand to pull Brezan's cloak more tightly around my shoulders. I feel his warm knuckles graze my chin, but the rest of me is numb.

'To survive the cold, you must find a way on board the *Ebisu*. That's Helacth's flagship—it'll be grounded not far from the drop zone. I've heard tell that there's a panel that's been disabled. You must find it and get inside. There are Rhemans living in hiding from Helacth aboard the ship. They're your only hope; you must find them.'

I'm sure there are questions I should be asking, but I can't shake the dread long enough to think what they are.

'You're stronger than you know,' Kranik says, brushing his thumb over my Stain.

I don't feel strong. I cover his hand with mine and push my face into his palm. If I can just keep hold of him, perhaps he won't slip away. He puts his arm around me and pulls me into him. I close my eyes.

'Tell me I'm not your nightmare,' he whispers. 'It's the worst of my fears.'

'The only nightmare is losing you,' I say.

He doesn't respond, and something changes in the way he's holding me.

I pull back, and my breath hitches.

'What's this?' he says abruptly, squinting at my face. 'Do I dream?'

It's not Kranik's way of speaking. Merrick is back.

I bundle my disappointment, somehow, and bind it close, to be dealt with later.

I don't want to scare Merrick, but he needs the truth. 'This is real.'

'Where's my Rheman?' he demands. Merrick agreed to be a body donor, not an active participant in this mission. Terrifying as our predicament is for me, it must be a complete shock for him.

'He's gone. Drawn back to his Sorb. It's just you and me now.'

'Where are we?' Merrick says. 'I never agreed to this.' He moves, trying to pull away from me. Then he's writhing in the ghoragall's claws, trying to open them.

'Stop!' I tighten my arms around him to prevent him loosening the claws and tumbling free. 'Please, you'll get us both killed.'

'Don't touch me,' he roars, fighting an impossible battle to get away from me. 'Don't you ever touch me.'

'I don't have a choice,' I say.

He grows still. It's a moment before I get up the courage to say anything else.

'Don't you even want to know what happened, or where we're headed?'

'Why bother? I already know I'm not going to like it. You'll be there,' he says.

'Well, that's mature.'

After our brief spat, we lie silently against each other, each of us trying not to look at the other's face. Neither of us speaks for a long while. I know we can't go on like this. I must convince Merrick of the truth, even if it means telling him it was Serain who put the infatuation potion into his drink. If we're going to go through this thing together, we must trust each other. Finally, I think of some news that might lift his dark mood. He lost a brother to the Tarrohar. No one could hate their species more than he does.

'We killed the Tarrohar. The Vigilance Men and the Charmores together slayed all five leaders. They're dead,' I tell him.

He perks up, staring at me with bright, watchful eyes. 'You're lying.'

'I'm not lying. My father figured out a way to block the Mind Pain.'

He stares at me blankly, then adds, 'I know.'

'How could you know?' I ask.

'I've been helping him test it. Why do you think I kept signing up for that awful Body Trust? It was the only way to get near them. You helped me there.' He snorts, but not unkindly. 'I couldn't figure out how to get them mad enough to use the Mind Pain on me, but not enough to wipe out my mind if the pills didn't work.'

'You mean, the day on the green, you were—'

I don't get the words out because the ghoragall opens its claws, and we tumble free, falling into the freezing sky.

We hit the ground hard. It's covered in luminous, spongy moss, but the impact takes my breath anyway. We bounce, knocking into hard ice, and then slide down an increasingly slippery slope. It's dark, and cold air rushes all around me, making my eyes water; I'm still screaming when I fly out the other end. We land on more fuzzy moss, where I sit shaking, trying to get my breath back. I touch my face; my skin is totally numb. I'd freeze if it weren't for Brezan's cloak. I clamp it around me with a quick motion that makes my hands ache. The stiffness in my fingers and the accompanying pain remind me that Merrick is wearing even less than I am.

I get to my feet and call out to him. 'Merrick?'

'Here.'

I turn toward the noise and make out a deeper shadow in the darkness. The moss doesn't offer much light, but I can just about get a sense of the dome's curvature. We must be in some sort of ice cave, beneath the snow.

'So . . . cold,' says Merrick, shivering badly. It's absolutely freezing, and my teeth are chattering.

I hold my hand out to him and help him get to his feet. 'Here,' I say, throwing Brezan's cape partially around his shoulders. He's so tall that my legs are suddenly exposed. My shivering picks up a notch, so much so that my bones ache.

'Thank you.' With his other hand, Merrick wraps an arm around me beneath the cape and pulls the front of the thick cloth tightly around us with the other. I feel slightly warmer. 'Now what?' he asks, still shivering.

I peer around the gloomy dome. Kranik said I should hide until the Rhemans finished searching the place, but I don't see any obvious hiding spots.

'We need to stay out of sight,' I tell him, still scanning the arched enclosure. 'If we can find their ship, we could get warm.'

I pull him toward the darker side of the ice cavern, where I think I spot a fissure, perhaps even a tunnel. We walk together, but it's awkward with the cloak pinning us against each other. Still, we're making progress until voices echo through the freezing chamber. It sounds like they're coming from the exact spot we're headed.

Panic-stricken, Merrick and I separate.

'Hide,' I whisper, expecting him to take off and leave me to find my own hiding place.

Instead, he grabs my arm and draws me, running back toward the chute. We hit hard ice, stagger against the edge of the ice chute, and then peer upwards. The moss offers a little light, but it's impossible to see very far, and I can't get a feel for how steep the incline is. What's clear is there's no traction to be had; the sides are slick with ice. Regardless, Merrick grabs me by the waist and shoves me inside. With his hands on my thighs, I try to scramble forward, but any progress I make is lost the instant he loosens his hold.

'It won't work,' I hiss back at him. 'It's too slippery.'

'Grab hold of something,' he urges, giving me another shove.

'There's nothing here. We need another plan.'

He releases me, and I slide into his arms. The moment my feet hit the ground, we run, scrambling to find a nook or corner to disappear into, but the dome is cleanly sculpted, and there are no natural hiding places—at least none visible in the weak light. With the voices closing in on us, I grab Merrick's hand and pull him onto the moss, throwing my cape over him, hoping we'll go unseen. The voices get louder and more distinct until it's clear that whoever they are, they're inside the dome, searching for us.

I hold my breath, drawing on all my strength to stop myself from shivering. If Kranik were here, he'd know what to do, but Merrick has no reference point for this, and is probably still reeling from shock.

When I hear the soft crunch of boots near my head, I know our time is up. Someone grabs me tightly around my middle and hoists me into the air. I have no choice but to let go of Merrick's hand as they throw me over their back, knocking the wind out of me. I beat the Rheman with my fists, not caring that my efforts are wasted. There are only two of them, but that's all it takes. Merrick is lifted and carried just as easily as I am, but we aren't quelled. I assume these Rhemans aren't the ones who'll make use of our bodies. They already have their own.

They carry us through the tunnel and out into the snow. I can't see much—just legs walking and a vista of white. There's a pause, and then we're slung into some kind of holding cell, and the door clangs shut. Golden filaments—probably zionate—line the holding cell, but the structure itself is far too sleek and shiny to be Aurora Saurin made. It makes me wonder if we're already captives on Helacth's flagship, the *Ebisu*, but then the room starts to move. It's not the slow, rumbling pace of Aurora Saurin-made wagons but a light, zipping slipstream, barely discernible from inside. There are two small windows on either side, but from the corner where we huddle, all we see is a white blur.

Several furs cover the floor, something taken from an animal with a thick pelt that I don't recognise. Merrick grabs one, throws it over me, and then selects another and pulls it around himself. Wearing nothing but a light desert weave, he's still shivering all over. We huddle together, trying to keep ourselves warm.

'Why didn't they quell us?' he asks through chattering teeth.

'We're not meant for them,' I tell him.

Merrick peers at me through the plush silvery fur. His words come clearer now; his shivering is subsiding. 'Who are we meant for?'

I shrug. 'I don't know. Does it matter?'

We're silent for a while, and then I decide it's time to clear the air. If we're both going to be quelled, I want to settle things between Merrick and me.

'You still believe it was me who put that potion in your drink?'

'Well, I don't think it was your stepfather,' he says wryly.

'Is it really that horrible?'

I'd hoped to lighten the mood, but now worry I've belittled his experience.

'Try it and see,' he scoffs. 'I sent you a vial.'

As my hand goes to the ampule at my throat, I recall the snarl of a misspelt word scrawled onto its label.

Vengance.

'Your vengeance is an infatuation potion?' I ask, surprised.

'What else could it be? Did you think I'd poison you?' He stares at me, still hurt, but I swear he's warming to me.

'It was my stepfather's niece,' I say. 'She's genuinely fond of you.'

'Serain?' He thinks I'm joking, but still manages to look pleased.

The vehicle glides to a stop, halting our conversation. We share a glance, huddled beneath the warm furs, and then the door opens, and two hooded figures peer in. They're wearing snow-coloured furs, their faces covered by red cloth masks and dark goggles. It's better this way; I'd hate to recognise either of them.

One of them is wearing cracked goggles; he starts to speak in a language I don't understand. It's a rasping, death-rattle murmur, barely audible above the whistling wind. The other, whose red mask is smeared with something that could be dried blood, responds in the same grim dialect. When the blood-smeared Rheman reaches for me, I scream. His hand wraps around my leg and jerks me across the space. Merrick keeps hold of me, his arms clamped around my waist. Kicking and yelling, we're surprised when the blood-smeared Rheman releases me in response to some booming utterance from his companion. Merrick and I scoot backwards and bunch together in the farthest corner of the compartment, while the Rhemans confer.

Then the Rheman with the dark smear across his mask leans in again, reaching for Merrick. I grasp Merrick tightly, refusing to let go as he slides across the pile of furs. When we reach the exit of the cargo hold, the blood-smeared Rheman swipes me across the face. I careen backwards, slamming my head against the side of the vehicle. Instantly, my vision goes dark.

When I come around, Merrick is gone. My cheek pulses hotly where the Rheman slapped me, and there's a large welt at the back of my head where it connected with the vehicle wall.

I try the vehicle's door, but not surprisingly, it's locked. So I scramble to the window and peer out across the moonlit snow. I don't spot Merrick or the Rhemans anywhere, but there's a dark silhouette on the right, blotting out Urther's light. I lean into the window, trying to get a better look. The shape is vast and unnaturally large. My first impression is of a mountain, but a mountain would have gathered snow. This structure, jutting straight up into the sky, hasn't accumulated any.

It can only be the *Ebisu*.

Home to Helacth.

Shakily, I draw back. Where's Merrick? The ship is at a distance; they wouldn't expect him to walk all that way in this weather, would they? On hands and knees, I shuffle across to the opposite window and stare out.

He's there! Being dragged across the snow by his feet. He's struggling against the Rheman's strength, clawing at the snow. The Rheman drags him until they reach a small gathering. There are five of them, including Merrick. One of the men—I assume he's ferrying a Rheman—lies prone in the snow. The moons are bright, so I can see that he's in some sort of trouble. He barely moves, and when he manages to grope at one of his fellows, his movements are jerky and strained.

The blood-smeared Rheman who hit me across the face drags Merrick to the spot where the ailing man lies. I beat my fist against the window, yelling for Merrick to get out of the way, but he can't hear me through the barrier, and it's not as if he has a choice. The Rheman with the bloody mask takes hold of Merrick's arm and forces Merrick's hand toward the ailing Rheman in the snow. When the two connect, a wretched, wet rasp escapes me, and I drop to the floor, unable to watch. I'm curled into a ball when the door to my compartment opens. The two Rhemans load the ailing man's body into the cargo hold. One look at the face of my new companion and all my self-pity is forgotten.

29

KYJTA

My stepfather lies perpendicular across the furs. He appears dead, but for the rise and fall of his chest. I should comfort him, but I'm pressed into the corner, my arms wrapped tightly around my knees. Silent tears pour down my cheeks.

I'm desperate to look away but I'm static with shock. His body may be motionless, but that doesn't make him any less terrifying. There's a black crater where his nose once was, and his cheeks are nothing more than bloody sacks of flesh. I imagined him quelled, but nothing like this. My breath is ragged, my chest heaving. Did I do this to him? I draw my shaking hands up around my head. How long have they left him out in the cold? Couldn't they tell he was dying?

I snatch at the sudden notion that what I'm looking at isn't real. It's a vision of madness brought on by shock. Every mind has its limits, and mine has reached it and snapped.

If only that were true.

A murmur escapes his lips, causing me to retract farther into the corner, horrified that he might actually be trying to speak.

'Cold . . .' he manages through shivering lips.

This basic utterance finally breaks the rigor mortis of my fear. I reach over to pull a fur out from beneath my stepfather's stiff body and tuck it around his middle. He opens his eyes then, and I yelp in surprise, falling back to my corner.

His pupils slide to the side, searching for me. I sit as still as possible, hoping he won't realise I'm here.

'Hello?' he croaks.

I know I can't sit here and let him believe he's alone, but how much of a hypocrite do I have to be to act like I'm here for him after what I've done?

'I'm here,' I say, moving closer, taking his head onto my lap.

'Kyjta, is it . . . really you?' he says, looking up at me. I stare back at him, searching his expression. I expect condemnation but find only regret.

'Yes.' My voice cracks.

'Then they have everyone,' he says in a barely audible whisper as his eyes cloud with tears. 'You must get away. The girls . . . they go to Helacth.' He tries to get up but barely manages to lift his head before slumping back into my lap. 'You must get back . . . to Merrocha.'

'Rest,' I say, trying to keep my cascading tears from landing on his ruined face. 'Moving will only make it worse.'

I untie his red scarf and make a bad attempt at bandaging the blackened fingers of one hand. I can't see what I'm doing through all the tears, but I must do something.

'I tried . . .' he says, the words catching in his throat.

'Don't speak,' I tell him, my tears plopping onto his brow. There are too many of them for me to catch.

'It was . . . hard. I lost my Berda, and I couldn't look at you without . . . I tried. Please . . . you must save yourself.'

These final words impale me. I hunch over, convinced that the pain is physical—pure sentiment can't hurt like this; my heart feels shredded in my chest.

My stepfather lets out a long breath, and his gaze goes flat.

'I'm sorry,' I manage, regret crippling me with savage sobs.

My stepfather's head remains on my lap. I can't bring myself to move it. When the door finally opens, and the Rheman with the bloody smear leans in, I think he's coming for me. Instead, he lifts my stepfather's body and carries it away. My reactions are retarded by the dead weight of clinging desolation. I watch silently as the body is taken, only launching into protest when it disappears from view. I scramble for the door and go sprawling face-first into the snow. When I look up, the other Rheman is standing over me, expressionless beneath his cracked goggles and mask. He leans down and lifts me onto my feet. I pull the fur around me and stare after my stepfather's retreating form.

Beyond him, a smudge blackens the horizon and blurs everything behind it. It's hovering above the ground like a trick of the light, a smoky grey swirl at its centre. I stand, momentarily stunned, wondering what it could be. A handful of Rhemans are gathered around it. When they spot my stepfather's body, they suddenly become animated. The Rheman being ferried by Merrick helps with the body while another two skirt the aberration, relocating to some point beyond the swirling blur so that, when I look through it, I see fuzzy, blackened figures. The remaining two Rhemans make their way to a black chest set a few paces back from the blur, atop a scattering of rocks. The one to the left opens the chest and fiddles with the contents. The one on the right checks the chest's contents and then instructs the others. I watch as they lift my stepfather's body, a Rheman at either side, and feed it into the swirling darkness.

'Wait,' I whimper, 'what are they doing to him?' I peer up into the cracked goggles, hoping I'll find the answers there.

The Rheman holding me by the arm doesn't respond; he might not even understand me. I try to walk forward, but he holds me back, and though I twist against his strength, my movements are listless and dreamlike. This may be some kind of Rheman burial, and while I know I ought to say goodbye, I don't feel I've earned that right.

Perhaps it's my fresh tears—maybe he takes pity on me—but Cracked Goggles walks me closer to the shimmering veneer. His cohorts don't look up from their task of feeding the body into the swirling haze.

I watch my stepfather go, feeling as if the darkness that's swallowing him is taking me too. When the last of his body is through, I blink, as if waking from a dream. His words sound in my head like a death echo.

Save yourself. The girls, they go to Helacth.

It comes to me that I'm standing around, waiting to be bundled back into the vehicle and delivered to the Rheman overlord. It's a fate better avoided, but what choice do I have? Even if I could get free of Cracked Goggles, I'd freeze to death before the day was out. I'm already so cold that the idea of being quelled holds almost no horror. It's abandoning Merrick that terrifies me. That, and leaving Calipsie to grow old, or die, as one of the Quelled.

I'm drawn to look at Merrick, wondering whether I have the strength to leave him. Though he's barely recognisable beneath his newly acquired furs, goggles, mask, and hood, I can see his curly blond hair peeking out from the thick fur. At least the Rheman quelling Merrick has outfitted him with full protective gear. My stepfather may have had the same protection before they stripped him of it. How long does that give Merrick? What's the life expectancy of the Quelled out here?

I'm too busy obsessing over Merrick's limited longevity to notice what's going on beyond the swirling black circle. I don't know what I imagined, probably that his body would disintegrate, turn to dust, but whatever I thought, it wasn't this. The movement grabs my attention, a shifting dark mass beyond the blur. The Rhemans standing on the other side of the murky sphere back away from it, whatever it is. I can't make out the shape, not clearly, but it seems to hold a hobbled, horrible form. I lean out as far as my Rheman captor will allow me, to take a closer look.

Partially obscured and beyond the dusty sphere, a slick, glossy mound has emerged. I stare at it, still not comprehending. Then I spot a flicker of movement, and my stomach clenches. I look on as the contorted shape twitches and shudders. Something black, slick, and glossy stretches out and pulls back in again. Then a long, pale hind leg, jointed backwards, scratches against the snow, exposing a waxy talon.

With a swift breath, I realise I'm witnessing the birth of a ghoragall. In my mind, I've always referred to the beasts as Helacth's grim creations, but I wasn't prepared for this. The cycle has a sick neatness: taken, quelled, mutated, then sent back to the towns for more.

My dead stepfather, the ghoragall, lifts its head and turns its blind eyes on me.

This is Helacth's legacy, our dead hunting us down and passing on the atrocity that got them killed.

My stomach twists and I retch into the snow. There's nothing in my stomach; all I manage is a dry, hacking sound. When I look back, the ghoragall is struggling to its feet. The Rhemans all shout and point at me. I have no idea what they're saying, but Cracked Goggles grabs my chin and stares down at my face.

Not my face, I realise, but my Stain.

Being stained, without being quelled, must make me a target for the hatchling because, instead of taking to the skies, the ghoragall staggers toward me. The horror is worse now that I know what it is. I flash back to the splinter of barn door that I plunged into one of the beasts, wondering who it had been before being turned.

The ghoragall's legs waver; the creature spreads its dark wings.

My captor still holds me, and running, he jerks me along after him. He's heading for his comrades, who stand shouting behind the peculiar black chest. The ghoragall finds its legs and lunges after us. Panicked, the Rhemans scatter. My captor releases me and sprints for the vehicle.

I hold my ground, turning slowly. I'm finally ready to face my stepfather. The ghoragall is almost upon me, haltingly figuring out how to work its back-jointed legs. Still, it has speed, and I don't have many options. When the creature is a few paces away, it brakes with a reverse flap of its wings and releases an ear-splitting caw. Its sightless eyes, the colour of things long dead, roam the space around me. Although it can sense my Stain, it can't see me. Gingerly I step behind the alien chest, with its myriad silver buttons neatly spaced on a shiny black plate.

The ghoragall charges, a blur of motion so fast that there's no dashing out of its way. I brace for the stabbing pain, but instead, there's an explosion of light as its beak strikes the chest, shattering it into pieces. Behind the great wings, the black smudge winks out. Then a talon reaches forward and grips me around the middle. With a flurry of matted feathers, I'm lifted free of the ground.

30

KRANIK

I can sense the men gathering, hundreds of them, their minds hot knots of agitation in the quiet expanse of desert. Why the Zhu committed an entire army to destroying twenty-three Sorbs is not something I'll ever discover.

I don't doubt that the Vigilance Men will find the hidden compartment; I instructed them on its location. They're probably tearing away the panel, unsheathing their swords. Soon, it will all be over.

Soon.

Such a corporeal word! Inside a Sorb, time is meaningless. Its progression can't be measured or felt. I either exist, or I don't. I suppose that, this time, I exist as a version of myself who has loved.

Who does love.

Next time, that will be lost. Ezerya will wipe it all away in preparation for rebirth.

I wish it were just my Sorb. But I've condemned twenty-two of my fellow Rhemans to the same oblivion. I should have tried harder to resist, but even if I had the strength, that would have meant Kyjta and her father's lives. Still, I wouldn't have dropped off that cliff edge if I'd held out, forcing Kyjta to leap after me. Now she'll have to face the Ice Realm without my help, and I can't change that. Time doesn't work that way, no matter where you are.

A shadow passes over my Sorb, and I brace for the end. I hope they take me first; I don't want to be present while the others are extinguished. It's not easy to understand what's happening outside. Sound and movement blur, overlapping and indistinct. I hear voices, but I can't tell what they're saying. There are echoes, abrupt and vital, then smooth and soft. Then more voices, a cacophony with a soaring cadence.

Then, abruptly, I'm losing space and finding shape. It's like falling into water from a height. I'm funnelling from one reality and flowing into another. My essence now has hands and feet, a mouth, and a face.

Eyes.

With these, I scan the formidable gathering of Vigilance Men, searching for an explanation. I think I've found one when I spot the Zhu and the Young Soro standing shoulder to shoulder. Have these forces now aligned?

Someone reaches for me, wrapping his hand around my lower arm in a Rheman greeting and pulling me toward the others. The contact enables me to recognise him as my friend, Lakhan. One by one, I link arms with my fellow Rhemans. Tiberico, Wixnor, Noon, Fiderly, Amasue, Allora, Rhytheus, and on and on.

'The Tarrohar are dead,' Lakhan says. 'The Zhu and his men accept the Soro as their rightful sovereign.'

I watched the Tarrohar die, so news of their demise is no surprise. Still, the unity of the Young Soro and the Vigilance Men is a relief. I was worried that the Zhu would usurp control himself.

'That's good news, my friend,' I say, drinking it all in.

Lakhan claps a hand on my shoulder. 'We're going after Helacth. All of us: the Rhemans, the Vigilance Men, and what remains of the Young Soro's men.'

Lakhan steps back, revealing Rhytheus, holding a large zionate vat. 'What's this?'

'Think of it as the access codes to a breezy shuttle service,' says the captain, cracking the lid.

Inside, a silvery liquid sloshes from side to side.

'Shot me down a ghoragall. Had a sack full of Stain in its belly.' Rhytheus grins, turning to face the others. 'Men, dunk a hand and hitch a ride. On with it!'

Already the Vigilance Men are lining up. They're happy to take on Helacth's brand if it means a swifter end to the quellings. It's not the same for the Rhemans; the ghoragalls are blind to us. It makes no difference if our bodies are stained. Ghoragalls don't spirit Rhemans away. Lakhan has a solution, though. He pairs each of us up with a Vigilance Man, whose job is to lure a ghoragall down from the sky.

Surveying my clothes, I realise I'm wearing the uniform of a Vigilance Man. I take a moment to inspect my face in the reflective surface of the zionate vat. I'm being ferried by Brezan, I realise, so it's no surprise when Lakhan pairs me up with the Zhu.

The head of the house ushers me away from the crowd of Vigilance Men, one of his hands gleaming silvery white. We're spreading out, every Vigilance Man looking for a patch of sand where they can wave down the next ghoragall that flies by. The Zhu and I stand together, peering up at the great expanse of blue. When he finally speaks, it's with great solemnity.

'My son killed one of the Tarrohar before it took his mind.' There's a pause as he tries to find the rest of what he wants to say. 'It wasn't his idea. I know the potion master's daughter put him up to it, but I believe the Hands guided him, and I take pride in his sacrifice.'

I stare at him, waiting for the rest.

'I want his life to mean something. You may use his body, but I expect a great deal from you. Are you sure you're up to this, Rheman? Helacth was your master.'

'I wouldn't be standing in these boots if you believed I held any loyalty to him,' I respond.

The Zhu nods thoughtfully; then he leans in to mimic the Rheman greeting, wrapping his hand around my forearm and touching his right shoulder to mine.

'Then we'll face the monster side by side.'

31

KYJTA

'm gliding over the snow, clutched to the warm breast of the ghoragall. The pleasant whomp of its wings is somniferous, like a heartbeat. I wonder if it knows who I am, and if it does, how long before it forgets? Where will it take me? Back to the ice dome, where the past day can play out over again, only this time I'll face it alone, or does it have other plans? Perhaps it'll just loosen its claws and drop me from a deadly height.

We soar over the moonlit snow until a dark shadow looms, vast and proud, stealing the light. I look to the side, getting a scrolling view of the expansive hull, dark as death's looming portcullis. A construction of this size can only be the *Ebisu*. In the near distance, I see an opening, a large square of white light at the ship's base. A few Rhemans stand around, illuminated in the ghostly light, while others track back and forth through the open portal. I'm convinced this will be the spot my stepfather's ghoragall chooses for me.

When we fly by without slowing, I sigh with relief and snuggle into the ghoragall's feathers, revelling in their warmth. I toy with the ridiculous notion that my stepfather's ghoragall is taking me home.

I'm heady with the idea until I slip my hands into my pockets, and my fingers brush against Calipsie's shells.

With sudden brutality, my sense of purpose rushes back.

I struggle against the mighty talons, shouting to be released. Impossibly, the ghoragall responds, swooping low and loosening its claws. I land with a soft plop, my feet driving deep into the snow. Almost all the way covered, I have to fight to free myself, clawing at the snow until I've dug myself out. When I look up, the ghoragall is circling overhead. Though I know the creature is blind, I still raise my hand in thanks. It breaks away with an eerie sense of timing, heading for Merrocha.

When I can no longer make out its silhouette, I turn my attention to the ship. It looms over me, monstrous in both girth and height. I try to recall what Kranik told me. There's a disabled panel—a second entrance used by Rhemans who prefer to go unnoticed. I stare up at the monstrosity. The task is made all the more daunting because I'm utterly freezing. My body aches with the chill. I hunch over, deeply regretting the loss of my fur when I first fled the ghoragall. After pulling Brezan's cloak around myself, I attack the closest panel, but the lipped edges are freezing. I push my fingers into the gaps with Brezan's cloak wrapped around them, but still, it's like touching raw ice. My fingers are numb and stiff.

The metal panels form a patchwork that seems to span forever; I'd need days to find the right one, but I don't have that kind of time. Already I'm shaking so hard I can barely control where I put my hands. My feet feel wooden and heavy. I have no choice but to cry out for help. If I'm quelled, so be it. Nothing the Rhemans can do to me could be worse than this. I pound on the panels until my fists feel lacerated by the cold. Finally, overcome by exhaustion, I drop to my knees. When the Rhemans finally do get my body, it'll be useless to anyone.

I'm seated at a small table with my hands and feet in bowls of warm water. The Rheman fussing around me with furs is very old, or their body is anyway. There are four of us in this peculiar space, which is too narrow to be a room. It feels more like a corridor, but a corridor would have smooth walls, and these are anything but. The enclosure is a confusion of piping, coiled filaments, and boxlike protrusions. I get the feeling these Rhemans live between the walls of the ship, which makes sense. What better place to hide if they want to escape Helacth's attention?

I continue to scan the misshapen room. Every utility is moulded into the ship's workings or grown from the floor. It's as though the silvery-white material that makes up the walls and floors is vegetation, shaping itself into tables and chairs, basins, and hooks.

The Rhemans are also strange, their features almost identical, making it impossible to tell if they're male or female. The smallest one can't stop staring at me. All three are shorter than me, but the little one is roughly Calipsie's height. Its tiny stature doesn't hold with its age, though, since the three appear equally wizened. They each have spiralling alabaster hair that gleams brightly in the unnatural light, and pearly skin, fragile enough to appear transparent. I don't know how long Rhemans live, but these three have been at it a while. They're obviously not cycling through Aurora Saurin bodies at the rate their friends are outside. They're not even using Aurora Saurin bodies, by the look of things. The low-slung ears and wide-set eyes are unlike any I've ever seen.

The third Rheman, also sitting at the table and facing me, but not looking at me, is engaged in rapid conversation with the one who's fussing around me. One of its eyes is a dark, homey brown, while the other is a simmering yellow, like flame. I don't understand a word the two are saying, but it's easy to see that the third Rheman is agitated. I suspect it's my arrival that has them so worked up. If I could speak Rheman I'd reassure them that I'm only here to rescue my friend. I won't give them away.

Throughout the rapid exchange, the small one stares at me. I can't be the first Aurora Saurin it's seen. I worry that the cold has damaged my face like it did my stepfather's. A blackening facial wound would transfix just about anyone. I raise a hand to check my face. I can feel my nose, though it's still numb. My cheeks feel thick to the touch, like ice is layered between bone and flesh. Still, nothing feels too off. I lower my hand back into the warm water. The painful, hot-needle sensation has started to subside. If I'm lucky, I'll keep all my fingers.

For a long while, I sit listening to the quarrelsome exchange. It's an odd interplay of relationships. One might think a family is gathered here—father, mother, child—but the pattern doesn't fit. The fusser is maternal, replacing the cooling water in my bowls with that from a freshly warmed pitcher. And Fire Eye is patriarchal in his aggression. But they appear to continually defer to the small one. Every so often, they turn to the little runt as though seeking approval. They're not rewarded with words but with modest, inconspicuous gestures. The raising of an eyebrow, the dip of a head, and once, the pursing of stone-coloured lips.

Since the small one continues to look at me, I decide to say something. If I want the Rhemans to help me find Calipsie, I'll need to engage with them somehow.

'I'm Kyjta,' I say. 'Do you understand Asaurin? Can you tell me your name?'

The aggressive exchange between the larger pair quickly fizzles out. The fusser looks over sharply. Then, surprisingly, the fusser answers for the small one, speaking in halting Asaurin.

'Nietsy no speak.'

Startled, I mutter something regretful about never having learned Rheman.

'Nietsy no speak Rheman. No speak.' The fusser holds three fingers in front of its mouth for emphasis. Her mouth, I decide. She is quite obviously maternal.

Nietsy may not speak Asaurin, or anything, but the fusser can. It's more than I could have hoped for. I'll be able to ask after Calipsie. I might be able to find out where to look for her. I hesitate with my questions because I'm worried the small one's inability to speak might be a delicate topic, and it would be insensitive for me to bombard the fusser with all my demands, but I can't wait forever.

'There's a young girl here,' I start tentatively. 'She's only nine alignments.'

I hold out my hand to indicate her height from the ground. 'She's about this big, with copper hair, and lilac eyes, like mine. Do any of you know where I can find her?'

I'm looking at the fusser while doing my best to ignore the flame-eyed Rheman glaring at me from across the table.

The fusser doesn't answer me, walking to the opposite wall where there's a small alcove between the piping. Here, the Rheman layers a set of furs into the hollow.

'You sleep.' It waves me toward the furs.

Fire Eye stands, looking disgusted, and yells another stream of aggressive Rheman, then turns and exits the space through a small, incongruous passageway.

The fusser mutters something in Rheman and then makes 'hurry' movements. I don't want to offend these Rhemans, given they saved my life. Also, I don't want to give up this little space out of the cold, and the furs look inviting. I can't remember the last time I slept in something resembling a bed. In the desert, I spent most nights tied to a chair.

I stand and walk over. The fusser pulls back the fur and gestures for me to crawl in. My legs feel weak with anticipation. Kranik said I'd be safe if I found these Rhemans. If they wanted to quell me, it would be done. If I go much longer without rest, I'll be no use to anyone, including Calipsie. I could really use the sleep.

I climb into the horizontal shelter and pull the top fur around me. The Rheman tucks the fur in at my sides.

'The girl,' I whisper, my eyes impossibly heavy. 'I must find the girl.'

'If here, she tested.' The fusser pats my furs, but it's too late. Wide awake, I struggle to get upright.

'Tested? What do you mean?' I demand, perched on the ledge of the little alcove and ready to spring into action.

'Nothing to do. If arrived before today, test is done.'

'But what if she failed?' I ask.

'She did fail. I hear if anyone succeed.'

'What does it mean? What'll happen to her?'

'You fail, you not chosen.'

'Chosen for what?'

'Enough. Rest,' says the fusser, coaxing me back under the furs.

Not chosen—that has to be better than being chosen, surely. If Calipsie was already tested and wasn't chosen, she'll be all right, won't she? I cling to that thought while I'm tucked back into my furs. I hadn't anticipated that the pipes would be warm, and the heat is like a sleeping draught. I close my eyes, and the quirky room with its curious inhabitants quickly melts away.

I wake to darkness, too afraid to move. I have the panicked sensation that something sinister is lurking nearby. My skin grows clammy while I wait for my eyes to adjust. Just ahead, I make out a mound and a pair of eyes staring back at me. A jolt of panic shakes me, and I try to sit up, but I hit my head, forgetting about the pipes overhead.

Something touches my hair, and I jerk back. My breath hisses.

The thing is closer now, and I can see the contours of its face more clearly.

'Nietsy. Is that you?'

Did the Rheman come to quell me while I slept? I was careless, passing out like that. Too tired to care if I never woke again.

Nietsy doesn't answer. We stare at each other while I take deep breaths and try to steady my heart. If the Rheman wanted to quell me, it could have easily achieved that while I slept. Instead, I get the eerie sense that it's been watching me.

'Do you know something about Calipsie? Have you seen her?' I ask.

Nietsy's hand materialises from the darkness, and I jerk back. I can't be sure it doesn't want to quell me; maybe it just needs a good grip. The little runt quickly retreats, and the bright, blinking eyes fall into shadow.

I wonder whether it can understand me, even though it can't speak.

He, not it. The Rhemans may not conform to genders, but this once has a certain masculinity.

'I'm worried that if you touch me, I won't be me any more,' I say.

Nietsy's face is in darkness, so I can't read the little Rheman's expression, but something in his posture changes. His shoulders fall back, and I get the sense he's receding, trying to show me he's not a threat. That might have been easier if he hadn't attempted to make contact in the dark. The next time he raises his hand, he grabs a handful of his own hair and lifts the snowy mess, so it hovers above his head.

'You like hair?' I ask. 'Right, you like my hair. That's what you've been staring at?'

I wonder if I could use my hair as a bargaining chip. If I had a knife, I could saw it off and make a gift of it in exchange for information.

'Can you help me, Nietsy? Do you know where Calipsie is? Tell me that, and I'll shave off the whole lot for you, I swear it. Can you take me to the place where Helacth keeps the girls?'

The small Rheman looks startled, stepping back and checking down the corridor. Probably worried old Fire Eye is about to scold us.

I fluff my hair, trying to make my offer as appealing as possible.

I must appease the little Rheman, somehow, because he beckons to me, like he expects me to follow. I struggle out of my awkward nest; I've never been so sorry to leave a place. Cramped and strange as it was to curl up between the furs and huddle into a gap between some pipes, it was still the best night's sleep I've had for the longest time.

I follow Nietsy at a safe distance. We walk for a long time, always in the narrow spaces between the walls or through the larger pipes. Nietsy knows these routes intimately. We zig left, then zag right, drop down a shaft, scale inexplicable protrusions from the walls, and on and on until finally, we stop at a dead end. Things get really strange in this sawn-off space, aglow in the light from a floating white orb that hovers nearby, like Nietsy's personal sun.

Nietsy squats and places his palm on a metal section at his feet. The metal warbles as though repelled by his hand. I stare incredulously as it ripples and thins until it's almost entirely transparent. When Nietsy beckons for me to squat beside him on the floor, I do so cautiously, afraid the entire structure might fall apart. I settle into position, tentatively touching the affected area and finding it cool. Hardly daring to trust that the landing will hold my weight, I lean over and peer into the peculiarity of the room below.

32

KYJTA

The window onto the room below is roughly the size of my hand. Through it, I glimpse a very different world. Everything is excessively smooth, like a cloth or a layer of snow has settled over it all. The ceiling is high, possibly as high as the ceiling in the House of Judgement. The walls curve into bright little alcoves, and though there's light everywhere, I can't find its source. I sweep the scene from one end of the room to the other. Roughly thirty women are gathered below, seeming to form two groups. One set is being ushered into a winding queue while the other does the ushering. The women being physically directed into line are skittish, like forest animals trying to shelter from a storm. They wear an assortment of dresses, tunics, and shawls. Not one of them is dressed for the snow. The ushers wear thick trousers with boots and fur strapped to their torsos with hide. Red bandanas are tied around their necks, much like those worn over the faces of the Rhemans that Merrick and I encountered in the snow. I assume anyone wearing a red bandana must be quelled.

I search for the glimmer of copper hair that might reveal Calipsie, but she's either tucked behind one of the older women or not in this room at all.

Something—a Sorb, I realise—nestles in a circular depression in the centre of the room. Its spherical sheath is transparent, revealing innards that glow with a sickly yellow light. Periodically the luminosity shifts, like a cloud shadow passing over the ocean.

Seeing the Sorb, it's impossible not to think of Kranik. He was drawn back to his Sorb, hidden in the secret compartment of a wagon somewhere in the desert. He'll be completely defenceless when the Vigilance Men arrive, charged to destroy all twenty-three Sorbs. I'll know when that time comes. I'm sure I'll feel it. I pull my focus back to the room. I can't let thoughts of Kranik paralyse me. I have to find Calipsie.

Another group of red bandanas enters from the right. I can't see the door from my position, but there must be one. They carry trays piled high with . . . what? Snow, I think. I sit quietly, watching them walk the circular white walkway that leads up to the Sorb. One by one, they tip their trays into the moat that rings the Sorb. The snow slides around the furrow and banks around the Sorb like a snow castle. I can't think what they're up to. Do Sorbs need to be preserved? Are they trying to freeze it? That makes no sense, given that Kranik's Sorb survived the desert.

The red bandana wearers carrying the trays exit the way they came, while the other set of red bandanas continues to align the queuing women with the swirling white pathway that leads to the Sorb. The women in the queue are frightened, clinging to one another, or trying to filter back up the line. None of them gets very far; the red bandanas seize them and wedge them back into place.

A shape rises from some unseen resting place, startling me. The form seems incongruous; the only male in the room. From my vantage point, I can't see his face; I only get an impression of strength and masculinity. He's much larger than any of the women, giant by comparison. His broad shoulders are draped with fur, but his arms are bare and ripple with muscle. At his approach, the women whimper and fall back. He rambles around the depression, gesticulating with his arms. When he turns, I get my first frontal view of him. He's talking, though I can't hear him through Nietsy's manufactured window. Still, he must speak Asaurin, because the women are paying careful attention to his words. During his speech, they look increasingly panicked, and most attempt to get farther away from the front of the queue. Despite their fear, he beckons them forward.

The first in the queue, a young woman, thin to the point of breaking, falters and is prodded by the statuesque red bandana stationed at her side. Another red bandana steps forward, taking her hand and leading her along the path. Together they walk the ring, getting progressively nearer the centre. Behind them, more and more red bandanas step forward, each taking and guiding one of the women. When the first woman reaches the Sorb, she stops. The red bandana then takes the woman's hands and draws her forward. The Sorb grows fractionally brighter, as though the future contact excites it. From within, something sparks against the enclosure. The frail woman jerks back, but the red bandana is strong and holds her in place, forcing her hands against the Sorb.

Although I don't hear the frail woman's scream, her pain reaches me; she's writhing in the red bandana's grip. It's over quickly, and the red bandana plunges the woman's hands into the snow. Even from up here, I see the steam rising.

The man—Helacth, I assume, given my stepfather's warning— walks over to where the injured woman lists against the red bandana, weeping, her hands still buried in the snow. He takes her by the shoulders, turning her to face him. She won't look up at him, so he shakes her until she does. Whatever he sees disappoints him. He shoves her aside and beckons to the next.

The small Rheman is at my hair again, and without thinking, I swat his hand away. Belatedly, I realise that he was trying to communicate something to me. One hand points to my hair, and the other points to the women queuing up to touch the Sorb. Finally, it clicks. Calipsie's copper hair. I mentioned it the first time I described the girl to the Rhemans, and all along, Nietsy has been trying to tell me she's here.

I'm right up against the window now, peering through it, trying to get a better sense of the room. I need to get down there and get Calipsie. But where is she? I push the transparent rectangle, wondering if I can loosen it and jump down, but the drop would probably kill me. I'd be doing the red bandanas a favour. I turn to face Nietsy. Sweet Nietsy, who I assume brought me here against advice. The little Rheman even snuck in to help me in the middle of the night, so its defiance would go unnoticed. I'll need a little more of that defiance if I'm to get inside.

'Make me a door,' I implore. 'I have to get down there.'

Nietsy looks uneasy. He squats and puts a hand on the floor. The metal gathers beneath it as though summoned.

'Wait!' I yell, hammering at the metal, trying to break through. 'Open it back up. I need to get down there.'

Nietsy is unmoved by my performance. When I look at him, finally convinced that the floor is conclusively solid, he points back the way we came. Could the runt plan to take me to an access point closer to the ground? One where I'm less likely to break my neck? It can't hurt to follow the Rheman; he's gotten me this far.

We travel back the way we came. I recognise the inexplicable protrusions from the wall and realise that, given Nietsy's talent, the Rheman probably constructed them. I stop when I realise we're not looking for a lower access point. We're headed back to the narrow room with my cosy bed, where the fusser and Fire Eye might already be bickering across the table. I stop dead, refusing to take another step.

Nietsy turns back, urging me to follow. Why won't the runt just take me to Calipsie? Unless . . . Unless Calipsie isn't there. What was it the fusser said? If Calipsie arrived before today, she's failed the test already. I flash back to the woman with the steaming hands. How she screamed and writhed in pain. Did the Rhemans do the same to a little girl of only nine alignments?

Nietsy beckons to me again.

'I won't go back. Not without the girl.'

Nietsy makes some complicated hand gestures, and I realise that he isn't taking me back to the cramped passage-like room. He's taking me in a different direction. Maybe Helacth is holding Calipsie somewhere else.

I follow Nietsy along another series of tunnels, until the little Rheman stops and puts his hand on a wall. The metal shrinks back, exposing a hole large enough for us to crawl through. The room beyond is some kind of storage space; shelves line the walls, each laden with jumbles of rich materials. Clothes, bags, equipment—it's not easy to make out anything distinctly. I walk to one of the shelves, wondering if I'll find anything useful, like a weapon.

I'm traversing the shelf when I come across a transparent box. There's a collection of fire sticks jumbled together inside. My limbs stiffen. There, among the mishmash of plain colours, lies one made distinct by its drained pigment. It was my mother's, bleached by a puddle of potion. My stepfather had it in his pocket the day he was carried away. My stomach twists and I realise that this isn't storage space for clutter from the Rhemans' planet; it's a dumping ground for junk from ours. The room is filled with all the things Aurora Saurins were wearing, or carrying, the day they were taken. My hands rest on either side of the box, but I can't open it. If I take the fire stick, it will only remind me of what I've done.

I step back, knocking into Nietsy. I've lost a grip on where I am and what I'm supposed to be doing. The Rheman seems oblivious to my state, shuffling through piles of clothes, searching for something. The room feels tight, the smell of stale sweat overwhelming. It's difficult to breathe. I want to leave. I'm craving the snow and fresh air; I need the cold to numb me again.

Nietsy distracts me by waving a red scarf in my face. I must be staring at the runt with blank incomprehension because he makes a pageant of tying the loose material around his neck.

It's a disguise, I realise with a jolt.

The small Rheman stands on his toes to secure it around my neck. Satisfied, he grabs a tarnished mirror from a shelf and holds it up for me. The silvery sphere reflects a girl covered in cuts and bruises, with raw, chapped skin. She looks both determined and fierce. I hardly recognise her. She's nothing like the broken, tormented wreck I know is wallowing on the inside. If I can be her for just one day, maybe I'll have a chance to do this one thing right.

When we make it back to the crazy room between the walls, I stall at the entrance. The fusser and Fire Eye stand in discussion beside my empty bed. Both turn to stare wide-eyed at the pair of us. My outfit must confuse them because they look shaken.

'It's a disguise,' I say, holding up my hands to show them I mean no harm.

Nietsy must have done a good job making me look like one of the red bandanas. The disguise isn't even complete—I still need the fur—but already the two Rhemans look completely spooked.

Fire Eye picks up where he left off earlier, an aggressive torrent of Rheman streaming from his lips. I tuck Nietsy behind me to shield him from Fire Eye's hostility.

'It was me,' I say. 'I insisted on finding the girl.'

The fusser barks something at Fire Eye, who turns from us. Then we're ushered to the table, where a meal is laid out. With a rush of gratitude, I notice there are four steaming bowls, one in front of each of the strange grown-from-the-floor seats. The fusser waves me forward, and we each take a seat. Sharing food feels strange; I've taken my meals alone for as long as I can remember. It's different when I visit my father; when I'm with him, we sit around the small spit he's set up outside. It's not as though he can fit a table and chairs in his tiny shack. But my stepfather and I never shared our meals. I haven't had a proper family meal since before my father was encircled.

The food is odd. Soft when I expect it to be firm. Sweet when I anticipate savoury. I most enjoy something small and moulded into a ball, which reminds me of something Maisi served us, though it's lumpier. Nietsy must notice how hungry I am; he returns the serving bowls to me whenever my plate runs low.

The fusser explains that their food is grown on the ship. I make small attempts at conversation, complimenting the food and making a big deal about how well I slept. At the end of the meal, I drop the big question.

'Is the test the real reason your kind came to Aurora Saura?'

Old Fire Eye slurps the dregs from his bowl.

'Is it why you're still here?' I push.

Surprisingly, it's not the fusser who answers me. It's Fire Eye, and the feisty Rheman does so in near-perfect Asaurin.

'It is the reason for everything.'

Nietsy and the fusser stare at him, looking as surprised as me.

'You have your Sorb inside you,' he tells me. 'It is connected. Our Sorbs were separated by Ezerya. They wanted us to live eternal.'

My mouth opens and closes, but no sound escapes. I don't have enough information to form a response.

'With each generation, it gets more difficult to connect Sorb to body, body to Sorb. Ezerya is needed once more.'

The fusser stands to clear the table. I get the uncomfortable sense that I've outstayed my welcome.

'Nietsy will take you to the Carathim,' continues Fire Eye. 'Then you will leave us alone.'

The Carathim. Could that be where Helacth is holding Calipsie?

I stand and try to help with the clean-up, but the fusser ushers me toward Nietsy, and I understand it's time to go. Nietsy snags one of the furs from my cosy bed and straps it around me with yarn. As for my possessions, I have a small tilling rod and a tub of calming balm that I found in a satchel in the storage room. I hope the cream will help alleviate Calipsie's pain if her hands are burned. The rod's purpose is to make a hole in tilled earth for sowing seeds, but I have another use in mind.

I thank the Rhemans for their hospitality, and soon after that, Nietsy leads me through the spaces between the walls. We take a different route from the one we travelled earlier. Although I don't recognise anything, I spot Nietsy's trademark adaptations. Rungs protrude from the walls to help us climb onto the larger pipes, and there are slipways to get us back down again. Eventually, Nietsy stops to assess one of the walls. First, the small Rheman thins the metal to make a peephole and then peers through it. I stand, fidgeting impatiently, desperate to have a turn. When the little runt steps back, I finally get a sweeping view of the Carathim. The space looks like nothing more than a large dining hall. Red bandanas are everywhere, eating and drinking at long tables. I see women without bandanas too, huddled at tables in the back. There are very few children and none with Calipsie's copper hair.

'I can't see her,' I tell Nietsy. 'I need to be in there. It's the only way I'll find her.'

Nietsy scans the wall, looking for a discreet entry point. When he's satisfied, he liquefies the metal, moulding an opening just large enough for me to crawl through. I climb in without hesitation but feel lost when the hole closes behind me. Without Nietsy's special ability, I've no way to rescue Calipsie. I survey the room, trying to catch a glimpse of her copper hair, but I can't see her anywhere. I'll have to move around the room if I want to find her. Taking a fortifying breath, I strut forward on shaky legs, trying to look like I belong. I'm searching the faces of the women sitting on benches, eating their morning meals, when I see her.

Calipsie!

I rush over and am about to whisper her name when I freeze. There's a red bandana around her neck.

I shrink back, my heart hammering.

Calipsie is quelled.

My mind goes blank. I can't rescue her if she's ferrying a Rheman. Failing the 'test' must not preclude you from being quelled. Maybe everyone who didn't pass it ends up quelled. Kranik might have known how to force this Rheman to vacate Calipsie's young body, but I don't. I step back, needing time to think.

Then, surprising me, someone taps my arm. Spinning around, I recognise my assailant as the statuesque red bandana from Helacth's Sorb room. My breath comes sharply, and I try to muster the right expression. She's gesturing to a group of red bandanas behind her, like she's rounding them up.

I turn and walk toward the group, focusing on steadying my breath. If one of them tries to talk to me, my deception will be plain. When I reach the group, I stand with my back to them, trying to look as unapproachable as possible. Then, Calipsie is striding toward me, looking far older than her nine alignments. I stifle a whimper when she positions herself beside me, our arms almost touching.

The red bandana who recruited me leads us toward a door that retracts into the wall at our approach. She must have been a Charmore before she was quelled; her head was shaved not long ago. We travel down a wide corridor with smooth, tapered walls and stop in front of a set of double doors. Beyond the doors lies Helacth's Sorb room. Roughly fifteen women in the room aren't wearing red bandanas. My team quickly ushers them into a queue. I've seen the barbarity from above, so I know exactly what's coming. With mounting trepidation, I help to line the women up with the circular pathway that leads to the Sorb. This time around, I must endure each scream as the women are forced to sear their hands against the scorching Sorb.

When it's my turn to lead one of the women forward, I take her hand. She's older than I am, a farm worker, judging by her sturdy build. She curses me, but when I pull firmly on her hand, she walks forward, following me along the path. By the time we reach the Sorb, my palms are slick with sweat. The Sorb's dirty-yellow glow brightens as we approach. The strands of light simmering at its base a moment ago start to climb the walls. It might be my anxiety, but the brightening of the strands seems far more dramatic than before. They traverse the inner housing with increasing agitation as we draw nearer.

I drop the farmer's hand, and we regard each other. She has pale eyes, and she uses these to convey her disgust.

'Go on,' I say quietly. Because I can't bring myself to force the woman's hands against the Sorb, essential as that step is to my act.

'You go on!' she bellows in my face, shoving my chest with both hands.

I lose my balance and topple, hitting the floor hard. The farmer seizes the opportunity, leaping over me and running for the door. She manages only a few steps before one of the red bandanas brings her down and drags her back to the Sorb.

I'm getting to my feet when I notice the statuesque ex-Charmore standing over me. Her fuzz of regrowth shimmers in the Sorb's light, still pulsing excitedly behind her. She pulls me up by my wrists and examines my hands. At first, I think she's looking at my Stain, but then I realise her palms are both charred while mine show no signs of trauma. It's an element of my disguise I overlooked.

I twist against the ex-Charmore's impossible strength as she drags me toward the Sorb. The skin on my wrists feels stretched to the point of tearing. Every lost foothold takes me that much closer to certain agony.

Ezerya is needed once more. That's what old Fire Eye said. Was he referring to this Sorb? If I fail Ezerya's test, will my hands be burned? The alternative is far more terrifying. What might become of me if I pass? My muscles tremble, straining against the Rheman, but it's no use. My fear is no match for her strength.

Then, something halts our progression. The ex-Charmore tilts away, and I get my first close-up of Helacth. I can't think where he came from. I didn't see him when I entered the room. He towers over me, his expression set. He looks eager. I was right to think of him as a giant. I can't imagine where he found his Aurora Saurin host, but the man is built like a mountain of rock. He looks utterly indestructible.

Helacth takes my hand and inspects my palm. His fingers are rough and warm—markedly warmer than mine. He might run at a different temperature, or maybe all the blood has drained from my hand.

'You're a clever one,' he says. His voice might be charming, if not for the hunger brightening his eyes. He speaks Asaurin, his manner calm and self-assured. He turns to the Sorb, its pulsing, sickly yellow light, and a strange, satisfied expression takes him.

'There's a reason we only test the women.' Helacth's thumb finds the centre of my palm. 'Would you like to hear the story?'

I don't respond. What would I say?

'Mental pliability,' he says, pushing his thumb deep into my flesh. The pressure lights a path of fire all the way up my arm. I grit my teeth, convinced his thumb will exit on the opposite side of my hand, splitting flesh and splintering bone. There seems no escape from the pain.

'Women must survive to protect their young,' he goes on. 'This is the driving force that makes them malleable. They adapt and accommodate. They make concessions in the name of stability, taking the smallest share of everything to reduce strife. It's the same on any planet that services more than one gender. Women fall in.'

I try to find that fierce girl I saw in the mirror. She could face down Helacth, but she's gone. The pain has vanquished her.

'Ezerya requires an accommodating mind. One with the fortitude to endure her.' He twists my body, using my throbbing hand to guide me to the Sorb. 'If you fight her, she will hurt you,' he whispers. 'But if you're strong enough to accept her and take on her burden, she will protect you.'

Amid the agony, I struggle to take in the meaning of his words. He's giving me the answer, but I'm still not sure I understand. Somehow Ezerya is at the centre of things. If I pass the test, it means I'm capable of ferrying Ezerya. That is the test. According to Fire Eye, Ezerya is the reason for everything.

The Rhemans need Ezerya, and Helacth believes I might deliver her. But I won't give him what he wants. I will fight Ezerya even if it means incinerating my palms.

Helacth drags me like a mewling pup toward the Sorb. Terrified as I am, my body recoiling from the threat, I can't slow my approach. Soon, my hands hover over the Sorb, almost brushing the surface. My heart races, hammering in my throat and drowning out the surrounding sounds. Heat radiates from the Sorb, warming my face and hands. It must be scalding hot, the way the snow around its base continues to liquefy and drain away. A chunk of ice collapses and is replaced by more, sliding down the purpose-built architecture.

My time is up. My skin is about to connect. I'm so transfixed by the Sorb, so tensed against the contact, that I barely notice Helacth's grip loosening. With the threat subsiding, my surroundings suddenly come back into focus.

When I look up, Vigilance Men are swarming the room with their swords drawn. Some are already doing battle with the red bandanas. I see the Zhu among them, with both blades unsheathed, and beside him is Brezan. My mouth goes dry. If Brezan and his father are here, they'll make me pay for what I did.

I'd hoped Brezan's mind would be obliterated by the Mind Pain, but it seems not. He's crossed the Ice Realm to take his revenge. His arrival is good for one thing—Helacth is distracted, dropping my hands.

Although the red bandanas don't have weapons, they don't appear to need them. They rush the Vigilance Men, leaping onto them like frenzied animals. Swords clatter to the ground. Then, Helacth is gone, clambering in to join the fight.

I look around, trying to spot Calipsie. Instinctively, I want to protect her, but how can I when she's ferrying a Rheman? A mental image of her impaled on one of the Vigilance Men's swords gets me moving. I'm running through the foray, screaming her name, when someone grabs me.

'It's me, Lakhan,' says the man. 'Are you all right?' I stare into the unfamiliar face. I don't recognise the Vigilance Man, but I remember Kranik's friend.

Am I all right? I hardly know. I look down at my hands, surprised to find them undamaged, and when I look up again, Lakhan is locked in battle with another of the red bandanas. She's baring her teeth at him, looking like she might use them to rip him apart, while battling him for the sword in his hands.

I scan the faces in the room, then realise that I'm no longer looking for Calipsie. It's Merrick's wavy blond hair I'm trying to pick out in the crowd. It's a senseless act because Merrick isn't ferrying Kranik any more. Still, I'd thought Kranik's Sorb was destroyed by the Vigilance Men, along with the others, but if Lakhan survived that attack, might Kranik have lived through it too?

Something like hope flutters in my belly.

Then Lakhan flies past me, looking like he's been thrown. He crashes into the snow castle, dislodging a mountain of snow onto the floor. Ezerya wobbles on the dais but doesn't fall.

I turn to check if his attacker will pursue him and am winded to see that it's Calipsie. She's joined forces with one of the red bandanas, and the pair charge after Lakhan, who's scrambling to get to his feet.

If Calipsie attacks Lakhan, he might kill her. He's locked in battle with Calipsie and the other red bandana now, and I know I should do something to help, but it's impossible if I don't want to injure either of them.

I realise there's one thing I can do. It might not help Lakhan, but it could help many others. Ezerya's Sorb sits defenceless, only a few paces from where I stand. If I can destroy the test—destroy Ezerya—that would end the maimings, and if the test is the reason for everything and the test is gone, Helacth might finally leave us in peace. Getting to my feet, I dig around in my pocket for the tilling rod I scavenged from the storage room. Once found, I draw it high over my head, then plunge.

I'm seized by the wrist just before impact. It's Helacth; the entire left side of his body is covered in blood, but I can't see any wounds.

Helacth twists my arm. The searing pain forces me to drop the tilling rod. I yelp, gritting my teeth against the agony as I'm drawn back toward the Sorb.

By some peculiar twist of the Hands, Brezan saves me, charging out of nowhere, and attacking Helacth with two swords. When the Rheman overlord drops me, I grapple on the ground until I grip the tilling rod in my good hand. My other arm throbs painfully, and I pull it protectively to my body.

'She must be tested!' Helacth roars, knocking one of Brezan's swords flying. The blade only just misses impaling me before it clatters to the ground.

I'm on all fours, reaching for the sword, when from somewhere behind me, Brezan screams, 'Run!'

When I turn, Helacth is charging me, and there's nowhere for me to go. No time to run. Then the floor gives way, and I plummet through the ship's innards.

———

Strong hands break my fall, lowering me onto a broad pipeline. In the light of a familiar floating orb, I recognise Nietsy's pale face, with its rough-stone countenance. The supporting pipe is almost as wide as the space between the two opposing walls, but it's good that Nietsy caught me, because there's a drop on either side that might lead anywhere.

I lost the tilling rod when I fell. I heard it clatter against the pipe and hit a hard surface below. The drop didn't sound very deep, and I consider going after it. Nietsy looks nervous, though, gesturing for me to follow the pipe into the tunnelled alcove ahead.

I point to the ceiling. 'I need to go back. Calipsie's up there.'

Nietsy jabs a stocky finger toward the alcove, hurrying me along.

I stand firm. I can't leave Calipsie.

'I know you're scared, and you don't have to come with me; just get me back inside.' I put a hand on the wall. 'You can build a ladder here. Make a hole up there.' I point again.

Nietsy's expression is grave. I can tell I'm not getting anywhere. I grab the small Rheman's hand and attempt to push it against the wall, but Nietsy is far too strong, and when the little Rheman jerks away, I lose my balance and fall.

I'm quickly swallowed into the gap between the pipe's sloping smoothness and the bone-cracking solidity of the wall. When I hit the ground, the impact jars my wrist. Crouching in the near darkness, I take a few deep breaths, gradually recovering from the shock. I'm getting unsteadily to my feet, mentally preparing for another confrontation with Nietsy, when something terminates my direction of thought. It's the eerily familiar glow reflecting off the walls; the way it oscillates from purple to white. I turn slowly, shocked by what takes shape from the dark.

As far as the eye can see, there's nothing but Sorbs. Hundreds, maybe thousands of them. The chamber is vast but cramped, with a low ceiling. It's as though the room has been crammed between the Sorb room and another chamber below. A hidden vault, lined wall to wall with transparent, egg-like encasements, glistening as light filaments ebb and surge within. My breath comes shallow as I absorb what a discovery like this means.

Without taking my eyes off the Sorbs, I feel around on the floor for my tilling rod. When my fingers locate it, I grasp it like a dagger.

Yes, warring with the Rhemans is futile, when every Rheman life taken claims the life of an Aurora Saurin, but this . . .

This is different.

For every Sorb I destroy, I can reclaim a life. I can restore women to their homes. Men to their wives. Children to their mothers. I can take back some of what was taken with just a few well-placed strokes.

I crawl on my hands and knees, gripping the tilling rod in my white-knuckled fist. The Sorbs are beautiful. Beautiful and terrible. Some ripple with light and life, while others burn dim. It's toward these dimmer vessels that I make my way. The gloomier globes must belong to Rhemans currently inhabiting bodies. Every Sorb destroyed represents someone's freedom. One stroke might even liberate Calipsie.

Rising to my knees, I raise my tilling rod in both hands. It hangs in the air like a dagger over a sacrifice. I take a deep breath and plunge downward, not wanting to look but unable to tear my eyes away. The tilling rod strikes the Sorb with lethal force, but the springy substance absorbs the impact. For one horrible moment, I imagine that the alien material will resist me, but then it explodes. Gelatinous liquid gushes up from its apex like pus from a ruptured boil; then the wreck collapses, flooding the floor and soaking my knees. I gasp, startled by the blowback. Shaking, I scrape at the mess, frantic to get it off my face and neck.

In the dusky light, I whisper assurances to myself.

Nothing here can hurt me.

Not the gel, not the Sorbs, nothing.

I can keep going.

I must keep going.

Time is something I don't have. There are thousands of Sorbs and only one of me. As soon as Helacth realises what I'm doing, he'll come for me. It won't be long. Someone's bound to notice the personality switches as Rhemans vacate their stolen bodies.

I crawl through the space, quickly manoeuvring into position. The rod is sticky in my hand. I raise it above a dusky sphere and strike. I attack another Sorb and another until the slippery wetness of five Sorbs drenches me. The act is exhausting, and my breath is rasping.

As I position myself in front of my next kill, a cold realisation grips me. Nietsy is Rheman. The destruction of any of these Sorbs could mean Nietsy's life.

I might have killed the little runt. The fusser and old Fire Eye, too.

The realisation changes nothing. At least, I can't allow it to. This is the only way to save Calipsie, Merrick, and others. I must keep going but my arm feels unnaturally heavy. I lift the rod, and the violence of my next blow is inadequate. The rod bounces back. I'm about to make a second attempt, drawing my arms higher this time and rising as high as I can on my knees, but I freeze, tilling rod poised above my head. There's a presence nearby.

I turn to find Nietsy standing in the shadows.

Watching me.

For a moment, we regard each other. I can't see Nietsy's expression, but I don't need to. I can tell what the little runt thinks of me by the slope of his shoulders and the droop of his head.

I drop the rod, but it's too late. Nietsy is gone.

I'm on all fours in a flash, crawling out of the space, calling Nietsy's name. When I reach the area with the pipe, I stand and try to get a grip on it and hoist myself up, but my hands are slippery, and the pipe is too smooth.

'Nietsy?' I try again.

Silence.

'Nietsy, please,' I beg.

I collapse to the floor, unable to think. If I'm left here long enough, I'll build up to destroying more Sorbs—I know I will. But right now, I can't get Nietsy out of my head. The little Rheman has been nothing but good to me—how can I keep going, knowing my actions might end his life?

A soft plop behind me announces that I have company. I tense up, thinking of Helacth, but the giant would surely have made more noise. Turning slowly, I'm relieved to find Nietsy standing there. I'm about to speak, wanting to explain myself—what my people have been through—but the small Rheman puts a finger to the wall and writes two Asaurin words in the malleable metal.

"Helacth come."

My heart goes quiet. We must run. I follow Nietsy down the passage, our footfalls echoing all around. I hope the noise won't give us away. I've reached full speed when something shoots through the wall. It's a hand, I realise, as I skid to a stop. The hand is enormous, definitely Helacth's. Nietsy darts to the side, using his whole body to create a hole in the wall. Quickly, I follow. Then Nietsy melts it shut. We take off down a slim corridor that runs between the walls. Nietsy's intimate knowledge of the ship's innards is our advantage.

When Helacth next finds us, his impossibly large arm shoots from the wall, and he grabs Nietsy around the neck. Nietsy spreads his stubby fingers out against the flat metal surface, and the fabric instantly thickens, bubbling around Helacth's arm. I think the Rheman overlord will let go, but the metal buckles, rippling away from the giant's bulging bicep. Then, the circle tightens again, contracting into the giant's flesh until the pressure is too great. The skin splits, disgorging blood that pours down his arm and onto the floor.

Maybe it's just my wishful thinking, but it looks like Nietsy has greater control of the metal than Helacth. What else could be preventing Helacth from simply climbing through? Helacth must realise it's a competition he can't win. His hand encircles Nietsy's head, gripping the small Rheman's crisp white hair, and slams it against the solid wall. Nietsy's head rebounds from the surface as if on a spring. Helacth's grip loosens, and Nietsy slumps to the floor, his head dropping onto his chest.

I grasp Nietsy beneath the arms and run backwards, dragging the limp little body. Helacth's arm retracts and disappears, but I'm acutely aware that it could shoot out again from anywhere. When my energy is entirely spent, I lower Nietsy to the floor and hunch over the injured Rheman, panting. Nietsy doesn't look well. His skull is caved in on one side, his expression weak, and his chalky skin turning a bruised grey.

Nietsy is fading, eyes fluttering against the desire to sleep.

'What can I do?' I ask.

One of the Rheman's hands flops against the wall, and a hole opens up. Nietsy whispers something I can't hear, so I crawl through the hole and pull the slack body after me. We're in a large room, no longer a space between the walls. The room has a door, and its presence scares me. I've grown accustomed to the ship's secret spaces.

I don't like knowing Helacth and his red bandanas could so easily enter here. I look around, wondering how safe we really are.

The room is flooded with natural light, filtering through a transparent wall. I leave Nietsy, skirting a broad pyramid dominating the centre of the room, to look outside.

It's the middle of the day, and the sheen off the snow makes it difficult to see. Slowly, the dark shapes speckling the pale landscape resolve themselves. They're Vigilance Men, I realise, and they're helping the rescued women from the Sorb room to make their way across the snow. I follow the line to see a gathering of men handing out furs and blankets. The women wrap themselves up warmly before trudging on. At the bottom of the next slope is another way station. It looks like Vigilance Men here are waving ghoragalls down from the sky. When the beasts land, the men use nets to trap them. One of the men attaches a harness to a ghoragall as it's held down by others. The harness is similar to the contraption the Grulo used to control their satermijtes. Pretty soon there's a smoking sack of feather dust dangling just below the ghoragall's head.

Someone has figured out how to control the ghoragalls! I scour the snow, automatically searching for my father. I'm squinting, trying to make out faces, clothing, anything that might help me identify him, when I see Brezan, his wavy golden-brown hair glinting in the sunlight. I follow his progress. He's carrying a sack of feather dust, and when he reaches the gathering, he hands it to a man. The man is my father, and my heart stutters, seeing him not only alive, but unhurt and no longer captive. Brezan claps my father on the shoulder, pointing at the ghoragall as it lifts from the snow. The great beast soars away with a rider and three rescued women on its back.

My father looks pleased, clasping Brezan by the upper arm and pulling him into a congratulatory embrace. The upper arm greeting is pure Rheman and my throat constricts; cool fear wicks through my limbs like yesterday's blood. If there's anyone in the world my father despises, it's Brezan. There's only one explanation for his behaviour.

My father is quelled.

Before I can see more, movement at the scene's periphery snags my attention. At first, I can't make sense of the droves of silver pellets streaking inward across the snow. Then, when the sleek capsules stop and Rhemans tumble from their doors, I recognise them. I'd been transported in one of the Rheman carriages myself, and now here are more of them. I count at least forty.

It's quickly clear that the Rhemans are here to prevent the rescue. They point strange devices at the Vigilance Men, who crumple and fall to the snow.

On impulse, I put a hand to the transparent barrier, and the view goes dark. I tap the window repeatedly, but it remains stubbornly black.

No, no, no.

I fall back, angry and cursing the Hands. Why did I touch it? I search the window, trying to find some lever or button that might undo what I did. That's when I notice that the window isn't completely dark. Hundreds of different-size globes are spread across the panel, interspersed with bright balls that seem to burn. Stepping back, I recognise the constellations of stars, but more detailed than anything I've witnessed staring up at the sky.

Behind me, Nietsy groans.

I quickly trace my steps back to the Rheman's side and lower myself to my knees.

'I'll carry you,' I say. 'I'll take you to your friends.'

In my head, I'm running through the reasons my offer isn't possible. I don't know the way, and small as Nietsy is, I can't carry him as I scale a ladder or crawl through a tunnel. But Nietsy is dying; the Rheman's flat grey eyes are losing their lustre.

Then I realise I already have everything Nietsy needs. Gently, I raise the Rheman's infantile hand in my own.

'Use my body,' I say. 'I give you permission.'

Nietsy's eyes flutter at the sound of my voice.

'You can get us back to Fire Eye and the fusser. They'll know how to help you.'

Then, my world goes dark.

33

KYJTA

When I come around, I'm back in the room between the walls, sitting with my back to one of the incongruous pipes. Old Fire Eye looms over me, his golden eye gleaming bright. The gruff Rheman grasps my arm and pulls me to my feet. He looks older, somehow. Wearier.

'I told you to leave us alone.'

'Is Nietsy all right?' I ask, spotting the fusser disappearing into one of the lopsided tunnels, carrying something. Possibly a Sorb.

Whatever Fire Eye thinks of me, it's clear my question doesn't warrant an answer.

'I will take you as far as the hidden exit. Then you make your own way.'

If only I'd listened to Nietsy. If I'd just left when he asked, the little runt might still be here. But the fusser was carrying a Sorb, wasn't she? There's still a chance.

'Why won't you tell me?' I demand. 'Is Nietsy alive?'

Fire Eye practically incinerates me with his amber glare.

'Never mind Nietsy. Do *you* want to live?'

It's a question I've never asked myself. Hearing it now, I come up empty. I want to survive, but living isn't the same as surviving. Living is bigger than that.

The closest I think I've come is that day on the beach, leaping from the rocks with hands clasped in anticipation rather than fear. Bizarrely, Brezan's face fills my mind, and I finally grasp what my subconscious must have known already. Brezan could never have withstood the Mind Pain.

Brezan is Kranik.

Kranik saved me, first fighting off Helacth, then yelling for me to run when the Rheman overlord was about to grab me. Brezan would never have done any of that. I thought my father was quelled, playing friendly with Brezan outside, but I got it backwards. Brezan is quelled, and my father was showing respect for Kranik, greeting him with the Rheman handshake. Fire Eye is offering me the chance to reunite with them. My mother might be there too. I can picture us climbing onto the back of a subdued ghoragall and flying home, the icy wind rushing through our hair.

But my mother is quelled, like Calipsie. And it's not only them. Every red bandana Helacth sends to fight the Vigilance Men is quelled. If Helacth succeeds, we lose, and if Helacth fails, we lose. I can't just fly away. I came here to save a single soul, but I can do better than that. I have something unique to bargain with.

I hold Fire Eye's incongruous gaze. The flaming iris burns with impatience, while the restorative brown one convinces me that the Rheman will hear what I have to say.

'Will the quellings end when Helacth finds someone to ferry Ezerya?' I ask.

'I do not speak for Helacth.'

'Do you recommend I try it if I want to stop the quellings?'

'I recommend you take my offer,' Fire Eye tells me.

The temptation is there, tugging at me like a barbed wire anchored in my heart. But what if the real reason for the Rhemans' invasion isn't bodies? What if all they've ever wanted was to find a single host? Someone to resurrect Ezerya so she can fix whatever's broken. That person could end the war. I saw how Ezerya's Sorb reacted to me, and so did Helacth. He might consider a trade.

My stepfather's dying wish was for me to save myself. This is my chance. Maybe I can't save my body, but I could save my soul.

'Can you take me to him?'

Fire Eye regards me with grave indifference.

'It's your body.'

I smile grimly and stand to my full height, ready to face my fate.

The fusser calls out as we exit the cosy hideaway. She tries to hand a bulging backpack to Fire Eye, but the Rheman refuses to take it.

'The girl can get Nietsy safe.' The fusser pushes the backpack against Fire Eye's barrel chest.

'The girl's not going anywhere safe. She's giving herself to Helacth.'

The fusser takes a step back, regarding me with fierce bewilderment.

'No. Must not. Must go, and take Nietsy too.'

I stare at the backpack. Nietsy must be inside it.

'You must convince her,' the fusser implores, shaking the backpack straps in Fire Eye's face.

'She has her own mind. Maybe she'll change it.' Fire Eye slings the backpack over one shoulder.

I throw my arms around the fusser, suddenly sad to leave this place.

'Time to go,' old Fire Eye says, breaking things up.

When the fusser pulls back, her eyes are crystal bright. 'You must look after you,' she says.

Fire Eye puts a hand on my shoulder and leads me away.

34

KRANIK

We are fifteen Vigilance Men and three Rhemans. That's all the Young Soro could spare from the war raging outside. I don't know how many Aurora Saurins Helacth is keeping quelled aboard the *Ebisu*, but at the rate the Vigilance Men out there are falling, the vast majority must've joined the fight. The Rhemans on snow patrol were first to arrive, piling out of their silver metzes before the vehicles could come to a stand; their handheld kwondors indiscriminately discharging lethal laser-burn, far outmatching the Vigilance Men's swords. With Lakhan's help, we secured a small stash of the handheld weapons from one of the stationary metzes before the fighting got too bad. The kwondors have a non-lethal setting, so we were able to stem the tide without killing very many.

The war would already be lost if not for the potion master and the stash of supplies from his desert tent. Not only bags of feather dust for controlling ghoragalls, but Rheman-strength smokers, like the kind he used on me. It took some doing to commandeer one of the metzes and set the potion master up on its voice amplification system, but we managed it. I can't hear the Hok's calming mantra from within the ship's walls, but before I left, he had the advancing Rhemans docile once they got in range of the smoke.

Still, I was lucky to get the Zhu, Lakhan, Rhytheus, and the others. I'll need them if we're going to face Helacth. We check the Carathim first but find it empty. The inhabitants must've left in a hurry; the long tables are still littered with half-eaten meals. Next, we check the Sorb Room, since it's the last place I saw Helacth. The room is quiet and empty, but for the twisted bodies lying lifeless on the pale floor. I check each one without acknowledging what I'm looking for: a body, smaller than the rest, with a sheet of rich copper hair.

I'm steadier on my feet once the gruelling task is done and I don't find Calipsie, so I join Lakhan beside the spiral pathway. The dais that held the diseased Sorb sits empty. All that remains is the snow shored against it, but even that is diminished. A great deal of snow must have come loose because the spiral pathway is deep with water.

Lakhan and I step over the low repeating walls until we reach the centre.

'I'm starting to think this stuff is more than just a garnish.' Lakhan lifts a fistful of crystals from the moat encircling the dais.

'It might be for preservation,' I suggest, thinking how unhealthy the Sorb looked.

Lakhan doesn't respond, and there's a shift in the air. I can't describe the sensation, but when I look up, Kyjta is standing, immobile, in the doorway. Beside her is a Rheman in one of the original animation cask-grown bodies. The Rheman passes Kyjta a backpack and disappears.

I'm instantly on the move, stepping over each low wall in turn. I can't go fast enough. I'm so absorbed by Kyjta's sudden appearance, so reassured at seeing her alive, that I don't notice the crouching figure as I hurdle the next wall. When she fires, it's too late to react. The laser slices through Brezan's thigh, sending me sprawling. I'm flat on my stomach, water leeching into my clothes, but there's no pain. I roll onto my back to get eyes on my attacker. She's hunched over me, pointing the kwondor at my head, but it's not the weapon that paralyses me; it's the face.

Calipsie's face is fully intact, bearing not a single scratch, copper hair cascading around her shoulders. Only it isn't her. She's wearing one of Helacth's signature bandanas, and those eyes—no way do they belong to a young girl. Not what's behind them, in any case.

Fortunately, Lakhan and Rhytheus aren't as stunned as I am. Between them, they tackle the Rheman, wrestling her to the floor. The kwondor glides across the pathway. I lift it out of the water, wondering if it'll still fire.

I look down at Brezan's leg. There's so much blood. The water surrounding me is swirling with it. Lakhan undoes Calipsie's red bandana and ties it around my wound.

When I look up, Kyjta is leaping the wall. She stops just an arm's breadth away and stares at me uncertainly.

'Kranik?' she asks.

'You guessed?'

Kyjta drops to her knees beside me, the water soaking her clothes. 'You're alive,' she says as she wipes Brezan's wet hair out of my eyes. Her touch is mild, but I should feel it—given how damp I am. I don't. All I get is that familiar sense of proximity.

'You came after us,' she says, searching my face, looking right through Brezan and finding me.

'Well, we were mid-conversation,' I say with a small smile.

She laughs. Then leans in, putting her forehead to mine and closing her eyes. Nothing.

She must see something in me—disappointment, sorrow—because she pulls back, bumping my leg in her haste and embarrassment. Then she's apologising, worried about causing me pain.

'It doesn't hurt.' My trousers are soaked, but I can't feel the wound.

'You don't feel anything?' says Kyjta, surprised. She looks around the rippling surface of the pool that's soaking my clothes, and at my dripping hair.

'Even with all this water?'

'Not in this body,' I say. I'd take the pain if it meant feeling her fingertips trailing the hair out of my face.

Kyjta's gaze drops to my hand, resting below the water's surface, and her expression grows determined. Even without a sense of touch, tension builds as she pushes her fingers between mine. She hasn't given up yet.

'What about now?' she asks.

My response needs no words.

Kyjta's face drops, and a small part of me rejoices. She wants me to experience her touch.

My leg is a bit stiff, but with Kyjta's help, I manage to get to my feet.

Rhytheus has hold of Calipsie, and I can tell the tight grip makes Kyjta uncomfortable, but we can't let down our guard.

'Can you get her onto a ghoragall?' I ask Lakhan. If we can get Calipsie far enough away, the Rheman will be pulled back to their Sorb, and we'll finally get Calipsie back.

'Shouldn't be too much trouble.'

'Do it,' I say. 'Take Kyjta with you.'

'And you?' says Lakhan, as Calipsie's Rheman squirms in Rhytheus's grip.

'The rest of us will stay to finish what we started.'

But we miss our chance, because a body hurtles into Rhytheus, knocking the captain down, and Calipsie darts free.

'Don't make any special arrangements on my behalf.' The voice is low, coming from the doorway.

Helacth has seven red bandanas flanking him, blocking the only exit. Each of the Rhemans holds a kwondor, aimed and ready to fire.

I look for Calipsie, but the Rheman has already scampered back to its master.

So I lunge for Kyjta, throwing my body over hers. There's a series of sizzles as lasers burst free of the kwondor's apertures, but they're no match for the terrinium walls. We must have just missed being hit, but when I look down, there's so much blood. For one torturous moment, I think it's Kyjta's, but her expression is filled with fear, not pain. There's a hole in Brezan's shoulder, and blood pulses from the wound, pouring onto her wet clothes.

'Run!' I yell. 'Get out of here.'

She doesn't run. Instead, she takes my hand and pushes it flat against the floor, then looks at me like she's urging me on. I stare at her, dumbfounded.

'Make a hole,' she hisses. 'We can go somewhere safe.'

'A hole?'

'Melt the metal. Dissolve it. Whatever.'

'Melt the terrinium?' I'm still confused. Terrinium is the most durable substance I've come across in my limited lifespan.

'I can't,' I say.

'What do you mean, you can't?' she asks, accusingly.

Now is not really the time to discuss my shortcomings. With a hand on Kyjta's shoulder, I force her to stay low as I peer over the wall. Helacth is lumbering toward us, batting aside Vigilance Men as they attempt to attack. I raise the kwondor and fire.

Ducking back down, I motion for Kyjta to stay low and traverse the wall. Then I fire three more shots, hitting Helacth in the arm and the rib cage. The Rheman overlord keeps coming.

Kyjta and I keep low, moving away from the location Helacth last had eyes on us, but our progress is slow. My vision is blurred, and my breathing is unsteady. Brezan's body is feeling the strain. I know this without pain as my barometer.

Before very long, we come across Lakhan. My friend is on the ground, wrestling Calipsie.

'She won't listen,' strains Lakhan. 'Keeps joining in the fighting.'

'You have to get her out of here,' says Kyjta.

'I'm trying,' Lakhan's teeth are gritted as he struggles to keep Calipsie under control without hurting her.

I look down at my kwondor. There's a switch on the side, and I flick it to the non-lethal calibration, raise the muzzle, and fire. Calipsie goes limp. Kyjta jerks back, glaring at me with blank incomprehension.

'It's just to knock her out,' I explain.

'Thank the stars aligned,' says Lakhan, throwing the limp body over his shoulder.

'You've still got to get her out of here,' whispers Kyjta. 'Helacth isn't just going to let you go. Not unless we distract him.'

Kyjta slips the backpack from her back and hands it to Lakhan.

'This is Nietsy,' she says. 'Someone else you need to keep safe.'

Turning back to me, she says, 'We have to draw Helacth's attention, and the others too.'

I'm trying to figure out a way to keep both girls safe when Helacth grabs me from behind and pulls me over the wall. Kyjta is screaming for Lakhan to run. Helacth crushes my hand, forcing me to drop the kwondor. With three fingers bent out of shape, the hand stops responding. I punch Helacth in the head with my good hand. Pretty soon, we're both on the floor, kicking and pummelling each other. Throughout our brawl, the Rheman shows no sign of weakening, while Brezan's body is sluggish from blood loss, and my punches grow weaker with every strike. Helacth pulls back, raising both fists, hammer-like, above his head.

He's going to crush my skull with his fists, I think, but, just then, a star hammer slams into Helacth's side. The Rheman overlord rocks in place, checking the bloody gash with the tips of his fingers. The blurred figure holding the hammer comes slowly into focus—it's Kyjta. Then five Vigilance Men leap the wall with their swords drawn.

Kyjta grabs me and pulls me to my feet. The floor is wet and, for a moment, I think I'm going to lose my footing, but then Rhytheus takes my other arm and we're moving. We make it to the door before things get too fuzzy, but when we reach the hall—

35

KYJTA

Rhytheus lifts Kranik into his arms. He's lost a lot of blood and he slumps, unconscious. My father might be able to save him, but we need to be quick.

I hear footfalls behind us and imagine the worst, but when I spin around, I find the Zhu, pale and panting—staring wide-eyed at his son. Kranik is probably the only thing keeping Brezan alive. The shock alone could kill him. The Zhu runs a hand over his son's bloody hair. He looks heartbroken; it's the second time losing his son.

'Tiberico has a medical station outside,' says the Zhu.

'Let's go,' I say, suddenly energised.

Together, we run. The corridors are long, and it seems to take forever.

Rhytheus leads us down a few levels, and then we're racing along another corridor. Occasionally, a door will open as Rhytheus approaches it. At first, this frightens me; I think someone will rush out, but the farther we go, the more I feel the ship is deserted. Everyone must've been ordered outside to fight the Vigilance Men. I hope my father found safety. And my mother; I still don't know where she is.

When the next door opens, I glance quickly to the side, and stop dead. It takes Rhytheus and the Zhu a few more steps before they realise they've lost me. By then, I'm already in the room, staring at the familiar myriad of planets and stars covering one wall.

'Lost something?' says Rhytheus, peering inside.

The Zhu has retraced his steps and stands with his back to Rhytheus, keeping a lookout.

'This was a window,' I tell him, indicating the planetary display. 'From here, you can see everything that's going on outside. We could prepare ourselves, check that the way to the medical station is clear. You're the captain of the *Rhema Bolajio*—you must know how it works.'

'Every ship has its master,' responds the captain. There's a gash beneath one eye, and the dusting of dried blood gives Rhytheus a grimy countenance. 'While my Sorb survives, the *Rhema Bolajio* responds to me, and only me. It's no different for Helacth and the *Ebisu*.'

I growl in frustration, but my outburst is short-lived. There's a sizzle, and the Zhu twists violently to the right, then collapses. One of his swords comes spinning into the room and clatters across the floor. I can't see Helacth from this side of the door, but by the look on Rhytheus's face, I can be sure the giant is coming. I run forward to grab the Zhu under the shoulders and drag him out of range. By the time I look up, Rhytheus has vanished and taken Kranik with him.

Something hits the door, and the reverberation is so loud that I stumble backwards. I look for some way to close the doors. I find a rectangular panel, but it doesn't respond to my touch. Then I notice that the Zhu's lower leg is still outside the room. I duck down to drag his leg through, and as I do, Helacth fills the doorway. Shocked by the bloodied form looming over me, I fall back, landing awkwardly on my wrist. He looks like something that escaped from a nightmare.

Blood gushes from his temple, and his left eye is swollen shut and seeping. His functional eye has no trouble locating me, though.

This is it; time to make my offer. Just give Helacth what he wants and pray he leaves everyone I love alone. Staring up into that lone eye, I struggle to recall why I thought my plan would work. I'm not in a strong bargaining position, lying on the floor with my one remaining ally wounded and pulsing blood from a shoulder wound.

When the giant steps in, the door closes, and silvery metal sluices into the seams. The Zhu screams, and I realise that his foot is still outside. I didn't get him all the way through. He tries to free himself, gritting his teeth and grunting like an animal, but it's no use; he's trapped.

Helacth regards the Zhu. His lone eye has a terrible, greedy sheen. Is he assessing the Zhu's bodily condition? Trying to figure out which host has the greater longevity? The Zhu may be my father's age, but he has the physique of a much younger man, and Helacth's body has taken too many deadly blows. The shot that dropped the Zhu may have been purposefully non-lethal. But now, with the loss of his foot, the Zhu's chances of being a viable alternative are shrinking.

'An interesting companion you chose. The Zhu, isn't it?' The black cape with its red trim must give the Zhu's title away, but why that's interesting is lost on me.

It's impossible to imagine Helacth's body holding out much longer. One of his arms is a mess, hanging loosely at his side; I'd be surprised if he could wield it. There's a chunk of flesh missing from his right side, exposing his ribs and seeping fluid onto his tunic. If he weren't ferrying a Rheman, he'd surely be dead. His clothes are soaked through, though it's hard to say how much is blood and how much is water. He must have gone a few rounds in the river of melted snow; his clothes are dark and dripping with liquid.

I grope at the floor, trying to find the Zhu's illing sword. It's nearby, but I don't dare take my eyes off Helacth. When I locate the hilt, I get to my feet, holding the sword in both hands, and brace to use it. I've never used a sword, and I don't expect my performance to reflect any innate talent, but I can't beat the giant with my fists. One touch and the Rheman could transfer.

Ruined as he appears, Helacth still manages to look amused.

'You're dying,' I tell him hotly. 'There's too much blood.'

'Dying's not so bad,' he says.

I suppose it's not, when you're immune to pain and doing it in someone else's body. Still, without the pain, he might not notice himself slipping. He might fall dead at my feet, if I can distract him long enough.

A sudden movement takes my attention. The Zhu swings his other sword, targeting the giant's Achilles tendon. It's a brilliant move, designed to cripple the Rheman, but it doesn't work. The Zhu is too weak, and the sword is too heavy. It slips from his grip and skitters into the wall. Then, the silvery floor morphs and swallows the blade.

Moving backwards, I position myself behind the central pyramid, out of Helacth's reach. With him now on one side and me on the other, we lunge in opposite directions, him feigning one way and then the other and me darting away. I can keep this up indefinitely, and soon his body will give out. Kranik got him to this point, and I owe it to Kranik to complete what he started. Soon, there won't be enough blood circulating in Helacth's borrowed body, and he'll surely die. Helacth must sense that I'm stalling; he stops and stares down at his bloody torso.

'Flesh. Such a fragile thing,' Helacth says. 'Ezerya might have designed you better.'

Tensed as my body is, I still stagger where I stand. Ezerya can't have designed *me*. The Hands are responsible for life on Aurora Saura; Ezerya can't be the Hands. Ezerya is Rheman.

My racing thoughts are cut short. Helacth raises a hand and utters a single command.

'Stay.'

The floor surges around my feet like flood water. I try to move, but I'm trapped in boots of silvery metal. I pry at the substance with the sword, but it has no give. My only defence is to stall him, but how?

The Zhu comes to my rescue with a comment that makes no sense. 'We had an agreement. You have what you want. Now you must go.' He's weak and still bleeding, but his voice is focused and steady.

'An agreement,' says Helacth, pulling on the cords that hold his threaded furs in place. The weight of the garment seems too much for him. Beneath it, his tunic is soaked through. 'Yes, I recall. I get what I want and go. You and the rest of your kind get to live; but soon, you'll be dead, and death is the leveller of all alliances.'

I stare at the Zhu, remembering the day he stood outside my father's shack, claiming to be puppet to no man or beast. Things are falling into place.

'You gave away the bunker locations,' I accuse. 'It was you all along, with your three-pronged approach.'

The Zhu raises his grey eyes. There's no remorse in them—it's more like pride.

'Fight, control, surrender,' he says. 'It's the only way to win.'

'But you didn't fight!' I shout. 'When the Tarrohar sent the Rhemans into the desert, you were counting on the Old Soro to kill them. Not once did you rally your own men against the Tarrohar.'

I'm breathing hard, but there's so much more I have to say, and if my words hold Helacth's attention, so much the better.

'You may have wanted to control the Tarrohar, but my father never made smokers potent enough. You failed. Is that why you surrendered our people? Telling Helacth where our bunkers were?'

'I did not fail. If the girl from the bunker hadn't been taken, the Charmores would never have hatched a plan to kill the Tarrohar with your father. Those pills made them powerless.'

'You couldn't have known that would happen. Why share the bunker locations with the Rhemans?' I ask, my voice raw.

'Azaire's contacts said the Rhemans were here to find someone to ferry their deity, and then they'd leave. Something about building better bodies; I didn't care. My job was to get them away. The sooner they had what they came for, the sooner they'd leave.'

Old Fire Eye said something about it getting progressively more difficult for each generation to connect body to Sorb. Is that why the Rhemans are unable to feel, and why Nietsy can't speak?

I turn my attention to Helacth. 'Is that why you need Ezerya? To design better bodies for you?'

Helacth chuckles softly and shakes the last of the strips of tattered fur from his shoulders. He might not feel pain, but his body is weakening.

'You are the better design,' he says. 'You're the replacements.' He raises a hand to indicate the wall of planets and stars. 'Seeded across the universe for our guaranteed existence. By keeping all of you connected to your Sorbs, Ezerya designed you never to become incompatible, ensuring that we Rhemans would always have an unlimited resource.'

There will be no appeasing Helacth. Even if I gave him Ezerya incarnate, Rhemans would still need our bodies. Sacrificing myself would serve no purpose except to satisfy his greed for everlasting life.

Helacth lumbers forward. I pull at my legs, desperate to free myself and run.

'I guess it didn't work out so well,' I stall. 'Can't be much of a life without a sense of touch.'

'Ezerya will correct that.' The comment is dismissive, but I can tell it irked him.

Helacth summons the silvery metal from the floor. It flows up his body, slipping around his form to craft a chest plate. Next, it forms a mask with slots for his eyes and a slim hole over his mouth. His body wouldn't survive another blow, and he's not taking any more chances. With the pale silver-white mask melded to his face, he looks like the ship personified.

I flinch when he reaches forward, but he's targeting the pyramid. Something happens when his hand connects—the material wavers, oscillating in colour. From nowhere, Ezerya's Sorb appears at the pyramid's apex. The Sorb glimmers dirty yellow as the strands of light lift and fall in a lazy, haphazard pattern.

'It's time you played your part.' Helacth's gaze brims with reverence. He's transfixed by the Sorb, but the comment is directed at me, I think. How long has he searched for someone to ferry Ezerya?

When he turns his full attention to me, I know precisely what's coming. My life will end, and Ezerya's will recommence. Helacth will win.

Air whistles through his mouthpiece as he approaches. I swing the sword when he's close enough, but he bats the blade away. The sword goes flying and is swallowed by the ship.

Helacth has me by one wrist, and his grip is impossibly strong. I'll likely break my arm battling to free myself, but that doesn't stop me from trying. With a flick of Helacth's hand, my feet slip free of my metal boots, and I'm jerked forward. I try to summon the defiance I felt in the Sorb Room. I was sure I could resist Ezerya before I knew what it was. Now, with this new knowledge, I'm no longer convinced. How do you resist your creator?

The Sorb's pallor hasn't improved since I saw it last. It was a sickly yellow then, and the lacklustre glow is nothing like the dazzling purple-white luminosity of the many thousands I came across in the space below the Sorb Room. Still, sensing my presence, it starts to revive. The sticky strands of light, twitching near the Sorb's base, begin to climb the sides.

My free hand instinctively reaches for my throat, but my satermijte wings are long gone, and they'd be little use here. Instead, my fingers brush something else: the leather cord and its little memento.

If Merrick could see me now, he might finally feel avenged. Only Merrick wasn't after vengeance; he wanted empathy. He thought I'd understand what I put him through if I dosed myself with the adulation mixture. He wanted me to suffer the same effects as any Aurora Saurin taking the elixir. Any Aurora Saurin . . . But, if I can trust my intuition, the results differ for a Rheman.

Helacth forces me bodily toward the Sorb. The closer I get, the higher the light streams climb the Sorb's encasement. Ezerya's ecstasy at my proximity is evidenced by the increased vigour of the luminous strands clambering to greet me. Every breath whistles through the mouthpiece of Helacth's mask, and the tempo increases. He thinks he's finally going to get what he wants.

I have other ideas.

Tugging on the vial of vengeance, I snap the string and pop the cap.

Helacth has to tilt his head. He can't easily see what I'm doing over the ledge of mask below his good eye.

His movement is my invitation to shove the unstoppered vial through the hole in his mask.

I may not be any good with a sword, but I have some skill when it comes to potions. Taking aim, I shunt the vial through the hole with enough forward momentum to force a decent dose into Helacth's mouth.

Helacth tries to spit it free, but the jar is lodged inside the mask.

Struggling for breath, he drops my hand and stumbles backwards. The terrinium falls from him like silver water.

The violence of his scream seems to gut him from the inside.

He collapses at my feet, clinging to his injured side and baring his teeth against the pain. I back away as he roars in agony. His good eye, unfocused at first, finds me. I'm paralysed by the change in him.

Merrick drank the elixir and was overcome by a desperate need; but the same wasn't true for Kranik. In Merrick's body, Kranik could feel; and feeling anything is just a gateway to pain. I know that from experience.

'What . . . have you done?' I can barely hear the strangled words escaping Helacth's clenched jaws as he struggles to withstand his terrible injuries.

I stagger backwards, wanting to put space between us.

'Make it . . . stop,' he whispers, lying on his back and rocking side to side.

I search the space for something lethal, anything long enough to do the job of killing him while keeping me out of range. One accidental touch and it would all be over. The swords are gone, and I must act quickly. Helacth's clothes are wet now, but they will dry. When they do, his suffering will end. Kranik couldn't feel a thing without the water, and neither will Helacth.

I turn to the Zhu, desperate for advice. He's managed to pull his leg free of the door, but his foot is a mangled mess, trailing a river of blood. He's taken up with fashioning himself a tourniquet, and I decide I don't want advice from him anyway, knowing the monster he truly is.

'It's a potion . . .' says Helacth. 'Potions have . . . antidotes. I'll give you anything . . . anything you . . . want.'

Anything I want?

Helacth must never have experienced pain and has no mechanism to deal with it—I've lived my entire life under threat of physical suffering, and I have a solid hold on the concept.

'Anything?'

'Anything.'

'Will you fly your ships away from here?'

'Yes,' he stammers.

'And you swear you'll never come back.'

'Never.'

I drop my head. 'I could never trust you.'

'There are other places . . . other worlds,' he gasps.

Other worlds where Helacth and his Rhemans can repeat exactly what they've done here? My stomach twists, thinking about the horrors he might inflict on other civilisations. It's no hero's solution, but I am no hero. Everything I love is here, and I need every ship motivated to leave. Killing Helacth isn't enough, another Rheman will simply take his place.

If I give them what they came for—if I give them Ezerya—and Helacth delivers on his promise of getting all of his ships off my world and headed for a more hospitable planet, then what reason would they have to return? They may truly never come back.

There's no time for negotiations. The longer the war rages outside, the more of my people will die.

'Do it,' I say.

Helacth grimaces as he gets to his knees. He crawls forward until he reaches the pyramid. He uses it to pull himself onto his feet. I worry that his pain is already subsiding. His movements are less strained. What if he becomes accustomed to the pain and reneges?

'Choose your destination.' Helacth touches the pyramid, and a rotating display expands from the central beacon. I see hundreds of planets. Are they all populated? Will each one be as easily conquered as ours?

Helacth looks at me, poised for my response. He's toying with me. If there are planets besides ours, and it's me he needs to ferry Ezerya, then this is no concession for him at all. I'm giving him exactly what he wants.

Deciding to let the Hands guide me, I find my fingers hovering over a red planet. I'm about to touch it when I rethink my strategy. It shouldn't be the Hands. Not if the Hands are Ezerya. I scan the globes and find one that looks like it primarily consists of water. There are small islands, but nothing like the vast expanses of land here on Aurora Saura. Perhaps the ship will land in the ocean, and that will be that.

'That one,' I say, pointing.

It takes time for the rotation to reach him, but when it does, he raises his large bloody hand and fingers the globe as it slides by. The procession stops, freezing the world in place. I study it, hoping it will be the final resting place for Helacth and his fleet.

'Earth,' says Helacth, touching the globe.

Earth. The name is meaningless, and I don't think about it any more, because the floors are vibrating. Everything is vibrating. My legs can't hold me, so I sink to my knees, using the floor for support. We're leaving Aurora Saura. The walls are ringing, and vibrations pound in my ears. I try to crawl across the floor to find something to hold on to, but the floor is tilting, and I'm sliding. I raise my hands to protect my head, but I'm slammed against the wall.

When I open my eyes, gasping with remembered panic, the Zhu is hunched over me, looking concerned. The ship still seems airborne, but the turbulence is muted, more of a dull thrumming in my bones.

Still panicking, I search the room for Helacth. His body lies lifeless near the door. Relief makes me weak, but I push myself onto one elbow to get a better look. I need to be sure.

'Is he dead?' I ask.

The Zhu stares at the crumpled and bloody body.

'Depends who you mean,' he says.

My stomach tightens. It's not the Zhu hunching over me; it's Helacth.

He has what he came for. We're leaving Aurora Saura, heading for Earth. A planet I expect I'll never see, though my eyes may roam its waters, and my feet may comb its sands.

36

KRANIK

I stand in the Eye, centre circle, with eleven others. This small band is all that remains of the twenty-three Rhemans who set out across the Parched Lands. We are ringed by five podiums, though only one is occupied. Spectators fill all the seats; it's a busy day for the House of Judgement. I suspect anyone within a day's travel has made the journey.

The sun is shining, and the sky is clear. The ghoragalls don't bother with Merrocha any more; instead, they keep to Thormyth, where they're left in peace. There's a lot of energy in the little seaside town. For the last three nights, I've listened as the townsfolk attend the night markets, dancing and singing until the early hours. Of the six ships that landed on Aurora Saura just over twenty alignments ago, the *Rhema Bolajio* is the only one that remains. It couldn't leave without its captain.

The Young Soro looks regal, presiding over us from above, but after today, Nija has promised to convert the Eye into a hospital, where she and the potion master will treat the sick and injured with their potions and elixirs. Where those fail, they'll use the traveller's restoration equipment that was confiscated from Tiberico when the fighting finally ended and all the wounded were seen to. I've Rhytheus to thank for making sure Brezan was one of them.

It's Brezan's body I stand in now. It has more scars than it did when I first transferred. The traveller's restoration equipment isn't nearly as powerful as the restoration pallets on the ship. Still, the tight wound in the shoulder is loosening every day, and the one in my leg only gives me a slight tilt to the right.

The outcome of our encirclement is predetermined, agreed between the Rhemans and the Young Soro in advance. We are to be pardoned for our original crimes but held accountable for others. Helacth escaped, and for that, we are responsible. Every Rheman spacecraft to leave the planet blasted off with a crew. There's no way to calculate the number of lives that have been lost, but it's significant.

I doubt Nija could have persuaded the Young Soro and his aides to let us live if it wasn't crucial for everyone to watch the last ship depart their world. Without that constant visual reminder, they will start to forget, and the healing can begin.

It helps that terrinium is close to indestructible, and hundreds of Sorbs are stowed inside the ship. Their proximity makes people edgy.

The twelve of us have been given bodies to use indefinitely, but this came at a cost. They belonged to the Vigilance Men who lost their minds during the attack on the Tarrohar. Their families have all agreed to the handover. I'm sure some acted out of appreciation, knowing we'd rid their planet of Helacth, but most probably can't afford to look after an incapacitated relative.

The Young Soro stands, and the crowd stops stomping their feet. There are fresh sea crawlers on the ground around us, but there are petals too. Many people here had loved ones return home with us, and that's something.

The Young Soro's key advisor, Nija, positions herself at his right shoulder. She is especially keen to see us off the planet; I suspect she's the brains behind this entire show.

'People of Sojour, thank you for gathering here today to bear witness to this historical event,' the Young Soro begins.

Merrick stands at the very perimeter of the circle, looking on. He returned to Merrocha on the fifth wave of ghoragalls. I remember seeing him briefly after the fighting ended. There's a girl with Merrick too. She's pretty, with a red dress and a matching hair tie. When he takes her hand, she smiles and leans into him.

I search the crowd for Calipsie's face, but I can't find her anywhere, though it's enough to know she's safe. Lakhan made sure of that.

'As the people know, under Sojour law, a wrong must be put to right,' continues the Young Soro. 'For this reason, and for the love of other species in the broader reaches of space, we charge these twelve Rhemans with a duty of honour. Much as they travelled across the Parched Lands to deliver us from our Rheman oppressors, they must now travel farther. They must ensure that no other species is subjected to the same punishments we endured under Helacth's nightmarish reign.'

A roar rises from the crowd.

It's a great story, but I doubt anyone believes twelve Rhemans will put up much of a fight against Helacth and his hordes. Still, legends have been borne on more fragile wings. Nija thought it would help the people come to terms with not delivering a more visceral punishment on those Rhemans who remained and could be disciplined.

'That is their burden, and they have agreed to bear it. We have gathered today to see them off and to wish them fair favour,' he concludes.

The Vigilance Men soon arrive to march us to a wagon that waits in the square. The wagon will transport us to the *Rhema Bolajio* for our final send-off. As we walk down the yellow sandstone steps of the House of Judgement, I spot Calipsie. She races across the paving, oblivious to the Vigilance Men who flank us on either side. She collides with me, throwing her arms around my waist. As I kneel to tell her goodbye, she smiles and loops her arms around my neck, so her mouth is close to my ear.

'You're going after Kyjta,' she says. 'I know you are.'

I squeeze her small body against my shoulder, smiling.

'I'll find her,' I say. 'You can count on it.'

One of the Vigilance Men grabs my arm, forcing me to stand and move along. I adjust my backpack and march forward. There's a Sorb inside it—one Kyjta insisted we protect. Not a monster to her, not a nightmare, but something precious that requires care. It gives me hope.

When we reach the wagon, I turn and wave to Calipsie before climbing in alongside my eleven Rheman companions. Not all of them are eager to leave Aurora Saura. Few are motivated to perform the mission the Young Soro and his advisors have set for us. Still, together, we'll face whatever comes our way. Who knows, perhaps we'll all find some way to survive without inflicting damage on another.

I sit in a chair alongside Azaire, who is ferried by a striking Vigilance Man with gleaming bronze skin and chiselled features. He was one of the victims of the Tarrohar, completely incapacitated by the Mind Pain, but left alive after the Charmores slayed the ruling party. Tiberico explained how the Zhu used Azaire to make contact with Helacth, claiming that he was working on a treaty that had to be kept private until it was sealed. When Azaire finally figured out that the Zhu was using the channel to leak the bunker locations, he was already implicated, and the Zhu threatened to expose his involvement if he ever told. At least Azaire managed to get Nija back safely. I'm thankful for that. When I find Kyjta I'll be able to tell her the lengths her mother went to, to send this Rheman search party after her.

Strapped into my seat, I remove a sheet of rolled paper from the pocket of the backpack. I've read through the lyrics a thousand times. Nija wrote them down in a tidy, tear-splattered print. She told me they're the words to a song she used to sing when Kyjta was young. I feel like the song—its essence—is something Kyjta will need when I find her. If I can deliver these words, maybe I can deliver Kyjta from some of her suffering, and together we might do something more than just survive this planet they call Earth.

THE FORGOTTEN SONG

A drop of dark, a flash of light
A circle's essence swirls with life
And comes to be, all things right

In the night when stars align
Our fates connected like the moons
We'll always be as one to me

I watched you burn like the brightest star in the sky
Follow your path, defying earth, wind, and fire

When I look upon the stars
Wishes are like curses, rough and cruel
When fate divides
You must decide
My search goes on and on

When it's dark and you're alone
I will be the light to guide you home
Renew my stone heart
Don't keep us apart
My quest goes on and on

Across the lands, of seas and sands
Or still as statues on their shores
Your energy calls out to me

A ring of stone, some fully grown
A web of life runs right through these lands
And offers you my hand

I watched you burn like the brightest star in the sky
Follow your path, defying earth, wind, and fire

When I look upon the stars
Wishes are like curses, rough and cruel
When fate divides
You must decide
My journey goes on and on

When it's dark and you're alone
I will be the light to guide you home
Renew my stone heart
Don't keep us apart
My crusade goes on and on

I know you're out there, somewhere out there
Can you feel me reaching out

I know you're out there, somewhere out there
Can you hear me now

When I look upon the stars
Wishes are like curses, rough and cruel
When fate divides
You must decide
My chase goes on and on

When it's dark and you're alone
I will be the light to guide you home
Renew my stone heart
Don't keep us apart
My hunt goes on and on

ACKNOWLEDGMENTS

My greatest thanks go to Hal Duncan, whose developmental edit breathed a fiery life into the manuscript back when it was still painful to read. Hal—your wit and satire got me through many isolated days of editing. Thank you for your brilliance and your brutal honestly. You're one seriously smart human, though you never let that interfere with your eloquence.

Thank you to my team at Greenleaf who crafted a bridge from manuscript to publication as though the act required no magic at all. Ava Coibion, for her enthusiasm and editorial wizardry. Aaron Teel, for his divination of errors and omissions. Lee Reed Zarnikau, Sally Garland, Leah Pierre for the alchemy of making-it-all-happen. And to David Endris, for picking up the manuscript in the first place.

Thanks goes to my talented brother, Christopher Taljaard, the boy whose beautiful mind conceived the trilogy's covers. And to another creative spirit, RAYM, who wrote the original version of 'The Forgotten Song,' which I played around with to accommodate the story.

I also want to thank my family. My husband, who is my lighthouse—thank you for looking after my brain. And my children, who missed me in the mornings and sometimes didn't see me for entire weekends while I wrote—thank you for every 'I love you' and 'Mummy, you're the best' that saw me through.

JOIN THE CREW

If you enjoyed this book, you'll want to join The Crew and get notified when the next instalment hits. For a limited time, Crew Members will receive two exclusive items of fan memorabilia. Firstly, an audio file of 'The Forgotten Song,' unavailable on mainstream media. Secondly, an undisclosed map of Merrocha, shared exclusively with members of The Crew. Don't miss this chance to sign up for these exclusive items, available for a limited time to subscribers via my website:

www.CLLauder.com/reader-sign-up

LEAVE ME
A REVIEW

I f you're enjoying this series and want to help it succeed, you can make all the difference by leaving a review on my book's Amazon page and on Goodreads here:

https://www.goodreads.com/book/show/199213298-the-quelling.

Reviews help draw the attention of other readers, and readers are fuel to writers like me.

ABOUT THE AUTHOR

 **C. L. LAUDER** grew up in South Africa before immigrating to the United Kingdom, where she attended the University of London to complete an MA in Creative Writing. She now lives at the foot of a lush mountain in Hong Kong with her husband and two rapidly lengthening sons, who all enjoy their newfound proximity to nature, and especially the sea.

The Quelling is the first novel in this trilogy, a dystopian fantasy series set in a futuristic universe, both on Earth and Aurora Saura, and the author looks forward to furnishing you with the next instalment, coming soon.

It's possible to catch her online here—

www.cllauder.com/

www.instagram.com/c.l.lauder/

www.facebook.com/c.l.lauder

www.twitter.com/c_l_lauder

Printed in Great Britain
by Amazon

36927027R10209